THE CLASSICAL
COUNTRY HOUSE
IN SCOTLAND

THE CLASSICAL COUNTRY HOUSE IN SCOTLAND
1660–1800

James Macaulay

faber and faber
LONDON · BOSTON

First published in 1987
by Faber and Faber Limited
3 Queen Square London WC1N 3AU

Printed in Great Britain by
Butler & Tanner Ltd Frome Somerset
All rights reserved

*The publisher acknowledges a subsidy from
the Scottish Arts Council towards the
publication of this volume*

British Library Cataloguing in Publication Data

Macaulay, James
The classical country house in Scotland
1660–1800.
1. Country homes—Scotland—History
2. Neoclassicism (Architecture)—Scotland
I. Title
728.8'3'09411   NA7334

ISBN 0–571–14616–3

In Memory of my Mother
Maisie Macaulay
Who Loved the Beauty of the Past

CONTENTS

LIST OF ILLUSTRATIONS

All the measured drawings are $\frac{1}{8}$th of an inch to 1 foot imperial scale or 1:96 metric scale.

ACKNOWLEDGEMENTS

When a work, long years in the making, is complete the anxieties and difficulties, which once beset every turn of the way, quickly disappear. Yet, before remembrance dims, it is an honourable duty to consider others, strangers sometimes, who materially forwarded this work.

The prime acknowledgement must be to Miss Aléxandra Artley (herself an authoress and now Mrs Gavin Stamp) who first suggested the title. However, given the geographical extent of the subject, the field-work and the research, frequently beyond Scotland, would have been impossible but for the good fortune of having relatives and friends in strategic localities. Those who provided hospitality, often on numerous occasions and without complaint, would include my brother and sister-in-law, Mr and Mrs Douglas Macaulay, the Marquess and Marchioness of Huntly, Sir Nigel and Lady Henderson, Mr and Mrs A. Munro Ferguson of Raith and Novar, the late Major and Mrs J. Stewart of Ardvorlich, Miss Mary Anderson, Mrs Sheila Fais (now Mrs G. Munro), Mr and Mrs Hector Macdonald, Mr Michael Player, Dr and Mrs Grant Simpson and Mr and Mrs Hamish Stirling.

Most of the research material has been culled from family archives, and those who allowed access to their papers included the Duke of Abercorn and the Deputy Keeper of the Records, the Public Record Office of Northern Ireland, the Duke of Buccleuch and Queensberry, the Duke of Hamilton, the Duke of Roxburghe, the Marquess of Bute, the Earl of Cromartie, the Earl of Haddington, the Earl of Kintore, the Earl of Rosebery, the Earl of Southesk, the Earl of Wemyss and March, the Viscount of Arbuthnott, Lord Home of the Hirsel, Sir John Clerk of Penicuik, Sir Houston Shaw Stewart, Sir James Marjoribanks, Mr Keith Adam of Blairadam, Mr Patrick Buchanan of Touch, Mr Malcolm Colquhoun, Yr. of Luss, Miss M. V. Gordon of Cairness, Miss Anne Graham of Mossknowe, Mr John Home Robertson of Paxton, Mr John Johnstone of Glenae, Captain Patrick Munro of Foulis, Mr A. Munro Ferguson of Raith and Novar, Mrs D. Pringle of Torwoodlee and Captain A. Ramsay of Mar. Archival material was also made available by the Haddo House Estate, the Hopetoun Papers Trust and Pollok and Corrour Ltd.

With many collections of family papers held in the Scottish Record Office, I am indebted to the numerous owners and to the Keeper of the Records of Scotland for allowing extracts to be published and to the following members of staff for their especial assistance: Dr P. Anderson, Dr I. Barnes, Mr J. Bates, Dr I. Grant, Mr C. Johnstone and Mr G. Mackenzie. From the labours of her own research Miss Aerne Grant generously provided many new facts.

Acknowledgements

Dr Iain G. Brown was an assiduous guide to the holdings in the National Library of Scotland from which material is reproduced by courtesy of the Trustees. Other documentary information was supplied by Dr Marinell Ash, Dr John Frew (University of St Andrews), Mr N. Higson (University of Hull), Miss A. Kerr and Miss H. Kearsley (Kirkcaldy Art Gallery), Mr C. McLaren and Dr D. Johnston (University of Aberdeen), Mrs A. Mace (British Architectural Library: Manuscripts and Archives Collection) and Miss C. A. Parker (Royal Academy). The late Miss C. Armet and Mr J. Hunter at Mount Stuart always made the visits there enjoyable. Information was also received from Major C. Innes, Miss J. Kinchin, Mr W. J. Mair, Mr W. Marjoribanks of Marjoribanks, Mrs D. Morgan and Mr J. Nightingale.

Material from the Boswell of Auchinleck collection is printed with the permission of Yale University and the McGraw-Hill Book Company (William Heinemann Ltd). Other source material is published by permission of the Perth and Kinross District Archive and the Strathclyde Regional Archives.

For anyone interested in architectural history a primary source is the National Monuments Record of Scotland where I have been the recipient for many years of good cheer and advice from Mr Ian Gow and Miss Catherine Cruft who also read the typescript. Others who have cast a critical eye over it include Mr H. M. Colvin, Dr Malcolm Higgs, Miss Anne Riches and Mr Ian Mowat each of whom has a specialist knowledge of Scottish architecture.

Though many owners have given access to their homes, it would be uncharitable not to single out Mr A. Bell Macdonald of Rammerscales, the late Mrs C. Burnett-Stuart and Mr J. Burnett-Stuart of Ardmeallie, Mr G. Gordon of Letterfourie, Major F. Irvine of Straloch, Mrs M. Fleming, Dr David Hannay, Mr John Mackintosh, Mr J. W. Ogilvie, the late Mr A. Parkin-Moore of Newton, Mrs I. Skene and Mrs A. Stancioff.

Drawings of individual houses were supplied by Mr R. Beaton, Mr Ian Begg, Messrs Bell Ingram, Messrs Groves-Raines and Spens, Mr John Laurie, the Lobban and Mullineux Partnership, Mr Ian Lowden, Mr John A. Smith, Mr J. A. Terrace and Mr A. C. Woolfe. It was from these and from his own field-work notes that Mr William Lippe painstakingly prepared the many line drawings which add so much interest to the text. Many of the photographs were prepared by Miss Katharine Harrison.

One must record the interest shown in this work by Mr Giles de la Mare of Faber and Faber Ltd and acknowledge with gratitude a research grant by the British Academy and the financial contributions made to the publication costs by the Scottish Arts Council, the Russell Trust, the Carnegie Trust for the Universities of Scotland and the Governors of the Glasgow School of Art.

Finally, to Ann, Rosemary and George I owe a private familial debt of thanks.

JAMES MACAULAY
Glasgow

PHOTOGRAPHIC ACKNOWLEDGEMENTS

3, Earl of Strathmore and Kinghorn
6, 11, 15, 26, Gregg International
14, 17, 19, 23, 30–2, 41, 48–9, 56, 58, 63, 70, 83, 102–4, 106–7, 110–12, 115–18, 122–3, 126–32, 134–6, 138, 140–1, 143, 145, 148–9, 157, 164–7, 172, Crown Copyright: Royal Commission on Ancient Monuments, Scotland
24, Ashmolean Museum, Oxford
34, 35, The British Architectural Library, RIBA, London
37–9, 105, *Country Life*
41, The Duke of Hamilton
56, 76, Historic Buildings and Monuments, Scottish Development Department
86–7, Glasgow Museums and Art Galleries, Pollok House
89, National Trust for Scotland
91, By permission of the Executors of the late Lord Cochrane of Cults
103–4, The Duke of Atholl's Collection at Blair Castle
106, Mrs David Stogdon's private collection
107, The Marquess of Bute
111, P. Buchanan of Touch, Esq.
115–16, Earl of Seafield
117, J. Home Robertson, Esq., MP
118, 145, 148–9, Sir John Clerk of Penicuik, Bt
123, 126–30, 132, 134–6, 138, 140–1, By courtesy of the Trustees of Sir John Soane's Museum
125, G. Gordon of Letterfourie, Esq.
143, By permission of the Earl of Wemyss and March
150, Reproduced by courtesy of the National Galleries of Scotland
158–60, Aberdeen University Library, Gordon of Cairness Collection, reproduced with the permission of Miss M. V. Gordon
162–3, The Trustees of the National Library of Scotland
164, Tom Scott of Edinburgh
165–6, In the collection of the Duke of Buccleuch and Queensberry, KT
172, The Earl of Cromartie
175, A. Stewart of Ardvorlich, Esq.
177, Yale Center for British Art, Paul Mellon Collection

ABBREVIATIONS

AR	*Architectural Review*
CL	*Country Life*
DNB	*Dictionary of National Biography*
NLS	National Library of Scotland
NMRS	National Monuments Record of Scotland
NRAS	National Register of Archives (Scotland)
NSA	*New Statistical Account of Scotland*
PRONI	Public Record Office of Northern Ireland
PSAS	*Proceedings of the Society of Antiquaries of Scotland*
RCAHMS	Royal Commission on the Ancient and Historical Monuments of Scotland
RHP	Register House Plan
RIBA	Royal Institute of British Architects
SA	*Statistical Account of Scotland*
SHS	*Scottish History Society*
SM	Soane Museum
SRO	Scottish Record Office
VB	*Vitruvius Britannicus*
VS	*Vitruvius Scoticus*

PREFACE

In any history concerning the architecture of the late seventeenth and eighteenth centuries, the names of Colen Campbell, James Gibbs, Sir William Chambers and Robert Adam will feature prominently. Although these four architects were each of Scottish descent, little attention will be given to whatever work may have been commissioned from them in Scotland, let alone to the general run of architecture north of the Border. Sir John Summerson, in his balanced and finely expressed *British Architecture, 1530–1830*, condenses Scotland's architectural development in the period after 1660 into one short section including a summary account of William Adam and before him of Sir William Bruce. Even in more detailed studies there is often a lop-sided approach in assessing architecture north and south of the Border. A. T. Bolton, in *The Architecture of Robert and James Adam*, devotes less than a third of his second volume to Scotland and that mainly to public buildings in Edinburgh and to Mellerstain in Berwickshire and Culzean Castle in Ayrshire, both essays in the castellated pictorial style. One chapter only is given over to a classical country-house, Newliston in West Lothian. As Bolton wrote: 'Turning to other examples in remoter parts of Scotland, a great list of designs exists, but, in the main, they are for unrealised projects.' That is not quite true. Twelve castles were built to the designs of Robert Adam; and, although many classical designs remained unfulfilled, eighteen classical country-houses were constructed. That list would include Gosford House, East Lothian, which ranks in interest with any of Adam's greater country-houses in England, but which Bolton dismissed as 'a good, if late, example'. Indeed, he postulated that 'the Adam work in Scotland does not show the same fine quality as that executed in the South'. The contention can at once be disproved by glancing even at an early work, Dumfries House, Ayrshire, where building began in 1754 under the superintendence of Robert Adam. While it is true that in Scotland no domestic commission by Adam displays the princely splendour of Syon House or the wealth of Osterley Park, that does not mean that his work lacks interest. His lesser country-houses are an original genre not found south of the Border. Why? Is it because Scottish clients were not prepared to spend lavishly on architectural embellishment? Undoubtedly it is a Scottish trait to equate plain living with elevated thoughts; scarce funds should not be spent on beauty and adornment unless these are allied to utility. Another consideration is that, while some aristocrats were as affluent as the richer English peers, there was in Scotland a large class of country gentlemen of good family but with little income. Estates could be small and overburdened financially by inherited debt and family commitments. Many a landowner had no option but to live quietly at home. Even then it was often impossible to make ends meet without external funding from a government post, military service, the law or perhaps trade in the subcontinent of India. Thus, when necessity demanded a new house, the lack of spare capital cut out all the trappings of classical architecture. Instead, the hint of an entablature, the suggestion of an order would be received appreciatively and intelligently understood, since classical studies were the stamp of educated men in all classes of Scottish society. Hence, affinities between architecture, philosophy, history and literature abound, though today they may have little significance.

It is still not fully realised, even in art-historical circles, that the brave insignia of Renaissance ornament, dating from the early sixteenth century, which bedeck the palaces of Falkland and Stirling Castle, pre-date any similar system of Renaissance design in England. Unfortunately, political instability in Scotland, the schism provoked by the Reformation and the removal of the royal court to London in 1603, followed by civil war, prevented the permanent rooting of Renaissance art. Only after the Restoration of 1660 did it begin to take hold. Then Sir William Bruce came to the forefront. Yet the paucity of evidence must not obscure the fact that Bruce was but one of a small band devoted to the promulgation of classical architecture which, by extension, included landscape gardening. It is distressing that all too often architectural writers, when looking at the British scene, have failed to perceive the pioneering nature of his work. Or consider James Smith and the novelty of his villas, such as Newhailes, East Lothian, which bespeak a familiarity with those in the Veneto. When it is remembered that Smith was the probable mentor of Colen Campbell, the former becomes worthy of a place in the pantheon of British architecture.

Any intelligent observer, looking at Scottish architecture, must be fascinated by the persistent duality between stylistic conservatism and innovation. While the Scots were ready to pick up new ideas, such as James Playfair's pioneering essay in the Greek Revival at Cairness, Aberdeenshire, they were just as happy using tried and tested formulae, such as the small country-house of three storeys with triple planning divisions running from front to rear, from one end of the country to the other and from the reign of Charles II up to the early days of the Regency.

However, even before the eighteenth century had expired, stylistic unity was fracturing. In 1745 Inveraray Castle, Argyll, the first major Gothic Revival mansion in Britain, was under way. All the same, the complex mingling of social, antiquarian and literary impulses which prompted the desire to recreate the middle ages in stone and lime is not only beyond the scope of this book but has been adequately dealt with in *The Gothic Revival, 1745–1845*. Even within the classical system divisions began to appear, and just as the Gothic Revival would be carved up by nomenclature, so the stirrings of the Greek Revival would undermine the supremacy of Rome. Nevertheless, before these divisions occurred there was an architectural philosophy and attendant style which, taken with the number of buildings executed, makes the time-span covered by this book attractive to the scholar and, hopefully, to the general reader.

CHAPTER ONE

'The introducer of Architecture in this country'

Although classical architecture had made sporadic appearances in Scotland, it was not until after the Restoration in 1660 that a system of architecture, in which symmetry was allied to classical details and the use of the orders, was to become general both in Scotland and in England. That the dissemination was less rapid north of the Border was in part because of the absence of a royal court and the widespread impoverishment of the country as a consequence of the debilitating religious and civil wars. The nobles, who could have been expected to set the architectural pace, had had to bear the fines and impositions levied by the Interregnum government[1] and were so reduced that, according to one contemporary, one half of their number was bankrupt while of the others few were worth more than £500 a year.[2] In such straitened circumstances little could be expected in the way of architectural innovation particularly when the tower-house, the almost universal dwelling of the land-owning classes, was still capable of evolution in detail and in plan. LESLIE CASTLE, Aberdeenshire, begun before 1661 as 'the last fortified house in Scotland',[3] has gun-ports on the stepped entrance elevation to defend the single doorway [1] but beyond it the introduction of a generous scale and platt staircase and the direct communication between the principal apartments [2] bespeak a desire for greater ease and comfort.[4]

1 LESLIE CASTLE, Aberdeenshire

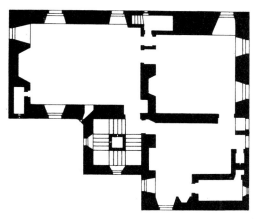

2 LESLIE CASTLE, Aberdeenshire, plan of the principal floor

3 GLAMIS CASTLE, Angus, by Charles Reddie, 1686

Almost contemporary with Leslie Castle was the remodelling of GLAMIS CASTLE [3] by Patrick, Earl of Strathmore who, on coming into his inheritance not only had to pay a £1,000 fine to the Cromwellian government for his father's royalist activities[5] but found his estates and houses in great disorder. It was not, therefore, until 1670 that he could begin the reconstruction of Glamis where the changes included raising the height of the main roof and the great staircase tower. It must have been considered that the days of warring factions were past as all the iron window grills were removed[6] and gun-loops were omitted. With little money the work went on piecemeal so that the earl 'did not call (in) such as in this age were known and reput [sic] to be the best judges and contrivers'[7] and perhaps as a result, although he 'did covet extremely to order my building so as the frontispiece might have a resemblance on both syds',[8] the detail on the whole is old-fashioned which is, perhaps, to be expected since the earl was intent, not on introducing new ways, but on restoring old forms, being 'inflam'd stronglie with a great desyre to continue the memorie of my familie'.[9] Even so the mature calculation and sophisticated invention make Glamis the swan-song of the native castle style so that Defoe was nearer the truth than he realised in rhapsodising over it. 'When you see it at a Distance it is so full of Turrets and lofty Buildings, Spires and Towers, some plain, others shining with gilded Tops, that it looks not like a Town but a City.'[10] He might have been describing the palace of a Tudor or early Stuart monarch.

Although Lord Strathmore, living in more settled times, would one day write that castles were out of fashion, wishing 'that everie man who hes [sic] such houses would reform them, for who can delight to live in his house as in a prisone',[11] castles continued to be inhabited. Even the nobility, as Celia Fiennes heard on the Border, lived in 'all kind of Castles'[12] and as late as the second decade of the next century a traveller in the western Scottish borders could remark that the lairds' houses were 'most of them old Towers of Stone'.[13]

The first country-house to be completed in the new mode, a large, undefended residence of classical inspiration, surrounded by formal gardens and set in an agricultural estate, was LESLIE HOUSE, Fife, which, significantly, was commissioned by a member of the government, John Leslie, 7th Earl and later 1st Duke of Rothes. As chancellor of Scotland he would doubtless have been able to meet the building costs from the rewards of his office rather than from estate income or by borrowing on the security of his land. 'An able and magnificent man',[14] Rothes was prepared, like fellow Restoration peers, to spend lavishly on sumptuous display, inclining, as Lord Strathmore wrote of himself, 'to be very profuse upon all things of ornament for my houses'.[15] Sinces Rothes spent much time in London, where he would be aware of the latest fashions in architecture and decoration, it was the countess who, remaining in Scotland, supervised the changes at Leslie House while contending with the inevitable delays. As she wrote in October 1670, 'I shall acquaint Mr Mill [Mylne] concerning the chimney-piece, and the painter with what relates to his Work, but it will be martinmas before he has finished the Galarie.' She was worried, too, because 'there is no Word neither do I know whom to inquire at about the stones, from Holland, and the black and white tiles'[16] which were, presumably, for the entrance hall. Such anxieties were transmitted almost weekly throughout the autumn of 1670, when Leslie House was being fitted up, to her near neighbour, Sir William Bruce, then in London. He was a trusted ally who could be asked to select some ordered items since if Lord Rothes did so that 'would but make them the dearer';[17] a month later and her ladyship was fretting about some hangings her husband had seen. Would they be the correct length for the room for which they were intended?[18] The correspondence, which gains interest since it is usual for the husband, as employer, to write, shows Lady Rothes as intelligent and hard-working but, above these gifts, as a wife anxious to do her best for her husband whose absence leaves her

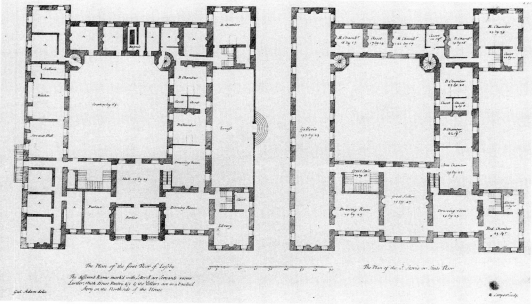

4 LESLIE HOUSE, Fife

feeling lost and lonely.[19] Yet she could still think of other people. Having received hangings, chairs and looking-glasses, costing 3,000 marks, she was distressed that the account could not be settled at once, especially as the supplier 'hath laid out that much for us already and is to furnish us with what will come to much more'.[20] Then Mylne had to be paid, for 'I know he is pinched for munie and looks more Melancolie than he used to doe.'[21] With so much to do and remember the countess sat down on one occasion and composed a memorandum, presumably for Sir William Bruce. 'Forget not to inquire after what fashion the windows are to be painted. If they be but white and gilded I think the man that painted the Cross of Edinr. may do that kind of work as well as the other.'[22]

As three-quarters of Leslie House was destroyed by fire in 1763,[23] early descriptions, such as by John Macky, are invaluable. 'You enter the Palace by two spacious Courts, with a Pavilion at each end of the first Court; the House is a large Square, with a paved Court in the middle; You enter it by a Vestibule Ballustraded with Marble, into a large Hall, pav'd with black and white Marble.'[24] Immediately above the hall, and extending the full depth of the west range, was a saloon set between two drawing-rooms one of which led into the gallery, 157 feet long, which filled the entire north range [4]. Even Defoe, eager to prick Macky's pretensions to aristocratic Scottish domestic grandeur,[25] was impressed by Leslie's magnificence and especially the gallery[26] which was hung, as can still be seen at the near contemporary Ham House, Surrey, with portraits of relations and friends, including Sir William Bruce. There were besides, 'Three resting chairs covered wt. Red Damask. One Seatie wt. a gilded frame covered with a Gilded stuff cushion of the Same, One Carpet resting chair.' Other public rooms were as richly decorated: the dining-room was hung with twelve panels of the fashionable gilded leather, more of which covered the three dozen walnut chairs,[27] while in the principal bedroom there were to be half a dozen chairs, two with arms, and the same number of stools, the frames of which were to be sent from London 'as there is none in Scotland can turn them in that fashion'.[28]

Despite its modern furnishings, Leslie, by contemporary English standards, was somewhat old-fashioned. True the rooms were connected en suite in the modern manner and there was some distinction between state and private apartments while each bedroom had its own closet. Nevertheless, the courtyard with protruding angle towers, containing spiral service stairs, was a bygone relic without any of the continental influences which distinguished the earlier and later courts of Heriot's Hospital and the palace of Holyroodhouse, both in Edinburgh. The main elevation, as originally built, also looked backwards with skewputs and gabled chimney-heads although the formal arrangement of projection and recession, the grouping of the chimneys in regularly placed stacks, the pronounced horizontality, emphasised by string-courses, and the tall windows on every floor, all showed an awareness of new ways [5]. Perhaps these were borrowed in part from Serlio's treatise[29] in which one elevation [6] seems to echo, though in a foreign tongue, the main elevation at Leslie where the innovation of a loggia and, more importantly, its outward mask of pilasters and entablature, are further evidence of the same Italian source.[30]

Although Leslie House was completed by 1672,[31] the gardens, including a fountain with a statue of Apollo, were still unfinished five years later.[32] The building contract had been drawn up in the summer of 1667[33] and reflected in the principal signatories the future and

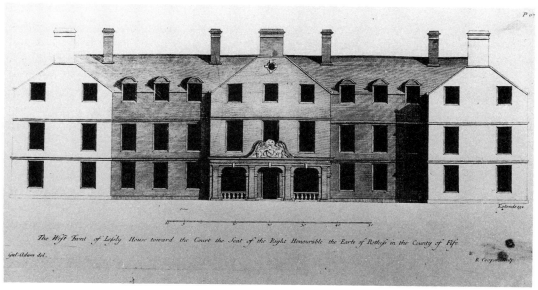

The West Front of Lesly House toward the Court the Seat of the Right Honourable the Earle of Rothess in the County of Fife

Gul: Adam del.   *R. Cooper sculp.*

5 LESLIE HOUSE, Fife
6 Design by Sebastiano Serlio

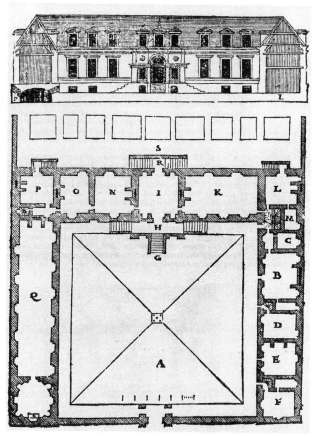

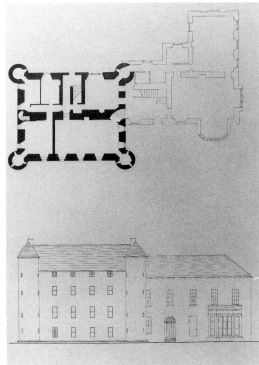

7 METHVEN CASTLE, Perthshire

8 METHVEN CASTLE, Perthshire

the past in Scottish architecture. Sir William Bruce, soon to emerge as Scotland's first architect, is mentioned for the first time in an architectural role and one of some standing since he was to act as custodian of the working drawings for John Mylne, the royal master mason. When the latter died at the close of the year, his commissions were inherited by his nephew, Robert Mylne. While it may be to the latter that the more progressive architectural details at Leslie House are due, it should be noted that his uncle had spent a year in London during the Interregnum.[34] Yet if stylistic analysis has any validity it may be that John Mylne is more truthfully represented by the reconstruction sometime after 1664 of METHVEN CASTLE, Perthshire[35] as a tall, square house, rubble built, of four floors with, at each corner, a round angle tower rising above the plain wallhead [7]. Methven is a transitional house [8] displaying what little was new on the north elevation where twin crow-step gables are held apart by a balustraded lead flat, as at Drummonie House, Perthshire, and more elaborately and less articulately at PANMURE HOUSE, Angus.

The 1st Earl of Panmure had wanted to build a new seat but, having been frustrated by the civil commotions of the middle years of the century, it was left to his son to carry out the father's intention[36] and commence building the first country-house in Scotland. The contract of February 1666 is of great interest since it not only establishes that the intended house would be 'as set down by the said John Mylne in draughts' but outlines the organisation for the construction. Twelve masons were to be supervised by an overseer who, over and above his wages, would have 'his bed and board in his Lordship's house'. Mylne was to supply 'four good able barrowmen, pioneers skillfull to make morter and bear stones long or short at the rate of fourtie eight shillings Scots per week'. Lord Panmure provided all the building materials including the scaffolding. As was customary the building season began no later than early April and finished in October with the hours being from 5 a.m. to 7 p.m. which included three breaks, one of which, at midday, was for 'dinner and some rest'. In the autumn the workmen would be dismissed except for those masons needed, at a reduced rate of pay, to win the stone for the next building season.

After John Mylne's death he was succeeded by another Edinburgh mason, Alexander Nisbet, who may have completed the carcase of the house by the time the earl died in 1671. By then it had been agreed that the great oak staircase would 'be made up after the order of the staircase at Donybryssel' by James Bain, the royal wright, who later undertook to plaster 'the withdrawing-room in rich fruit-work', probably in the fashion of the ceilings at Holyroodhouse.[37]

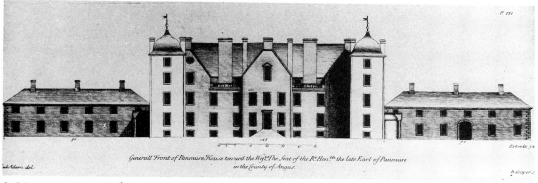

Generall Front of Panmure House toward the West. The Seat of the Rt Honble the late Earl of Panmure in the County of Angus.

9 PANMURE HOUSE, Angus

As shown in *Vitruvius Scoticus* [9] Panmure was, for it was demolished in 1955, a composite of the Methven and Leslie House elevations. There were three gables but with the outer ones cut into by square, five-storey towers, which restored the Scottish desire for strong corner verticals, evoking memories of Heriot's Hospital but without its decorative bravura. The towers, with ogee pyramidal roofs, were the first of their kind in Scotland, copied perhaps from the early Jacobean Charlton House in Greenwich, the plan of which, with five divisions from front to rear, may have influenced that of Panmure [10]. Set over a half-sunk basement,[38] the loggia, as used at Leslie, had become an enclosed vestibule, doubtless in deference to the Scottish climate, and with a long inner hall may indicate an arrangement shown by Serlio [11] whose plan also has square angle towers.[39] It may be no coincidence that the Serlian undertones occur at Leslie House and Panmure House, both commissioned by aristocratic patrons and where, on each occasion, Sir William Bruce was involved. At Panmure not only did he design a gateway in 1672[40] but in 1693 he was consulted about the offices, 'which are yet to build',[41] which presumably were the two rectangular courts linked by quadrant corridors to the rear of the house and added by the 4th Earl.[42]

The establishment of the canons of classicism as the regulator of architectural activity in Scotland was accomplished by Sir William Bruce (c.1630–1710). That his role was para-

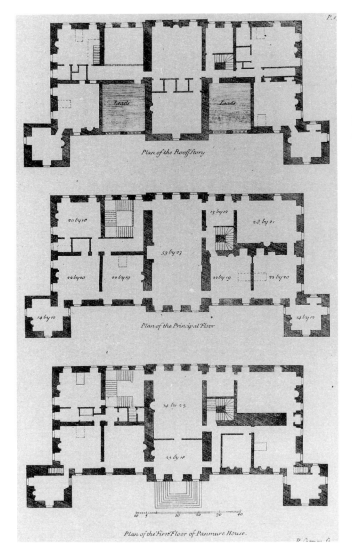

Plan of the Roof Story

Plan of the Principal Floor

Plan of the First Floor of Panmure House.

10 PANMURE HOUSE, Angus

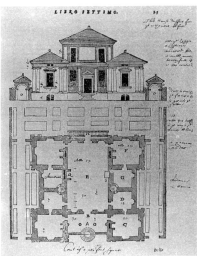

11 Design by Sebastiano Serlio

mount was recognised within a few years of his death when a leading architectural savant, Sir John Clerk of Penicuik, dubbed him 'the introducer of Architecture in this country'.[43] Bruce was not a craft-trained mason who rose to become a builder. Born the second son of a minor Perthshire laird he seems to have owed his rise to political fortune by his support for the exiled house of Stuart, for shortly after the Restoration he was knighted, becoming a baronet in 1668. As a protégé of the Earl, later Duke, of Lauderdale, Bruce received the post of surveyor-general of the royal works in Scotland from which he was to be dismissed seven years later in 1678, although by then the major royal work, the building of the palace of Holyroodhouse, was almost complete. With the accession of James VII in 1685 Bruce lost all his remaining government offices and entered a long old age of political, personal and financial difficulties. Bruce had established himself as a landowner first at Balcaskie,

8

Fife, in 1665 and ten years later at Kinross, which he seems to have purchased cheaply,[44] where he commenced a magnificent family seat. By birth, position and the marriages of himself and his children (his son, John, married a younger daughter of the Earl of Rothes) Bruce was either related or otherwise connected to his architectural patrons. For example, Lauderdale's second wife, Elizabeth Murray, Countess of Dysart and owner of Ham House, was a distant cousin of Bruce, who was called upon to design a gateway for Ham in 1671.[45] As a gentleman with an interest in architecture it was seldom that Bruce personally superintended the execution of a project.

In the absence of other evidence it has to be assumed that Bruce developed a theoretical understanding of architecture from such sources as Serlio, Le Muet, whose *Manière de Bien Bastir* of 1647 first appeared in an English translation in 1670, as well as from Du Cerceau, Fréart, published in English in 1664, and Palladio. Such a literary education was reinforced and extended by travel to the Low Countries and France. In addition visits to England in the decisive years after the Restoration provided an awareness of the classical style, not as grafted on to old buildings or ancient crafts, but as a concept for achieving a philosophical ideal of perfection in the integration of plan and elevation.[46]

Bruce's first substantive architectural role, one recorded in correspondence, was at THIRLESTANE CASTLE, Lauderdale's imposing family seat in Berwickshire. Built in the previous century, it had an unusual plan, being a long rectangular block with, at each corner, a three-quarter engaged round tower terminated by a square, crow-stepped cap-house. On each flank there were three half-round turrets.[47] All in all it must have seemed very out of date to be the chief residence of the king's first minister in Scotland and although it has been suggested that the ambitious building programme on which Lauderdale embarked, which included Lauder Church and Brunstane House, was prompted by his future wife,[48] it seems more likely that he felt urged by aristocratic competition, always a powerful motivation, to follow and to outclass such co-peers as Rothes and Panmure and indeed his own brother at Hatton.

Work on refashioning Thirlestane seems to have started in 1670, as early in the following New Year Bruce could write to Lauderdale at Whitehall, 'Mr Mylne hes [sic] promised nixt week to come hither and go with me to Thirlston Castle: says the work advances well.'[49] Clearly, the relationship between Bruce and Mylne was much the same as at Leslie House with the former exercising a supervisory role over Mylne's contractual activity. It was an arrangement recommended to a prospective patron by another gentleman architect, Sir Roger Pratt. 'If you be not able to handsomely contrive it yourself, get some ingenious gentleman who has seen much of that kind abroad and been somewhat versed in the best authors of Architecture: viz. Palladio, Scamozzi, Serlio etc. to do it for you, and to give you a design of it in paper',[50] while for those lacking 'skill, time or patience' he advocated the employment of a surveyor.[51] Perhaps Lord Lauderdale had little patience. Certainly, he not only complained bitterly to Bruce about Mylne, for 'taking so false measures and keeping to time so very ill as to my house', but told the former in no uncertain terms that any failure 'will be at your door'.[52]

At Easter in 1671, when good progress was still being maintained, Lord Lauderdale had bargained for half a dozen marble chimney-pieces 'and three of them are finer than any I see in England'. Lauderdale had paid for two and reckoned that he had got a bargain not only because, as he perhaps naively believed, the Italian merchant 'let me have them as he payed for them in Italie with the customes and charges', but they were cheaper and finer than the Lord Chancellor's.[53] Yet Lauderdale was more than simply concerned at going one better than a ministerial colleague, such as the Earl of Rothes, for he took both a serious and a practical interest in the alterations which were so contrived that comfortable use was as important as fashionable concerns. That London was the touchstone of taste appears repeatedly in the minister's correspondence. Thus at Brunstane one room was declared to be 'as broad as the galleries at Whitehall',[54] while for a third property, Lethington (later renamed Lennoxlove) in East Lothian, Lauderdale purchased a brass chimney-piece with pillars like the one in the queen's privy chamber.[55] A similar concern led him to write in May 1671 from Ham House where he had been considering Thirlestane and the proposed pavilions 'which are absolutely necessary to make a front at the entry'. He had decided that similar pavilions should be attached to the rear of the castle so that the four elevations would appear uniform while there would be a practical gain since one of the pavilions could house the library, which would save him from having to climb to the third storey 'which frights ane old man'. Even so, there would be problems such as the ground fall at the rear of the castle and the dimensions of the projected pavilions as well as their convenient junction with the main structure. Lauderdale, however, felt that he need not worry about overcoming such difficulties since Bruce had 'ane excellent faculty at all that'.[56] Although the king's chief minister was eagerly awaiting by midsummer 'a rough draught of my new Pavillion',[57] the proposed rear addition was postponed for two years, before being eventually abandoned, as Lauderdale was once again fretting about the pavilions on the entrance and the 'absolute necessity' of raising them a storey higher using the existing roof timbers and slates.

Lauderdale's attention to detail led him to employ foreign artisans, including two joiners (probably Dutchmen) who, having worked at Ham House, where they had made the new-style sash windows[58] and, it would seem, the wainscoting,[59] would sail to Newcastle and then proceed overland to Thirlestane and go on to Brunstane. The Dutch painter 'with paterns'[60] may have been Edward Kickius, whose name appears in the building accounts along with the English plasterers George Dunsterfield and John Hulbert who had already worked at Holyroodhouse.[61] Yet it is interesting that for the gateway, proposed to be designed for Ham by Bruce, inquiry was made as to whether the ironwork could be made in Scotland.[62]

Thirlestane Castle is the first country-house, for that is what it became, where considerable surviving documentary evidence indicates in detail the relationship between the client and his architect and the considerations prompting the internal and external changes. Once these were complete Thirlestane was as fine as the king's palace of Holyroodhouse so that Bishop Burnet, despite his admiration for the duke's scholarship, may well have stated the truth when he described Lauderdale as 'haughty beyond expression' and one who, having 'delivered himself up afterwards to luxury and sensuality ... stuck at nothing that was necessary to support that'.[63]

Although Thirlestane is yet one more example of an old structure being enlarged and remodelled, the changes, particularly if the unexecuted ones delineated by the Dutchman

12 THIRLESTANE CASTLE, Berwickshire, entrance elevation

John Slezer are included, are perhaps more significant than those at Holyroodhouse. At Thirlestane [12] there is, for the first time, a show parade of graduated pavilions to support the old house, now transformed into a *corps de logis*. The entrance, elevated on a terrace, is approached by a central staircase, leading to a pedimented doorway, perhaps copied from

13 THIRLESTANE CASTLE, Berwickshire, side elevation

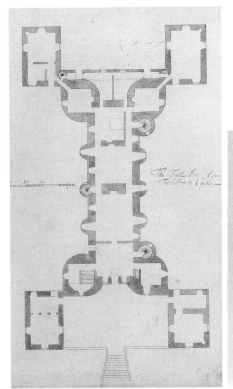

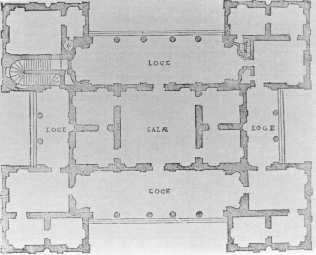

14 THIRLESTANE CASTLE, Berwickshire,   15 Design by Sebastiano Serlio
late seventeenth-century ground-floor plan

a French source,[64] while on the wallhead a pediment spans the two central bays. None of the features is outstanding; taken together they reveal a determination to reproduce classically inspired tenets north of the Border. For example, the pavilions on the garden side of Thirlestane [13] are copies of the loggias at Ham. Even at second hand such an Italian derivation may provide a clue to the ultimate source of the carefully marshalled components. Perhaps in elevation but more so in plan [14] the architect has not only turned to Serlio [15] but has modified the sequence of family rooms used at Leslie House so that, by borrowing from its south range, he has reinforced the processional character of the long axis of Thirlestane, where not only is the drawing-room in the same place as Serlio's *sala* but so too is the staircase, tucked into the pavilion to the left of the entrance, while the loggia becomes an ante-room.[65]

Perhaps it was a knowledge of Serlian planning that allowed for the expansion of BRUNSTANE, on the outskirts of Edinburgh, into a U-plan, which corresponded quite closely to a plate in Book Seven[66] even to the infilling of the internal angles, which at Brunstane was done with polygonal stair turrets, and at the rear a central passage communicating with the courtyard and with the garden.

As Brunstane had been built only thirty years before,[67] Lauderdale, in the autumn of 1672, determined that 'I will only patch what is already built and make myself a very convenient

12

lodge'[68] so that, as he had written a week before, 'I mean to finish Brunsten first of all, after Thirlestane Castle, and let Lethington stand ablow.'[69] Accordingly, the alterations were essentially practical. There were to be no bedrooms on the first floor where one wing was given over to the great chamber which was positioned, not on the west side where it would look into yards, but on the east 'where I shall have three fair lights looking upon the sea and upon Fife, and the fourth light looking upon the garden'.[70] In order to 'make the sight of the house much more fine' the elevations were to be regularised by the addition of two more towers in one of which there would be a chapel with a loft reserved for the duke and duchess[71] as at Thirlestane. Despite the labour of his ministerial duties, Lauderdale was not content to leave architectural decisions to Bruce. From the south there flowed a stream of suggestions and ideas and Lauderdale even made copies of drawings so that, as he wrote to Bruce, 'We may convers upon the alterations without sending draughts any more' and, with almost housewifely concern, he marked on his own plan, 'C my tobacco room ... G, for keeping of the sweetmeats ... K for keeping candle-sticks, brooms, etc.'[72]

Lauderdale was not the only member of his family to delight in building and may have caught the contagion from his younger brother, Charles Maitland, who was not only a member of the Scottish Privy Council but, more usefully, controlled the Mint. Although Lord Hatton, as he became, had married the heiress of Hatton in 1653 there could be no building there until after the Restoration. Between 1664 and 1675 there was added to the L-plan tower an extended south-facing screen of three storeys set over a basement.[73] Because it incorporated work from a previous generation the façade was not symmetrical[74] although unity was imposed by a square central tower, containing the entrance, and circular terminal towers. Much was traditional in the elevational treatment although on the east elevation the interlocking towers and gables were a reminder of both Leslie House and Panmure House. Most striking, however, was the entrance staircase possibly copied from the garden front at Ham but originating from numerous examples in Serlio. Although there is no evidence associating Bruce with Hatton House, it would be improbable if he, and possibly the Mylnes, were not involved.

The houses with which Bruce has so far been connected conform to one pattern. Lying in the fertile eastern plains they belonged to hereditary landowners, usually enriched by the profits of government office. Architecturally, there was a modest alliance between native ways overlaid with a touch of classicism but scarcely sufficient to justify the later assertion by Colen Campbell that Bruce was the best architect of his time in the kingdom.[75] Even if the new design of Holyroodhouse is taken into consideration, the claim had to be substantiated by a more radical architecture which first appears with two new country-houses in Perthshire, DUNKELD and MONCREIFFE.

The former, which replaced a house destroyed by troops in 1654,[76] was in 'a warm winter situation'[77] so that the Marquess of Atholl and his family could escape the rigours of living in the larger and more elevated Blair Castle. A plan, prepared by Bruce, was ready in the spring of 1676[78] and work started in the summer, for materials had been ordered, so that at the close of the building season, with the masons and others having to be paid, £200 would have to be found[79] which, for a highland estate with most of the rents paid in kind, would have been a problem. The next mention of Dunkeld House is in the autumn of 1684

16 DUNKELD HOUSE, Perthshire. The wings are later additions

when the marquess sought permission to have stones hewn 'in the new church of Perth'.[80] Even allowing for a shortage of cash, it is difficult to believe that Dunkeld House [16] took eight years to construct, especially as it was 'not larg and it will not cost much expences ether'.[81] Uniquely, it was of brick with a white render[82] so that, although the stone may have been for dressings, it is more likely to have been for additional work.

Contemporary with Dunkeld was Moncreiffe House finished in 1679[83] for Thomas Moncrieffe of that Ilk who seven years before had witnessed the building contract for Holyroodhouse.[84] Although the evidence linking Bruce with the design of Moncreiffe [17] is circumstantial a comparison between it and Dunkeld makes his authorship indubitable.

Both houses were, for both have been demolished,[85] rectangles of seven by five bays with basement, two floors and an attic storey below a hipped roof with chimney-stacks set on a central flat. Apart from a modelled cornice there was no other decoration save for quoins, a string-course and a pedimented doorcase. Moncreiffe, which was 73 feet long by 60 feet broad, making it 5 feet longer on each side than Dunkeld, was described by John Macky as 'a neat little Seat ... built of Freestone after the Manner of the Country-Seats in the Villages about London, with a Glass Cupola or Lanthorn at top, and very neatly wainscoted and furnished within'.[86] It is an apt description, for the closest parallel to both Moncreiffe and Dunkeld is the near contemporary Chevening in Kent, which has the same general outline and number of bays on each elevation while displaying such Italianate undertones as a suppressed attic storey below a bracketed cornice,[87] features which were illustrated in conjunction above an astylar elevation in Rubens's *Palazzi di Genova*[88] and in Serlio where the corresponding plan has a tripartite division from front to rear.[89] Such an arrangement was found in Bruce's two Perthshire houses and was not only repeated by him at a later date but became a standard layout with later generations of house builders.[90]

14

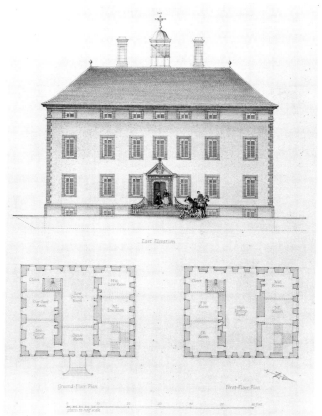

East Elevation

Ground-Floor Plan   First-Floor Plan

17 MONCREIFFE HOUSE, Perthshire

Clearly, at both Moncreiffe and Dunkeld, where there were new sites, Bruce was released from the controls imposed by existing ancestral piles and could adopt, both in plan and in elevation, up-to-date English models as he was free to do at his own house of KINROSS. Although Bruce had enlarged Balcaskie in the early 1670s,[91] the general tenor of the internal and external changes, with one significant exception, can be compared to his commissioned projects of that period. Having a virgin site at Kinross, however, Bruce could introduce an entirely new type of house into Scotland while displaying a facility in massing and detail which can be seen as the culmination of early endeavours. As ever there is the debt to Serlio which is most obvious in the low attic common to nearly all the Italian's inventions. Along the principal elevation [18] of eleven bays the two main floors are tied together at the angles, not by quoins, but by a giant order of Corinthian pilasters. Set over a rusticated basement, these support an entablature spanning the full elevation, which is, therefore, divided into three framed rectangles, all of which is certainly Serlian,[92] although some of the details, such as the carvings over the pedimented doorcase, could have been seen at the Mauritshuis at The Hague.

But Kinross would be neither so interesting nor so sophisticated if Bruce had not married to his Serlian block an extended layout derived from Palladio. Bruce purchased a copy of the Italian's celebrated treatise in 1676[93] but, before then, at Balcaskie he had fastened to the high crow-stepped house curved screen walls ending in two-storeyed pavilions to provide not only an open, cheerful space but a fluidity of movement in marked contrast with Thirlestane where the stepped towers and tight geometry of the forecourt have a French

18 KINROSS HOUSE, Kinross-shire

air as though they were blood kin of the château of Balleroy designed by Mansart about 1626. The Palladian scheme at Balcaskie was not only unique in Scotland but, even more remarkably, and so far unnoticed by historians, it was the third in Britain since its introduction by Inigo Jones sometime after 1629 and its next appearance at Berkeley House, Piccadilly in 1665.[94] Late in the next decade Bruce reworked the concept, perhaps too arcane for his London-orientated patrons, for Kinross where, and it may be of some import, it was the forecourt that was completed first by 1686.[95] Possibly there was a financial reason or a practical one since the outbuildings could provide some accommodation. Certainly, one is aware of an order of priorities.

The construction of the mansion occupied the second half of the building programme after 1686. The walls must have been rising fastest in 1688 when twenty-two masons' accounts were paid ranging from such a small sum as £8:17:0 to nearly £1,000 for Tobias Bauchope, the chief mason, and his men. Altogether the total came to over £3,500 Scots which was one-twelfth the value of sterling. By 1690 'windows of the upmost storie' and chimney-heads were being put in place.[96]

By 1692 the furnishings were under consideration and, as might be imagined, they were every bit as smart as those for Lady Rothes and included numerous sets of stamped and gilded leather hangings which came, not from London as might be supposed, but from Alexander Brand, a merchant in Edinburgh, who, in the midst of retailing the latest war news from the Continent, would give as his opinion that leather was cheaper than the 'coarsest arrasse' and longer lasting. In the drawing-room at Kinross [19] there were gold

19 KINROSS HOUSE,
Kinross-shire,
the drawing-room

and pearl-coloured hangings with a vivid blue, crimson and gold set in the 'little tobacco room' and a plainer set in the low dining-room. However, one set had to be returned because the gold was blemished and Brand 'ordered that there should be nine skines Gilded and stamped and that there should be great ceare taken to doe them exstordinary well'. There also came painted overdoors and overmantels and Bruce paid £6:10:0 for '2 picktors of fruit' and a quarter of that for 'architectorie wt. a frame'.[97]

Kinross, begun in 1679, the year after Bruce was stripped of the office of surveyor, and not completed until 1693, was an enterprise, not only of his sere years, but of studied care and protracted consideration. There are no hurried judgements at Kinross, no aesthetic doubts but instead sober judgements with every line, stone and detail breaking from inner contemplation and a calculating eye. While Bruce was striving to establish a seat worthy of himself and of his heirs, he must have considered Kinross to be his last testimony, the summa of what he most valued in architecture. It should, therefore, be of note that the plan [20] was the Restoration ideal for an English country gentleman's house as developed by Sir Roger Pratt and Hugh May. Indeed, the Englishness of Kinross was recognised, albeit indirectly, by John Macky who not only rated it as 'the finest Seat I have yet seen in Scotland',[98] an opinion shared by Defoe,[99] but noted that the saloon, which filled the five central bays on the first floor, was 'two Stories high, with a Lanthorn on top, as at Montague-House in London'.[100] Yet Montagu House, rebuilt, after a fire, between 1686 and 1688 by a francophile nobleman,[101] drew many of its chief features from a purer English source, Clarendon House by Sir Roger Pratt which, though demolished in 1683, less than twenty years after its construction,[102] was widely influential, one reason being that as the grandest London town-house it was the cynosure of fashion's eyes and, indeed, it is conceivable that Bruce may have been a visitor.[103] Thus at Kinross the wings and slightly recessed centre

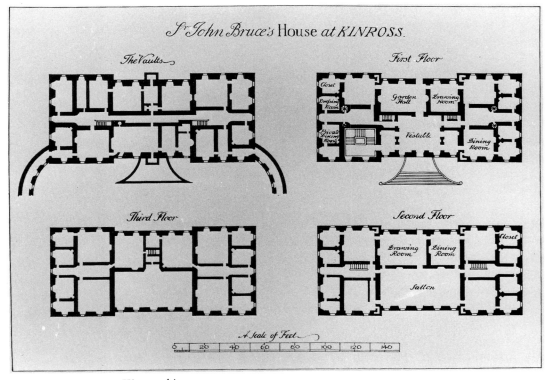

20 KINROSS HOUSE, Kinross-shire

hark back to Clarendon House and, although its elevations and those of Pratt's earlier Coleshill House, Berkshire, had a familial resemblance, it is in the double-pile plan, with two lines of rooms, parallel to the principal elevations and separated by a corridor, that Kinross accords most closely with Coleshill. For example, the largest dining-room is placed, in the English fashion, on the first floor where, however, even after Bruce's death, 'Many of ye Rooms ... are not finish'd',[104] for Bruce, who calculated in 1700 that Kinross had cost him in excess of £10,000,[105] had been caught in the familiar trap of those who build. As Pratt wrote: 'Their designs are generally too big for their purse so that in the end they are either forced to leave them imperfect, or whilst they strive to finish them they ruin themselves.'[106]

The double-pile plan was considered by Pratt to be 'the most useful' being not only compact and, therefore, economical to build but warm, comfortable and easy to service.[107] These qualities were displayed at Harden (now called Mertoun), Berwickshire which William Adam ascribed to Bruce.[108] Although Harden is a more compressed version of Kinross, it is closer both in plan and in elevation to the chief works of Pratt. For instance, the plan not only has the through vista from front to rear, which Celia Fiennes commented on at Coleshill,[109] but like that paradigm Harden has its service stairs placed at either end of the service corridor. Then, too, the hierarchy of parts, which Pratt had ordained,[110] also occurs at Harden with the largest, public rooms in the centre, family rooms on either side and beyond them the closets over which Bruce set, in Serlian semblance, a mezzanine.

18

Harden is Pratt's 'oblong square',[111] a nine-bay pedimented block which in elevation is Clarendon House minus the wings. Thus the central three bays of Harden break forward to carry the pediment, a standard design component in all Bruce's houses, with one exception, after Kinross.

Bruce had first made use of a pedimented centre, as a dominant feature, at Craigiehall on the north-western outskirts of Edinburgh. In 1694 he had promised Lord Annandale, 'I shall designe your lo. a convenient little house, gardings and courts'[112] but it was not until 1698 that the building contract was signed with Tobias Bauchope for a house which was to be 64 feet long, 46 feet broad, 28 feet above the ground and 6 feet below. There were to be four chimney-stacks, each 8 feet high and 'caped like the Chimlay heads at Kinross with windows and doors according to the modell of wood and the draught signed by Sir William Bruce of Kinross'. Apart from the stipulated cash payments, Lord Annandale agreed to supply four bolls of oatmeal and salmon when it was required.[113] Two informative, though undated, letters also cast some light on Bruce's involvement with Craigiehall. In one letter Lady Annandale writes of practical matters 'and approves much of your method both for preventing smel and nois',[114] which echoes Pratt's recommendation for 'a half ground storey' or basement so that 'no dirty servants may be seen passing to and fro by those who are above, no noises heard, nor ill scents smelt'.[115] The earl's concerns were aesthetic: he wanted the entrance hall to be open to the stairs since 'the lesse your look be bounded att your first Entrie the greater is the satisfaction'.[116]

It must surely be of some significance that during the erection of Kinross House Bruce had no country-house commissions and that when they do reappear after 1693 his designs, though more suave, show none of the innovations which make his first period, in the decade after 1670, so exciting. At Craigiehall, despite the novelty of a pediment, awkwardly seated over a two-bay centre, the plan has the tripartite division as at Dunkeld and Moncreiffe and as repeated at Auchendinny, Midlothian, a plain five-bay house raised after 1702 for an Edinburgh merchant.[117] Yet, that the spirit of invention had not finally deserted Bruce was shown at HOPETOUN HOUSE, West Lothian.

In an age of grandiose house building by the aristocracy Hopetoun [21] was to become one of the most extensive seats, taking its place alongside such English palaces as Castle Howard and Wentworth Woodhouse and for size and interest rivalled in Scotland only in the nineteenth century by the large additions to Hamilton Palace. Alike by its extent, its decoration and the reputation of its architects, Hopetoun is the key work in the

21 HOPETOUN HOUSE, West Lothian, by Sir William Bruce.

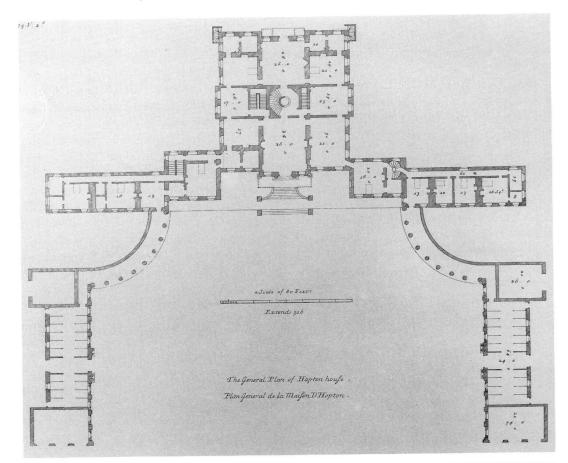

22 HOPETOUN HOUSE, West
Lothian, by Sir William Bruce

23 HOPETOUN HOUSE,
West Lothian, the garden parlour

20

understanding and appreciation of eighteenth-century classical country-house architecture in Scotland.

The building contract was signed in 1698 by Lady Margaret Hope[118] for her son, Sir Charles Hope, then a minor, who was elevated to the peerage five years later. Lord Hopetoun, who would marry a daughter of Lord Annandale,[119] was, like his father-in-law, a virtuoso while, through a series of relationships, he was connected to Bruce.[120] The architect's plan [22] was a Greek cross-in-square, the first to be used in Scotland, with the public rooms [23] grouped around an octagonal staircase well with the more private apartments filling in the corners of the square. Such a plan, though it would first suggest an analytical combination of Serlian and Palladian elements, with the Villa Rotonda as the leitmotif, seems to have had a nearer and more novel source for there is a striking similarity to the château of Marly [24] begun only twenty years before and drawn out with room dimensions by Alexander Edward,[121] who acted as Bruce's architectural amanuensis. Externally, the overall effect is Palladian with an easy horizontality, aprons below the windows, and statuary atop the unbroken parapet. The Villa Marcello may have been the inspiration for the triple-arched entrance although Bruce substituted pilasters, as was permissible in the Palladian canon, for the terminal columns. Yet the French influence was not entirely suppressed and is most evident in the banded ashlar[122] and more vividly on the garden front where the tight little semicircular pediment could have been devised by Le Muet himself. The house was finished by 1703,[123] leaving the attendant stables, other offices and colonnades to be completed. According to *Vitruvius Britannicus*[124] the last were convex, not the usual concave, and may have been the first of their kind in Britain.

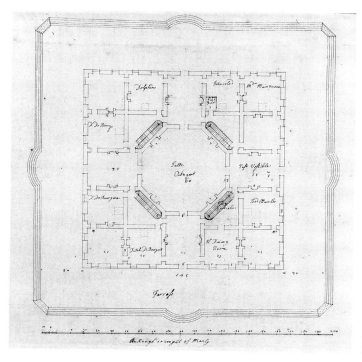

24 CHÂTEAU OF MARLY,
from a drawing by Alexander Edward

As was so often the case with a Bruce work, the master mason was Tobias Bauchope who received a first payment, of £50, at the end of December 1698 with regular payments following in the months and years ahead. By 1701 the building work was sufficiently far advanced to allow contracts to be placed with the finishing trades, including one for wright work with Alexander Eizat[125] while in the following year the contract between 'the laird of Hopetoun and George Humphray plaisterer' was witnessed by Bruce.[126] Finally, Thomas Warrander the painter was paid 'for Collering the Balcony roume in the 3rd story three tymes over wt. ane pearle collour in oyll and marbelling the Chimney'. In the bedroom of the countess the panels were rendered 'in fyne Landscap work of walnuttree Colloure in oyll, and the styles japand on ane blak ground' although in the dressing-room the styles were tortoiseshell on a gold ground. Externally, too, there was some paintwork including 'the four lead pipes for receaving the water from the roof of the timpons (i.e. pediments) on the front and back of the house 3 times over wt. a stone collor in oyll'.[127]

Hopetoun, Bruce's last major work, marks in the architect's oeuvre a definite break with what had gone before. True, it may be seen as the culmination of a process whereby Bruce's early commitment to Serlio is overtaken by his French and English experience and, finally, by his conversion to Palladianism. The appearance of the last at Hopetoun is extraordinary since Palladian layouts in English country-houses had appeared only at Hackwood Park and Burley-on-the-Hill. With Bruce their use, including convex screen walls at Kinross, was both tentative and not wholly satisfactory aesthetically; at Hopetoun there is a harmony of the parts whether it is the dignified scale of the masses or running the cornice of the colonnades through the main block as a string-course. At Hopetoun, an Italian evocation by the shore of the Firth of Forth, the creative vision would seem to have been that of an old but experienced hand pulling out all the stops, perhaps as a response to the grandeur of the concept but perhaps to prove to younger architects, and possibly to James Smith in particular, that new tricks were to be had from an old dog.

Notes to Chapter I

1. J. G. Fyfe (ed.), *Scottish Diaries and Memoirs*, vol. I (1928), p. 179; R. Marshall, *The Days of Duchess Anne* (1973), pp. 30–1.
2. W. C. Mackenzie, *The Life and Times of John Maitland, Duke of Lauderdale* (1923), p. 338, n. 1 quoting Wodrow; Fyfe, op. cit., vol. I, pp. 173–4.
3. S. Cruden, *The Scottish Castle* (1963), p. 220.
4. D. MacGibbon and T. Ross, *The Castellated and Domestic Architecture of Scotland* (1887–92), vol. II, pp. 198–9; Cruden, op. cit., pp. 155, 188; J. G. Dunbar, *The Historic Architecture of Scotland* (1966), p. 75.
5. 'The Book of Record. A Diary Written by Patrick, First Earl of Strathmore, 1684–9', *SHS*, vol. IX (1890), p. xiii; A. H. Millar, *The Historical Castles and Mansions of Scotland* (1890), p. 229.
6. 'The Book of Record', pp. 37–8; Millar, op. cit., p. 225.
7. 'The Book of Record', p. 42; Millar, op. cit., p. 232.
8. 'The Book of Record', p. 41; Millar, op. cit., p. 230.
9. 'The Book of Record', p. 19.
10. D. Defoe, *A Tour through the Whole Island of Great Britain* (1927), vol. II, p. 798.
11. 'The Book of Record', p. 33; Cruden, op. cit., p. 151; Dunbar, op. cit., p. 75.
12. C. Fiennes, *The Journeys of Celia Fiennes* (1947), pp. 205–6.
13. J. Macky, *A Journey through Scotland* (1723), p. 7.

14. R. Chambers, *Domestic Annals of Scotland from the Reformation to the Revolution* (1859), vol. II, p. 426.
15. 'The Book of Record', p. 32.
16. Countess of Rothes to Sir William Bruce, Balgonie, 19 September 1670, SRO, GD29/1901/2.
    R. S. Mylne, *The Master Masons to the Crown of Scotland* (1893), p. 217 refers to Mylne finishing the gallery which is a misreading of Lady Rothes' letter.
    In July 1668 black and white floor tiles had been supplied by Sir William Bruce. See J. Dunbar, *Sir William Bruce, 1630–1710* (1970), p. 10.
17. Countess of Rothes to Sir William Bruce, Balgonie, 19 September 1670, SRO, GD29/1901/1.
18. Ibid., 19 October 1670, SRO, GD29/1901/4.
19. Ibid., Balgonie, 10 October 1670, SRO, GD29/1901/3.
20. Supra, n. 18.
21. Ibid., 22 October 1670, SRO, GD29/1901/5.
22. 'Ane note of thes(e) thing(s) which are to be sent from London', SRO, GD29/1901/9.
23. J. Fittler and J. C. Nattes, *Scotia Depicta* (1804); *SA*, vol. VI, p. 53; *NSA*, vol. IX, p. 116; J. M. Leighton, *History of the County of Fife* (1840), vol. II, p. 188; A. H. Millar, *Fife: Pictorial and Historical* (1895), vol. II, p. 75.
24. Macky, op. cit., p. 169. The contract for the two pavilions and for finishing a gardener's house was signed on 16 August 1671. Robert Mylne was the mason and Sir William Bruce was a witness. Rothes MSS, 40/69/1.
25. Defoe, op. cit., vol. II, p. 689.
26. Ibid., vol. II, p. 778. See also 'Journal of Henry Kalmeter's Travels in Scotland, 1719–20', *SHS*, 4th Series, vol. XIV (1978), p. 25.
27. Inventory of *c*.1722–50, Rothes MSS, 40/58/1.
28. Supra, n. 22.
29. S. Serlio, *Tutte l'Opere d'Architettura et Prospetiva* (republished 1968), Bk. VII, p. 57.
30. Ibid., Bk. III, p. 122.
31. Accounts for the building of Leslie House show that as late as April 1677 money was still owing to Robert Mylne. Rothes MSS, 40/69/3.
32. P. Hume Brown, *Tours in Scotland, 1677 and 1681 by Thomas Kirk and Ralph Thoresby* (1892), p. 17.
33. Dunbar, ibid. Leslie House was to be built by 1 September 1669 at a cost of £3,000 sterling. W. Bodie, 'Introduction to the Rothes Papers', *PSAS*, vol. 110 (1978–80), pp. 408–10 wrongly gives the building dates as 1677 and 1679.
34. *DNB*; H. M. Colvin, *A Biographical Dictionary of British Architects, 1600–1840* (1978), p. 569.
35. MacGibbon and Ross, op. cit., vol. IV, p. 278. The Methven estate was purchased in 1664 by Patrick Smythe of Braco whose descendants in 1815 commissioned neo-Jacobean designs from James Gillespie (Graham). *NSA*, vol. X, p. 150 states that Methven Castle was completed in 1680.
36. J. Stuart, ed., *Registrum de Panmure* (1872), vol. I, p. xliii.
37. SRO, GD45/18/565. Mylne, op. cit., pp. 153–7; Stuart, op. cit., vol. I, pp. xliv–xlvi; A. H. Millar, *The Historical Castles and Mansions of Scotland*, pp. 289–92; Colvin, op. cit., p. 570.
    It is interesting to note that seventy years later, when Duff House, Banffshire, was being built, the masons worked a twelve and a half hour day with an hour off for breakfast and another one for dinner. 'State of the proof in the process William Adams Archt. in Edinr. agt. William Ld. Braco. 8 December 1743', SRO, CS230/A2/1.
38. *VS*, pls 129–31.
39. Serlio, op. cit., Bk. VII, p. 25.
40. Stuart, op. cit., vol. I, p. xlvi; Mylne, op. cit., p. 157.
41. Earl of Panmure to Sir William Bruce at Kinross, Panmure, 12 February 1693, SRO, GD29/1944. Mylne, op. cit., p. 232.
42. Ibid., p. 156. The 4th Earl of Panmure succeeded in 1686 and came out in support of the Old Pretender in 1715. Macky, op. cit., p. 99, compared the offices at Panmure with those at Yester House, East Lothian.
43. J. Fleming, *Robert Adam and His Circle* (1962), p. 331. Quoted by Dunbar, op. cit., p. 2.

44. 'The Book of Record', p. 28.

45. Mylne, op. cit., p. 167.

46. The best-informed account of Sir William Bruce's life appears in Dunbar, op. cit., pp. 1–2. See also *DNB*; J. Dunbar, *The Historic Architecture of Scotland*, pp. 93–4; Colvin, op. cit., pp. 151–3.

47. MacGibbon and Ross, op. cit., vol. IV, pp. 335–9; 'Thirlestane Castle, Berwickshire', *CL*, vol. XXVIII (6 August 1910), p. 196.

48. J. Dunbar, 'The Building Activities of the Duke and Duchess of Lauderdale, 1670–82', *The Archaeological Journal*, vol. 132 (1975), pp. 202–13 gives the fullest account of the progress of the improvements at Thirlestane Castle. M. Binney, 'Thirlestane Castle, Berwickshire', *CL*, vol. CLXXIV (11 and 18 August 1983), pp. 336–9, 410–13.

49. Sir William Bruce to the Earl of Lauderdale, Edinburgh, 3 January 1671. Mylne, op. cit., p. 164.

50. R. T. Gunther, *The Architecture of Sir Roger Pratt* (1972), p. 60; O. Hill and J. Cornforth, *English Country Houses. Caroline, 1625–1685* (1966), p. 37.

51. Gunther, ibid., p. 48; Hill and Cornforth, ibid.

52. Lord Lauderdale to Sir William Bruce, Ham, 19 October 1671, SRO, GD29/1897/4.

53. Lord Lauderdale to Lord Hatton, 4 April 1671. Mylne, op. cit., p. 167.

54. Lord Lauderdale to Sir William Bruce, Ham, 24 December 1672, SRO, GD29/1897/7. Mylne, op. cit., p. 184.

55. Supra, n. 53.

56. Lord Lauderdale to his overseer, Thomas Cassill, Ham, 4 May 1671, SRO, GD29/1897/3. Mylne, op. cit., p. 168.

57. Lord Lauderdale to Lord Hatton, Ham, 2 June 1671. Mylne, op. cit., p. 174.

58. Lord Lauderdale to Sir William Bruce, Ham, 15 April 1673, SRO, GD29/1897/9. Mylne, op. cit., pp. 185–6.

59. Lord Lauderdale to Sir William Bruce, Whitehall, 3 April 1673, SRO, GD29/1897/8. Mylne, op. cit., p. 185.

60. Ibid.

61. J. Dunbar, *Sir William Bruce, 1630–1710*, p. 12; G. Beard, *Decorative Plasterwork in Great Britain* (1975), pp. 82–3.

62. Mylne, op. cit., p. 175.

63. Fyfe, op. cit., vol. I, p. 277; Mackenzie, op. cit., p. 496.

64. Dunbar, op. cit., p. 13.

65. Serlio, op. cit., Bk. III, p. 122.

66. Ibid., Bk. VII, p. 13.

67. MacGibbon and Ross, op. cit., vol. IV, p. 180; G. Good, *Liberton in Ancient and Modern Times* (1893), pp. 81–3; J. Dunbar, 'The Building Activities of the Duke and Duchess of Lauderdale, 1670–82', pp. 214–17 describes fully the changes at Brunstane House.

68. Lord Lauderdale to Sir William Bruce, Ham, 23 October 1672, SRO, GD29/1897/6. Mylne, op. cit. p. 182.

69. Lord Lauderdale to Sir William Bruce, York, 16 October 1672, SRO, GD29/1897/5. Mylne, ibid.

70. Supra, n. 56.

71. Lord Lauderdale to Sir William Bruce, Whitehall, 3 April 1673, SRO, GD29/1879/8. Mylne, op. cit., p. 184.

72. Supra, n. 56.

73. MacGibbon and Ross, op. cit., vol. III, pp. 268–73; 'Hatton House, Midlothian, *CL*, vol. XXX (16 September 1911), pp. 410–12; T. Hannan, *Famous Scottish Houses* (1928), pp. 97–9; C. McWilliam, *Lothian* (1978), pp. 247–8.

74. Hannan, ibid. The south-east corner of Hatton House was built in 1640 and incorporated in the later rebuilding which began in that corner and progressed towards the west. The house was demolished in 1955 without having been properly recorded.

75. *VB*, vol. II (1717), p. 4: *DNB*.

76. Duke of Atholl, *Chronicles of the Atholl and Tullibardine Families* (1908), vol. I, p. 172.
77. R. Pococke, 'Tours in Scotland, 1747, 1750, 1760', *SHS*, vol. I (1887), p. 226.
78. J. Dunbar, *Sir William Bruce, 1630–1710*, p. 14.
79. Atholl, op. cit., vol. I, pp. 172–3.
80. Lord Atholl wrote to the Provost of Perth from Dunkeld on 29 September 1684: 'Sir, Being informed that is is customarie to heugh stones in the new church of Perth, I intreat you will allow John Smith, meason, libertie to heugh some for my house at Dunkeld.' Ibid., vol. I, p. 199.
81. Dunbar, ibid.
82. Atholl, op. cit., vol. IV, p. 388; J. Mitchell, *Reminiscences of My Life in the Highlands* (1883), vol. I, p. 107. D. Wordsworth, *Recollections of a Tour Made in Scotland A.D. 1803* (1874), p. 211, described Dunkeld House as 'an ordinary gentleman's house ... and whitewashed, I believe'. In 1758 Sir William Burrell found that 'large Offices' were being built 'into every Part of Which Water is conveyed in Leaden Pipes at the distance of almost an English mile'. NLS, MS 2911, f. 16.
83. The date was carved above the entrance. *NSA*, vol. X, p. 804; F. Moncrieff and W. Moncrieffe, *The Moncrieffs and the Moncrieffes* (1929), vol. I, p. 304.
84. Ibid., vol. I, p. 294. It was from the Moncrieffs that Bruce purchased the Balcaskie estate in Fife in 1665. 'Balcaskie, Fife', *CL*, vol. XXXI (2 March 1912), p. 318.
85. Dunkeld House appears in the background of the portrait of John, 1st Duke of Atholl by Thomas Murray, 1708, at Blair Castle, Perthshire and in J. Slezer's *Theatrum Scotiae*. At each corner of the wallhead there were curious projections like a classical rendering of angle turrets and on at least two of the elevations there was a pedimented dormer.

    Dunkeld House was condemned in 1827 by Thomas Hopper and replaced in the next year by a large Gothic mansion, of which he was the architect, which was begun for the 4th Duke of Atholl but left incomplete, and eventually demolished, after his death in 1830. Atholl, op. cit., vol. IV, pp. 388, 392–3.

    The remains of Moncreiffe House were taken down after a fire in 1957.
86. Macky, op. cit., p. 159.
87. Hill and Cornforth, op. cit., p. 25.
88. P. P. Rubens, *Palazzi di Genova* (republished 1968), fig. 3.
89. Serlio, op. cit., Bk. VII, p. 103.
90. J. Dunbar, *The Historic Architecture of Scotland*, p. 96.
91. Ibid., p. 94; J. Dunbar, *Sir William Bruce, 1630–1710*, pp. 10–11.
92. Serlio, op. cit., Bk. VII, pp. 37, 103.
93. Dunbar, op. cit., pp. 2, 7.
94. J. Summerson, *Architecture in Britain, 1530–1830*, 4th edn. (1963), pp. 80, 109.
95. Dunbar, op. cit., p. 14. See also M. Girouard, 'Kinross House, Kinross-shire', *CL*, vol. CXXXVII (25 March and 1 April 1965), pp. 666–70, 726–9; J. Dunbar, 'Kinross House, Kinross-shire', *The Country Seat*, ed. by H. Colvin and J. Harris (1970), pp. 64–9.
96. SRO, GD1/51/62; *CL*, vol. XXXII (20 July 1912), p. 93.
97. SRO, GD29/432/1–7. It should be noted that in 1686 at Craighall, Fife, which was remodelled a decade later by Bruce, there was only one set of 'Stamped Hangings'. The hall had 'five pairs of new Arras hangings which were bought when the house was taken up' and there were five other pieces, which had cost £47, in the drawing-room. 'Inventor (sic) of the Furniture of Craighall House', SRO GD242/Box 40.
98. Macky, op. cit., p. 171.
99. Defoe, op. cit., vol II, p. 777.
100. Macky, op. cit., p. 172.
101. J. Lees-Milne, *English Country Houses. Baroque, 1685–1715* (1970), pp. 39, 41.
102. Hill and Cornforth, op. cit., pp. 28, 134; Summerson, op. cit., pp. 87–8.
103. General Monck, who was known to Bruce, having been instrumental in bringing about the Restoration, was created Duke of Albemarle by Charles II in 1660. Monck was a friend of Edward Hyde, Earl of Clarendon and unsuccessfully tried to save him from the wrath of Parliament before the earl fled abroad,

dying in exile in 1674. According to Evelyn, his son sold Clarendon House, which had cost £50,000, in 1675 to the 2nd Duke of Albemarle for half that sum. Gunther, op. cit., pp. 16, 137–8.

104. J. Loveday, 'Diary of a Tour in 1732', *Roxburghe Club* (1889), p. 129.

105. J. Dunbar, *Sir William Bruce, 1630–1710*, p. 15.

106. Gunther, op. cit., p. 54.

107. Ibid., p. 24.

108. *VS*, pl. 142. The foundation stone is dated 1703. See J. Cornforth, 'Mertoun, Berwickshire', *CL*, vol. CXXXIX (2 June 1966), pp. 1392–5; Dunbar, op. cit., p. 19.

109. Fiennes, op. cit., pp. 24, 61.

110. Gunther, op. cit., pp. 27–8, 64–5.

111. Ibid., p. 62.

112. Sir William Bruce to Lord Annandale, Kinross, 3 September 1694, Hopetoun MSS, bundle 470.

113. 'Contract Betwixt the Earle of Annandale and Tobias Bachop. 1698', Hopetoun MSS, bundle 355.
A volume, belonging to the Earl of Rosebery, of drawings of Craigiehall includes a basement and first-floor plan (f. 59) which seem to be preliminary studies for the final design. Stylistic analysis indicates that they are by James Smith who prepared 'Ane estimat of the hous' as did Robert Mylne. Hopetoun MSS, bundles 1768 and 472.
The outworks of Craigiehall were being considered in 1708 when Alexander McGill and Lord Mar exchanged designs for the inner and outer courts, the railings, piers and gates, using as a model for the last 'one of J. Tijou's plates or prints'. SRO, GD124/15/752/1 and 2.

114. The Countess of Annandale to Sir William Bruce, SRO, GD29/1955/1.

115. Gunther, op. cit., p. 27.

116. The Earl of Annandale to Sir William Bruce, Craigiehall, 13 September, SRO, GD29/1955/2. Mylne, op. cit., p. 232.

117. The tradition that Bruce was the designer of Auchendinny must be an old one since Henry Mackenzie, the author of *The Man of Feeling*, who lived in the house, praised Bruce for the construction of chimneys that did not smoke. H. W. Thompson, *The Anecdotes and Egotisms of Henry Mackenzie, 1745–1831* (1927), p. 216; McWilliam, op. cit., p. 83.

118. Ibid., p. 251; *VB*, ibid. See also A. Rowan, 'The Building of Hopetoun', *Architectural History*, vol. 27 (1984), pp. 183–9.

119. *DNB*.

120. Dunbar, op. cit., pp. 6, 17.

121. Gibbs drawings, III, 49, Ashmolean Museum, University of Oxford. The drawing is undated but probably belongs to Edward's continental journey of 1701–2 when he visited several of the French royal châteaux, including Marly. Clearly, however, Bruce must have known of the plan of Marly before Edward's visit. See Colvin, op. cit., p. 282.

122. *VB*, ibid.

123. Dunbar, op. cit., p. 17.

124. *VB*, vol. II, pls. 75, 76. McWilliam, op cit., p. 253 suggests that the colonnades were never built. Although there is no mention of them in the accounts there is a reference to 'Guilding the Globs and Thenes of the two pavilions'. 'Account Be the Earl of Hopton to Thomas Warrendar painter. June 1701 to December 1703', Hopetoun MSS, bundle 3025.
Macky, op. cit., p. 205 records that, 'The Court-Yard is collonaded (sic) and adorn'd with Statues and Vases; but since the Building the two Wings, the Court is to be extended to the Breadth of them, and proportionably longer.'

125. Hopetoun MSS, bundle 626.

126. Ibid., bundle 627. On 7 July 1714 Lord Roxburghe wrote to his mother recommending that, 'Mr Humphrey' should undertake plastering at Broxmouth, East Lothian. Duke of Roxburghe's MSS, bundle 768.

127. Supra, n. 124. Hopetoun MSS.

CHAPTER TWO

'A Mr Smith, a Popish Architect'

With the appearance of James Smith the question of the origin of Palladianism in late seventeenth- and early eighteenth-century Britain becomes a matter of debate.[1] Unlike Bruce, whose knowledge of Palladianism was not graced by the benefit of foreign travel, Smith, who claimed in old age to have had 'a liberal education at schools and Colledges at home and abroad', may have spent the years between 1671 and 1675 in Rome, thus enabling him to develop a precocious interest in Palladian concepts as shown in drawings later held by Colen Campbell.[2] Smith would, therefore, merit Pratt's approbation since, when it came to house building, 'No man deserves the name of an Architect, who had not been very well versed both in those old ones of Rome, as likewise the more modern of Italy and France.'[3] Even so it has been suggested by one authority that Smith was content to follow in the footsteps of Bruce, producing 'plain, handsome and for the most part undemonstrative houses'[4] with the unqualified exception of DRUMLANRIG CASTLE, the massive red sandstone mansion [25], which, with its galleried and columned show front, rises from the Dumfries-shire hills like a pink marble palace in the steaming heat of the Indian subcontinent. That Colen Campbell included Drumlanrig Castle in the first volume of *Vitruvius Britannicus* must surely have been a gesture of loyalty or friendship for not only is it the sole Scottish specimen but it is the only non-classical building. The dated lintels on the courtyard towers

25 DRUMLANRIG CASTLE, Dumfries-shire

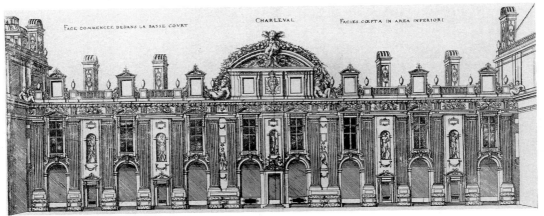

26 CHÂTEAU OF CHARLEVAL, by Jacques du Cerceau

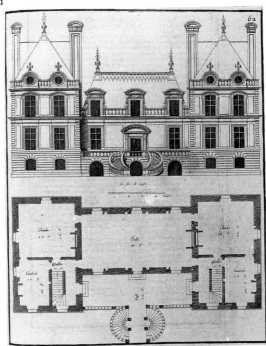

27 CHÂTEAU OF PONTZ, by Pierre le Muet

are evidence that work was in progress at Drumlanrig in 1679 and continued for eleven years, with William Lukup as clerk of works under the direction of James Smith, who supplied plans which, in essence, were inherited from a much older scheme,[5] comparable to Heriot's Hospital. However, the early seventeenth-century scheme was brought up to date by incorporating a loggia looking into the inner court. More interesting, though, are the changes, which must be Smith's, on the show front. The open parapet and central cupola, bearing a ducal coronet, make due obeisance to the newly finished palace of Holyroodhouse, while the pilasters, pediments and richly swagged porch must surely come from Du Cerceau's château of Charleval, of a hundred years before, which may even have

28

28 MELVILLE HOUSE, Fife

influenced the plan [26]. Finally, the whole robust assemblage sits above an arched basement and a horseshoe staircase taken, without any pretence of concealing the plagiarism, from Le Muet.[6] Although the purist may sneer at such borrowings [27], sheltering beneath Gothic turrets, or carp because 'every where is a wearysome profusion of hearts carved in stone',[7] Drumlanrig is thrilling. Smith welded his elements to dramatise a unique composition on which he scored his classical vocabulary with lugged window architraves, bands of triglyphs and basement niches which, in *Vitruvius Britannicus* at least, shelter coy but scantily clad statuary figures.

As the last of the medieval courtyard mansions and in a late transitional style Drumlanrig is apart from the sequence of Smith's domestic architecture as, indeed, is MELVILLE HOUSE, Fife [28], not least for its Englishness. Colen Campbell noted succinctly that 'it was designed by the most experienc'd Architect of that Kingdom, Mr James Smith'[8] and it was one of two Scottish seats, the other being Hopetoun House, which found a place in the second volume of *Vitruvius Britannicus*. The preamble of a lawsuit sets on record, 'That in the year 1697 George, Earl of Melvil ... entered into Contract wt. Mr James and James Smiths [sic], for building a new house at Melvil ... there was a draught of ye sd. house and intended building made out' which did not include the colonnade and pavilions.[9] Clearly, Smith was the builder. But was he the architect? In April 1697 Sir William Bruce wrote to Lord Melville: 'I have painfully improven the draught I designed for your Lo.'s house, and kept the bearer Mr Edward from morning till night close at work to extend the whole Stories and the elivation [sic] of the fronts of ye whole' which 'will provide a convenient good house', which was perhaps more than could be said of a scheme by Smith since Bruce could make nothing of his 'draught' which was perhaps a lesser consideration than that 'it was high time for him to repair to Minomoall [Monimail, near Melville] and set about, and give directions for preparing and providing materials for founding, such as ston [sic], lime, sand and utensiles for ye work'.[10] Two years later, when the plumber's contract was

29

29 MELVILLE HOUSE, Fife

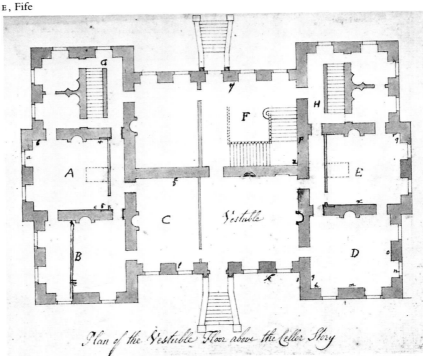

30 MELVILLE
HOUSE,
Fife, late
seventeenth-century
ground plan

Plan of the Vestible Floor above the Celler Story

signed,[11] the construction work must have been nearing completion with the finishing trades taking another three years so that it was probably with some thankfulness that Lord Melville could have the year 1702 carved on the oak mantel in the saloon.

As built, Melville [29] is an H-block resembling Belton House, Lincolnshire, which had been completed less than ten years before near Grantham[12] on the eastern route between

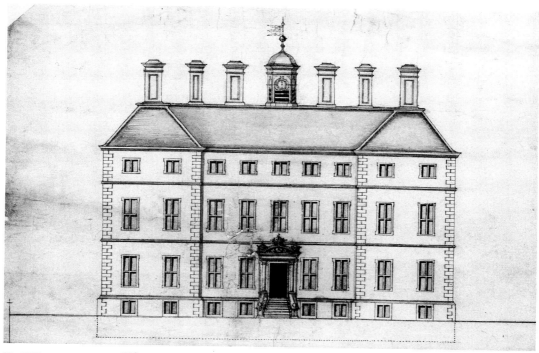

31 MELVILLE HOUSE, Fife, 1697

London and Scotland. In plan, however, Melville is both shorter and more compact so that the elevations have more mobility, especially on each side where a pediment breaks forward over two bays, a favourite Bruce arrangement. Indeed, there are numerous cross–references to Kinross for not only does Melville have an attic storey and a five-bay centre, as against seven at Belton, but its plan can be regarded as a loosening and expansion of the more controlled Kinross. Lastly, the entrance floor, with a saloon of identical area above, is an arrangement [30] that occurred at Kinross and afterwards at Hopetoun House. On stylistic grounds, therefore, there is much to commend Bruce as the designer, a hypothesis which can be further tested by considering the elevational drawings relating to Melville. The drawing [31] which approximates most closely to the finished building, with a weather-vane which appears to be dated 1697,[13] must be the 'unsubscribed plan which agreed with the Contract in every point', referred to in the lawsuit.[14] However, two other drawings, the more finished of which is annotated by Smith, are of more interest because of the design concept and the design source.[15] The former has a six-bay centre with a two-storeyed loggia which, in the second drawing, has sufficient detail to show the capitals of the order [32]. This Italianate façade recalls the Villa Trissino, built by Palladio's first patron at Cricoli, near Vicenza, which Smith may have visited. As Palladianism it not only goes beyond anything yet attempted in Scotland, or indeed in England since Jones, but the loggias and their flanking towers are handled so convincingly – it is the Caroline cupola that is the oddity – that one has the feeling that here is an interpretation of Palladianism seen in Italy.

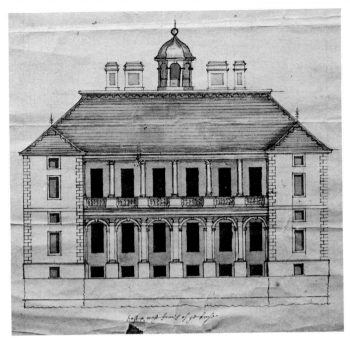

32 MELVILLE HOUSE, Fife,
preliminary design,
late seventeenth century

Such a point of view can be fortified by turning to another design[16] which must, to judge by the massing and the rhythm of the bays, be for Melville. An attached tetrastyle portico rises through three storeys with an entablature and pediment riding over the wallhead so that the whole frontispiece has the awkward air of having been imposed on an existing elevation. There are two versions of the corresponding plan in which a central, top-lit hall is either square or circular with four openings alternating with niches and columns so that the Pantheon is brought to mind.[17] If the Italian origin of the schemes is correct then not only does Smith's work after Melville become more significant but Melville, as it stands, should be removed from the list of his designs leaving him the role of executant architect.

The earliest houses where Smith had a free hand were his own home, Newhailes (originally Whitehill), Midlothian, and Raith House, Fife, to which may be added, on stylistic grounds, STRATHLEVEN HOUSE, Dunbartonshire, a modest-sized mansion of c.1690[18] and hitherto without a proven architect [33]. All three houses may be examined together, being of approximately the same overall dimensions and composed of seven bays with the central three edging forward below a pediment with quoins as the only other diversion. NEWHAILES, 'first made by a Mr Smith, a Popish Architect'[19] for which the plans and an elevation [34] are among the Campbell drawings,[20] is a single-pile plan, which

33 STRATHLEVEN HOUSE, Dunbartonshire

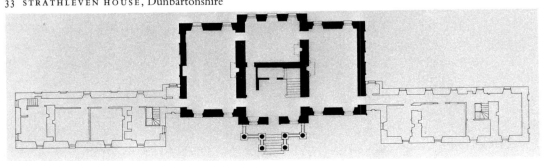

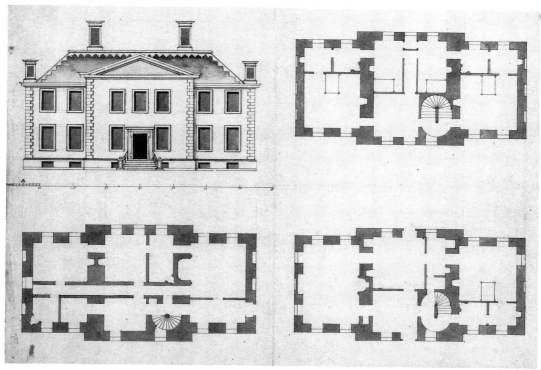

34 NEWHAILES, Midlothian, by James Smith

Pratt condemned since the rooms would 'lie open to all winds, and weather, and having through lights, look too glaring, and be inconvenient for the most part for pictures, beds, etc.'.[21] RAITH, which bears the date 1694, making it two or three years later than its counterpart, has been remodelled internally but can be ascribed to Smith for not only does his name recur in the building accounts but there is a site plan in his hand.[22] One should also take into consideration two previously unidentified drawings.[23] The first shows a seven-bay house with a portico and cupola with a weather-vane incised with the initials A M, presumably for Alexander Melville, Lord Raith (1655–98), the eldest son of Lord Melville and treasurer depute of Scotland. His monogram, similar to one on the Raith datestone, is in the tympanum of the second design [35] which, although not executed with all the rich external detail, has a plan very like that of Newhailes and, in its essentials, of the modified Strathleven.

At Raith the most novel feature is the tympanum with blind *oculi* which compares with the same feature at Belton before it was reshaped,[24] making the Scottish link with that house earlier than was suspected. Or is the Raith tympanum another credit in the calculation of Smith's Italianism? For example, Strathleven [36] has a full entablature over the centre but with the frieze and cornice scaling the wallhead to support the pediment in which *oculi* partner coats of arms. Similarly, the Villa Rotonda has *oculi* and though each pediment is bound to a portico, Smith's practice of using the pediment alone was justified by Palladio for 'such frontispieces shew the entrance of the house, and add very much to the grandeur

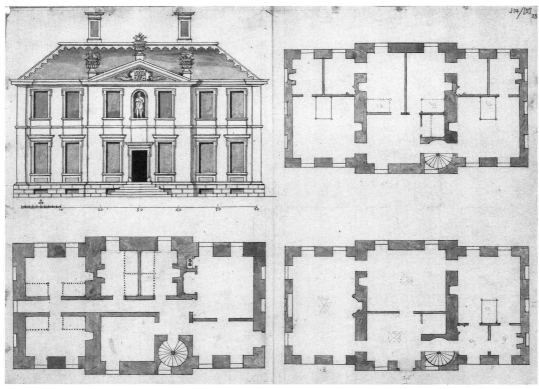

35 RAITH HOUSE, Fife, by James Smith
36 STRATHLEVEN HOUSE, Dunbartonshire

37 HAMILTON PALACE, Lanarkshire, south elevation

and magnificence of the work. Besides, the fore-part ... is very commodious for placing the ensigns or arms of the owners.'[25] Newhailes, Raith and Strathleven are harled, a practice which was becoming less common with quality building in Scotland and may, therefore, be yet one more evocation of Italy. Certainly, if a distinction can be made between Bruce and Smith it would be that the former came slowly, and perhaps reluctantly, to Palladianism through study whereas the latter may have seen Palladio's works. One can then understand why the prim little pediment at Craigiehall sits awkwardly while Smith's settle easily into the façade. Such reasoning also helps to show that Smith's two major works, Hamilton Palace and Dalkeith House, are consistent with his development as a Palladian architect.

Although HAMILTON PALACE, Lanarkshire [37], was torn down half a century ago, after generations of ducal extravagance and latterly indifference, there is sufficient in the way of engravings, accounts and correspondence to reform its late seventeenth-century genesis from the palace of a hundred years before. Then it was quadrangular, mostly three storeys high and with a square, platformed tower protruding at either end of the north front where the entrance led into the Horn Hall, so called because it was hung with antlers. Immediately to the west was the Laigh or Low Hall from which the Great Stairs in the corner tower led to the gallery filling the entire north range and containing, not only prized family portraits, but masterpieces by, amongst others, Rubens and Raphael. The west wing held the important chambers, such as the High Dining Room and the High Drawing Room.[26]

It may seem surprising that in an age given over to aristocratic building, because of the status implied by houses of magnitude and richness, the Hamiltons who, by their station and the extent of their possessions, were without equal in Scotland, should have continued to live in a residence which was not only old-fashioned but awkward in circulation and management. Yet the civil war had wrought havoc with the family finances for, besides debts, there were fines and even the sequestration of estates so that any thoughts of rebuilding

35

had of necessity to be postponed until there was a recovery of prosperity. In the meantime architecture was becoming a public art in which gentlemen ought to be interested and knowledgeable. On his journeys into England, therefore, the 3rd Duke of Hamilton inspected houses, such as Hatfield, purchased architectural treatises and doubtless perused with some eagerness the description of French mansions sent home by his eldest son.[27] When, finally, the reconstruction at Hamilton did get under way it began, as at Kinross, with the offices and after 1684 stables and kitchens were erected before work started at the end of 1691 on demolishing the west range with careful instructions that the good stone was to be retained.[28]

Meanwhile the duke had turned to Sir William Bruce for advice and he recommended Tobias Bauchope as 'a fit person to build your palace at Hamilton'.[29] A year later, in March 1692, Bruce was again consulted and this time sent his mason to Hamilton; the duke then went to Kinross House and in the autumn Bruce and Bauchope were at the palace. Even after the building contract for the west wing was signed with James Smith and his cousin of the same name in March 1693 the Duke paid 'Mr Banks the king's carpenter for drawing some draughts of the Palace at Hamilton'. According to the Duke's heir, Sir Christopher Wren was 'one my father used to consult with' and when the duke went south, taking Smith with him, the latter went to see Wren's work at Hampton Court.

After a year's labour the west wing was being roofed. Speed was of the essence for as the duke wrote: 'I do not intend to pull down a stone more until we are living in that now in hand.'[30] When the duke died shortly afterwards the duchess persisted with what her son called 'the Great Design'[31] so that within two more years the east wing was complete. Only then was attention given to the intervening north range which was to be renovated internally.[32] Still, there were numerous consultations and exchanges of drawings, with Wren being asked for his opinion,[33] so that Smith's design, as he wrote in May 1696, 'is the result of all that we can look upon, either related to our invention or by comparing the designs that came from London with the work which is already done'.[34] It soon became clear, however, that, except for the north wall and the towers, the entire range would have to be taken down and, although there was a set-back, there was a gain as the new work could be tied in fully with the new west and east wings. By the close of the building season in 1697 the stonework was finished, with the exception of the new stair and the carving of coats of arms, crests and ciphers,[35] although it was to be another four years before the interior was complete. Certainly Hamilton Palace was everything that could be desired of a ducal seat. The largest new house in Scotland, it was impressive alike for its architectural control of massing and of detail whether in the armorial tympanum or in the sumptuous display of carved woodwork with soberly panelled rooms [38] made joyous by frames of fruit, flowers and game cascading from carved cornices to marble chimney-pieces set between oak pilasters and surmounted by coronets and collared arms [39]. The gallery, in particular, was, and continued to be, admired by all, while Defoe rated the apartments as 'fit rather for the Court of a Prince than the Palace or House of a Subject'.[36]

Because of atavism and with piecemeal building the old plan was reproduced in broad measure with numerous rooms being found in their former positions [40]. Although the palace may have appeared, therefore, old-fashioned in plan, when compared to other

38 HAMILTON PALACE, Lanarkshire,
bedchamber in the west wing

39 HAMILTON PALACE, Lanarkshire, bedchamber

contemporary Scottish houses, it was suited to the grandeur of the family, for as Pratt noted: 'Concerning the building about a court, it is without all doubt fit only for a large family, and a great purse.' Still, his reservation about the possibility of shade being cast by the wings[37] was certainly a criticism of Hamilton. The plan, which was not, one suspects, of

40 HAMILTON PALACE, Lanarkshire

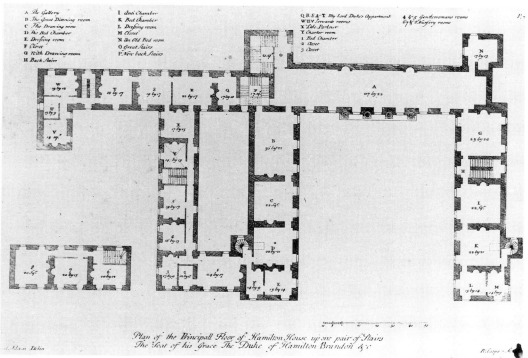

41 HAMILTON PALACE, Lanarkshire, the entrance portico by James Smith

Smith's choosing, can be related, if one is looking for an antecedent, to one by Le Muet whose style is accurately represented on the return elevation of the wings.[38] However, the chief external interest must be the tetrastyle portico [41] which, with its half-engaged columns on high plinths, rose through three storeys. Nothing like it had yet been seen in Scotland nor, for that matter, in England although Wren had introduced a portico at Chelsea Hospital in 1682 and a hexastyle one, rising through two floors, at Winchester Palace begun in 1683. So far as Hamilton Palace is concerned the closest stylistic sources would appear to be some of Palladio's villas. Yet none has the scale of Smith's portico, which bears closest comparison with the front of the church of San Giorgio Maggiore, Venice. As it was not illustrated by Palladio can one assume that Smith had been to Venice?

Doubtless Smith would have been well pleased with the novelty of the Hamilton centre-piece and, not surprisingly, repeated the formula, as has been mentioned, in a design for Melville House. However, Lord Melville, a lawyer, was probably a cautious man not given to expensive foreign ways and the next commission which warranted a portico was DALKEITH HOUSE, Midlothian, for which an agreement for repairs was drawn up in March 1701,[39] no doubt so that the old house could receive the Duchess of Buccleuch on her return to Scotland after an absence of forty years. She stayed with Lord Melville, her financial adviser,[40] with the result that when an estimate, 'for the reparations and new additions to be made to ye Castle of Dalkeith', was prepared in February 1702 James Smith was 'to heighten the walls of the old house at ye same rates that he build ye new. The Hewen work must either include the winning of ye stones or so much must be rebated of the Price.'[41]

38

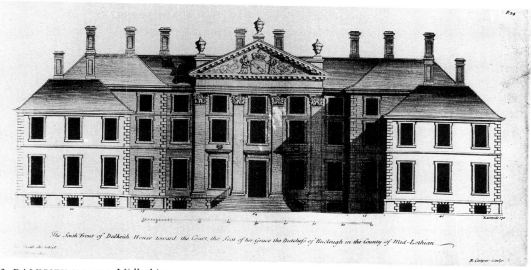

The South Front of Dalkeith House toward the Court, the Seat of her Grace the Dutchess of Buccleugh in the County of Mid-Lothian

42 DALKEITH HOUSE, Midlothian

The masonwork cost almost £3,000 Scots with other payments for lime, totalling over £500 Scots, for almost 5,000 bricks, an early use in such a prestigious affair, and for lead from the 'laird of Hopton' who owned the Lead-hills mines. Timber arrived from Norway in 1702 and two years later three shiploads came from Holland with an additional entry in the accounts recording, 'Bout. at Montross of ye Dutch Timbr. yt was Wrecked there, 1709 ... £186:9:0.' The names of the craftsmen are also listed. William Morgan, the wood-carver, who had worked at Hamilton Palace, was paid in 1704 and in 1706; there was

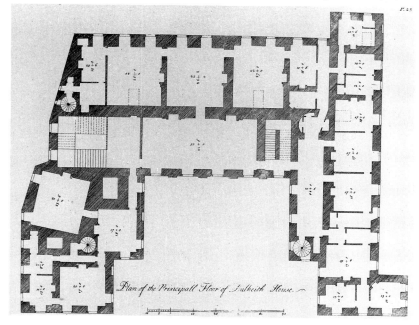

Plan of the Princepall Floor of Dalkeith House.

43 DALKEITH HOUSE, Midlothian, principal floor plan

The North Front of Yester House toward the Court The Seat of the most Honourable the Marquis of Tweeddale in the County of East-Lothian

*...smith &
...x^t Mc Gill* *Architects*

... Outer and Stair & Pilasters with the Attick were added by Willm Adams

R. Cooper Sculp^t

44 YESTER HOUSE, East Lothian

plastering by John Sampson, the gilder was 'Mr Hew' and Isaac Silverstyn, the stone-carver (who was later employed at Mavisbank by William Adam) was paid in 1708. In the next year Richard Neale came from London to cut marble, the patterns for which had been fetched from Holland. After eight years of expense and of effort the old castle had become the 'Palace at Dalkeith'.[42]

There was a magnificent extended show front [42] of three, then four storeys stepping up to a tetrastyle engaged portico of fluted Corinthian pilasters. With that exception, everything is once again taken from Le Muet even to the placing of the gallery [43] in the right-hand wing.[43] Externally, the chief feature was originally to be a three-bay centre with a pediment as at Raith and Newhailes.[44] However, the duchess, who held the title in her own right, like the 3rd Duchess of Hamilton, and had royal connections by her marriage to the Duke of Monmouth, would require, not only costly variegated marbles for floors, doorcases and the principal staircase, but also the expensive effect of a portico, with all its implications of semi-royal state, even though it meant a reduction in the fenestration to admit the pilasters. The elevation has often been cited as being of Dutch stock. Certainly, for Macky, Dalkeith was 'the very Model of King William's Palace at Loo',[45] an English description of which was published in 1699, to which Smith's receding planes seem to make more than a passing acknowledgement. If the Dutch palace lacks a portico then there is the Cloth Hall at Leyden of 1639,[46] although the Trippenhuis, Amsterdam (1662), with its fluted Corinthian order, would be closer. Yet neither of these has the scale of Smith's portico which, rising through three floors, has a modelling, as against the flatness of Dutch classicism, to be found with Palladio who used pilasters on the façade of Il Redentore, Venice and in certain villas.

Hamilton Palace and Dalkeith House represented ducal state and there were few, if any, in the land who could match the titles and estates of their owners. As houses of the first rank Hamilton and Dalkeith introduced new standards of aristocratic grandeur, breaking away from the cautious, aloof classicism of Bruce, which could not be emulated by lesser

40

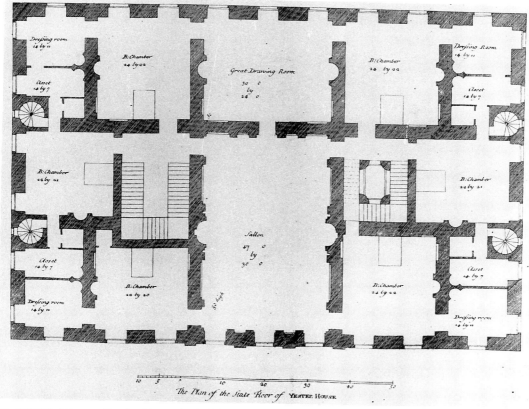

45 YESTER HOUSE, East Lothian, principal floor plan

nobles.[47] Thus, YESTER HOUSE, East Lothian [44], is a nine-bay, hip-roofed block supported by three-storey, ogee-roofed pavilions and devoid of ornament save for ornamental lead flashings, a detail found in the Smith drawings in the Campbell collection and copied from Le Muet, as was the channelled masonry although that had been used at Kinross and Harden. The plans of these houses are somewhat similar to Yester, with closets and service stairs on the outer edges of the plan, although its interior must have been more dramatic since the hall and saloon were both double height [45]. Building began at Yester with the offices but it was 1710 before the main block was started [46], after which the succession of a minor five years later brought the work to a halt leaving the apartments above the ground floor 'not yet so much as floored, although the House is entirely covered at Top'.[48]

It has already been seen with Bruce that for a Scottish architect the nexus of familial relationship among noble clients was of much importance. Doubtless the commission to build Hamilton Palace had gone to Smith because the duke's sister, the Duchess of Queensberry, was the wife of Smith's patron at Drumlanrig, just as at Yester the 3rd Marchioness of Tweeddale was a Hamilton by birth and the sister-in-law, by her first marriage, of the builder of Strathleven House.

Smith was assisted at Yester, according to *Vitruvius Scoticus*, by Alexander McGill,[49] who

46 YESTER HOUSE,
East Lothian,
original entrance front

had links with Bruce's circle[50] and designed a number of houses, after leaving Yester, in a manner reminiscent of Bruce's style although rather than being considered primarily as independent blocks they were conceived as the final unit in a Palladian assemblage. BLAIRDRUMMOND, Perthshire [47], was the first of these in 1715. Unusually, it was a new house set on 'a bare moorish farm' so that, as a neighbour criticised, 'It was a bold, and in some measure a disinterested undertaking, for one to set down such a house in a situation where he could hardly expect to be sheltered by trees of his own rearing.' As the stones were of 'bad quality'[51] there may have been harling which would have been a play for the many windows for there were seven bays of three storeys and a basement. What distinguished Blairdrummond, and so puts McGill in a class of his own, is the grandiose series of courts[52] perhaps inspired by the extensive outerworks planned for Castle Howard but having their source in Palladio's designs for the Villa Pogliana and the Villa Barbaro. On entering a reversed semicircle there is an outer court, with stable yards on either side, leading to a screen of railings and pillars and so through to an inner court, again with parallel courts to the sides, giving almost a royal approach to the tall plain house. Something of the same effect but in reverse occurs at DONIBRISTLE HOUSE, Fife, built four years later.[53] Though more extended in plan and plainer in silhouette,[54] it was comparable to Melville House but was entered on the north side below a pediment. To the south there lay a long garden court descending by terraces to the shore of the Firth of Forth where two L-shaped blocks of offices are comparable in size to the *corps de logis* of Blairdrummond. As an ensemble Donibristle may have been inspired by the plan of Palladio's Palazzo Valmarana.

The same trick of returning the offices so that they were advanced from but parallel to the main element was repeated at MOUNT STUART[55] which, being on the island of Bute, caused the wright, John Blaikie of Dalkeith, to disclaim responsibility for damage to his sash windows 'by the overturning of the Carts that carry them or by wreck at Sea'.[56]

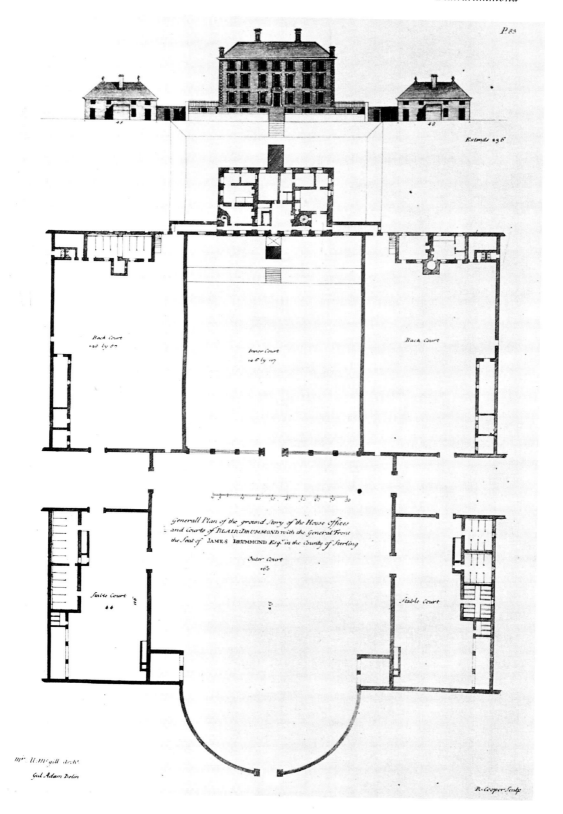

Extmds 296

Back Court
146 by 80

Back Court

Inner Court
146 by 117

generall Plan of the ground Story of the House Offices
and Courts of BLAIR DRUMMOND with the General Front
the Seat of JAMES DRUMMOND Esq.r in the County of Sterling

Outer Court
166

Stable Court
44

Stable Court

Mr. W. M.c gill Arch.t

Gul. Adam Delin.

R. Cooper Sculp.

48 CAROLINE PARK, Edinburgh

McGill, who 'knows his busines [sic] verie weell', seems to have been first consulted by Lord Bute in the summer of 1716[57] when he produced drawings which again, both in their general form and in the use of advanced double-bay ends, are a reflection of Melville, although a gallery, running the full length of the topmost floor, would have been old-fashioned in that situation. The liking for a gallery persisted and it appeared, in the executed scheme, at the rear of the basement, overlooking the garden, with a parlour next to it and the more formal dining-room directly above as the fulcrum of the rooms of parade. Externally, the scheme was quite up to date with a pedimented centre-piece although the introduction of a staircase tower on either side of the block was a feature copied from the House of Nairne, Perthshire, on which McGill had worked with Bruce.[58] The signal for the commencement of building operations at Mount Stuart was the signing of an agreement in the summer of 1718 for the supply of timber.[59] McGill was paid some time afterwards for 'Suptring. [superintending] and drink money and founding',[60] which prompted the Duke of Argyll to write to Lord Bute, his brother-in-law, 'I am astonish'd to hear that you have at last laid the Foundation of a House, having I confess taken it for granted that we should never see it but in black and white.'[61]

In investigating the introduction and establishment of classical architecture in country-houses in Scotland after 1660 it is easy to forget that 'a very mean style of architecture, both in public and private buildings, prevailed in Scotland between the Restoration and the Union. In many cases there was a motley compound of Gothic and modern – turrets and

49 CAROLINE PARK, Edinburgh, the saloon

battlements being affected by people that never dreamt of defending their houses.'[62] Thus, although the achievements of Bruce and of his disciples, Smith and McGill, were exceptional in the general run of building it would have been odd if there had been no imitators. Who they were is not known but their products are found from the south of the country to the far north-east. Around Edinburgh, two houses, Prestonfield (often attributed to Bruce) of 1687[63] and the near contemporary Cammo[64] displayed a fashionable Dutch taste for curling gables duplicated on either side of a lead flat in the manner of Robert Mylne. Gradually, however, such exuberance was checked as patrons saw the new classicism of the great nobility so that at Denbie, Dumfries-shire, said to have been built by Bruce in 1706, there are bold window dressings and a fine pedimented doorcase. Perhaps, however, because of his reserve, Bruce was less copied than might have been expected when one considers his dominant position in official and social circles. What was most appealing was that lingering love of strong vertical corner features. The façade of CAROLINE PARK, near Edinburgh, was an example in miniature where a two-storeyed mask with ogee-roofed towers [48] was added to an older courtyard house by George, Viscount Tarbat who, rather engagingly, inscribed his name and title on the architrave of one tower and his wife's on the other. On the north and entrance side a balustraded parapet between two gables, an arrangement reminiscent of Panmure and Methven, houses a tablet with a Latin text, part of which read in translation, 'Enter then, O guest, for this is the place of hospitality. Now it is ours, some day 'twill be another's, but whose afterwards I neither know nor care for abiding dwelling there is none.'[65] Like a distant respond the words seem to echo Pliny. Sadly, this rare

50 GALLERY, Angus

51 GALLERY, Angus

mansion, so evocative, with its academic allusions and fine interiors with wreathed plaster ceilings [49] and curled ironwork, of Restoration culture, has been engulfed by an industrial wasteland. Less exclusive is Black Barony, Peebles-shire, whose owner, Sir Alexander Murray of Blackbarony, became Master of Work after the 1689 Revolution[66] and, therefore, would have been in a position to employ Robert Mylne. That may explain why an older

52 and 53 THE HA' HOOSE, Raemoir, Kincardineshire

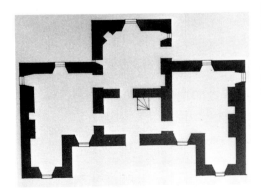

46

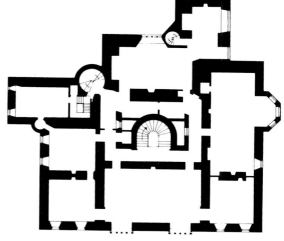

54 KEITH HALL, Aberdeenshire
55 KEITH HALL, Aberdeenshire, principal floor plan

structure was screened with what, in the last decade of the century, was a somewhat out-of-date formula of four-storeyed towers, with ogee slated roofs and fancy lead flashings, standing sentinel over a five-bay centre.[67] The same additive process may have occurred at GALLERY, Angus [50], which has advanced towers, with pyramidal roofs, and a five-bay centre [51] with a saloon on the first floor reached by a central enclosed staircase.[68] Similar characteristics are to be found at the charming and diminutive HA' HOOSE at Raemoir, Kincardineshire [52], where there is a paved terrace between the projecting wings [53]. The walling is of pinkish granite rubble setting off the oval windows and armorial panel above the door, points of interest which are repeated at Skellater further to the west in Aberdeenshire. However, the most intriguing of the northern houses is KEITH HALL, Aberdeenshire [54], the ancestral seat of the Earls of Kintore. The first of that creation submerged the old castle of Caskieben in a new casing [55] which was regular on each elevation and although there are frontal towers they are singular in being locked within the main fabric yet given a vertical expression by rising above a wallhead crowned by an urn-capped balustrade. There is much here to take the mind back thirty years or so to the building of the now-vanished Panmure House. Despite being robbed of some its classicism a century ago, Keith Hall remains a unique, if little known, specimen of its class and though the state rooms have lost their original decoration the enfilade arrangement and the processional duplication of apartments, even to the use of double closets to close the sequences, on either side of a saloon, all point to the acceptance of the traditional building date at the close of the seventeenth century.[69] Then Keith Hall, rising from amidst the treeless wastes and boulder-strewn fields of the north-east of Scotland, must have seemed a wondrous phenomenon to the castle-dwelling lairds.

The last variation on the twin-towered theme is BRECHIN CASTLE, Angus, the secondary seat of the 4th Earl of Panmure, whose countess was a daughter of the 3rd Duke and Duchess of Hamilton. Of the earl's many alterations and additions at Brechin it may be of some note that the work which has consequence and real beauty is the west front, begun within a few years of the completion of Hamilton Palace although the final plan was

47

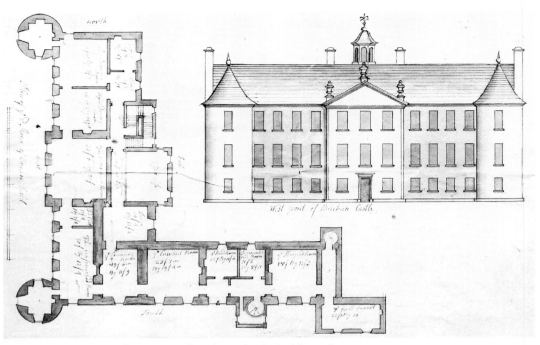

56 BRECHIN CASTLE, Angus, west elevation and principal floor plan

not settled until 1704. The architect, Alexander Edward, Bruce's assistant and himself an Angus man, provided a long horizontal façade of three storeys [56] all in fine ashlar with an advanced centre of three bays below a pediment, dated 1711, and with a circular tower retained at either end of the elevation.[70] Such atavism was not only justified by Bruce's repetition of circular towers at Holyroodhouse but perhaps by Edward's observation of *tourelles* in France while on his Grand Tour in 1701. Although his elevation at Brechin [57] displays a sophisticated competence, as opposed to the rather tough vernacular quality of the earlier Hatton House, which has the same components, the juxtaposition of towers and pediment is evidence of the tension in Scottish Restoration architecture between old and new ways. By the early eighteenth century the former were an anachronism in the development of the classical country-house and were eschewed by the next generation of architects who looked first to England for ideas and then to Italy. Such had been the pattern for the past two generations, at least for the higher nobility whose standards in building, decoration and manners were metropolitan. Writing to his lady from Bath in 1693, the Marquess of Lothian condemned his ancestral home, Newbattle Abbey, for 'When I see houses heir it seems a skandalous thing to keep that rotten thing upp'; but in 1696 he was more cheerful, reckoning that his refurbished great hall would be a better room than the king's new picture gallery at Kensington Palace.[71] There were royal standards, too, at Leslie House, from where the Countess of Rothes wrote, 'After having done the work of the fornoun, the ladys as to the drawing room at whythall all repare to my Chamber about two a clock.'[72] Although Leslie had family rooms for everyday use on the ground floor there was ranged over them the formal drawing-room, ante-chamber, bedchamber and

48

57 BRECHIN CASTLE,
Angus, west elevation

closet. As Macky noted at Dupplin House: 'On the First-floor there's a handsome Apartment of six Rooms.'[73] At Thirlestane and Hamilton, both of semi-royal status, the Great Apartment consisted of five rooms, the dining-room, drawing-room and bedchamber with dressing-room and closet. Yet an examination of house plans shows that the linear parade of rooms was becoming old-fashioned, so that at Melville House, as at Keith Hall and elsewhere, it is the saloon which is the fulcrum of the plan. Entered from the staircase, it has a drawing-room on either side leading at right angles to a bedchamber with the dressing-room and closet set side by side. At Kinross, on the other hand, while the double-cube saloon is placed, as one would expect, over the entrance, behind there lie a drawing-room and dining-room with, presumably, a bedroom between them and the closets. Interestingly, Kinross had three dining-rooms while at Raith there seems to have been a 'high dining roome' and another with a cupboard and 'lyned wt. wanscot', lesser rooms being lined with fir. In the 'low storie' the domestic offices were a milkhouse, wine-cellar, 'woman house', pantry and 'second table room'.[74] Great importance was given to bedrooms and their ceremonial role was emphasised not just by the magnificence of the furnishings, so that at Melville, 'The Bed of State is very noble, of Crimson Velvet, richly lin'd and adorn'd; the Chairs of the same',[75] but by their propinquity to the drawing-room and their size so that at Craigiehall and Melville the principal bedroom was larger than the drawing-room. There was strong English influence, too, in the details of houses. At Raith an additional cost was altering 'ane Lantrone turnpyk to ane open stair Lyk to ye monument of Londone'.[76] Lord Lauderdale, it will be recalled, imported Italian and English chimney-pieces. These would be for the public rooms. For the closets [58], such as the tobacco-room

58 KINROSS HOUSE, Kinross-shire, south-west closet

at Kinross, the practice was to follow what had been introduced at Holyroodhouse where 'His Majestie likes very well to have chimneys in the corners of roomes where it is not so convenient to sett them in any of the sides; and hath made his new House at New Markett with all the chimneys in the corners.'[77]

Although none of the houses described retains its original furniture and furnishings *in situ*, enough has been said to show that they were of the richest kind with sumptuous materials and bold colours being in vogue. As Lady Rothes wrote of one bed: 'I wold have all the fringes for this bed very slight, but let them be of as gadie colers as ye please to set the stufe.'[78] Such demands must have helped to stimulate the trade in luxury goods. Camlet was hung in one room in Brechin Castle where there was a 'Morehair Room',[79] with another one at Leslie which also had a red damask room,[80] while in 1707 the Duchess of Buccleuch paid £1:5:0 'for Printing Velvet'.[81] When Lord Melville was building his new house he attended an auction in Edinburgh, 'Over against Gladstones Land, in the Land Mercat', of 'a curious Collection of Pictures, of all sorts and sizes, some fit for Halls, Stair-Cases, Chambers and Closets', which were mostly by Dutch artists[82] while in London Lord Lothian 'lookt for Cabinetts, Glasses etc. and bespoak 4 good Statues' for Newbattle Abbey.[83]

Though initially many items were imported into Scotland there were local manufacturers. As has been seen, Alexander Brand supplied Bruce with leather hangings and in 1678

Quintin Adam was supplying chairs to Lady Haddington from the Canongate in Edinburgh.[84] Likewise there was an early dependence on foreign craftsmen for the new sash windows, for wainscoting and plasterwork. Yet in 1722 John Blaikie of Dalkeith agreed with Lord Bute 'to lyne and floor the gallry in the Earls new house at Mount Stuart and the drawing room on the north end thereof . . . so as no naill may appear according to ye English manner'. It should also be noted that the joiner was to be supplied with candles 'during the usuall time of working with candle light'.[85]

Almost without exception the patrons of Bruce, Smith and McGill were government ministers and their relatives. Provided with funds from public office, they were enabled to build on such a scale that their homes were not to be surpassed until the Victorian era. Within Scotland Leslie House, Thirlestane Castle, Hamilton Palace, Dalkeith House and others are a match, perhaps not always in size but certainly in the quality of the details, for the Wren works at the royal palaces of Kensington and Hampton Court; and if the Baroque is of little moment in late seventeenth-century Scotland, the use of Palladianism by James Smith was both more mature and more novel than anywhere else in Britain, a fact hitherto unrecognised by the generality of historians bemused by Scots Baronialism and the castles of the later sixteenth and early seventeenth centuries in which, even a hundred years later, the great majority of Scottish landowners still lived. Nevertheless, once the means to more elegant and more spacious living had been shown by the higher ranks of the nobility, the lesser nobles and the gentry, who, remaining on their estates, lacked direct contact with court circles, would inevitably consider and then obey the command of fashion and practical necessity and, in time, abandon their castles.

Notes to Chapter 2

1. H. M. Colvin, 'A Scottish Origin for English Palladianism?', *Architectural History*, vol. 17 (1974), pp. 5–13.
2. H. M. Colvin, *A Biographical Dictionary of British Architects, 1600–1840* (1978), pp. 755–8.
3. R. T. Gunther, *The Architecture of Sir Roger Pratt* (1972), p. 23.
4. Colvin, op. cit., p. 756.
5. M. Girouard, 'Drumlanrig Castle, Dumfries-shire', *CL*, vol. CXXVIII (25 August 1960), pp. 378–81.
6. P. le Muet, *Manière de Bien Bastir Pour Toutes Sortes de Personnes* (1681), pl. 62.
7. T. Pennant, *A Tour in Scotland and Voyage to the Hebrides: 1772* (1790), vol. I, p. 122.
8. *VB*, vol. II (1717), p. 3. Colen Campbell's opinion was shared by Lord Lothian who wrote on 3 September 1693 that James Smith 'hath really the best skill of them all'. SRO, GD40/Portfolio VIII/58.
9. SRO, GD26/6/164.
10. SRO, GD26/13/272, 440.
11. The contract is dated 25 July 1699 and was witnessed by 'Mr James Smith of Whitehill'. SRO, GD26/6/158. For a description of Melville House before it was emptied of its contents see 'Melville House, Fife', *CL*, vol. XXX (30 December 1911), pp. 1006–12.
12. O. Hill and J. Cornforth, *English Country Houses. Caroline, 1625–1685* (1966), pp. 193–202.
13. SRO, RHP 4093, an elevation and five plans, is marked: '4 July 1721. This is one of the draughts relative to Mr James Smith's oath of this date in his process against the E. of Leven.' Corresponding plans are in the RIBA drawings collection, J14(4)1, 2.
14. Supra, n. 9.
15. The simpler drawing belongs to Mr A. R. Conlon with a photograph in the NMRS. Smith's annotated drawing is SRO, RHP 35813.
16. RIBA drawings collection, J14(2)4.

17. RIBA drawings collection, J14(5)27 and J14(5)22.
18. The builder of Strathleven House was William Cochrane, second son of the 1st Earl of Dundonald, Sheriff of Kilmarnock and joint Keeper of the Signet. He married Lady Grizel Graham, a daughter of the 3rd Marquess of Montrose, and it is their joint arms which are displayed in the tympanum. J. B. Paul, *The Scots Peerage*, vol. III (1906), pp. 350–1; *Burke's Peerage, Baronetage and Knightage* (1970), p. 868.
19. A. Allardyce, *Scotland and Scotsmen in the Eighteenth Century* (1888), vol. I, p. 411, n. 3. The estate of Whitehill was purchased by Smith in 1686. See Colvin, ibid.
20. RIBA drawings collection, J14(5)30.
21. Gunther, op. cit., p. 24.
22. The accounts show that building began in 1693 and continued until 1698 when 'Mr James Smith his men' were paid £198:18:4 Scots. In 1696 the account for plasterwork was £598:6:10 and four times that sum was spent on carpentry including a Doric chimney-piece at £24. SRO, GD26/6/152; 157/1, 5 and 8. 'Vouchers for Building the House of Raith in 1693, 1694 and 1695' and 'Mr James Smiths draght of ye yard of Raith' are among the Raith MSS.
23. RIBA drawings colection, J14(5)51, 33.
24. Supra, n. 12.
25. A. Palladio, *The Four Books of Architecture* (republished 1965), Bk. II, p. 53.
26. R. Marshall, *The Days of Duchess Anne* (1973), pp. 37–8.
27. Ibid., p. 191. The Earl of Arran to the Duke of Hamilton, 3/13 July 1676 and 5 June 1677, Hamilton MSS, C1/8449, 6685.
28. Marshall, op. cit., p. 192. Hamilton MSS, F2/454, 458, 494, 538.
29. Sir William Bruce to the Duke of Hamilton, Kinross, 10 March 1691, Hamilton MSS, C1/9766.
30. Marshall, op. cit., pp. 193–5. The contract drawings for the west, east and north ranges, dated 1693, 1695 and 1696 respectively, are among the Hamilton MSS.
31. Marshall, ibid, p. 191.
32. Ibid., p. 203.
33. Hamilton MSS, C1/8453, 4140; F2/591.
34. Marshall, ibid.
35. Ibid., pp. 204–5. Hamilton MSS, C1/4171.
36. D. Defoe, *A Tour through the Whole Island of Great Britain* (1927), vol. II, p. 750.
37. Gunther, op. cit., p. 25.
38. A copy, now in the National Library of Scotland, of the English translation of Le Muet is inscribed: 'Boght. at Hamilton Nov. 10th 1698 by me James Smith', who was perhaps the cousin of the architect.
39. SRO, GD26/5/489.
40. 'Dalkeith Palace, near Edinburgh', *CL*, vol. XXX (7 October 1911), p. 517.
41. SRO, GD26/5/492.
42. SRO, GD224/625/1.
43. In more recent times the saloon at Dalkeith House, which is on the first floor over the entrance hall, has been called the gallery.
44. Drawing in the possession of the Duke of Buccleuch. A photograph is in the NMRS. Other drawings are in the RIBA drawings collection, J14(2)2, 3. See also *VS*, pls. 22–4.
45. J. Macky, *A Journey Through Scotland* (1723), p. 50; J. P. Neale, *Views of the Seats*, vol. I (1818), p. xvii; J. Small, *Castle and Mansions of the Lothians* (1883), vol. I.
46. C. McWilliam, *Lothian* (1978), p. 159.
47. James Smith may have been responsible for Dupplin House, Perthshire, destroyed by fire in 1827. It was a hipped roofed block of three storeys with an engaged tetrastyle portico of fluted Ionic pilasters. The house is said to have been built between 1688 and 1690 with offices, including a two-storeyed kitchen which was added c.1720 by James Smith 'who lives there till he finishes it'. Macky, op. cit., p. 149. To judge from a letter of 1707 (SRO, GD124/15/663) and contemporary descriptions of the interior comparing it, for instance, with Hamilton Palace, it seems reasonable to suppose that Smith was responsible for the earlier work. See J. Loveday, 'Diary of a Tour in 1732', *Roxburghe Club* (1889), pp. 133–4; Colvin, op. cit., p. 758.

Other works which may be by Smith include Broomlands, Longformacus and East Park, all in the past credited to William Adam because of their appearance in *Vitruvius Scoticus* although Adam did not claim to be the architect. Broomlands, Roxburghshire, dated 1719, had an octagonal hall behind which was a top-lit tribune which could be related to Smith's Italianate planning exercises. Longformacus, Berwickshire, was (for it has been altered) a seven-bay house with a plan akin to the Newhailes type. East Park (or Smeaton House), Midlothian, of *c.*1710 has planning similarities with the adjacent Dalkeith House. McWilliam, op. cit., pp. 161–2.

Finally, there is Dryden House, Midlothian, with an H-plan resembling Melville House. On the entrance front, as shown in *Vitruvius Scoticus*, pl. 80, there was an Ionic tetrastyle portico, set over three arches and rising through two storeys with the entablature passing above the wallhead as at Hamilton Palace and Dalkeith House.

48. Macky, op. cit., p. 32. See also Defoe, op. cit., vol. II, pp. 697–8; 'Journal of Henry Kalmeter's Travels in Scotland, 1719–20', *SHS*, 4th Series, vol. XIV (1978), p. 45.

For a full account of Yester House see J. Dunbar, 'The Building of Yester House, 1670–1878', *Transactions of the East Lothian Antiquarian and Field Naturalists' Society*, vol. XIII (1972), pp. 20–5; A. Rowan, 'Yester House, East Lothian', *CL*, vol. CLIV (9 August 1973), pp. 358–61.

49. *VS*, pl. 23.

50. Colvin, op. cit., p. 530.

51. Allardyce, op. cit., vol. II, p. 111; J. Burke, *A Visitation of the Seats and Arms* (1852–3), vol. II, p. 76.

52. *VS*, pl. 83.

53. Building materials for the new house of Donibristle were collected in spring 1719 when William Adam supplied bricks and iron (Moray MSS, vol. VI, box 16). Macky, op. cit., p. 179; Colvin, ibid.

54. *VS*, pls. 92, 94.

55. Ibid, pl. 31 shows the plan of Mount Stuart and an elevation which was an unexecuted restyling by William Adam of McGill's design. The main elevation, as designed by McGill, is shown by W. Watts, *The Seats of the Nobility and Gentry* (1786). However, see Colvin, op. cit., p. 58 and J. Simpson's introduction, p. 31, to the reprint of *VS*.

56. 'Article of Agreement Betwixt E. of Bute and John Blaikie, 1720', Bute MSS, Mount Stuart.

57. Ronald Campbell, W. S. to Lord Bute. Edinburgh, 30 July 1716. Other letters which refer to McGill are dated 7 and 20 November 1716 and 29 October, 7 November and 1 December 1717. Bute MSS, Mount Stuart.

58. The appearance of the House of Nairne, which was built *c.*1710 and demolished half a century later, is known from a drawing at Blair Castle. See J. Dunbar, *Sir William Bruce, 1630–1710*, p. 20.

Gray House, Angus, has similarly placed staircase towers and in plan and elevational details accords closely with known McGill work. *NSA*, vol. XI, p. 577 gives the date as 1716. See also Macky, op. cit., p. 138.

59. 'Agreement with Adam Boyle of Borrowstoness', 26 May 1718, Bute MSS, Mount Stuart. See *NSA*, vol. V, p. 88.

60. The 2nd Earl of Bute's accounts, Bute MSS, Mount Stuart.

61. Bute MSS, Mount Stuart.

62. Allardyce, op. cit., vol. II, p. 95.

63. In a letter of 3 February 1687 Sir James Dick announces that he is going to build a country-house. W. Baird, *Annals of Duddingstone and Portobello* (1898), pp. 121–3. See also T. Hannan, *Famous Scottish Houses* (1928), p. 153; J. Dunbar, *The Historic Architecture of Scotland* (1966), p. 98.

64. *VS*, pl. 141. *NSA*, vol. I, p. 597 gives the date as 1693 which is recorded on a datestone above the entrance lintel.

65. The tablet on the north front of Caroline Park recorded that the house was built in 1685. The south front was refaced and the towers added in 1696. Later Lord Tarbat claimed that he had expended £6,000 on the house. See 'Caroline Park, Midlothian', *CL*, vol. XXX (19 August 1911), pp. 276–84; *NSA*, vol. I, p. 596; W. Fraser, *The Earls of Cromartie* (1876), vol. I, p. 305; vol. II, pp. 451–4. Plans, prepared in 1835 by William Burn, are in the possession of the Duke of Buccleuch.

66. R. S. Mylne, *The Master Masons to the Crown of Scotland* (1893), p. 230.

67. RCAHMS, *Peebles-shire* (1967), vol. II, pp. 284–6.

68. A weather-vane at Gallery is dated 1680. Comparable U-plan mansions are Bannockburn House, Stirlingshire (*c.*1680) and Bargany, Ayrshire which is dated 1681.

69. Keith Hall is supposed to have been given its present form between 1697 and 1699. The architect may have been James Smith. As 'overseer of His Majesty's works', he received a commission in 1685 from Lord Kintore and others to provide granaries in the royal castles of Stirling, Dumbarton and Edinburgh. Lord Kintore was a kinsman of the 11th Earl of Mar among whose artistic circle James Smith was included. In the Kintore MSS a letter of 6 August 1729 refers to a plan by William Adam which may be the unexecuted scheme shown in *VS*, pls. 143–4. Changes and additions made in the early and later nineteenth century have removed some of the interest from Keith Hall.

70. The plan of 1704 is in Edward's hand, SRO, GD45/25/4. See J. Stuart, *Registrum de Panmure* (1872), vol. I, pp. lxiv–v, cl–li; D. Walker and J. Dunbar, 'Brechin Castle, Angus', *CL*, vol. CL (12 August 1971), pp. 378–81; Colvin, op. cit., p. 282.

71. The Marquess of Lothian to the Marchioness, London, 3 September 1693 and 3 February 1696, SRO, GD40/Portfolio VIII/53, 108.

72. The Countess of Rothes to Sir William Bruce, 22 July 1671, SRO, GD29/1901/6.

73. Macky, op. cit., p. 154.

74. 'Dimensions of the roumes in the Raith measured by John Ogstoun 5 March 1697', Raith MSS. For an analysis of the arrangement of rooms and their use in the later seventeenth century see J. Fowler and J. Cornforth, *English Decoration in the 18th Century* (1974), Ch. 3.

75. Macky, op. cit., p. 160.

76. 'Ane Accompt to My Lord Raith of Additione of Meason work', Raith MSS.

77. Mylne, op. cit., p. 170.

78. 'Ane note of thes(e) thing(s) which are to be sent from London', SRO, GD29/1901/9.

79. The mohair room in Brechin Castle was above the entrance hall and is marked on an early eighteenth-century plan. SRO, GD45/25/47.

80. Rothes MSS, 40/58/7.

81. Supra, n. 41.

82. SRO, GD26/13/271.

83. The Marquess of Lothian to the Marchioness, London, 23 December 1693, SRO, GD40/Portfolio VIII/76.

84. Rothes MSS, 40/47/3.

85. 'Agreement between the Earl of Bute and John Blaikie, 1722', Bute MSS, Mount Stuart.

CHAPTER THREE

'Mr Adams, a skilful Architect'

It would not be beyond the truth to state that Sir William Bruce of Kinross had effected, almost alone at first, a complete and irreversible revolution in Scottish architecture. On a footing of social equality with his patrons, he was enabled to build a series of country-houses which loosened Scotland's dependence on old and well-tried forms not only in design and in construction but in the departments of plasterwork, woodwork, decoration and furnishings. It was a stupendous achievement. Yet to Scotsmen today the name of Sir William Bruce is little known and all because of William Adam (1689–1748) and the architectural dynasty which he founded. No other family can ever have so dominated the architecture of their native country as did the two generations of Adam architects whose practice, as a contemporary shrewdly noted, 'seems to involve the whole history of British Architecture during the improving period of the Eighteenth Century'.[1]

As his father was a builder[2] so it was that William Adam's early years were spent in the obscurity of the building trade.[3] Thus, unlike Bruce, he lacked, initially at least, the advantages of a well-connected social station and a theoretical study of architecture although, apart from lack of opportunity, it would seem that he was by temperament a notionalist in things architectural for William Adam was, and would remain, a practical, bustling man of business whose numerous and expanding ventures included bringing 'a Modle of a Barley Miln from Holland . . . and also the making of Dutch Pantiles in Scotland'.[4] More ambitious were his industrial concerns, so that he could charge the Duke of Hamilton £200 for his 'going frequently to Bo'ness during the Course of Six years Superintending the fitting of the Coal and Salt Works and erecting the fire Engine'[5] and from there on one occasion, doubtless to save time, 'I sent My Lad out to Niddrie on Monday to goe on with the Survey about the House and Gardens.'[6] Elsewhere he was prepared to take the management of industrial works into his own hands so that he 'surely should be a Considerable gainer considering the Certain Expences and Hasard he runs'.[7]

Adam's first recorded experience of architecture, when he was thirty-two years old, was the remodelling and enlargement of FLOORS CASTLE, Roxburghshire, for the 1st Duke of Roxburghe. Although, as the young Lord Roxburghe on the Grand Tour in 1701, he had roundly declared, 'The more fine houses and the more fine gardens I see, the more am I determin'd neither to build, nor make gardens,'[8] ten years later the surviving correspondence between Lord Roxburghe, living in England, and his mother shows a constant pre-occupation with the need to bring his Scottish seats up to date. At Broxmouth in East Lothian, for example, there was a concern to replace the newel stair with a modern 'narrow skale stare'. Something of the same kind, but with an iron rail, was also being proposed for Floors although there was the possibility of re-using the staircase from The Friars in nearby Kelso according to 'a draught of Mr Maguill's showing how it can be done'.[9]

Whatever the changes at Floors there was ever the thought in Lord Roxburghe's mind that, 'I shall certainly be obliged to add to it one day, and the only reasonable way of doing that is, to be sure, by adding the Friars to the Floors' by making use of the better materials. 'The sash windows should be numbered and carefully taken down and laid by' with the hewn stones for 'they never belonged to the church, not that I am scrupulous myself on this point, but I would not offend my brethren'.[10] However, there was no major rebuilding at Floors until it failed demonstrably to match the grandeur of the owner's dukedom and the sparkling novelty of the architectural concepts displayed after 1715 in the first two volumes of Colen Campbell's *Vitruvius Britannicus*, to each of which the duke subscribed for two copies.

On 18 May 1721 a neighbouring laird recorded, 'This day I goe to the Floors, to see the ground start of the new building laid.'[11] The year's building account more accurately itemises 'for diging [sic] the foundation of ye Adition [sic] £184:11:0 [Scots]', while distinguishing William Adam with the notation, 'To Mr Adam for mason work £1,725:17:8 [Scots].' That was a third of the year's expenditure which included the carriage of timber from the ports of Berwick and Eyemouth as well as materials from The Friars and Cessford Castle. Adam's standing is further highlighted when it is seen that other masons were paid 'at a Merk Scots a day' with additional money being paid at harvest time to retain the labour force.[12]

Although Floors, a rectangle of eleven bays on the entrance front and with a protruding tower at each corner,[13] has been in the past credited to Sir John Vanbrugh it is Adam who lays claim to the design in his *Vitruvius Scoticus*. Undoubtedly, the elevation of Floors [59] lacks the boldness, the sky-rocketing swagger or the powerful detailing associated with the English maestro; instead the design has the air of one who, having stepped into the Palladian stream, is uncertain how to proceed. According to Pococke, 'The whole is built of rough stone, but with window cases of hewn stone. It is strange so large a house should not afford one good room.'[14] There was the rub. There was no axial vista, no saloon on the garden side and no ranked suites of rooms [60]. Externally, too, there was gaucherie for there was neither order nor portico so that, for the Palladian, the saving grace could only be the pedimented corner towers rising above the wallhead in the manner of Wilton, although another source which might be considered, despite its commencement in 1722, is Houghton Hall, Norfolk, where the proposed towers and the projecting corners and framed window cases could be some justification in Palladian terms for the same features at Floors. Certainly, Adam's time at Floors marked the period when he emerged from the dust of the builder's yard to become the architect not only at Hopetoun House but soon at Mavisbank, a property in Midlothian of Sir John Clerk of Penicuik, Adam's single most important patron.

Despite the praise accorded the architect, it was perhaps the appearance of HOPETOUN HOUSE in *Vitruvius Britannicus* that made Lord Hopetoun dissatisfied with a house completed only a little more than a decade before. When compared, say, with Wanstead, the touchstone of Palladian 'Antique Simplicity',[15] Hopetoun, with its roofs bobbing above the

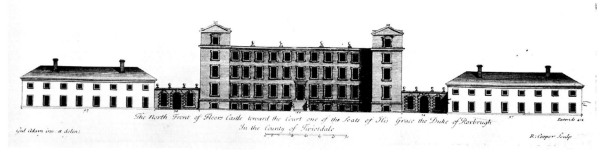

59 and 60 FLOORS CASTLE, Roxburghshire

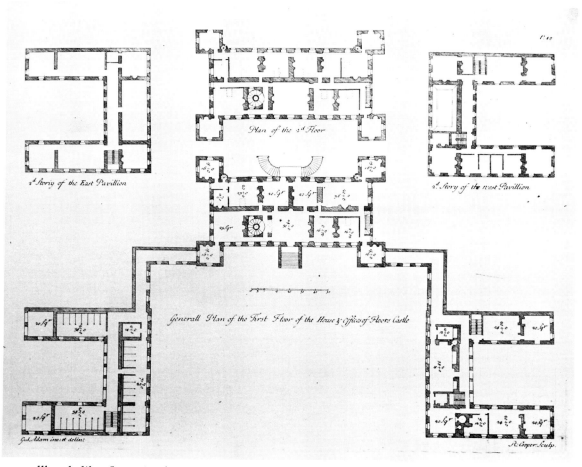

wallhead, like floats in the sea, its windowed pediment, its underlying verticality behind the French rustication and, perhaps most glaring because they were almost alone in the two volumes, the expansive convex colonnades, all, in Campbell's curt phrases, were 'excessive Ornaments without Grace' and 'wildly Extravagant'.[16]

At Hopetoun one can see the upset which Palladianism caused in fashionable taste for not only was the saloon on the upper floor, when it should have been behind the hall, but there was a marked lack of public rooms arranged *en suite*. Instead the rooms had the

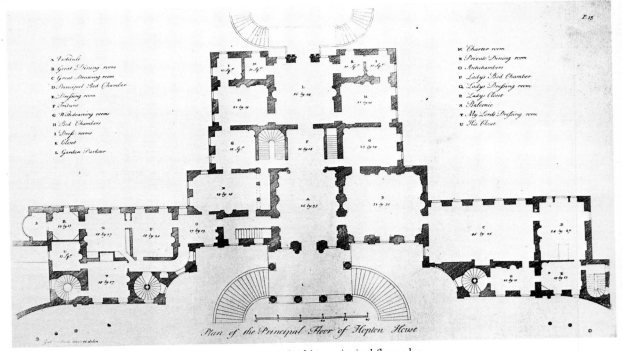

Plan of the Principal Floor of Hopton House

61 William Adam, HOPETOUN HOUSE, West Lothian, principal floor plan

appealing Caroline intimacy and the umbered comfort that comes from honey-streaked oak panelling and chimney-pieces, dark as dross, providing a background for furniture which would have been similar to that in Lord Hopetoun's uncle's house at Craighall, Fife, where 'in the Little dining Roome there was a dozen of Rushie Leather chaires, Two wainscot Tables and a Chimney ... In my Ladys own Chamber ... There was a Blue Stuft bed and hangings which is a little black [i.e. tarnished], A fine Cabinet and a Chist of drawers, A Glass and a Cloak. Six chaires covered.'[17] By these standards Hopetoun would have been not only old-fashioned but displayed solecisms which must have been acutely embarrassing to the Palladian eye. Clearly, what was required was 'an Addition of Beauty and Majesty'.[18]

Accordingly, William Adam was paid £96 in 1721 'to Takeing down of old house'[19] which, in effect, meant removing in large part and expanding the entrance front [61] beginning at the south end with the family apartments. These were faced with '10 Key's Carv'd for the Arch'd Windows att one Guinea [each]' while on the angles there were '3 Capitalls, haveing 6 faces, each att 10 Guineas', although ten times as costly was the 'Enriching off principall Architrave and Cornishes, by Carveing'.[20] Not surprisingly, the remodelling does not seem to have been complete until 1725[21] when Lord Hopetoun turned his attention to the entrance, where Adam was 'to raise two Double Pilasters of the same Hight [sic] and Order as those in the South Building one on each corner of the present breaking or Portico'. The pediment was to go and the cornice was to be replaced by a full entablature carrying an attic storey crowned by an ornamental balustrade,[22] all of which must have been completed by 1732 when a traveller noted, 'Ye front most elegant, much exceeding Any We have seen in ye Kingdom ... Corinthian Pilasters in front, except in ye middle where are 3 Arches of ye Doric Order.'[23] Clearly, the north section must also have been rebuilt and indeed £5:18:0 was paid in 1733 'To Joysting the North Wing'.[24] However,

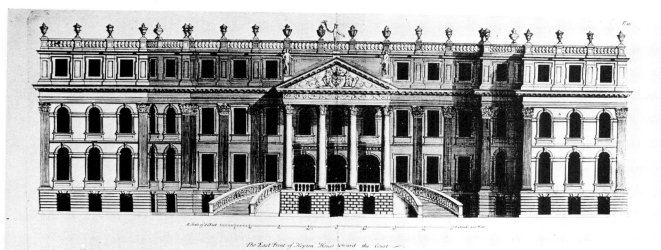

The East Front of Hopetoun House toward the Court

62 William Adam, HOPETOUN HOUSE, West Lothian

the entrance was to remain a design problem for many years to come.

An important element in lending scale as well as containing the spreading frontal screen were Doric colonnades, which in 1726 were priced at thirteen pence per foot,[25] hiding a jigsaw of interlocking back courts and poultry yards. Finally, there were the pavilions, seven bays long on the sides and designed from a distance to introduce the architectural themes while within the *cour d'honneur* their opposed pediments would be the precursors of the intended portico beyond and above them. The south pavilion contained what this unsophisticated age would call a leisure centre with a hundred-foot-long library (now the ballroom), a laboratory and billiard room while across the gravel the stables for hunters, coach- and work-horses were large enough to require a 'Mr. of horses' who had a room in the house.[26]

When the cost of the pavilions was totted up in 1746 there was a general reckoning of the accounts. Lord Hopetoun decided not to have the new work measured, in part because of the time required and partly because of 'the Opinion I have of Mr Adams Honesty'. So the account was 'made up by Mr Adam from the Plans and I have fill'd up all the blank Articles by Guess In which no doubt some may be too high and some too low, especially the Carved Work. But upon the whole I am satisfy'd his Profits are very moderate and therefore when I paid him the £4443 I made his Son John a Present of 50 Guineas.'[27] One would have thought that the work of reconstruction was complete and that Lord Hopetoun would have been tired of having builders ever round him. Yet not only had the large new public rooms to be fitted up but the Corinthian tetrastyle portico, rising through two storeys, had not been erected [62]. That was to be the crowning achievement and if not the first free-standing portico for a Scottish country-house, it would be the most magnificent.[28] Although some examples, mostly by Colen Campbell, had been illustrated in the third volume of *Vitruvius Britannicus* in 1725, Adam preferred for his main effects the stronger Handelian orchestration of Vanbrugh. Thus when Pococke wrote: 'You see through the rooms of the house to a window at each end about 300 feet,'[29] he might have been describing Castle Howard, the source for the Hopetoun window heads and the giant order of Corinthian pilasters. As these were details not fully shown in *Vitruvius Britannicus*, it can be supposed that Adam, perhaps on a journey to London,[30] had inspected Castle Howard as well as Vanbrugh's later northern masterpiece, Seaton Delaval, Northumberland, where pediments outstare one another across the vista of the *cour d'honneur*. Finally, Hopetoun's attic storey and the ground plan with its concave bays Adam drew from Blenheim Palace as it was shown in *Vitruvius Britannicus*. Indeed in 1721, when the remodelling of Hopetoun was begun, Vanbrugh was considering a design for one of his own commissions, 'Which consists, in altering the House both for State, Beauty and Convenience, And making the Courts Gardens and Offices Suitable to it'.[31] That, in essence, was Adam's achievement at Hopetoun.

For Lord Hopetoun to have employed Adam initially must have betokened confidence in his capabilities. Undoubtedly, Adam, like many another architect, could make a job grow so that Hopetoun House remained an Adam family monopoly for over thirty years; often, too, he became the social intimate of his patrons. That, however, was in the future so that the question remains. Why was Adam chosen for the work at Hopetoun? One reason may have been the interest of Sir John Clerk of Penicuik, the owner of the adjacent estate of Cammo until 1724.[32] In literature, art, architecture and politics, Clerk was the Maecenas of Scotland's burgeoning artistic self-confidence. Years after his Grand Tour he could recollect that, 'My two great diversions at Rome were Musick and Antiquities',[33] with the latter finding a practical expression in building although in the matter of style Clerk rejected the stony hallelujahs of Vanbrugh whose Castle Howard 'must displease any body of Taste'.[34] But then Vanbrugh was 'of an Odd sense', building houses above Greenwich with battlements and towers, 'which the Goths and their successors used to place in Castles and prisons'.[35] No, Rome *rediviva* would come from the study of the Palladian texts and as seen at Wanstead. It was much admired although Kent's painted ceiling in the saloon was 'a very indifferent piece of work',[36] a sentiment reflecting Clerk's belief, 'that there are more fine houses in England than in Italy, tho' all of them not so well ornamented'.[37] Despite such gratification, he could still be critical so that Amesbury, by John Webb, the pupil of Jones, had 'no great merit in it' while Chiswick House, built 'all in the ancient manner' by Lord Burlington, the high-priest of Palladianism, was 'rather curious than convenient'.[38]

That Clerk was a fair judge was because he himself had founded a villa at MAVISBANK, Midlothian [63], where the Clerks had coal interests. On inheriting his patrimony in 1722 he had intended to renovate the family seat at Penicuik as 'a very fine uniform house' but, as it was not worth repairing, he 'fell abuilding of Mavisbank which my father likewise intended as appears by the draughts of a house he has left'.[39] A number of designs between 1696 and 1698[40] show their author moving away from the notion of a traditional laird's dwelling with its turnpike stair in one corner giving access to the cellar and kitchen below and to a row of bedrooms, entered from a sparse corridor, above. There are no public rooms, save for a 'dyning roume and bedchamber' with a bed alcove, flanked by closets, as a concession to the new etiquette. An alternative scheme shows a scale and platt staircase, symmetry in the disposition of spaces and the separation of public and private chambers. Externally, angle quoins, a modelled eaves course and a piend roof, carrying a balustraded platform, betoken the Bruce idiom. Nevertheless, the Mavisbank schemes, conceived by

63 MAVISBANK, Midlothian

the father and realised by the son, show how, in the interval of one generation, Scottish architecture was attracted towards Italianate ideals.

Though using professional advice, Clerk, like Burlington, was his own architect and it was, therefore, no more than the plain truth when he recorded: 'In May 1723 I not only finished my design for the Ho. of Mavisbank, under the correction of one Mr Adams, a skilful Architect, but laid the foundation of the House.'[41] So began one of the most significant partnerships in Scottish architectural history. In the first surviving exchange of correspondence at the end of January 1723 Adam sent a draft of 'a Very Small Box, and Genteel too' with some comments about the situation of rooms and their ordering. It was standard stuff with 'a following of Rooms ... in the first floor above the Vaults. Here is also the Family Appartment in ye same floor, and the Lodgeing Rooms above, with a Billiard Table Room Serving for Ane Ante Chamber to the whole floor. On the Garrett Storrie I have introduc'd a parapett wall in form of ane Attick, which has a very good effect, and by which, there is so many windows as is Necessary for Lighting these Rooms plac'd in that wall. By which the Roof is Sav'd from Breaking by Storm Windows which Ye'l know proves commonly troublesome.' Despite the well-meant advice, it is, nevertheless, clear that it is Clerk who is the mentor for Adam will not only comply 'with any thing of Your own thought that may be judg'd Better than Mine', but concludes, 'In the Mean time any thing that Occurs to you – with respect to this Seat in any thing els, shall be glad to have your Mind their anent.'[42] Clearly, Sir John was no ordinary client, for not only could Adam ask for the loan of a copy of Palladio's treatise, 'because Your's has the Temples Mine has not', as well as Inigo Jones's works[43] but, on an earlier occasion, he apologised for the non-delivery of a drawing-board to the baron's lodging.[44]

With between nineteen and twenty-three masons, later reduced to eleven,[45] on hand the initial work at Mavisbank proceeded rapidly so that in the late summer of that first building season Adam despatched Isaac Silverstyn to carve 'the Cartouche for ye Entry Door which by the Draught Support ye Coat of Arms, which is now rady. There is also 2 festoons above ye Windows of ye Front to be Carv'd.' It was Silverstyn again who was to carve the tympanum at the end of the next winter. 'Ane window in the Middle of the Pediement will have the best Effect with a Large Peice of foliage on each Syde, and that all the Leaffs, flowers or fruits be very Large as being farr from ye Eye, and for that end 6 Inches of Rough Stone be Left Swelling without ye plain of the Pediement.'[46] Rapid progress continued and the roof was on by the summer of 1724[47] although it was not until four years later that Adam was finished with the carcase of the house.[48] By then Sir John had decided that the house, intended for occasional residence in the summer months, was too small. 'I found that a Kitchen and a Stable however they might be brought within the compass of one Large Roof yet they would never do under a small one.'[49] So pavilions had to be built to north and south although Sir John could take consolation in the thought that in the event of fire the entire house would not be destoyed 'but that two of the 3 parts remaining the family may safely retire into them'.[50] Adam himself would have preferred octagonal pavilions.[51]

Inside Mavisbank must have been light and attractive. The drawing-room seems to have had Corinthian columns with gilded capitals and a veined white marble chimney-piece, one of several, although for the children's room Sir John was content with a second-hand one at twelve shillings. In 1726 the painter James Norrie was paid £2:10:8, 'To painting a room Yellow Landscop', and other rooms had red and green landscape work; three years later he decorated in 'Landscap, whyte marble and Mahogany Colours' the hall and staircase, the ceiling of which had a gold sun on a blue and white ground,[52] decoration which may have been 'according to the old mode revived, of a whitish colour and all the carvings are gilt' which Sir John had seen in the octagon room at Orleans House.[53] Certainly his preference was for stucco rather than oak wainscot 'as being cheaper and safer against fire and all manner of Vermin Such as Rats, Mice, Bugs etc.'.[54] The stairwell had a pilaster in each corner and with these Sir John seems to have been content. Adam, however, was against 'Your finishing the Stair with plain plaister' and suggested that Calderwood, the stuccoer, be called. For once Adam had his way and, as the account in 1729 included 'foliage and flowers' at a cost of over fifty pounds,[55] one can assume that some of the decorative plasterwork must have equalled in richness and variety that still surviving at The Drum. That the finishing proceeded slowly suited Sir John since, being content to spend 'to the extent of about £200 stg. annually',[56] his salary, as a baron of the exchequer, 'did much more than answere all the Expence of my building and other embellishments'.[57] Indeed, one of his chief reasons for building was that he considered it only proper to support some of the king's subjects with a portion of the royal bounty. 'I knew no better way than to employ some masons and wrights and thereby give bread to their families for some years.'

While attending to his duties in Edinburgh, in June and July each year, Sir John resided at Mavisbank[58] which was, therefore, 'rather a summer pavilion than a family house'.[59] As an occasional residence it could be compared with the astylar Dunkeld House. There, however, the comparison stopped for the latter was conceived of necessity by climate and geography whereas the seed of Mavisbank was in the words of Pliny when writing of his villa near Laurentum, 'It is possible to spend the night there after necessary business is done, without having cut short or hurried the day's work.'[60] With banded pilasters, festooned

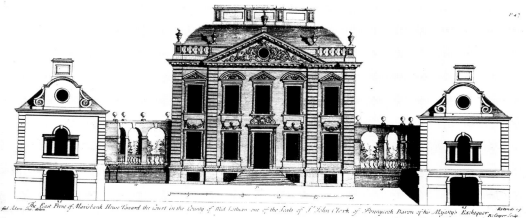

64 MAVISBANK, Midlothian

windows and a dentilled pediment, Mavisbank [64] showed how architectural syntax had been orchestrated by the garnered borrowings of antiquity. With a frontage of only fifty feet, it was perhaps over-rich for, as Clerk noted, 'No house can be sufficient which has too many external ornaments for the clime of Scotland will not bear it. Mavisbank errs in this particular.'[61] However, he did confess that, 'Since my house was to be but small I choised to make the Front as handsome as I could think of,'[62] which was allowing his Baroque heart to rule his Palladian head.

Throughout the second decade of the century there must have been discussion about the concept of the villa. Castell's *The Villas of the Ancients* was published in 1728. In the previous year Clerk 'saw several villas near Richmond but generally of a very poor sort of Architecture'[63] although by then the famous English examples, such as Colen Campbell's Stourhead, Newby Park and Mereworth (which alone preceded Mavisbank), Lord Herbert's villa in Whitehall and Lord Burlington's Chiswick House had been or were in course of erection. All these were larger than Mavisbank. Yet, when Clerk saw Chiswick, he could rightly observe: 'The whole situation of this villa is without any prospect'[64] and though, as has already been noted, he was critical of the architecture he must have recognised that in scale and the intellectualism of its parts it outdid Mavisbank. Even so, surely it was the latter which most matched Castell's Roman exemplar of 'a Place rather Proper for Study, and to retire to with a few select Friends, than for State and Shew'?[65] Such were the sentiments to which Clerk gave utterance in his poem 'The Country Seat' where, although he says nothing of its architecture, he conceives,

> . . . a little Villa where one may
> Taste every Minutes Blessing Sweet and gay,
> And in a soft Retirement spend the Day.[66]

If in the eighteenth century smallness was not necessarily a criterion of the villa one can accept that there were specific characteristics such as the triple divisions of the plan [65]. Mavisbank, however, is both more interesting and important in its external forms. For Clerk, whose 'time had been hitherto spent in reading the classicks',[67] it was easy to 'Mark

63

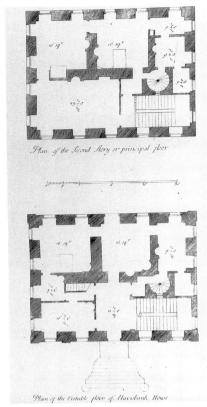

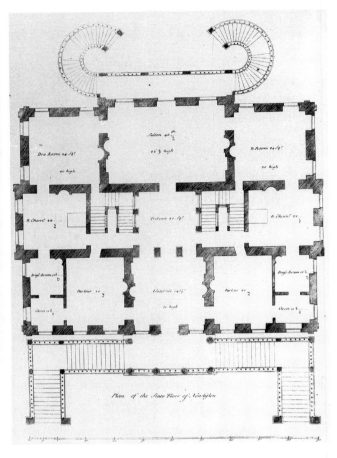

65 MAVISBANK, Midlothian
66 NEWLISTON, West Lothian,
   proposed principal floor plan

how the Plinian Villa was disposed'[68] from which it could be concluded that 'the antient Greek and Roman Structures, or the Designs of them by Palladio and others ought to be standards fit for the Imitation of our modern Architects'.[69] Not surprisingly, therefore, when William Adam wished to build Mavisbank a storey higher, his employer objected because 'the fabrick would have lookt like a Touer, and been quite spoiled'.[70] That was Clerk wearing his learning like a new coat and content though he was to have French pilasters, as most suited to 'rural Seats',[71] the Dutch influence, which one critic has professed to see,[72] would have been not only an anachronism but would have run counter to Clerk's desire to draw upon Palladio for the grand and suggestive ideas – the crescendo and the diminuendo of the pediments, the roof shaped like the Basilica in the square at Vicenza[73] and the pavilions, transalpine translations borrowed either directly from the Villa Barbaro[74] or indirectly by way of Raynham Hall, Norfolk, whose owner 'had been my Acquaintance in Leyden'.[75] Yet it is the colonnade which the cognoscenti would most appreciate for there, with the trees peeping shoulder high through the open arches, is Pliny's 'covered arcade ... [with] windows on both sides'[76] which transforms Mavisbank into the 'Villa Urbana'.[77] Though built near 'a little Farm House',[78] it was not the centre of agricultural operations, as were Robert Adam's villas later in the century, but 'a Country-House of Pleasure'[79] so that Sir John could rest easy as Horace had done with:

> A piece of land – not so very big,
> with a garden and, near the house, a spring that never fails,
> and a bit of wood to round it off.[80]

In the profession of architecture one has to be lucky in the choice of friends. In that respect William Adam was more than fortunate for, apart from Sir John Clerk, one of the more influential was the 2nd Earl of Stair, 'who seemed by a sympathy of character to be peculiarly destined for the friend and patron of such a man'.[81] Stair, who had won fame as a military commander and colleague of the Duke of Marlborough, became ambassador to France in 1715 but was recalled five years later. With his fortune impaired by his official expenses he retired to Scotland, spending most of each year at Newliston, West Lothian, which he had inherited from his mother. Like Cincinnatus, he there occupied himself in tending his estate, improving the farms and becoming the first Scotsman to plant turnips and cabbages on a large scale in fields,[82] activities which had a Roman sanction as 'it is from the farming class that the bravest and sturdiest soldiers come, their calling is most highly respected, their livelihood is most assured and is looked on with the least hostility'.[83]

It is to be regretted that Stair's commission for a grand country-house at NEWLISTON should have lapsed once the stable pavilion was complete. Newliston was Adam's first new project for an aristocratic client and, as he participated in national affairs as well as subscribing to *Vitruvius Britannicus*, it is likely that the strict Palladianism of the composition came from

67 NEWLISTON, West Lothian

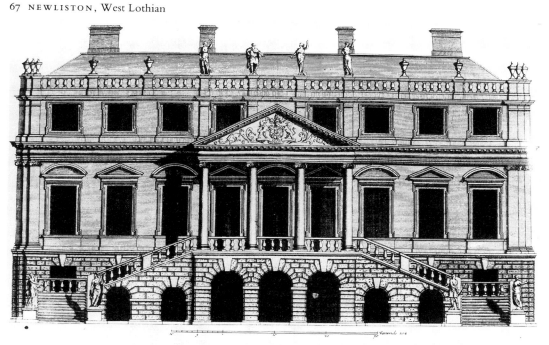

The South Front of Newliston toward the Court

a client who, like Sir John Clerk of Penicuik, had as much a hand in the design as did his architect. In consequence it is all the more unfortunate that there is no surviving exchange of correspondence, as in the Clerk of Penicuik papers, although these, unique in their completeness, perhaps give Sir John, his associates and activities an undue prominence.

In 1723 Lord Stair was 'making a Canal and several very grand Improvements' at Newliston.[84] While it was usual to erect the mansion later, Stair would have required to renew his fortune once he considered replacing the tall, turreted house,[85] not with William Adam's addition but with a new mansion[86] where the main block was 102 feet long and 80 feet deep. Advanced colonnades would curve out to hold the stable and kitchen pavilions. On the piano nobile [66] there was to be, for the first time with Adam, the standard Palladian plan of hall and saloon though interrupted by a tribune placed between twin staircases. Along each side there was to be a returned sequence of drawing-room, bedchamber, dressing-room and closet. This compact, stately plan owes everything to Italian models, such as the Villa Pisani,[87] with borrowings from Wanstead which Lord Stair inspected in company with Sir John Clerk, who admired the ground storey which was 'open quite through to the Gardens'[88] as was intended at Newliston. Externally, there is a confident handling of the profuse motifs [67] with the staircase pulling out the horizontality, since one 'will see in Paladio's Architecture that Stairs are very often the whole Length of the Front'.[89] The single disappointment is the diminished portico which, set against the windowed attic, is robbed of its culminating role in the composition. Although Palladio's Villa Foscari can be cited as a precedent,[90] it seems evident that at Newliston the intention with the portico was to reproduce, even to the rusticated basement arches, the central features of Lord Herbert's villa in Whitehall.

Possibly before the proposed mansion at Newliston was on paper, Lord Stair's brother, George Dalrymple, like Sir John Clerk a baron of the exchequer, was erecting Dalmahoy (originally Belvidere) five miles away in neighbouring Midlothian.[91] A plain, three-storey, seven-bay front, without the costly figure sculpture of Newliston, Dalmahoy has a balustraded parapet and a string-course above the basement, thus framing up the quoins, with the frontal plane broken by recessing the centre, which allows the end bays to be read as vertical accents. What is in the main an identical composition was used at Newhall, East Lothian,[92] but minus the parapet so that the gables of the advanced end bays read as their pediments. A third and even simpler variation was Balgregan, Wigtownshire,[93] where no attempt is made to disguise the true nature of the gables and though there is little external distinction for the piano nobile it is allowed full expression in the plan which is the counterpart of the Newhall plan. In both the Newliston saloon is replaced by a dining-room, since 'A family House especially for a Man of Quality ought to be large and to have in it ane good apartment at least comprising of a dineing-room, drawing-room, Bed chamber, dressing-room and Closet.'[94] The same order of decreasing volumes was planned for Makerstoun, Roxburghshire, where Adam seems to have built, probably when employed at Floors, a scheme first prepared in 1714 by McGill, who recommended that 'The Northwest end being very Crazy is to be taken down' and drew out a seven-bay front with a plan for the bedrooms that subsequently appears on a sheet of drawings subscribed, 'The Plans and Elevations of Makerstoun House, with improvements on the former by

Wm. Adam, Architect.'[95] That would confirm, what otherwise is inexplicable, that the platform roof with the elaborately cut ridges, the scrolled pediment over three bays, the sweeping screen walls and the pavilions *en face*, all hallmarks of the preceding age of country-house building, reveal Adam as the builder of a McGill design.

For all but the richest nobles a house built overall of dressed stone was too expensive so that rubble walling coated with harl and strengthened at the angles by quoins was acceptable at Newhall and Balgregan, as the drawings indicate, and at Makerstoun as well as at Craigdarroch, Dumfries-shire,[96] which belongs to the same group of houses, except that the 'one good apartment . . . comprising of a dineing-room, drawing-room, Bed-chamber, dressing room and Closet',[97] was on the second floor, which was unusual, with the dining-room overlooking the entrance. Craigdarroch was Annie Laurie's married home and it was her husband, Alexander Fergusson, the fourteenth laird, who commissioned Adam, whose estimate of £526:2:9 for the central block of a proposed tripartite scheme included '16 Chimney piecess at £1 [each]' as well as 'Boxing of 2d Floor' at £70 leaving the laird to provide some materials from his old home.[98]

For any architect the bread and butter of practice would be the alterations and additions to existing buildings; such commissions, usually given after a verbal recommendation, are, nevertheless, troublesome as they tend to overrun the allotted time and hence become increasingly expensive. A good example is Lawers, Perthshire, where large works, completed by 1724, totalled £703:19:0, more than the cost of Craigdarroch, for east and west pavilions although they were not floored or lined until eight years later.[99] As the two-storey pavilions were lateral extensions of the central block the height gradually rises to a pediment oversailing the wallhead and embracing three tall, round-headed windows lighting a saloon. In 1739 Adam was sending from Edinburgh 'a Draught of the Front as it is to be, I mean that toward the South As Also another Draught of the Front toward the North', although he retained 'a Section of the rooffs' to show to the wright, Archibald Chessells.[100] Seven years later, by which time Colonel Campbell, a relative by marriage of Lord Stair, had become a general, the final cost was over a thousand pounds, albeit that 'Mind Mr Chessells got Eleven dozen or thereby of the planks quh. Mr Adam's sent to Lawers about ye beginning of the Work.'[101]

Another Campbell property in Perthshire was Taymouth Castle which was probably an L-plan in origin that was extended until twin crow-stepped gables framed a row of roof dormers strung out, like abacus beads, between them. Perhaps Lord Breadalbane toyed with a fancy for a new family seat[102] but settled instead for pavilions, broad enough to require a central passage, tied to the castle by curved two-storeyed corridors.[103] Other projects, to add to and so disguise older and irregular fabrics, were for Elie House, Fife, where Ionic colonnades masked enclosed service passages,[104] and for Torrance House, Lanarkshire, for which the rare survival of a dozen drawings allows a glimpse behind the slick plates of *Vitruvius Scoticus*.[105] The ideal scheme was a square block connected to pavilions by curved or right-angled links, although the latter, which would have been cheaper, were seldom built which says much for the power of fashion and aesthetic theory. The cheapest version was to leave the 'Old House' and put up one pavilion with the stable yard close by although it would have been more correct to square the L-plan house with the 'addition proposed'

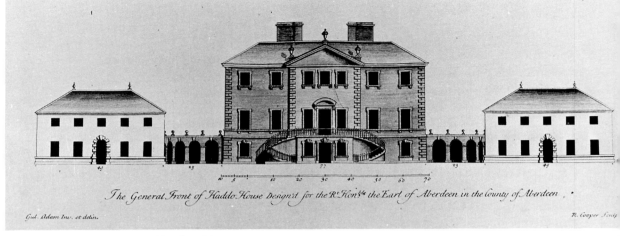

The General Front of Haddo House Design'd for the R.t Hon.ble the Earl of Aberdeen in the County of Aberdeen.

Gul. Adam Inv. et delin.   R. Cooper Sculp.

68 HADDO HOUSE, Aberdeenshire

and have east and west pavilions; if that cost too much then one could mark out 'The Outlines of the House' and erect the dual pavilions with the ground floor of one 'to be made use as a Stable for some time'.[106]

Such arrangements must have occurred at Mellerstain, Berwickshire, and at Lonmay, Aberdeenshire, for in both cases new mansions with service wings were planned although only the latter were executed so that at Mellerstain the family lived in the east wing with the servants across the court. At first there was only one pavilion. To obtain greater height part of the floor was lowered, which enabled Adam to contrive two 6-foot-high intersolls, 'which I Judge a great Conveniency for Sertts. [servants'] Lodgeing', while in the kitchen the $5\frac{1}{2}$ feet from the floor to the window sills 'is so much better that it prevents those in the Kitchin and Scullerie from Looking into the Gardens'.[107]

The design for James Fraser of Lonmay was probably produced in 1726. The layout was similar to the future scheme for Haddo but was less grand with a plain, three-storey block (with not even a pediment), short quadrants and Adam's customary two-storey pavilions, one to contain the brewhouse and bakehouse and the other the kitchen.[108] As Fraser died in 1729 the centre was never constructed once the pavilions, only one of which survives, were completed. The practice was to erect them first since the accommodation they provided allowed the owner to supervise the slower and more detailed work required for the main block. Thus, at Yester there 'are two Pavilions ... where the Lady Marchioness and her son the Marquiss reside, till the Body of the House is finished'.[109] But the Duke of Buccleuch outdid everybody else, as ever, by sending an invitation from East Park asking Sir Gilbert Elliot of Minto to dine at Dalkeith House for, 'I keep my Kitchen there, and Lye here'.[110]

If Adam was disappointed over Lonmay he was to receive a further reverse at HADDO HOUSE, a few miles to the south [68]. Late in 1731 the 2nd Earl of Aberdeen wrote to his friend Sir John Clerk acknowledging the receipt of a letter 'from the bearer Mr Baxter when he came north'. John Baxter, the mason in charge of constructing Mavisbank, would be free to return to the north-east in the following year to begin a new house according to Adam's 'Draught'. However, there were difficulties and Lord Aberdeen, 'so little knowen and unexperienced in Building', sought Sir John's approval for 'such alterations as shall appear necessary'.[111] In the spring of 1732 Baxter received £25:16:3 for taking down the old house;[112] by the early autumn its replacement was as high as the second storey despite

68

using 'whine asheller all wrought wt. hamers which is a longesom work'. With the building season drawing to a close, Baxter was preparing to go south, 'for I take the north to be a cold place'.

Like any amateur, Lord Aberdeen was 'very absolout in his oun opinion in building', so that Baxter found him a difficult client and if an idea came into his head 'the world nids not advance an arguement to put him of it'.[113] However, sufficient progress was made so that by midsummer 1733 the front wallhead was up, which prompted Baxter to hope that in another two months 'We will be Nier a Cloas with the hous so that they may have time eneugh for puiting on the Roofe and may gittet Sleted and leaded in deu time'.[114] Despite his optimism it was not until October that the mansion-house was 'now near Roffed'[115] with timber, which probably came from Norway[116] since, according to Baxter, the local wood was fit only for coal-pits,[117] although other local products were used. Lime came from Strichen and in 1733 rubble stone, probably from Pitmedden,[118] was to be cut for the offices[119] so that, twelve months later, one pavilion and the corridor to the central block was 'Joiste high'. It was roofed in the autumn and by the end of 1735 the second wing was being completed.[120]

Adam had designed a conventional block, seven bays wide and three storeys high with a piend roof faced by a pediment.[121] There were angle quoins and dressings around the windows, apart from which no decoration was intended although Lord Aberdeen and Baxter introduced a string-course between the first and second floors, a sculptured armorial panel and an octagonal light in the tympanum above the entrance.

As the designer, Adam had hoped to erect the new house of Haddo but was superseded by Baxter, perhaps on the recommendation of Sir John Clerk,[122] so that Adam's relations with his former employee became strained. So it may have been with some pride that Baxter, whom Lord Aberdeen had found to be 'very good of his Trade',[123] reported that the house 'Stanes weill without Crack or flau or the least Simptem of a Sitle in any pairt of the whoall so Mr Adams is disapointed who thought to have turned me of with disgrace and got the work in his oun hand'.[124] Yet, more than a year later, Adam was making a sketch for the roof.[125]

The failure to secure the contractual work at Haddo could only have been a minor irritant to Adam's professional pride for even ten years before he had, 'So many Real and so many Imaginary projects that he minds no body nor no thing to purpose'.[126] Still it was not without pleasure that the architect could inform Sir John Clerk in the spring of 1726 of 'Severall aqu's that have advertis'd me of their being quickly down from London as Mr Dundas of Arnistone, Lord Somervill etc. who are designing to build this year, and I have their Draughts rady for them'.[127]

Arniston and Somerville House (or The Drum, as it is usually called) lie respectively seven miles to the east and north of Mavisbank in the county of Midlothian. Although within the sphere of influence of Sir John Clerk, they each mark a departure in Adam's work, for gone are the restraints imposed by an unsullied imitation of Palladian forms, as at Newliston, or by a patron, such as Sir John Clerk, or by intractable building materials, as at Haddo. Instead there is a confidence, almost a bravura, indicating that assurance that comes from success. Some otherwise thoughtful critics have been harsh in their assessment of William Adam's abilities, seeing in him a provincial master whose chief glory was to be the father of a more famous son.[128] That underrates William Adam's achievement which, as a country-house builder, was demonstrated probably more to his own satisfaction at ARNISTON [69] than anywhere else so that it remains the mansion which approximates more closely to Palladian concepts than any other country-house of its period in Scotland. It also corresponds, therefore, to the ideas expressed by Sir John Clerk in 'The Country Seat', although the import of the lines should be treated perhaps with some reserve since, despite what has been implied, there is no evidence that Adam knew of the poem which remained in manuscript only.[129]

Arniston can be equated with Sir John's 'Usefull House' which is characterised by 'convenience and ease' and which 'may three Convenient Floors inclose'. Above the basement there should be:

> A Floor of well proportiond Rooms, to which
> By a large open stair or Portico
> We may ascend from a neat Spacious Court
> Here may a Loby or Salon be plac'd.[130]

Indeed, the hall at Arniston [70] is the most striking feature, being modelled in plaster by Joseph Enzer[131] who would later work at Yester House [71]. As a scaled-down version of Vanbrugh's stone hall at Castle Howard, it was the sole example by Adam which conformed to the cubic halls at the Queen's House, Greenwich, and at Houghton Hall, Norfolk, which 'serve for feasts, entertainments and decorations, for comedies, weddings, and such like recreations ... the nearer they come to a square the more convenient and commendable they will be'.[132] Palladio further considered, and at Arniston Adam obviously agreed, that 'in the private houses of the antient Romans', the entrance hall or 'Atrio' should have 'some pilasters' with 'an open terrace above', although 'The rooms on the side thereof, are six foot less in height'.[133] According to Sir John:

> Round the Salon may fitly be disposd
> Th'apartments for the Master's proper use.[134]

These Adam intended as a family bedroom and dining-room on the west side[135] and to the south what he would have called a garden parlour but which at Arniston is the Oak Parlour, its late seventeenth-century decoration reminiscent of the interiors of Drumlanrig and the vanished Hamilton Palace. Like many another country gentleman Robert Dundas had his own copy of Palladio – it was Leoni's edition[136] – in which he would have noted that 'Opposite to the entrance is the Tablino ... to place the images and statues of their ancestors in.'[137] Without such an acceptance of atavism it is difficult to account for the retention of the Oak Parlour.

> By a well lighted Staircase we ascend
> To the cheif Floor, with more capacious Rooms
> All made to entertain our better Freinds.[138]

For them Adam formulated on the west and south sides an apartment consisting of saloon, drawing-room, bedroom, dressing-room and closet. Of course a lawyer had to have a

69 ARNISTON, Midlothian, the garden front
70 ARNISTON, Midlothian, the entrance hall

71 YESTER HOUSE, East Lothian, the staircase ceiling

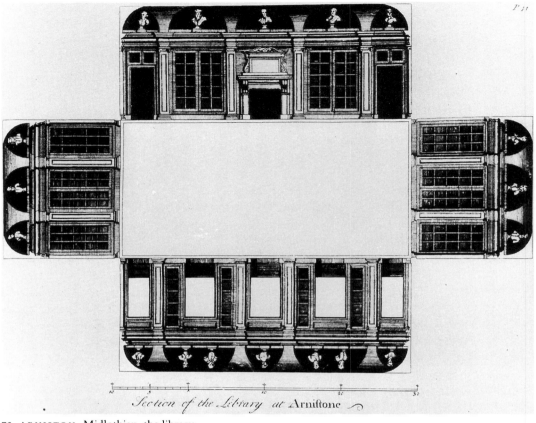

Section of the Library at Arniftone

72 ARNISTON, Midlothian, the library
73 THE DRUM, Midlothian

library and in several of Adam's houses it finds its place, not as a unit in the parade of public rooms on the piano nobile but placed privately, almost secretly, in the lodging storey, 'where the mind, fatigued by the agitations of the city, will be greatly restor'd and comforted, and be able quietly to attend the studies of letters, and contemplation'.[139] Just as the hall has its modelled reliefs of Roman emperors so in the library busts are set beneath the ceiling cove [72].

Such a complete Palladian programme is unusual in Britain and if it appears bookish that surely is because, 'Those who are unacquainted with the antient Greek and Roman Structures or the Designs of them taken by the best masters have no pretence to understand Architectory.'[140]

At Arniston, and even more so at THE DRUM, Adam was enabled to express his fascination for richly textured surfaces with a Vanbrughian diaper of stonework in which Gibbsian mouldings are pinned by triple blocked keystones with the larger design elements culled from the third volume of *Vitruvius Britannicus* published in 1725. Thus, at Arniston the engaged Ionic tetrastyle portico rising through two floors above a heavily rusticated triple-arched base is another reworked version from Lord Herbert's villa in Whitehall.[141] Even more derivative is The Drum [73] where, although the overall surface treatment imitates Palladio's Palazzo Thiene, there is the novelty of a Palladian window which, set above the entrance, would seem to be a more robust specimen than that in the 'New Bagnio in the Gardens at Chiswick'[142] although more useful examples would appear in James Gibbs's *A Book of Architecture* in 1728. More effective was the centre-piece of the elevation for Torrance House, Lanarkshire with a Palladian window, set between Ionic pilasters, resting on the Doric entablature of the entrance[143] which went against Clerk's injunction that although

> Some Architects effect to show their Skill
> By sevral orders, with Entablatures
> Above each other gradually pild
> Shun this mean practice...[144]

Adam was unsure of the treatment and use of Palladian windows so that at The Drum and in the Torrance design they illuminate hall landings and not a saloon or a library; at Dun House, Angus (1730), and in the design for Niddrie they are each recessed behind, and so repeat in diminuendo, the triumphal arch frontispiece, thus establishing horizontal as well as vertical movement. In the design for Cally House the Palladian window becomes the entrance, as at Gartmore where two Palladian windows sit one above the other while in the design for Castle Kenmore they appear in the end bays as at Burlington House in London. In general, however, Adam relegates the Palladian window to the pavilions or offices as at Mavisbank, Cammo, Broomlands and Preston Hall.[145]

When it was built The Drum was a show house re-establishing a family seat and probably reflecting in the profusion of decorative work the expenditure of a wife's inheritance. Certainly the construction must have been speedy since, perhaps at Lady Somerville's insistence, the London-trained Samuel Calderwood was hired late in December 1727[146] to conjure up pyrotechnics of plasterwork in the hall and adjacent dining-room. The latter

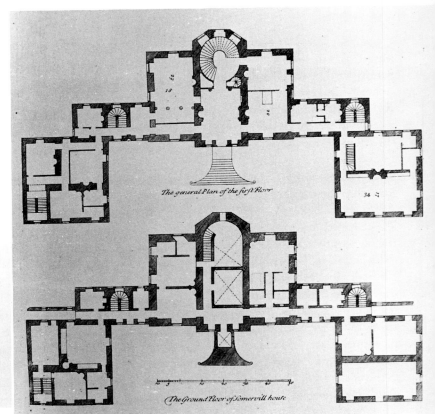

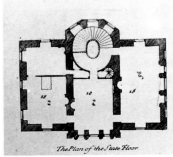

The general Plan of the first Floor

The Ground Floor of Somervill house

The Plan of the State Floor

74 THE DRUM, Midlothian

was balanced, on the plan [74], by the family bedroom. According to Palladio one practical reason for a symmetrical plan was 'that the walls may equally bear the burden of the roof',[147] although at The Drum they are continued externally to become a canted bay. That was not a feature found either in Palladio or in *Vitruvius Britannicus* but it was favoured by Adam and recurs at Cumbernauld House, Dunbartonshire, which was similar in many respects to The Drum, especially in the overall application of rustication,[148] and at TINWALD, Dumfries-shire, where there is a canted bay on each side elevation.

Tinwald is the smallest of a series of houses, beginning with Arniston and continuing with Dun, which Adam built for members of the judiciary. The client was Charles Erskine, Lord Tinwald, to whom Adam wrote early in 1739 promising to send masons to Dumfries-shire in the middle of February. Three months later he was writing at length from Dumfries where he and Lord Hope, a friend of the judge, were staying. They had been to the site where a new foreman had been appointed. A more serious problem was that 'Oak Timber for the Joisting and Rooff of the House is not to be gott to answer the dimensions Contained in the Note and Plan of the Floors Sent befor', so that Adam had pre-empted 'a parcell of Squair Timbers'. That was part of a consignment of fir imported by the provost of Dumfries who had also agreed to supply 'Flooring Dales . . . of Such Lengths as to Answer the Squair Rooms without a Joint', leaving some oak from the previous house to be utilised as joists on the first floor although 'the rest of the old Oak I propose to be us'd over the Arches of the Ground Storie'. Another difficulty was the lack of sound bricks, forcing the architect to order 'Stone work to be putt in place of Brick divisions'. Yet, once lime was fetched

74

across the Solway from England and the new building season was under way, Adam was confident that before its close the roof would be on with the window sashes ready to be fitted. Made in Edinburgh, they would be as good, Adam maintained, as the trial window his client proposed having made up in London.

Tinwald was perhaps unusual in that it was only the *corps de logis* which was being considered in 1739 and, although Adam was prepared to accept that the stables 'may be built either in the Manner design'd or in what other shape may be thought better, and at what time you Please after the House is finish'd', he was clearly disappointed that Lord Tinwald was not proposing to construct the pavilions and linking corridors. 'Yet its then that the necessary Conveniencys for a Family can be compleat.'[149] Likewise Sir John Clerk, when taking stock of the second category of country seat, reckoned that the 'Usefull House' with a front of between 80 and 100 feet and 'with convenient wings is judged of all others the most useful and commodious'. Arniston was 94 feet long and 68 feet deep whereas Tinwald is 62 feet long and 40 feet in breadth, although Clerk conceded that, 'Even Houses of Smaller Dimensions may be made very convenient where State is not required. The breadth of a usefull House should never fall under 40 foot.'[150]

Such a house was intended almost invariably by Adam to have the offices connected to the centre after the manner of Palladio's villa designs, in the majority of which the links form right angles although there are three examples with curved colonnades. With Adam the numbers are reversed so that Floors and Gartmore have right-angled links, at The Drum they are lateral and at Arniston they were to be set at an angle of forty-five degrees, an idea taken from James Gibbs.[151] Adam's preference was for quadrants. Usually one storey high, although there are two-storeyed examples, as was intended at Tinwald, they pay due heed to Scotland's climate, becoming enclosed passages communicating directly with the house. On the courtyard aspect there are three openings with the middle one being a doorway. For grand schemes an open colonnade was provided, as at Hopetoun and Newliston, but at Elie and Duff House it was backed by a covered service passage.

DUFF HOUSE, Banffshire, was Adam's last important domestic commission [75] and though work on the incomplete project ceased in 1740 the ensuing litigation dogged the last eight years of the architect's life. The client was William Duff of Braco whose father, by a variety of means, all of which were sagacious and some of which were ruthless, had acquired a string of estates, mostly in Morayshire, to which were added further substantial holdings, such as Balvenie in Banffshire, on the failure of the principal line of the Duff family in 1718. William Duff of Braco was the possessor not only of extensive unencumbered estates, to which he would continue to add in the years ahead, but of £30,000 in money. Some of this wealth he would expend in employing two celebrated architects, James Gibbs at Balvenie from 1724 and a decade later William Adam at Duff House. The latter, according to tradition, cost £70,000.[152]

Although Adam had been consulted in 1730, four years were to pass before William Duff, now retired from politics, 'resolved to settle at home and his family pretty numerous and yearly growing he also Resolved for his Amusement and better Accomodation [sic] to make Considerable Alterations to his principall Mansion house near to the Town of Banff' for which Adam was invited to produce drawings. That the scheme did not proceed was

75 DUFF HOUSE, Banffshire

because of two events in 1735. William Duff was rewarded with an Irish peerage, becoming Lord Braco, and he entertained at Banff 'ane honourable person of great Judgement and taste in Architecture as well as other more usefull things'. When the anonymous guest mooted that the old house should be abandoned in favour of a new one more distant from the town, William Adam was summoned by express to Perth 'and there settle the first draught of a plan and to bring it north to Banff . . . and the Iron Struck while it was hot', the foundation stone of a new mansion was laid on 11 June 1735. For the north and south elevations Morayshire freestone was used although for the show fronts stone was shipped from Queensferry 'at no very great Charge by the means of Boats or Barks that are frequently going from this firth [of Forth] to the north to fetch meall'. Timber from Lord Braco's newly acquired Mar estates was floated down the River Dee to Aberdeen for the voyage to Banff; more came from Norway while glass and nails were despatched from Edinburgh by William Adam.[153] No construction job is without its toll of delay, disappointment and ever rising costs. In the second year of operations when the barrowmen went on strike for a penny a day increase to sixpence Lord Braco refused to yield, sought for other men, 'And Sent Alexr. Rhind likeways to Auchterless Mercatt to Go about with a Pyper to Engage them', which broke the strike.[154] Another incident occurred three years later when Lord Braco essayed to have two barrowmen imprisoned for breaking their contract by leaving his service.[155] As Lord Braco himself admitted, 'I am like all Scotsmen,' which meant litigious, 'especially if he thought he had met with any Disingenuity, or been in the least imposed upon.'[156]

Once building was under way Lord Braco decided to omit the attic storey so that the house would be 'less exposed to Storms in a Situation very near the Northern Ocean'.[157] Yet, as Adam wrote to the clerk of works, John Burt, 'The Charge that My Lord made by his Letter to me, in takeing of the Attick Storie gave me fresh work to do.' And there was a further consideration, 'For tho' those that propose them may think the alterations, Yet Generale Speaking they disconnect other thing in a building and this is not ane affair to be Spoilt.'[158] Eighteen months later, in the spring of 1737, Lord Braco despatched to his architect further reflections about an attic storey 'because the want of it would Spoill the Looks of Such a Monstrous house and indeed I wish you and the house had been at the D— before it had been begun'.[159] Such were the storm signals that Adam, having loaded some newly cut capitals and keystones at the Forth, noted ruefully, 'I am only afraid that My Lord is not sensible of all the expense I am att.' Five months later, in August 1738, the front pediment was on its way and its companion was blocked out but Lord Braco had not decided on the coat of arms for the tympanum although the foliage was cut.[160] Although Adam maintained that the northern stone cutting could not compare with the Queensferry work for 'fineness, Trouble and variety', Lord Braco reckoned, 'that he should have made Bargain for every thing before the work was begun'. He was not only suspicious about 'a quarry Mr Adams had in Lease near Queensferry' but opined that his architect wanted, 'to make a good Estate for himself out of this Single Jobb'.[161] Thereafter, matters went from bad to worse and it was only with hindsight that the true cause of the ensuing legal suit was revealed. 'Mr Adams does not pretend that there was any explicit Agreement'[162] for it was customary not to have one, 'Because of the many Alterations which frequently and almost allways occur according to the fancy and Conveniencys of the builder' so that work was paid for on completion by measurement.[163] In the years to come Adam became 'Such ane abandoned Rascal'[164] and the unfinished mansion caused its noble owner such pain that the coach blinds were lowered whenever he drove past.

What interpretation can be placed upon the last of Adam's great country-houses? How does it compare, say, with Hopetoun House of the previous decade? Does it show a stricter adherence to Palladian principles? Or does it prove once more that Adam was a visual artist interested in the tactile values of the Baroque rather than in maintaining an intellectual ideology?

As intended Duff House is a block approximately 105 feet long and 85 feet broad including the corner projections from which expansive colonnades would have reached out to pavilions containing servants' rooms and a library above the stables and kitchen respectively.[165] It is unfortunate that the outbuildings were never constructed for they would have absolved the *corps de logis* of its 'naked look', about which Pennant commented,[166] and would have been the essential counter-balance to the compressed verticality of the centre [76] emphasised by the tight ranges of windows underscoring the Corinthian pilasters. Of their capitals Adam wrote, 'They gave the ffront a grand appearance',[167] thus echoing his claim that at Yester the intended tetrastyle frontispiece 'is much wanting to take off the Plainness of the ffront'.[168] Bishop Pococke was reminded at Duff House of Castle Howard and he was not alone in seeing a resemblance to Vanbrugh's work[169] for there is, behind the antique mask, a dour, powerful force while the projecting corners owe some debt both to Eastbury and to Castle Howard, although the belvederes with which they are crowned reinterpret the turrets which once sat astride the Pantheon.[170]

It has already been noted that Sir John Clerk prevented Adam from adding an extra

76 DUFF HOUSE, Banffshire

storey to Mavisbank; of Duff House the client wrote approvingly, 'With the Turrets upon each Corner to go up to the roof of the house, you have preserved the height and beauty.'[171] Yet should the apparatus of four floors be considered an aberration by Adam of the accepted formula, bearing in mind McGill's designs or Keith Hall, a possible prototype, some thirty miles to the south, for Duff House? Undoubtedly, Adam did like to introduce an attic behind a pediment as he had done at Hopetoun. A union of attic and pediment may not have been common in English practice although Adam could have found a source in Buckingham House.[172] Adam's clients likewise looked to England for their architectural standards and Lord Tweeddale certainly submitted one design by Adam for Yester to Lord Pembroke, with whose opinion Adam quibbled[173] although at Dun he utilised an elevation sent earlier from Paris by the exiled Jacobite Earl of Mar to his Erskine kinsman.[174] Lord

Braco also had opinions but these had less to do with aesthetic appreciation than practical considerations. He insisted that the library should be retained within the *corps de logis* where the first floor [77] was to be reserved for family use[175] with the state floor above, as at Yester, for the drawing-room and saloon, the latter being a 30-foot cube behind the attic. It would have occasioned no surprise to find the gallery, with a prospect over the town of Banff to the sea, on the attic floor, since to have the most magnificent room at the highest level was Scottish practice, as at Crathes Castle, Kincardineshire, in the late sixteenth century and over a hundred years later with McGill at Donibristle and in the first scheme for Mount Stuart. Indeed, in the planning of Duff House there is something of that earlier generation – formal but comfortable, dignified but practical – so that one senses that Adam was never the slave of Palladianism, with its tenets of correctness, but retained a sturdy independence.

Perhaps that is expressed, too, in the practicality, and even the homeliness which is integral in Adam's plans. At Lonmay, for example, the ground floor was to be given over to family use with the nursery and private dining-room on one side of the entrance and the family bedroom and dressing-rooms on the other. Cumbernauld had similar arrangements on the first floor with the addition of a private drawing-room and although no dining-room was specified there was an octagonal parlour, below which a garden parlour had an outside door. At Craigiehall a proposed parlour would have contained a bed alcove, although it was usual to have a family bedroom as at Dun where, from the basement, 'Closets and Back Stairs to the Ladys room above' led to a dressing-room.[176] Throughout the early eighteenth century it was, in Scotland at least, the family chamber which was the

77 DUFF HOUSE, Banffshire, principal floor plan

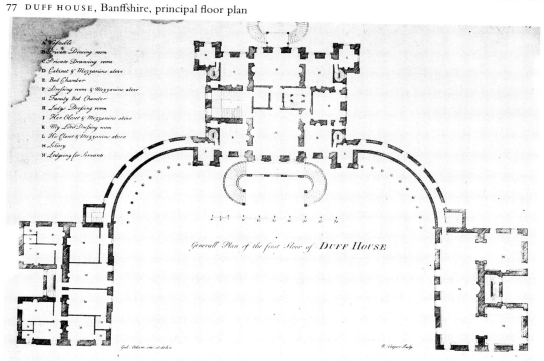

79

room of consequence. Few mansions were grand enough to warrant a saloon, let alone a state floor as at Duff House, and although Dun has a hall and saloon plan the day-to-day routine of living must have been in the linked parlour and family bedroom. The latter was often as large, if not larger than the drawing-room, which in turn was smaller than the private dining-room, with the need for table space, as at Newhall, Makerstoun and Balgregan. Probably the grandest dining-room was at The Drum, for not only is it ornamented overall with stucco-work but columns screen the servants' waiting area. Since no country-house could function without servants Adam considered that the second-table-room at Duff House should be vaulted so that 'the private Dining-room above would be the less troubled with the noice of the Servants below',[177] which may explain why the chaplain's room at Hopetoun was behind the servants' hall. To ensure peace and quietness libraries tended to be on the bedroom floor although that was where, at Mavisbank as at Makerstoun, Adam intended to place a billiard table. Another new but expensive taste is perhaps demonstrated by the tea-rooms at Lawers and Newhailes. More prosaically, and very Scottish, were the charter-rooms commonly adjacent to the master's dressing-room as at Newhall and Yester. Although every bedroom had its closet, stool-rooms are shown at Makerstoun where there were to be 'presses for house furniture' and, on another plan, 'two press beds in the Gallery for Stranger Servants'.[178] However, it is at Yester that the social distinctions of the age are most cogently summarised with 'A House of Office for Servants' in one corner of the courtyard, another one for gentlemen near the stables to be made of timber and enclosed by a hedge, while in the house there was to be 'a Water Closet with a marble Stooll' by the lord's bedroom.[179]

Apart from Hopetoun House and unfinished work, as at Duff House, or unexecuted work, such as Newliston, two-thirds of Adam's country-houses were for the middle rank of the landed gentry. In the previous century the patrons of architecture were drawn from the upper echelons of the Scottish aristocracy and though names like Hamilton, Atholl and Buccleuch are linked to Adam their commissions were either trifling or abortive. Now a middle rank of builders had emerged – men for whom close contact with England and the Hanoverian springtime of peace were bringing new ideas which, together with the more settled internal social and political conditions and wealth, either from soldiering or practice at the bar, allowed them to imitate an earlier generation of ducal builders. Adam and his clients were pragmatists. Few could afford the pediments and pilasters of Duff House but those of lesser means could utilise the fine building stone, whether the creamy sandstone of Queensferry or the red of Locharbriggs in Dumfries-shire, and still afford some carved embellishment. In style there is little evidence of that restrained horizontality, the limitation on the variety of elements, the decorative understatement that are the sterling stamps of English Palladianism. In a sense there is little advance in Scotland on the layouts of such pioneers of Palladianism as Bruce and Smith although the classical syntax is more extensive. Perhaps Adam's most signal contribution was to provide a new class of dwelling, which combined the practicalities of habitation with a more rhetorical classicism both in structure and in decoration, that found evident favour with his shrewd, undemonstrative, commonsensical and, on the whole, appreciative clients. Not for them the cerebral abstractions of Palladian concepts and harmonic proportions. Their objectives were both more limited and more practical; and if, in his heart, Adam ever retained a love for the sweeping chords of the Baroque in preference to the drier plainsong of Palladianism, he did establish new criteria in the planning and decoration of country-houses so that they might match Palladio's definition and 'in themselves contain beauty and be of credit and conveniency to the owners'.[180]

Notes to Chapter 3

1. John Clerk of Eldin, 'Life of Robert Adam', SRO, GD18/4981.
2. Ibid. The most complete account of William Adam's life and career is by J. Fleming, *Robert Adam and His Circle* (1962), pp. 2–3, 6–7, 33–75.
3. William Adam was 'bred a Mason and served his time as such'. 'Act and Commission William Lord Braco Against William Adam, 1743', p. 139, SRO, CS230/A2/1.
4. Supra, n. 1. Fleming, op. cit., p. 7. See also Sir John Clerk of Penicuik, 'An Account of Some Business made in Fife, 1728', for a list of Adam's industrial enterprises. SRO, GD18/2108.
5. 'Copy Report on the Claim John Adams Architect in Edinburgh for himself and in right of William Adams his father against the Duke of Hamilton', NLS, MS 8265. See also SRO, GD31/554.
6. William Adam to Lord Milton, Borrostoness, 6 March 1734, NLS, MS 16555, f. 6.
7. George Dundas to Lord Tweeddale, Dundas, 28 May 1739, NLS, MS 14429, f. 169.
8. Lord Roxburghe to his mother, Paris, 16 August 1701, Duke of Roxburghe's MSS, bundle 726.
9. Ibid., 30 October and 18 November 1712, Duke of Roxburghe's MSS, bundle 767. Doubtless McGill was employed at Floors because Lord Roxburghe was a first cousin of Lord Tweeddale.
10. Ibid., London, 26 February 1712, Duke of Roxburghe's MSS, bundle 768.
11. Sir William Bennet, Marlfield, 18 May 1721, Duke of Roxburghe's MSS, bundle 726.
12. 'Account of Disbursements at Floors, 1721' and 'Copy of the workmens Accts. att Floors from August 12th 1726 to Sept. 9th', Duke of Roxburghe's MSS, bundle 128.
    Adam was at Floors in the spring of 1723 and probably in May 1724 and again two years later. SRO, GD18/4724, 4728/4, 4729/2.
13. *VS*, pl. 49. Floors was roofed with a lead flat which evidently caused problems so that in 1745 Roger Morris was consulted and he, it was reported, suggested leaving 'the four Turrets standing and to take of the first Floor of the Body of the House and Turn it into Garretts with a Slated Pent house roof'. It would seem that the roof was releaded. Duke of Roxburghe's MSS, bundle 548. Palladio had made the point, which would not be lost on his eighteenth-century followers, that 'magnificent palaces ... are generally covered with lead'. *The Four Books of Architecture* (republished 1965), Bk. I, p. 4.
14. R. Pococke, 'Tours in Scotland, 1747, 1750, 1760', *SHS*, vol. I (1887), p. 330.
15. *VB*, vol. I (1715), introduction.
16. Ibid.
17. 'An Inventor of the Furniture of Craighall House at Sir Thos. Death which happened the 28th of March, 1686', SRO, GD242/Box 40.
18. Supra, n. 15.
19. 'Accot. the Earle of Hoptoun to Mr Adam, 1721', Hopetoun MSS, bundle 636.
20. 'Account of the Building of the new addition to the south side of Hoptoun House as given in by Mr Adames', Hopetoun MSS, bundle 636.
21. 'Attested Account of the Measur of the New building at Hopetoun House, 6th April 1725', Hopetoun MSS, bundle 636.
22. 'Heads of an Agreement between the Earl of Hopetoun and William Adam, Architect', Hopetoun MSS, bundle 636.
23. J. Loveday, 'Diary of a Tour in 1732', *Roxburghe Club* (1889), p. 144.
24. 'Accott. and Discharge The Deceast Jo. Niccoll', 1733, Hopetoun MSS, bundle 2946.

25. 'Note of Prices agreed between Ld. Hopetn. and Mr Adams, 1726', Hopetoun MSS, bundle 636.
   As the Bruce columns in the colonnades were the same height as the existing ones it is likely that they were re-used by William Adam which may explain the curious wording of the account, 'To New Additional hewn work in Arcad Bases and piers etc. including the steps. £62:11:6.' 'Accompt the Right Honble the Earl of Hoptoun to Walter Moreiss Mason. 1734.' Hopetoun MSS, bundle 3025.

26. VS, pl. 14. J. Fleming, op. cit., pp. 92–3 states that the pavilions are William Adam designs reworked by John and Robert Adam in 1751. However, in the 'Abstract of Mr Adams Accts. from May 1736 to May 1746' the library pavilion is costed at £1,225:8:1 with the stable pavilion costing £1,330:19:1 and there are references in 1747 and 1748 to 'the two Cupilloes', presumably the lanterns over the pavilions. Hopetoun MSS, bundles 636 and 385. VS, pl. 17 shows a pavilion design which is not dissimilar to what was built. See also C. McWilliam, Lothian (1978), pp. 253–4; A. Rowan, 'The Building of Hopetoun', Architectural History, vol. 27 (1984), pp. 189–94.

27. 'Abstract of Mr Adams Accts. from May 1736 to May 1746', Hopetoun MSS, bundle 636.

28. Dryden House, Midlothian and Elphinstone House, Stirlingshire were remarkable in that each seems to have had an Ionic tetrastyle portico. VS, pls. 80, 76. Dryden House, attributed to James Smith (Chapter 2, n. 47), belonged to George Lockhart of Carnwath who inherited a large fortune in 1689, was MP for Edinburgh from 1702–10 and was arrested at Dryden on the outbreak of the Jacobite rebellion in 1715 by which time, presumably, the house was structurally complete.
   Elphinstone House could be attributed to Alexander McGill as there were planning similarities with his first scheme for Mount Stuart. It may be significant that the wife of the 8th Lord Elphinstone, whom he married in 1670, was a daughter of Lord Hatton and a niece of the Duke of Lauderdale. Lord Elphinstone died in 1717 DNB.

29. Pococke, op. cit., vol. I, p. 297.

30. Adam was thinking of travelling to London in the winter of 1724–5 and was certainly there two years later in the company of Sir John Clerk of Penicuik. W. Adam to Sir John Clerk, 15 December 1724 and 'Journey to London in 1727', SRO, GD18/4278/6 and 2107.

31. Sir John Vanbrugh to Brigadier General Watkins, 26 August 1721. G. F. Webb (ed.), The Complete Works of Sir John Vanbrugh (1927), vol. IV, p. 138.

32. The estate of Cammo was purchased in 1710 and sold in 1724. J. M. Gray (ed.), 'Memoirs of the Life of Sir John Clerk of Penicuik', SHS, vol. XIII (1892), pp. 78, 113, 116.

33. Ibid., p. 28.

34. Sir John Clerk of Penicuik, 'Journey to London in 1727', SRO, GD18/2107.

35. Ibid.

36. Ibid.

37. Gray, op. cit., p. 219.

38. Supra, n. 34.

39. 'Memorandum of the building the house of Pennycuik', SRO, GD18/1758. See also 'Memorandum Concerning the Building of Mavisbank House . . .', SRO, GD18/1770 and Gray, op. cit., pp. 113, 114.

40. The drawings are in the Clerk of Penicuik collection. Photographs are in NMRS.

41. Gray, op. cit., pp. 114–15.

42. William Adam to Sir John Clerk, Links of Kirkcaldy, 30 January 1723, SRO, GD18/4719.

43. Ibid., Edinburgh, 5 May 1726, SRO, GD18/4729/2.

44. Ibid., Floors, 6 May 1723, SRO, GD18/4724.

45. The information is contained in the accounts, SRO, GD18/1767, bundle 2.

46. William Adam to Sir John Clerk, 21 August 1723 and 20 February 1724, SRO, GD18/4726 and 4728/3.

47. Gray, op. cit., p. 119.

48. Receipt by William Adam dated 20 February 1728, SRO, GD18/1767, bundle 1.

49. Supra, n. 39. SRO, GD18/1770.

50. 'Advice by Sir John Clerk on the building of a family house', SRO, GD18/1855.

51. William Adam to Sir John Clerk, Edinburgh, 15 December 1724 and 16 April 1725, SRO, GD18/4724/6, 12.

52. SRO, GD18/1767/bundles 2 and 4.
53. Supra, n. 34.
54. Supra, n. 50.
55. William Adam to Sir John Clerk, Edinburgh, 15 May 172– and 20 December 1727, SRO, GD18/4728/10 and 4729/5. Also SRO, GD18/1767/bundle 4.
56. Supra. n. 39. SRO, GD18/1770.
57. Gray, op. cit., p. 155.
58. Supra, n. 39. SRO, GD18/1770.
59. 'Advices Concerning Building and Planting', SRO, GD18/1395.
60. *The Letters of the Younger Pliny* (1974), Bk. II, p. 75.
61. Supra, n. 59.
62. Supra, n. 39. SRO, GD18/1770.
63. Supra, n. 34.
64. Ibid.
65. R. Castell, *The Villas of the Ancients Illustrated* (1728), p. 6.
66. Sir John Clerk of Penicuik, 'The Country Seat', f. 18, SRO, GD18/4404/1.
67. Gray, op. cit., p. 19.
68. Clerk, op. cit.
69. Ibid., f. 1.
70. Gray, op. cit., p. 115.
71. Sir John considered that there were two divisions of the 'Rustick Order', namely the Tuscan and the French which, since they were not so fine as the other more classical orders, were more suited to the British climate. Clerk, op. cit., f. 21 and n. 47.
72. McWilliam, op. cit., p. 315.
73. See also *VB*, vol. I, pl. 20.
74. Palladio, op. cit., Bk. II, pl. XXXIV; S. Serlio, *The Book of Architecture* (republished 1980), 5th Bk., p. 14.
75. Gray, op. cit., p. 141 gives a brief account of Clerk's tour of Norfolk in 1733. See also SRO, GD18/2110.
76. Pliny, op. cit., Bk. II, p. 77.
77. Castell, op. cit., p. 1.
78. Supra, n. 70.
79. Castell, ibid.
80. *The Satires of Horace and Persius* (1976), Bk. II, Satire 6.
81. John Clerk of Eldin, SRO, GD18/4982.
    In 1727 Stair's approach to Sir Robert Walpole to appoint Adam as Surveyor of the King's Works in Scotland was thwarted by the death of King George II. SRO, GD18/4730. H. Colvin, *A Biographical Dictionary of British Architects, 1600–1840* (1978), p. 56.
82. *DNB*; J. Graham, *Annals and Correspondence of the Viscount and the First and Second Earls of Stair* (1875), vol. II, p. 161.
83. M. Cato, *On Agriculture* (1934), p. 3.
84. J. Macky, *A Journey through Scotland* (1723), p. 325.
85. Graham, ibid.
86. *VS*, pls. 32–6. William Adam to Sir John Clerk, Links of Kirkcaldy, 30 January 1723, 'Ther's just Now among My hands a Design of ane addition to Newliston House.' A year later Adam was considering travelling to Galloway to see Lord Stair. SRO, GD18/4719, 4728/3. In August 1730 Adam wrote to Lord Milton from Newliston, NLS, MS 16542.
87. Palladio, op. cit., Bk. II, pl. XXX.
88. Supra, n. 34.
89. William Adam to Sir John Clerk, n.d., SRO, GD18/4735/2.
90. Palladio, op. cit., Bk. II, pl. XXXIII.
91. *VS*, pl. 72. Adam reported in 1724 that Baron Dalrymple was after some timber deals which the architect intended for Sir John Clerk. Some months later Baron Dalrymple expressed annoyance because his staircase

was not finished. SRO, GD18/4728/6, 10. In 1758 Sir William Burrell reported that the house was 'not yet entirely fitted up'. NLS, MS 2911, f. 19.

92. *VS*, pls. 73–4.

93. Ibid., pls. 127–8.

94. Supra, n. 50.

95. Copies of the drawings are in NMRS.

96. *VS*, pls. 77–8. The pavilions were not built.

97. Supra, n. 50.

98. 'Estimate of Craigdarroch, 1726', SRO, GD77/204/1.
  Sir John Clerk, travelling to south-west Scotland in 1735, halted at Craigdarroch which he described as 'a new convenient building of 60 feet in length and 40 in breadth'. SRO, GD18/2112.

99. 'Accompt the right Honourable Collonel James Campbell to Archibald Chessels. April, 1724' and 'Arch. Chessels Wright his Acct: 1732', SRO, GD237/99/1/46, 47.

100. William Adam to General James Campbell of Lawers, Edinburgh, 5 October 1737, Bute MSS.

101. 'Accot. of what Money Arch. Chessells has got preceeding the 1st Augt. 1744', SRO, GD237/99/2/31.
  General Sir James Campbell of Lawers was the third son of the second Earl of Loudon. A distinguished soldier, he fought at the Battles of Malplaquet (1709) and Dettingen (1743) and died at the Battle of Fontenoy (1745). *DNB*.

102. *VS*, pls. 51–2.

103. Ibid., pls. 50–1. William Adam's account was submitted in 1739. SRO, GD112/20/1/5/11.
  The foreman at Taymouth Castle was James Runciman, an Edinburgh wright. His receipts were made out in 1740. SRO, CS230/A2/1. During his tour of Scotland Sir William Burrell visited Taymouth Castle which 'has a great No. of Rooms, a Saloon 40F by 22 with a Recess of fluted Doric Pillars, a Drawing Room hung with Tapestry'. NLS, MS 2911, f. 15.

104. *VS*, pls. 88–9.

105. Ibid., pls. 139–40.

106. 'Plans for House at Torrance Made out by old Mr Adams Architect for Colonel Stuart of Torrence. Anno 1740', NLS, MS 8222.

107. William Adam to George Baillie, Edinburgh, 27 May 1726, Mellerstain Letters, vol. IX.
  The foundation stone of the east wing is dated 1725. Bishop Pococke, op. cit., p. 332 recorded in 1760: 'The offices are finished.' William Adam is credited as the designer of the undated plans and elevations still at Mellerstain which show a seven-bay pedimented house with a platform roof. A. Bolton, 'Mellerstain, Berwickshire', *CL*, vol. XXXVIII (13 November 1915), pp. 648–56; M. Girouard, 'Mellerstain, Berwickshire', *CL*, vol. CXXIV (4 September 1958), pp. 476–9.

108. *VS*, pl. 95.

109. Macky, op. cit., p. 31.

110. Duke of Buccleuch to Sir Gilbert Elliot of Minto, East Park, 23 July 1739, NLS, MS 11003.

111. Earl of Aberdeen to Sir John Clerk, Kelly, 5 December 1731, SRO, GD18/5005/1.
  Lord Aberdeen was considering a new house as early as 1724 and in the next year a model was prepared. However, three years later Adam was working on a 'new Draught'. SRO, GD18/4728/6 and 4729/6; Mellerstain Letters, vol. IX; C. Hussey, 'Haddo House, Aberdeenshire', *CL*, vol. CXL (18 August 1966), pp. 378–81.
  In the summer of 1731, when he was seriously contemplating building, Lord Aberdeen interviewed James Runciman but the latter was doubtful about his chances of employment since 'ther is another man of my busnes who is seting strongly up for it who imploys evry on he knows to recemend him.' He was referring presumably to John Baxter. James Runciman to Alexander, 2nd Earl of Marchmont, Edinburgh, 22 July 1731, SRO, GD158/1381.

112. Baxter was paid at regular intervals until 1 November 1735. Kelly building accounts and receipts, 1732–4, University of Aberdeen MS 2520.

113. John Baxter to Sir John Clerk, Kelly, 14 September 1732, SRO, GD18/5005/2.

114. Ibid., Kelly, 2 July 1733, SRO, GD18/5005/4.

115. Lord Aberdeen to Sir John Clerk, Kelly, 28 October 1733, SRO, GD18/5005/6.
116. Supra, n. 114. 'Commission The Right Honble The Earle of Aberdeen and Captain Stewart. 1733', SRO, GD33/30/55 and GD33/65/12.
117. Supra, n. 113.
118. Supra, n. 112.
119. Supra, n. 114.
120. John Baxter to Sir John Clerk, Kelly, 3 June 1734, also 4 and 25 September 1735, SRO, GD18/5005/7, 8, 12.
121. *VS*, pl. 56.
122. 'A Trip to the north of Scotland as far as Inverness in May 1739', SRO, GD18/2110.
123. Lord Aberdeen to Sir John Clerk, Kelly, 28 June 1733, SRO, GD18/5005/3.
124. Supra, n. 114.
125. Lord Aberdeen to Sir John Clerk, Edinburgh, 30 December 1734, SRO, GD18/5005/14.
126. Lord Annandale to Sir John Clerk, Craigiehall, 23 January 1724, SRO, GD18/4727.
127. William Adam to Sir John Clerk, Edinburgh, 5 May 1726, SRO, GD18/4729/2.
    Robert Dundas of Arniston (1685–1753) was a distinguished member of the legal profession becoming Lord President of the Court of Session in 1748. Having succeeded to the Arniston estate in 1726 it would seem that he lost no time in commissioning William Adam to design a new house and policies. J. Small, *Castles and Mansions of the Lothians* (1883), vol. I; G. Omond, *The Arniston Memoirs* (1887), pp. 42, 71, 74.
    Lord Somerville (1698–1763) was recognised as the 12th Baron in 1722. By his marriage to two heiresses he repaired the family fortunes, built The Drum and hence became known as The Restorer. H. More Nisbett, *Drum of the Somervilles* (1928), pp. 16–17.
128. A. Bolton, 'The Drum, Midlothian', *CL*, vol. XXXVIII (9 October 1915), pp. 488–92; Fleming, op. cit., pp. 67, 73–4.
129. A. Tait, 'William Adam and Sir John Clerk: Arniston and "The Country Seat"', *Burlington Magazine*, vol. CXI (March 1969), p. 132. Clerk wrote of 'The Country Seat' that, 'I have no Design to publish the following Essay.' Supra, n. 66. See also S. Piggott, 'Sir John Clerk and "The Country Seat"', *The Country Seat*, ed. by H. Colvin and J. Harris (1970), pp. 110–16.
130. Clerk, op. cit., f. 21.
131. A contract between Joseph Enzer and Sir Robert Dundas is at Arniston House. G. Beard, *Decorative Plasterwork in Great Britain* (1975), p. 218. See also M. Cosh, 'The Adam Family and Arniston', *Architectural History*, vol. 27 (1984), pp. 214–20.
132. Palladio, op. cit., Bk. I, p. 27.
133. Ibid., Bk. II, p. 43.
134. Supra, n. 130.
135. *VS*, pl. 40.
136. Tait, op. cit., p. 135.
137. Supra, n. 133.
138. Clerk, ibid.
139. Palladio, op. cit., Bk. II, p. 46.
140. Clerk, op. cit., n. 5.
141. *VB*, vol. III (1725), pl. 48.
142. Ibid., vol. III, pl. 26.
143. *VS*, pl. 140; 'General Front of Torrance House toward the North', NLS, MS 8222, f. 2.
144. Clerk, op. cit., f. 11.
145. *VS*, pls. 70, 115, 113, 52, 83, 47, 141, 119, 108. Dun House was built for John Erskine, later Lord Dun. There is a surviving account for wright work executed between 1730 and 1737 (SRO, GD123/428/1, 3) but, as at Haddo House, Adam was not the executant architect. 'Act and Commission William Lord Braco Against William Adam, 1743', SRO, CS230/A2/1.
146. William Adam to Sir John Clerk, Edinburgh, 15 May 172– and 20 December 1727, SRO, GD18/4728/10 and /4729/5.

147. Palladio, op. cit., Bk. I, p. 27.
148. *VS*, pl. 125. Cumbernauld House was built for the 6th Earl of Wigton in 1731. After a fire in 1877 the interiors were remodelled.
149. William Adam to Charles Erskine, 30 January, 10 April and 3 May 1739, NLS, MS 5074, ff. 93, 153, 194. Also Lord Hopetoun to Charles Erskine, Hopetoun House, 11 and 13 April 1739, NLS, MS 5074, ff. 163, 167.
150. Clerk, op. cit., f. 62.
151. J. Gibbs, *A Book of Architecture* (1728), pl. 58. Even as late as 1739 Arniston was still lacking one wing. NLS, MS 2145, f. 62.
152. J. Mitchell, *Reminiscences of My Life in the Highlands* (1883), vol. II, pp. 37–8: A. and H. Tayler, *The Book of the Duffs* (1914).
153. 'Act and Commission . . .', pp. 1–47.
154. 'State of the proof in the process William Adams Archt. in Edinr. agt. William Ld. Braco, 8 December, 1743', SRO, CS230/A2/1.
155. 'Inventory of the fitted Accompts and other writes betwixt the Lord Braco and those Employed by him in building his New house at Banff. 1743', SRO, CS230/A2/1.
156. Tayler, op. cit., vol. I, pp. 115, 109.
157. 'Act and Commission . . .', p. 75.
158. William Adam to John Burt, Edinburgh, 15 September 1735, SRO, CS230/A2/1.
159. 'Act and Commission . . .', p. 78.
160. William Adam to John Burt, Edinburgh, 1 April and 24 August 1738, SRO, CS230/A2/1.
161. 'Act and Commission . . .', pp. 16, 6, 73, 72.
162. Petition of Lord Braco, 30 June 1743, NLS, Kilkerran Collection, vol. IX, f. 18. Also 'Petition ffor William Ld. Braco. 2d July 1743', SRO, CS230/A2/1.
163. 'Act and Commission . . .', pp. 14, 28.
164. Lord Braco to Lady Braco, 16 March 17–, University of Aberdeen MS 2727/1/10.
165. *VS*, pls. 146–8.
166. T. Pennant, *A Tour in Scotland, 1769* (1774), p. 134.
167. 'Act and Commission . . .', p. 5.
168. William Adam to Lord Tweeddale, n.d., NLS, MS 14551, f. 30.
169. Pococke, op. cit., p. 195; H. Skrine, *Three Successive Tours in the North of England and Great Part of Scotland* (1795), p. 124.
170. Serlio, op. cit., 5th Bk., pp. 11, 15, illustrates pavilion-capped towers on either side of a temple front. They also appear in Leoni's revision of the Villa Valmarana where the plan has an affinity with that of Duff House. G. Leoni, *The Architecture of A. Palladio* (1742), Bk. 2, pl. XLIV.
171. 'Act and Commission . . .', p. 76.
172. *VB*, vol. I, pl. 44.
173. Lord Tweeddale to William Adam and 'Memorial relating to the Front Stair at Yester', 17 March and 9 April 1743, NLS, MS 14551, ff. 70, 72.
174. RHP 13288. For an account of the 11th Earl of Mar's architectural interests see Colvin, op. cit., pp. 295–7.
175. 'Act and Commission . . .', pp. 77, 75.
176. *VS*, pl. 58.
177. William Adam to John Burt, Edinburgh, 12 May 1736, SRO, CS230/A2/1.
178. Photographs of the plans are in NMRS.
179. 'Memorandum Relating to Some Work to be done at Yester. Edinr., 18 October 1734', NLS, MS 14551, f. 41.
180. Palladio, op. cit., Bk. II, p. 56.

CHAPTER FOUR

'A pritty amusement'

According to an eighteenth-century memorialist, 'After the Union [of the Parliaments in 1707] when, from a combination of causes, Scotland revived apace, our country gentlemen began to show some inclination for better houses. Architecture was now studied as a science by private gentlemen and by professional men.'[1] It was, therefore, with the eye of knowledge that, in 1719, Sir Archibald Grant of Monymusk considered the house of his ancestors 'with battlements and six different roofs of various heights and directions, confusedly and inconveniently combined, and all rotten, with two wings more modern, of two stories only, the half of the windowes of the higher riseing above the roofs, with granaries, stables and houses for all cattle and of the vermine attending them, close by'.[2] From Aberdeenshire to Ayrshire such were the homes of the generality of landowners, a social and economic group numbering no more than 5,000 of whom fewer than a hundred were nobles or powerful Highland chiefs.[3] Although a wealthy landowner might have a rent-roll of £500, 'many gentlemen of good degree and long pedigree had to preserve their station with £50 to £20 a year'[4] and at a time when 'money was very scarce in Scotland ... A great part of the gentlemen's rents were payd in kind'[5] which might be a half or even two-thirds.[6] When the Earl of Mar, one of the more substantial noblemen, claimed that his family was never rich enough 'to undertake the building of a new house all at once'[7] one can understand why the thirty-four datable country-houses, begun from scratch in the first two decades of the eighteenth century, numbered little more than the total for the previous twenty years. The same number was constructed in the decade after 1730 and, although the Jacobite rebellion of 1745 caused a fall, thereafter, 'when riches increased considerably',[8] the figure steadily increased in each decade until, in the final decade of the century, over sixty mansions were built.

With the death of Bruce in 1710 the leading practitioners were Smith and McGill. Although it is traditionally held that the former had largely given up architecture after 1715, that view should perhaps be modified when one considers three mansions in Ayrshire. The most novel is KILKERRAN which was developed as an H-plan *c.* 1726.[9] On the entrance elevation the most striking feature was the pediment held above the eaves, in typical Smith fashion, by the entablature, supported at each end by a pilaster rising through two storeys and framing four window bays. Once described as 'a slightly gauche display',[10] the elevation is, nevertheless, a neat display of visual balance for, while the double-windowed wings and six-bay centre hark back to various Melville designs, the composition of the centre, with its powerful uprights opposed to the horizontal sweep of the ground storey with its off-centre doorways, reads like one of Palladio's courtyard elevations and as such is unique in Britain. It seems likely that Smith was also the designer of Ardmillan, some ten miles to the south-west, which, though a simpler exercise, has a three-bay centre enclosed by a pediment and pilasters, as at Kilkerran, but here passing through all three storeys and matched in a lesser chord by a pedimented porch which, in its clean geometry, hints of Serlio. Northwards at Ayr there is the astylar Craigie where the integration of entablature and pediment with the roof must surely betoken Smith.

If the trio of Ayrshire mansions do date from the start of the second quarter of the century then a severe critic might find in them a lack of the continental inventions which so distinguished Hamilton Palace and the prototype villas; by the same test he would discern a staleness in the later work of McGill. Though a lesser architect certainly than Smith, the absence of classical detailing in McGill's elevations may have had more to do with economy than poverty of ideas for, only a few years before his death, he purchased a copy of *An Essay in Defence of Ancient Architecture* by Robert Morris[11] and subscribed, along with William Adam and the leading Scottish nobility, to James Gibbs's *A Book of Architecture*. It may be that McGill and Gibbs knew one another for both were members of a coterie which included Alexander Edward, Smith and William Adam as well as Sir John Clerk and which moved around John Erskine, 11th Earl of Mar, an architect *manqué* if ever there was one.

Despite a fatal predilection for political intrigue and his roles in London as a commissioner for the Union and principal secretary of state for Scotland, Mar (like the Duke of Lauderdale before him) found time to send despatches for the ordering and improvement of his Scottish properties, especially his seat at Alloa, Clackmannanshire, where his landscape garden was classed as 'the largest and the finest ... of any in Britain; it far exceeds either Hampton-Court or Kensington',[12] although offence was given to some by 'the filthy naked statues'.[13] On succeeding to the earldom in 1689, Mar found himself heir to 'more debt than estate',[14] because of the financial depredations caused by the civil wars, so that 'I was to blame as my father was, for going about repairing the old House of Alloa, which was more fitt to be made a quarrie' although, surprisingly, Mar accepted the retention of the fulcrum of the house, a square four-storey tower 'venerable for its antiquity'.[15]

If Mar built little it seems that he was not without influence in matters architectural both before and during his European exile following the abortive Jacobite coup in 1715. He 'was always ready to give his neighbours advice. Tullibody and Tillicoultry and Blairdrummond Houses are said to have been built upon his plans.'[16] As all three are within easy reach of Alloa, perhaps the claim is worth pursuing. While it is accepted that BLAIRDRUMMOND is by McGill, it should be noted that, throughout most of his working life, he had a close association with Mar who, in a design exercise for Dun House, proposed a series of surrounding terraces[17] as at Blairdrummond where the multiplication of forecourts is just the kind of paper exercise in centrality that was to occupy Mar when abroad.

Although there are masons' accounts for work in 1714 and 1715, there then seems to be a gap in the building programme at Blairdrummond, doubtless because of the Jacobite rising, until the delivery of two hundred planks from Sweden in June 1716[18] after which construction seems to have proceeded rapidly and uninterruptedly so that, within another eighteen months, the house was 'Slatted and the Plummer is now laying on the Lead. So

78 BRUCEFIELD, Clackmannanshire

all will be finished in a fourtnight.'[19] As always, fitting up the interior was slow work which continued until 1721 when the final surviving account included, 'The making of 27 Crooks for doors. £1:7:0.'[20]

As it was demolished in 1806, nothing is known of Tillicoultry; Tullibody, however, not only had the same plain, handsome countenance as Blairdrummond but the top-storey window lintels were run into the eaves course, a distinctive feature also occurring at Brucefield in the same county [78] in 1724.[21]

In the previous year, Lord Mar's kinsman, Lord Dun, had sent him 'Mr Mc—ls explanation' of a proposed new mansion which Mar thought 'is the same almost wth. ye house of Cragiehall but less and wou'd be attended wth. the Same faults if not greater' so that 'it would be fitter for a Gingate (as its named here) for a Burges near to a great town than for a Gentlemans Seat in the Country'. He sent back his own design which included an apartment of five rooms 'for parad [sic] and a principal Stranger when there comes any such' with the family lodging above to 'keep the rest of the House neat and clean'. The offices were to be in the basement except for the 'Woman-house where they work at flax and wool and by that often burn the house'. Although 'woman-house' was a common term, this is the only place where its function is explained. For the construction Mar insisted on stone dressings and though 'Pilasters be not much used in Scotland' he recommended them. Finally, the architrave and frieze would also be stone though, if 'the upper part of the cornish be thought too expensive of Stone' he suggested a painted wooden substitute. As to the cost, 'If it should chance to come to more than was design'd wch. Such things

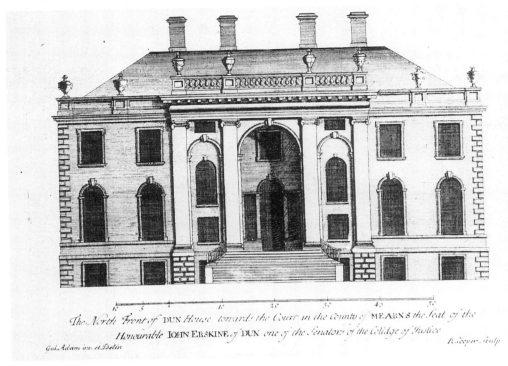

The North Front of DUN House towards the Court in the County of MEARNS the Seat of the
Honourable JOHN ERSKINE of DUN one of the Senators of the Colledge of Justice
Gul. Adam inv. et Delin   R. Cooper Sculp

79 DUN HOUSE, Angus

comonly [sic] do, it is but takeing the more time to do it in, or delay begining it for a year
or two, and Saveing the money til the next.'[22] Lord Dun took the last point so that it was
not until 1730 that Dun House was begun although, by then, it was to William Adam's
design to which Lord Mar, having been consulted once more, suggested amendments. He
placed the 'lady's apartment' over the ground floor, to 'be free of any company's noise',
and he removed Adam's billiard room as it would darken the entrance hall below. To gain
the necessary light, it was Mar who suggested the tetrastyle frontispiece [79] even although,
'It is foreseen that those not accustomed with Porticos will immediately exclaim upon seeing
the high one placed to the north.'[23]

Perhaps Mar's chief claim on the architectural historian is that he was the earliest patron
of James Gibbs and, though unable to bestow the largesse of patronage himself, he would
have been instrumental in introducing his protégé to his compatriots. Thus, in *A Book of
Architecture* by Gibbs in 1728, the Scottish subscribers, who included half a dozen dukes and
a dozen earls, totalled thirty-two of whom only two, William Adam and Alexander McGill,
were not hereditary landowners. If Gibbs had ever hoped for much work in Scotland, he
was to remain disappointed since he received two domestic commissions only. The first,
for William Duff of Braco, was BALVENIE HOUSE, Banffshire, a modest and somewhat
severe mansion set below the frowning bulk of Balvenie Castle which dominated Glen-
fiddich. That the castle might be modernised seems to have been considered[24] but, in the
event, a lower and more sheltered situation was preferred and the castle was robbed of

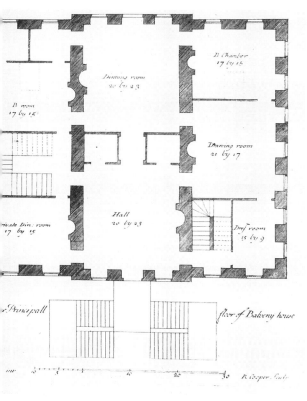

80 BALVENIE HOUSE, Banffshire, principal floor plan

81 BALVENIE HOUSE, Banffshire

materials which, in the spring of 1724, included floor timbers.[25] Two years later the new house of Balvenie was far enough advanced to allow for 'the Boxeing', that is lining with wood, of the principal floor [80] where the accommodation was set out as Lady Braco's room, a 'Bedchamber off the drawing room', a closet, blue room, a little dining-room and a great dining-room which, being almost cuboid and allotted the space usually given to a saloon, was the sole concession to formal entertaining which may partly explain the later need for Duff House.[26] To permit the hall and saloon plan the great stairs were placed to one side but rising, uncommonly, from the ground floor [81] with its stone-vaulted lower hall or common entry.[27] With half the accommodation on the ground storey taken up by nurseries,[28] the domestic offices were contained in pavilions for which plans were prepared by Alexander Fraser, who may have been a local mason, in 1725.[29] After the completion of the offices the accounts do not end. Early on there was trouble over the design of the platform roof for, with the lower ends screened by a parapet wall, water would collect so that in 1729 the parapet was removed;[30] even so there was more trouble with the roof ten years later when William Adam was called in.[31]

It may be that Gibbs was introduced to Duff of Braco by Andrew Drummond, the banker of Charing Cross and treasurer of St Martin's-in-the-Fields. One of his richest clients was the Duke of Chandos, builder of Cannons and patron of Gibbs, as was his friend and fellow picture collector, John Drummond, the youngest brother of James Drummond of Blairdrummond.[32] John Drummond was a member of the influential Scottish coterie ever present in London. Like many expatriate Scots he wanted a place in Scotland for his retiral and bought the 'prittie little estate', together with the coal rights, of QUARRELL (later Carron Hall) in Stirlingshire which in 1725 was described thus: 'As for the house and office houses of all sorts they are just as it were echoes of ruines hardly Slates or thack on anie of them, and for the house itself just four high walls and so but ane Roum above ane other ... four turrets to each room three Closetts the fourth turret being the stair.'[33] In addition, 'The halfe all the windows being timber without anie glass and their timber mostly rotten and some of the Casements quite out' it was not surprising that, 'Just now the Rain, and the pigeons confound the whole house.'[34] Nothing much seems to have been done for ten years when a detailed correspondence between London and Scotland not only reveals the age-old difficulty of doing up property from a distance but gives an insight into the standards of critical metropolitan taste.

From the outset Quarrell was to be 'a convenient little habitation ... done frugally and effectually'[35] so that the old part would only be repaired once the new front of 40 feet was habitable. Although John Drummond accepted 'that Mr Gibs plan has been and is the most reasonable for me to follow', he was not above amending it as he saw fit so that 'the ornament of the lowest windows to be as Mr Gib has made them, of the upper too as you have seen them at Scarburgh and not of all arch'd'. Then, too, 'I would carry the new building 2 foot further forward than Mr Gibs dos which will make the rooms 20 by 22'. He also altered the height of each floor while insisting that the attic must 'comprehend the roof'.[36] Drummond picked up ideas on his travels as 'at Kingsweston Mr Southwells new house where the first floor is 16 foot and I find 3 foot wainscoting is enough'[37] and he later recalled the 'good stone pavement in the entry and Lobey at Broxmouth' in East Lothian.[38] The flow of instructions not only depended on where Drummond had been but on whom he met so that 'in the presence of Mr Gib Sir Andrew Fountain and other persons of teast I was houted for talking of a room of 22 foot square and only $12\frac{1}{2}$ foot heigh',[39] although he later reckoned to mask the height of one small room 'by a Sort of Coving with painted canvas which is much used here'. If it was cheap he was prepared to consider marble for the chimney-pieces in the two public rooms as 'I should like it best for cleanness'.[40] While 'the mode is not the same here as in France' for chimney-pieces to be four or six inches broader than they were high,[41] for the fireplaces 'all tylls are now out of fashion, either free-stone, iron or clean brass Sides now all in fashion'.[42] That did not mean that one should not be practical and economical. The staircase, for example, was to have 'a partition wall and not a hanging stair with a rail, because its both safer and warmer than when its open, besides the Saving the expence of a rail'.[43] Likewise, 'I have no charters to keep and desire no more vaults nor any grates to the windows'.[44]

92

Meanwhile, the Duke of Chandos, having 'sold his great old house in St Jameses [sic] Square to a builder', had 'bargained for the roof painting of two rooms which is on cloth by Beluschi (Bellucci) for £70. They had cost him £300.' When the duke could find no use for them, one was despatched in two long boxes for the drawing-room ceiling at Quarrell.[45] So it was that there was no need 'for the Stucko man ... I shall wainscot or line the drawing-room 4 foot heigh and then put upon the plaister from that to the Cornish a plain green or red stuff or the new sort of paper painted like green damask to hang my pictures on which will have almost all gilded frames.'[46] As for the woodwork, 'I desire no wainscot door nor wainscot shutters, they are now all painted coffy Collour', while 'all nicety of flooring is left of ... because coverings or carpets are found absolutely necessary to keep rooms clean.'[47] Fortunately, there were already 'old carpets enough to keep the floor of the parlour room'.[48]

As Gibbs was the first metropolitan architect to work in Scotland it is regrettable that funds did not allow for the opulent sophistication which made his English works so influential. Balvenie was constructed of harled rubble with dressed stone margins and, although the centre was to be rusticated, the surviving portion is of rough-hewn ashlar. Alike by geographical location and economical simplicity, Balvenie could not direct the course of Scottish architecture. Perhaps Quarrell did even though, despite some Gibbsian accents, the plain mansion-house could have been the handiwork of any one of a number of Scottish builders operating on a client's instructions. Thus, it was John Drummond who stipulated, 'The 3 windows to the front of the new building to be large, that no Side windows be necessary'[49] while the one extant view shows that only the ground-floor windows have Gibbsian surrounds, as the client directed. To dramatise the skyline the chimneys were collected in one stack pierced by an arch just as Drummond would have observed at Vanbrugh's Kings Weston.[50]

It seems that the contractual work for Quarrell was under the superintendence of John Douglas, an Edinburgh master builder.[51] In demand in various parts of the country, he could produce Baroque decoration or save the plainest of building from architectural bathos by fine lines and proportions. A proven example is Finlaystone, Renfrewshire where Lord Glencairn, a brother-in-law of Sir John Clerk, signed a contract in 1746 within six weeks of the fateful Battle of Culloden. A 'New House', 46 feet by 37 feet and three storeys high, was to be linked by colonnades to 'Dinnistoun's Tower' and to the old house where the rooms were to be divided into bedrooms with all the rooms 'finished with Hard plaister Commonly Called Stucko'. Lord Glencairn allowed £1,100 for the addition and £200 for repairing the old house all of which would be finished 'by Lammas 1747'.[52] Four years later Sir John Clerk's daughter was a house-guest at Finlaystone which, she wrote home, was 'but badly executed but not so bad neither as some People represents'. The dining-room was 22 feet broad and half as long again 'besides a kind of Alcove in the Middle with a Venetian Window in it'. Off it there was a drawing-room 'and Lady Glencairn's Room is as handsome a well Lighted Room as ever I saw a Venetian Window in one end; and some towards the Clyde'.[53]

There must have been as handsome rooms at ARCHERFIELD, East Lothian [82], a late seventeenth-century mansion[54] improved in 1733 and again in 1744 and 1745 when John

82 ARCHERFIELD, East Lothian

Douglas was paid £465. In accordance with a contract of 1747 it was probably he who tacked on the extended frontal range[55] on which the confection of Gibbsian details read as trappings borrowed at second-hand. To create interest, in the now familiar study of a three-storey block, the centre-piece is a protruding half hexagon with the entrance at first floor. Such an intrusive compositional feature is not one found in Gibbs's works and probably derives from William Adam although with him it stands decently at the rear as at The Drum and Cumbernauld. These examples are plain in elevation; at Archerfield there is a wedding-cake display of a pedimented doorcase with Ionic pilasters, festooned armorial bearings, scrolls to support a window and finally a superimposed arch breaking into the

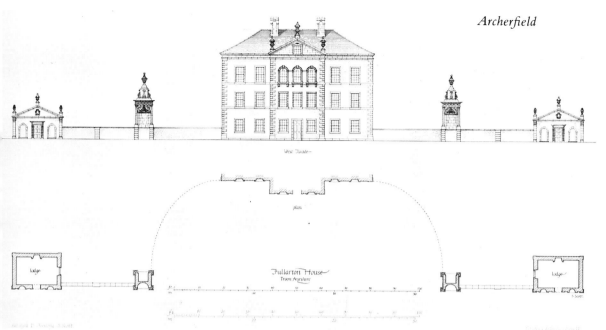

83 FULLARTON HOUSE, Ayrshire

wallhead parapet. On the sides circular niches are added to the disturbance of architectural syntax, doubtless to lessen the disparity of balance between the upper floor and the piano nobile, which, in turn, presses too heavily on the basement. A further plagiarism of Gibbsian details occurred at Fullarton, Ayrshire,[56] which was distinguished by a trio of round-headed windows connected at top and bottom by a string-course [83]. More novel were the low curved screen walls ending in ornamental piers, aligned with pedimented lodges which, flute-like, play against the bass chords of the house.[57] Yet, in plan and elevation, it tends to be *retardataire* since, in the setting-out of a three-storeyed, seven-bay block with the central bays bearing a sharply raked pediment, one has a standard design which, emanating with the Smith-McGill school, found favour throughout the century so that something of that earlier period also occurred in the adjacent county at Castle Semple, Renfrewshire, built in 1735, where the familiar sequence of seven bays had an even more acute pediment into which an arch obtruded to jostle with a pair of *oculi* below which the topmost lintels were aligned with the eaves cornice.[58]

Perhaps the Gibbs reflections at Archerfield and Fullarton were becoming common currency. His published designs, after all, were intended for 'Gentlemen as might be concerned in Building, especially in the remote parts of the Country, where little or no assistance for designs can be procured ... which may be executed by any Workman who understands Lines, either as here Design'd, or with some Alteration'.[59] Such was the case at LOCHNELL CASTLE, on the western seaboard of Argyll, where the wright, John Johnstone, was overseer for Sir Duncan Campbell who 'has though fitt to pull down and remove some of ye superfluous part of ye Old house and putt it in another order'. That was in 1738[60] and already Lochnell displayed, on front and rear, features, such as the canted bay to house the staircase, which would recur at Archerfield and Fullarton. On the neighbouring promontory there is Airds House, dated 1737, which is a well-assorted group of house, screen passages

84 AIRDS HOUSE, Argyll

and pavilions [84] with stone dressings and pediment with *oculi* highlighted by harling, giving a repose which belies the building difficulties in the west highlands for, as the laird wrote in 1738, 'The season has proved so cross that I have no expectation of getting the Rooff on my house this Year, all I propose is to be Sidewall height.'[61] Perhaps one can sympathise with Johnstone's simultaneous complaint from Lochnell, 'Yt. what time I shall have done heer, I will be heartily tyred of ye Highlands.'[62] That there is yet a third Campbell house dated 1737 on the same coastline cannot be coincidence. Although Ardmaddy Castle has design elements common to Lochnell and Airds, it is much smaller, being only two storeys, but with a deeply recessed pedimented centre borne on Ionic columns with half columns at the sides.[63] Clearly, somebody, thumbing through a copy of Palladio, hit on reproducing the plan and front of the Villa Emo[64] although the balustrades in the side intercolumniations hint at the Villa Chiericati-Porto.[65]

The spread of building in the western counties contrasts with the previous half century, when country-houses first arose in the fertile Lothian plains, and is indicative of the burgeoning commercial status of Glasgow whose mercantilist families bedecked the city's green environs with modest seats. Although most have been engulfed by subsequent waves of urban expansion, POLLOK HOUSE remains [85]. It is usually attributed to William Adam, since he was consulted in 1732[66] and again two years later when the laird paid '8d for the white iron case that holds the draught'. Work, however, did not begin until 1747[67] by which time Adam was a sick man burdened by commitments. Pollok, therefore, may have been erected by Allan Dreghorn, a Glasgow wright acquainted with metropolitan standards although the stylistic time lapse between London and Glasgow would account for the conservative handling.[68] Being a single block without supporting units, it was probably necessary to have four storeys, a practice to which Adam had occasionally resorted

96

85 POLLOK HOUSE, Glasgow
86 POLLOK HOUSE, Glasgow, the dining-room

87 POLLOK HOUSE, Glasgow,
the dining-room

88 CATTER HOUSE, Dunbartonshire

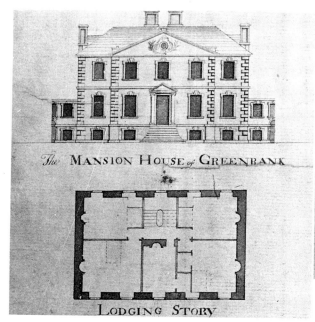

The MANSION HOUSE of GREENBANK

LODGING STORY

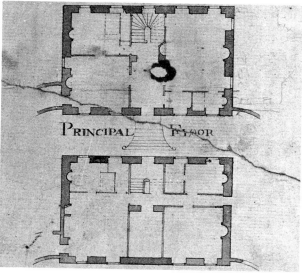

PRINCIPAL FLOOR

89 GREENBANK, Renfrewshire, detail from an estate plan of 1772

although he did once write to a client that, 'This Estimate Cutts of the 4th or Attick Storie, and gives Lodgeing in the rooff in place thereof'[69] and he would probably have deplored the platform roof. Because there are four storeys the accentuation of the piano nobile remains unresolved. The entrance front is pedimented but the garden elevation is plain except for a serliana which strains the vertical rhythm of the fenestration unnecessarily since the central space on the piano nobile was not a saloon but a small ante-room or garden parlour supported laterally by a drawing-room and dining-room [86], where the fashionable plasterwork over the china recess and chimney-piece [87] includes a tableau of field-sports incorporating a pair of ice skates, a golf club and a thistle, doubtless as a reminder of the rough. In searching for a design source the closest equivalent is a plate from Kent's *Designs of Inigo Jones* showing a four-storey block with four rooms straddling the cross passages and with overall dimensions exactly suited to Pollock.[70]

The local impact of Pollok was such that numerous details were exploited in other mansions. Cochno, on the north side of the River Clyde, has a pedimented front but a plain garden side though the centre is projected as a splayed bay, a device lifted from *The Modern Builder's Assistant* published in 1757,[71] the year in which Cochno was founded.[72] Closer still to the published elevation is Capelrig, Renfrewshire, where, with the entrance set in the bay, there is scope for some variety in the internal plan.[73] Next door to Cochno there is Edinbarnet, a five-bay house with chimney-stacks on the gables resting on stubby pediments as happened with other Glasgow houses.[74] Further north, Catter House is a modest block [88] made attractive by a curved double forestair and a tiny floating pediment.[75] It has the customary tripartite plan with a central enclosed staircase and, originally, two rooms on one side and, on the other, a panelled dining-room with Corinthian pilasters by the chimney with a shell-topped recess opposite. Much the same arrangement occurs at

90 GREENBANK, Renfrewshire

Greenbank, Renfrewshire [89]. The land was bought by a Glasgow merchant in 1763 who proceeded to erect a Palladian mansion[76] albeit on a small scale and with economy though allowing such flourishes as the carved mask and foliage round the *oeil-de-boeuf* [90] all of which is a straight copy from Gibbs.[77] Undoubtedly, however, the most interesting of the mansions in the Glasgow locality must have been Hawkhead [91] of which too little is known. Two fragments of information can be gleaned from Sir John Clerk's correspondence. His nephew, Lord Garlies, wrote in 1738, 'Mr Baxter will have time enough to finish the Master of Ross's house'[78] which Clerk saw in the following year when he noted that it was 'lately repair'd'.[79] That he did not enthuse about Hawkhead would be because the main block, to judge from the design mannerisms, was probably McGill's handiwork with Baxter softening its bulk with his lower wings.

91 HAWKHEAD, Renfrewshire

Sir John's first wife was a sister of the 5th Earl of Galloway whose chief seat was GLASSERTON, near Whithorn, of which Sir John wrote approvingly during a visit in 1721.[80] However, in 1734 there was a disastrous fire caused by Lady Galloway 'going up to one of her wardrobes at night' with a candle. Though the walls remained entire, Sir John attempted to dissuade his sister and brother-in-law from rebuilding partly because of the expense and because, too, 'The Situation is very bad.' In any case the earl's brother was declining (he died thirteen years later) and as the former would inherit his house Sir John suggested that his relatives live in Whithorn 'and in the meantime to build a family house at Clary', the home of the eldest son, Lord Garlies. Not that it was much of a place, being 'a poor habitation' with 'abundance of Lodging about it but ill disposed and ruinous', so that Lord Garlies was contemplating building a new house[81] and, therefore, turned to his uncle since, 'You have more experience in affairs of this kind than anybody whatever.'[82] While the ensuing correspondence of Lord Garlies might be compared with John Drummond's apropos of Quarrell there are significant differences for the former was not dispensing instructions and notions of metropolitan taste but seeking advice and even basic information. 'As to houses of office', he wrote on one occasion, '... knowledge of that kind would be useful for a Galloway man, for as yet we are absolutely ignorant of office houses.'[83]

Lord Garlies was of Sir John's opinion that Glasserton was 'a cold, unwholesome, most abominable place' but felt bound to support his father's inclination to build there although 'I can by no means approve of what you call a family house' since 'both my father and I have debt. Politicks, elections, different kinds of law pleas, and severall incidents have run out a good dale of money. Both of us have children's provisions to pay.' Regarding a scheme by John Douglas, Lord Garlies not only reckoned that the pavilions would be better left for a later generation to construct but 'when you mention Cubes and rooms of 18, 16 or even 19 foot high you write indeed like ane architect' when all that was wanted was accommodation with 'the fewer windows the better. The rooms may be perfectly well lighted, the house the warmer, looks as well and saves charges.' Yet, whatever the need, there could be no building except on borrowed money.[84]

With the next surviving letter, in August 1737, Lord Garlies was concerned about the economics of his own house. 'Its impossible to have what you call ane apartment in a little house, without taking up a whole story and that I cannot spare. Mr Adams plan with some amendments would do mighty well' although the one prepared by Douglas for his father would cost less. Despite those restrictions, Lord Garlies considered that, 'I cannot have less than eighteen rooms, with beds; closetts with beds will do as well as rooms for the one half of them' although there would be 'three tolerable bed chambers of about sixteen foot square, a drawing room of that size, a dining room as good as could be got not above twenty four or twenty seven at most', all at a cost of £2,000 including furniture.[85]

After the death of his countess late in 1737,[86] Lord Galloway finally abandoned the idea of replacing his family seat and contracted 'with a sort of Mason, no better than a barrow man, to build him a summer house' at Glasserton.[87] It seems to have been modest enough with the ground floor half vaulted, for a cellar and charter room, besides 'a low parlour' with two rooms, plus attached closets, and the entry above although it was lacking ancillary accommodation and offices.[88] Meanwhile, at Clary 'it's not only want of room to Lodge us, but the walls particularly are so insufficient that the rain beats in, and we are never dry'.[89] However, by the autumn of 1739 not only had Lord Garlies determined to remove from Clary and settle at Ponton, 'the healthiest, pleasantest, most agreeable and most convenient situation in our whole estate and so near the sea side that all materialls can be easyly imported', but his father had agreed to fund the move. Therefore, to fix upon the stance of the house and to lay out the grounds, Lord Garlies suggested that Sir John should come with John Douglas, and also John Baxter who 'would give his directions as to a quarry, and anything else relating to the masonry or building' as well as procuring materials at Whitehaven in Cumberland although the timber would be Norwegian.[90] If the optimism was dampened when Lord Galloway reneged on financial help, there was no stopping his son who wrote to his uncle, 'Its to your plan of a house we agree in the main, but not intirely ... A little house with good lodging pavilions is what I like best. I send you my plan ... I beg you may meet with Mr Douglas, and finally end it for me.' He also suggested that they could be joined by Baxter who was to have 'the absolute command, and intire direction to hire and turn off all workmen as he pleased'.[91]

With materials arriving in spring 1740, Lord Garlies was in a fix since his father, having retired to Glasserton, was using estate funds to build further leaving his son in debt. Unable to dispose of the materials, he ordered a start to the work[92] and, in consequence, needed 'a plan of the front' from Douglas which Baxter could bring 'into the country with him'.[93] By the next spring the house was well under way[94] so that, by the end of that year, Lord Garlies was prompting Sir John to talk to Douglas about the design of the pavilions[95] which were begun in the following building season[96] when Baxter reported of the house that, 'We are half up wt. the 2d story',[97] although it would be another three years before Galloway House neared completion.[98]

During the course of the work, Baxter had 'given my Lord Garlies a front of his hous ... and Corected his plans. I have taking out 24 windows and his Rooms [are] as well lighted as on[e] would wish.'[99] On the strength of that and earlier statements, Baxter's role in the design of Galloway House has been overrated.[100] There can be no doubt that the gestation of the final design was both lengthy and complex for, though Lord Garlies valued his uncle's opinion, the sage reflection by Sir John, that, 'Every man thinks himself a sufficient architect and will build in his own way,'[101] was certainly true of his nephew even if, at the end of the day, he seems to have accepted the compromises offered by Sir John and, to a greater extent, by Douglas. Baxter, on the other hand, was always classed as the builder. Perhaps he was never more in the eyes of Sir John since, for most of his career, he worked to other men's designs and if Ormiston Hall, East Lothian, in 1745[102] was the exception then the single, unadorned block serves to advertise his lack of creative design ability.

As it was first built,[103] GALLOWAY HOUSE [92] owed much to the wishes of the client. 'I propose', he declared sensibly, 'Only five windows, to witt, three in the middle, and one in each end division.'[104] What was not so sensible was the overall height which distressed Baxter. 'I begin to think that he should a Contented himself wt. 3 story in the whoal whereas he's to have four; ... I am sorry to build such a high Modrin Castell.'[105] To remedy such a defect the centre had pilaster strips, carrying an entablature across the entrance and supporting an attic topped by a pediment. The walling was whinstone with red freestone

92 GALLOWAY HOUSE, Wigtownshire

dressings shipped in (probably from Locharbriggs near Dumfries) which allowed good carved work on the central window with its egg and dart mouldings and bracketed scrolls reminiscent of those at Archerfield but here set in an elevation cobbled together from plates in *Vitruvius Britannicus*.[106]

While Galloway House has not one jot of originality, by its very conventionality it was bound to become the paradigm in south-west Scotland. Not only does it mark the social ascendancy and cultural awareness of a noble family but it is a further demonstration of the potent penetration of architectural classicism which became established in the north and west of Dumfries-shire at Craigdarroch in 1726, Tinwald in 1739 and at Springkell, a handsome, well-mannered house with an Ionic tetrastyle garden elevation dated 1734.[107] In the next decade there is Galloway House, the influence of which can be seen further along the Solway coast at ARBIGLAND reputedly completed in 1755 at a cost of £4,000.[108] The owner was William Craik who, as a noted improver, would include among his gentlemanly pursuits the proper study of architecture as did his contemporary George Ridpath, minister of Stichill in Roxburghshire, who recorded in his diary, 'Read some of Wolff's *Elem. Arch. Civ.*, being led to it by Sir H. Wotton's work' and on the next day, 'Read chiefly in Wolff's Architecture' and on the day following, 'Read some of Ware's Palladio, and looked to the cuts which are very beautiful.'[109] While such aesthetic appreciation must have been widespread, Craik could not have played the local Palladio without having to hand some of the practical manuals, published from the twenties onwards, which illustrated every branch of the art of building. Though *Rural Architecture* by Robert Morris was extended to include bridges, keepers' lodges and cold bath-houses, *The Modern Builder's Assistant* (to which Morris contributed) cast a wider net by including not only stables but chimney-pieces, staircases and wall and ceiling decorations, which were copied by architects, such as John Adam, and by tradesmen, such as Thomas Clayton, while the window designs with little modification could be adapted for doorways as at Duchal, Renfrewshire, or on the garden elevation at Pollok where the chosen model was 'Rustick Venetian'. For the setting-out of details, however, the publications of the Halfpennys and the Langleys must have been indispensable. Indeed, the latter's *The Builder's Jewel*, subtitled *Youth's Instructor and Workman's Remembrancer*, was closely packed with instructions for floors, trusses and coves together with twelve varieties of pediments not to mention windows and doors. The book must have had a wide distribution for Langley doorways are found at Rammerscales, Pollok, Kippenross, Dalvey and as far north as Ardmeallie in Banffshire.

Arbigland seems to owe the composition of its front to Galloway House. Single-bay links lead to pavilions which belie their appearance since the rooms are half octagons. Indeed the entire house is one room deep only and, what with the odd disposition of the stairs, indicates that, though one might compose a passable front, the sensible disposition of the internal volumes required rather more skill. There is an idiosyncratic air about Arbigland which recurs at Mossknowe slightly to the north near Gretna.

Writing from Arbigland in December 1763 to John Graham, the brother of the laird of Mossknowe, William Craik discussed plans, including 'Mr Irvine's plan' (presumably by the laird of nearby Bonshaw), as well as prices. Craik doubted if a house could be built for £600 and passed on a warning for the laird of Mossknowe that, 'If ever he settle in the country he will soon be convinced that the saving betwixt a commodious house and an inconvenient one is the worst saved money in the worlde to whoever can afford a tolerable one.' Accordingly, Craik had devised a fresh plan and elevation which, though it 'may be built at four or five different times',[110] had been costed by a local builder at £1,143:10:1½. It is of some note that, 'As it was proper to smooth the rooms for paper this I think makes the lining the walls with brick quite unnecessary and therefor there is no brick work except in the two cellars.'[111] However, such considerations were premature since Dr Graham could not afford to build although he was prepared to lay in materials in anticipation of doing so in the summer of 1765,[112] which he seems to have done so that by late 1766 the bulk of the house was complete leaving the wings to be begun.[113] Like Arbigland, Mossknowe does not fit easily into the pattern of current Scottish country-house practice. The obvious source is Palladio but so used that the body of the house is no wider than the pediment and hence runs back leaving the wings to establish a lengthy but thin frontage.

Given the activity of Craik as a designer, perhaps one might see his hand at Ardwall which had eccentric fenestration though details compare with Arbigland.[114] Ardwall could be dismissed as thoroughly *retardataire* if it was not for the overlarge, pedantic Tuscan doorcase which, with its pronounced frieze, is reminiscent, as are other features, of the tetrastyle porch at Knockhill, Dumfries-shire, which carries the date 1777 below the motto, 'To Small for Envy, for Contempt to Great.' The twin of that porch is at Rammerscales, the most bizarre of the south-western houses, which possibly dates from 1762 [93]. The

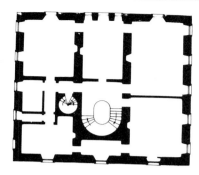

93 RAMMERSCALES, Dumfries-shire

estate was purchased as a retreat by Dr James Mounsey, a local boy who became physician
to the Empress Catherine of Russia but who, according to tradition, insisted on more than
one exit in each room, being fearful of enemies.[115] Generally speaking, the plan is the
standard one of two rooms aligned on each side of the staircase hall in which the unique,
inverted pendentives convert the upper hall from the round to the square, the kind of
statement that would delight the amateur designer. Unusually, Rammerscales is a detached
block little ornamented save for a triple window on the first floor, to light a small parlour,
and large but erratically disposed modillions below the pierced parapet.

A similar percolation of classicism through the strata of society occurs in the north-east
after the building of Haddo House. On the northern coast, Aberdour House has a garden
front very similar, even to the octagonal light in the tympanum, to the entrance elevation

94 WARDHOUSE, Aberdeenshire

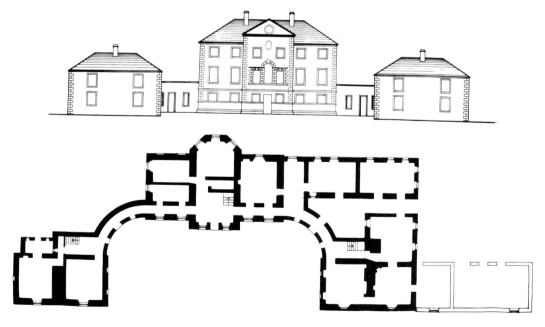

of Haddo. Yet the wings, instead of sweeping forward, are returned to the north to form a courtyard dated 1740. Another house with the same ground plan, though the details are closer to the vernacular, is Pittendrum to the east of Aberdour and dated 1734. It is only at Wardhouse, which, according to a surviving inscription, was built in 1757, that a fellow member of the clan Gordon attempted to emulate Haddo. The site of Wardhouse, near Insch, is a fine one, being elevated and commanding spreading views, with the mansion set on a natural berm on the hillside. Unroofed some thirty years ago, Wardhouse [94] is a ruin although the walls still stand to their full height. There are, however, variations on the Haddo plan. For example, the central portion of the main block not only breaks forward but overtops the wallhead. As is usual with the majority of Aberdeenshire mansions, there is no sunk basement, because of the need to excavate rock, which permits an entrance at ground level although the Palladian window above, with its Gibbsian surrounds, would seem to demand a grand outer staircase. Internally, the staircase was contained in a bow which was expressed on the rear elevation as a half hexagon. That was an arrangement which appears at nearby Newton, possibly the most familiar mansion in Aberdeenshire since it stands above the Aberdeen to Huntly Road. Newton [95] is exceptional in possessing a basement and so is minus service wings. Four storeys high and harled it is dependent for effect on balanced proportions since granite allows for little in the way of fine dressings. Esslemont House of 1769 was very similar, before it became a Scots-Baronial pile, although it was a storey lower[116] making it comparable with Ardmeallie House near Huntly [96]. One of the least altered of the smaller lairds' houses, it has a tripartite plan [97] but with the staircase housed at the rear in a projecting sweep leading up to a rather grand drawing-room with a coved ceiling.

The aristocratic assurance of Haddo or the mercantile extent of Wardhouse were beyond the means of most lairds. At Craig Castle, near Rhynie, where there was a substantial tower-house, the owner was content to erect close by, in 1767, a plain, three-storeyed rectangular block for sleeping and living accommodation leaving the old castle as a kitchen and service quarters[117] while at Auchanachy Castle, 'It is hard', as a modern historian has observed, 'to say where the tower-house finishes and the new laird's house begins.'[118] Indeed, classicism was catholic enough to accommodate some old forms with ease. Thus the nep-house, or central gable incorporating a chimney-stack, appears at Aldie House, near Cruden, as a

95 NEWTON, Aberdeenshire

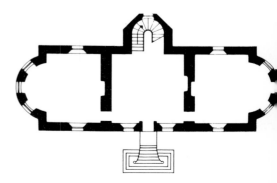

96 ARDMEALLIE HOUSE, Banffshire

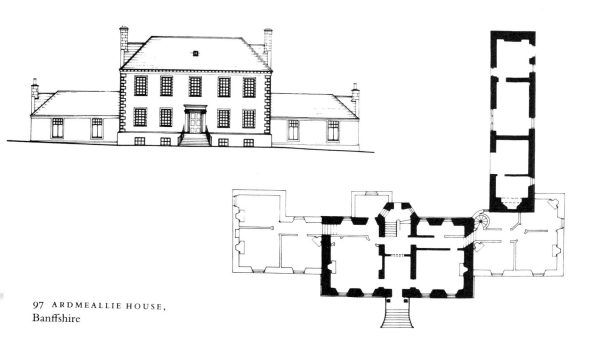

97 ARDMEALLIE HOUSE,
Banffshire

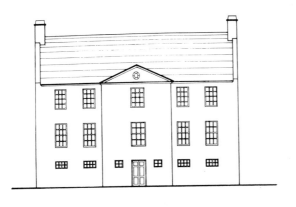
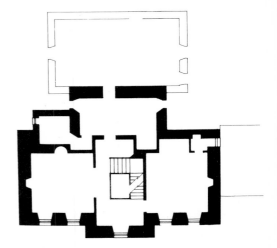

98 BOURTIE HOUSE, Aberdeenshire

rudimentary pediment while at Bellabeg in Strathdon it has a curved outline like a segmental pediment. A true pediment appeared at Whitehaugh House, near Alford, a place of modest proportions of 1745 to which wings were added half a century later.[119] Undoubtedly, though, the most interesting of the north-east lairds' houses is Bourtie, on the outskirts of Inverurie, which has survived remarkably unaltered [98]. Like Newton, Bourtie has a basement but here fully exposed. The short façade of five bays breaks forward in the centre to allow more internal space for a scale and platt stair to rise through all three floors. Unusually, Bourtie is a T-plan. It is dated 1754 on the neat pediment and the principal rooms have original panelling.[120]

Apart from the nobility and a few mercantile families, who could afford to spread themselves in building, the majority of country-house builders had to mind their pennies. For them the most economical form of building was the single oblong block, with the domestic offices in the basement and the servants sleeping in the garrets, which, by saving space, reduced building costs. It was commodious and convenient enough for the needs of the gentry or for those who, having made a modest fortune in other fields, sought a contemplative existence in the country. Thus Robert Craigie, successively Lord Advocate and Lord President of the Court of Session, bought the estate of Glendoick in east Perthshire in 1726 although it was not until twenty years later that he erected a new mansion.[121] Perhaps the bellcast roof and pair of massive chimney-stacks set over five bays are rather conservative although there are such dignified touches as pedimented windows and doorway. Such stone dressings stand out sharply against the white harling, establishing a mathematical precision in the placing of each design element whilst allowing the spectator to appreciate the overall harmony.

That such a class of house was still acceptable twenty years later is shown at Duchal, Renfrewshire, a plainer but almost identical example,[122] and at Old Allangrange in the Black Isle where the projected centre is crowned not by a pediment but a single chimney. Another variant on the five-bay theme is Stewart Hall, Bute, which, being only two storeys high, has single-storey lateral wings.

Although Kippenross, Perthshire,[123] is also of the five-bay pattern, the pediment is pulled across three bays and, with the end bays slightly recessed, the result is subtler modelling, although there was no departure from the usual tripartite division of the plan since there were two public rooms, with a smaller room behind each, separated by a hall with a rear staircase. Other houses in the same group would have been Strathtyrum, Fife, and Reelig, Inverness-shire,[124] both of which were T-plans. Perhaps the most lavish in this category, at least in external display, is Dalvey, Morayshire, where the entrance front is of dressed stone overall with pilasters, instead of angle quoins, which puts it in the same class as some of the mansions in the south-west. Dalvey has a Tuscan pillared porch with a full entablature bearing bucrania which reappear in the drawing-room and dining-room cornices and accord with the armorial insignia of the Macleods who later purchased the estate. Most lairds liked some heraldic display and though it was usually confined to a coat of arms in the tympanum, Henry Mackenzie's *Man of Feeling* 'had sewed the pedigree of our family in a set of chair-bottoms'.[125]

More popular, on the whole, than a five-bay composition was the grander seven bays. At Letham in Angus it is the central bay alone which is embraced by the pediment which is uncommon since the preference was for a three-bay centre. Since the history of most country-houses is clouded by the absence of both a building date and the name of a designer, special interest must be attached to the contractual specification drawn up in 1754 between the Viscount of Arbuthnott and the wright, John Ferrier of Montrose, for ARBUTHNOTT HOUSE, Kincardineshire [99]. Clearly what Lord Arbuthnott wanted was both a more convenient and more regular dwelling. Accordingly, some parts having been demolished,

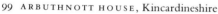

99 ARBUTHNOTT HOUSE, Kincardineshire

a new north wing of three storeys plus garrets was to be constructed to correspond externally to the gabled south wing. Such was atavism when one's horizons were constricted by narrow geography. 'And betwixt the said two Wings to Interject a Mid building of three storys High with garrets ... the Joinings of the Mid building of the Front to the Wings to be by hewen Stone in the Rustick order jeting out from the face of the walls.' The centre would be enriched 'with a timkin, And three Vases to be sette thereon'. The walls would be of polished ashlar and the window frames of oak with crown glass but with common glass on the ground floor and garrets; the chief rooms were 'to be sufficiently boxed with fir wood' and have plaster ceilings. The total cost was to be £480.[126]

With the sculpted lines of the gables enfolding the pediment and with the harled planes as a background foil for the dressed ashlar, Arbuthnott House combines a degree of informal softness with classical reserve. In the atavistic need for twin gables Arbuthnott House can be regarded as stylistically archaic, comparable to Leslie House of ninety years before; yet it can also be held that the variety engendered by a serrated skyline is in tune with the fantastical compositions set out in *Chinese and Gothic Architecture*. Certainly, when the rigours of classicism were becoming rigidities, it is a joy to view again the Scottish love for composing with vertical units, for the contrast of building materials and even for the continuation of the courtyard plan.

100 FOULIS CASTLE, Ross and Cromarty

Though such plans had been generally dispensed with, in conformity with politer living, there is a spectacular example at FOULIS CASTLE, Ross-shire [100], the new seat of the chief of clan Munro which replaced a castle burnt in 1750. With date stones marked as late as 1792, the protracted building sequence brings to mind the maxim of Mrs Grant of Laggan that, 'A Highland mansion is generally the work of two generations' being completed by the heir once he 'began to thrive in some lucrative profession or by some wealthy match'.[127] At Foulis the ochre-washed show front, rising above the verdant fields of Easter Ross, is evidence of wealth sufficient to enable Highland proprietors to compete for the first time in conspicuous building with their southern counterparts [101].

The show front is an immediate reminder of the long, low elevations in *Rural Architecture*. Yet, lacking the emblematic dignity of a portico, the central bays are overwhelmed by the unyielding horizontality and even the pediment is robbed of its dominant role being

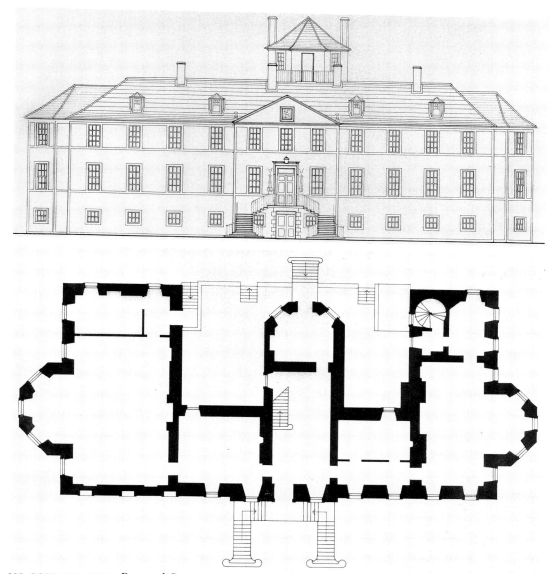

101 FOULIS CASTLE, Ross and Cromarty

overtopped by the staircase tower in the courtyard. The consanguinity of mansion and
extended outbuildings was uncommon for, as Macky had noted, 'The Stables, Hen-house,
and Coach-houses, are at a Distance in the Park, as is the custom in all the great Houses I
have yet seen in Scotland.'[128] To soften the rectangular plane of the show front the sides are
returned with splayed centres as had occurred once before at William Adam's Tinwald. If
that did provide the germ of an idea for Foulis then there was a theoretical justification in
The Modern Builder's Assistant where it was allowed that, 'For a Country Seat, situated on
an Eminence where there is an extensive view' the angles could be set out 'so as to command

a Prospect every way'.[129] If such permissible freedom was a factor in the genesis of Foulis then one has to look for an up-to-the-minute architect. Perhaps he was John Adam. Not only is it known that he travelled in the locality but the Adam brethren made use of *The Modern Builder's Assistant* and were subscribers to *Rural Architecture*. Then, too, there is the appearance at Foulis of Adam plaster decoration and ironwork. Certainly, if John Adam was the architect that would strengthen the possibility of his hand appearing in other work in the area. For the moment, however, it should be noted that two other Munro properties have affinities with Foulis. Novar has splayed side bays and a courtyard while at Poyntzfield, where a minute floating pediment is dated 1757, there is a polygonal tower on the rear elevation. Other courtyard plans occur at Ardovie, Angus, a tiny mansion of three bays but sporting outsize vases on the pediment, and at Hatton, Kincardineshire, where the architecture, while regularly composed, is so plain as almost to be classed as vernacular. Indeed, Balnakiel, on the most north-westerly point of the Scottish mainland, still displays crow-stepped gables.[130]

For the gentry the years after the Union, despite 'the triffling insurrections of 1715 and 1745'[131] were a period when material comfort gave substance to social graces for 'by degrees great changes took place in houses lately built and in such as were modernised. People got the ceilings lathed and plastered, their rooms finished with wainscot or fir, and sashed windows hung with pulleys.'[132] That was about as much as most lairds could afford. When it came to the more ornamental parts of architecture Sir John Clerk must be the touchstone of fashion. Taking a cue from Palladio and Jones, he liked to see in public rooms, and especially in the dining-room, a ceiling cove, of about 2 feet, which would ease the transition, in a room 18 or 20 feet high, between the walls and the ceiling flat;[133] for such a room the smart finishing was stucco. William Adam was enthusiastic about its properties as 'a plaister, Much us'd Now in Publick Rooms ... And My Lord Burlington has done the floors of Some of his rooms with it in imitation of Marble. It can be made of any Colour, or Vein'd as Marble ... Walls and Rooff being done ... is very prettie, and may have Pillasters, Capitalls, Architrave, freese and Cornish inriched by it.'[134] Some five months later, in May 1725, he could confide to a potential client that, 'Ive gott in to a Curious Secret, by a Swedish Gentleman, One of Our philosophy Masters who had dealt in that of Stucco formerly, And att My desire had made a great Many New Tryalls, whe[re]in we have had the greatest Success, in imitateing all kinds of Marble, Egyptian, Italian, English, Scotch, etc. Yea Lapus Lassulie Not excepted, and can make alls fine a Skin and Gloss upon itt, as Any Marble qt. Soever.' Not surprisingly, he was anticipating 'haveing our Country Ornamented by itt'.[135] Yet it must have been always costly and, as most country-houses lack ornamental plasterwork, its appearance can be read as a barometer of wealth. At Dun House [102] it was the dining-room (or saloon) that was enriched; at The Drum it was the processional route of hall, dining-room and upper saloon while at Blair Castle, Perthshire, two floors of an old castle were transformed in the mid-century into rooms of parade [103] culminating in the great dining-room [104], a double cube, which changes in fashion decreed should become the drawing-room [105] and be hung with crimson damask rather than compartmented by panels, although in the coved ceiling the Palladian and rococo ingredients are testimony to the deft inventiveness of such a virtuoso as Thomas Clayton.[136]

102 DUN HOUSE, Angus, the dining-room or saloon
103 BLAIR CASTLE, Perthshire, state floor plan by James Winter

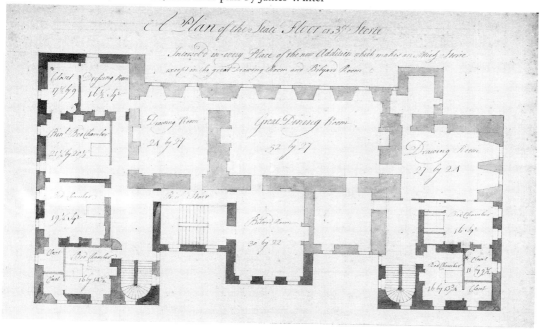

104 BLAIR CASTLE, Perthshire, proposed dining-room ceiling

105 BLAIR CASTLE, Perthshire, the drawing-room

106 NEWHAILES, Midlothian, the dining-room

Already, however, the modelled birds, masks, shells and foliage were losing their appeal so that for a visitor to Newhailes in 1757, 'The new drawing-room, bedchamber and closet are the finest things in point of high finishing, furniture etc. that I have ever seen'[137] rather than the earlier decorations by Clayton in the dining-room [106] and library.[138]

Though Adam claimed that plaster was as cheap as wood linings,[139] until its use became widespread, the walls of principal rooms were finished with oak wainscot until a more squeamish generation found that it 'harboured vermin; dead rats the greatest nuisance'.[140] The alternative was hangings which the Duke of Roxburghe was proposing in 1718 for the drawing-room and bedchamber at Floors but not elsewhere since 'Tapestrie in a little room never does well',[141] although within a few more years he would be having 'Severall rooms done up' with stucco.[142] After 1730 wallpaper, made in Edinburgh in two colours, was available at a shilling for twelve yards.[143] Lesser rooms were still painted. In 1729 a bedroom and the 'tea room' at Newhailes were painted 'olive Collour'.[144] If they could be afforded there were chimney-pieces of imported marble. At Dun House '2 white and Vein'd Chimneys' for the dining-room were part of a lot of five bought in Italy for £50. Two of them, one of purple marble and another dove-coloured, came with frames for glass. For the fireplaces, twenty-six dozen Dutch tiles, of two different kinds, were shipped in at a cost of £5:4:0.[145] Carpets were little used except in the drawing-room and dining-room[146] where there might be a recess for the china which was ousting Dutch delft and pewter ware.[147] 'A punch-bowl, and teacups and saucers of china ... were ostentatiously arranged in what was called the cupboard.'[148] Perhaps there was one at Blairdrummond in 1718 since an account itemises '4 pairs large polished hinges for glass doors in parlour'.[149] Certainly, the handsomest surviving example is at Glendoick where an Ionic tetrastyle pinewood frame with a scroll pediment has a stuccoed interior.

Being small, most lairds' houses were 'fitter for the reception of day than of night visitors'.[150] Even so, except on occasions of ceremony, the dining-room and drawing-room, in which the bed was 'the most showy in the house',[151] were seldom used for it was the family bedchamber that was in daily use and in which company was received. Overnight guests, even if unacquainted with one another, were often put two to a bed though it might be only a box-bed with sliding doors.[152]

Celia Fiennes had heard in Scotland that travellers mostly 'go from one Nobleman's house to another'[153] which remained the case throughout the eighteenth century in which, given the impossibility of communicating quickly from any distance, it is no surprise to learn that strangers, friends, and neighbours 'were welcome without previous invitation' although, in order to allow time for the preparation of a meal, it was considered polite to arrive early.[154] 'Jupiter' Carlyle recorded that, when he was visiting the Duke of Argyll at Inveraray in 1758, 'We Sate Down every Day 15 or 16 to dinner.'[155] While that was the daily occurrence of country-house living, there were times when an owner preferred a more private life. In the spring of 1745 the Duke of Roxburghe, then in London, forwarded instructions for the opening up of Floors Castle. 'You will take care to have all the Beds aired, and Small Beer and Ale Brewed, and write to Mrs Macdougall for half a hogshead of Claret; and half a hogshead of French white wine, and also to Edinburgh for twelve pound of large Wax Candles ... I don't know what we shall do for Cream and Butter. If there be no Cows ... some must be bought.' The ducal party would consist of 'twenty in Family, besides the Children' but the duke did not wish news of his intended arrival to be spread abroad 'for I chuse to be as little troubled with visitors as possible'.[156] House-parties were, however, the life-blood of country-house living, bringing news and information and promoting amusement. A typical gathering must have been that at Eglinton Castle, Ayrshire, in the early autumn of 1736, which included 'Lord[s] Cassels – Kilmarnock – Garles [sic] – Boyle – Eglintoun – Boyd – about a dozen of gentlemen, such as Fullarton, Mr Lockhart of Cambusnethan, Mr Cuningham of Caprington and all the young ladies'.[157] With some of the guests already committed to building anew, there must have been much talk of plans, elevations, publications and prices as well as of the latest material and decoration. For nobles and lairds alike, it was, as Lord Mar had written, 'a pritty amusement'[158] even if the Duke of Roxburghe did comment sourly, 'I hope the curiosity of my friends was fully satisfied in seeing Floors House, and that it would serve them at least for one days Table talk to find fault with every thing they saw, as is usuall in those cases.'[159]

Notes to Chapter 4

1. A. Allardyce, *Scotland and Scotsmen in the Eighteenth Century* (1888), vol. II, p. 97.
2. R. Chambers, *Domestic Annals of Scotland* (1861), vol. III, p. 418; T. Smout, *A History of the Scottish People, 1560–1830* (1970), p. 286.
3. Ibid., p. 135.
4. H. Graham, *The Social Life of Scotland in the Eighteenth Century* (1899), vol. I, p. 4.
5. 'Selections from the Family Papers Preserved at Caldwell', *Maitland Club* (1854), Pt. I, pp. 261–2.
6. Graham, ibid.
7. 'Lord Mar's Legacies' 1722–7', *SHS*, vol. XXVI (1896), p. 182.
8. Supra, n. 5.
9. A. Rowan, 'Kilkerran, Ayrshire – I', *CL*, vol. CLVII (1 May 1975), pp. 1114–17.
10. Ibid., p. 1116.
11. The copy is now in the Mitchell Library, Glasgow.
12. J. Macky, *A Journey through Scotland* (1723), pp. 181–2.
13. Sir David Dalrymple to the Earl of Mar, Edinburgh, 12 October 1708, SRO, GD124/15/897/2.
14. *DNB*.
15. Supra, n. 7.
    Surviving correspondence of 1706 and 1707 indicates that Alexander Edward, Thomas Bauchope and James Smith were amongst those employed in the improvements at Alloa. The house, which was three sides of a square, was a plain building of three storeys except at one corner which was dominated by the high bulk of the old tower. SRO, GD124/15/427, 440, 663/2.
16. Allardyce, ibid., n. 2.
17. RHP 13288/1. The terraces would have been made up with spoil from the foundations and ground storey. SRO, GD123/120/1. See also Lord Mar's comments in April 1731 in RHP 13257.
18. SRO, GD24/5/4/20, 21, 26.
19. William Drummond to John Drummond, Edinburgh, 30 November 1717, SRO, GD24/1/464D, f. 9.
20. 'Ane Accompt of work wrought by James McAlester, Smith', SRO, GD24/5/4/44.
21. Tullibody House (demolished in 1961) was begun in 1725 and had much in common with Brucefield. A. Drummond, *Old Clackmannanshire* (1953), p. 33; Allardyce, op. cit., vol. II, pp. 118–19.
22. SRO, GD123/120.
23. Lord Mar set down his reasons for his alterations in April 1732 a year after William Adam's first scheme for Dun House was drawn up. Therefore any work begun in 1730 could only have been preparatory. RHP 13257.
    Adam's alternative schemes are shown in *VS*, pls. 57–8 and 69–70. Work on fitting up Dun House seems to have proceeded slowly. Late in 1741 chimney-pieces were supplied and in the autumn of 1742 it was reported that, 'There is still some windows and window shutters to be hung, and locks to be fixed on some doors.' SRO, GD123/136/29 and /428/3.
    William Adam addressed letters to John Burt (the clerk of works at Duff House) from Dun House in July and October 1739. SRO, CS230/A2/1.
24. RHP 31393. The ground- and first-floor plans are unsigned and undated.
25. 'Ane Accompt of Work wrought Att the House of Balvenie Upon days Wadges to Braco Be Alexander Baillie Wright', University of Aberdeen MSS, 3175, f. 36.
26. 'Ane Accompt of the Boxeing of the house of Balvenie. June 22d 1726', University of Aberdeen MSS, 3175, f. 36.
27. *VS*, pl. 91.
28. Supra, n. 26.
29. RHP 31388, 'Ballvenie. May 3th 1725. Inventior Alex. Fraser.'
    The site architect was Alexander Jaffray (ex inf. Mr H. M. Colvin). The departures from the published elevation in *VS*, pl. 91, included heightening the second floor to correspond to the first floor and the substitution of a cast metal coat of arms (of Duff impaling Grant) for the *oeil-de-boeuf* in the south tympanum in 1729. University of Aberdeen MSS, 3175, f. 36.

30. 'Two Additional Accompts given in by Mr Lindsay, after he had given in the haill Accompts of the work to Braco, 1729', University of Aberdeen MSS, 3175, f. 36.

The parapets were never replaced and it must have been at this time that the coat of arms was put in place. Supra, n. 29.

31. 'Act and Commission William Lord Braco Against William Adam 1743', pp. 30, 89. Also William Adam to John Burt, Edinburgh, 2 July 1739, SRO, CS230/A2/1.

32. H. Bolitho and D. Peel, *The Drummonds of Charing Cross* (1967), pp. 31, 35 and 36. James Gibbs opened an account with Drummonds in 1723. Ibid., p. 30.

33. William Drummond to John Drummond, Edinburgh, 15 May 1725, SRO, GD24/1/464D, f. 31.

34. Ibid., Edinburgh, 28 August 1725, SRO, GD24/1/464/D, f. 45.

35. John Drummond to James Drummond, London, 3 January 1735/6, SRO, GD24/1/495, f. 20.

36. Ibid., London, 12 December 1734, SRO, GD24/1/495, f. 6.

37. Ibid., Bristol, 13 September 1734. John Drummond in this same letter mentions that, 'I got a great dinner yesterday from honest Mr Gib.', SRO, GD24/1/495, f. 17.

38. Ibid., London, 31 May 1735, SRO, GD24/1/495, f. 60.

39. Ibid., London, 4 January 1734/5, SRO, GD24/1/495, f. 27.

40. Ibid., London, 4 February 1734/5, SRO, GD24/1/495, f. 2.

41. Ibid., London, 21 June 1735, SRO, GD24/1/495, f. 35.

42. Supra, n. 35.

43. Supra, n. 39. The staircase and entrance hall were in the former tower-house. J. Fleming, *Ancient Castles and Mansions of Stirling Nobility* (1902), p. 197.

44. Supra, n. 36.

45. Supra, n. 38.

46. John Drummond to James Drummond, London, 3 June 1735, SRO, GD24/1/495, f. 37.

47. Ibid., 'Hotwell at Bristoll', 25 August 1735, SRO, GD24/1/495, f. 70.

48. Supra, n. 41.

49. Supra, n. 39.

50. *VB*, vol. I (1715), pl. 48.

51. Supra, n. 35. On 18 February 1734/5 John Drummond mentions a 'Draught' by 'Mr Douglas' and writes on 27 March 1735 that, 'Br. William has sent me Mr Douglass's draught of the addition to quarrel which I like very well.' SRO, GD24/1/495, ff. 33, 57. In 1739 there was an exchange of correspondence with William Adam about offices at Quarrel, SRO, GD24/1/500A, ff. 610–12.

52. 'Copy Contract twixt The Earl of Glencairn and John Douglas Architect 1746', SRO, GD39/6/3/4/1.

53. Jackie Clerk to Sir John Clerk of Penicuik, Finlaystone, 12 March 1751, SRO, GD18/5474.

54. J. Small, *Castles and Mansions of the Lothians* (1883), vol. I.

55. 'Measur of plaister, lyning and flooring work at Archerfield, 1733' and vouchers for payment in 1744 and 1745, SRO, GD6/1587/1 and /2115. C. McWilliam, *Lothian* (1978), p. 78, suggests that the canted bay may have been transferred from the courtyard (now the rear) of the seventeenth-century house.

'Contract Betwixt William Nisbet of Dirletone and John Douglas, 17th June 1747' is in NMRS.

56. J. Paterson, *History of the Counties of Ayr and Wigton* (1863–4), vol. I, pt. 2, p. 470; A. H. Millar, *Historical and Descriptive Accounts of the Castles and Mansions of Ayrshire* (1885).

57. J. Gibbs, *A Book of Architecture* (1728), pls. 43, 90.

58. All that may be deduced at present about the building of Castle Semple is contained in an account for £26:7:3 from John Craig (presumably the Glasgow wright) for oak and fir timber for 'making the raft'. SRO, GD237/139. G. Crawfurd, *A General Description of the Shire of Renfrew, 1710* (1818). p. 349; A. H. Millar, *Castles and Mansions of Renfrewshire and Buteshire* (1889).

59. Gibbs, op. cit., p. i.

60. John Johnstoun to Sir John Clerk, Lochnell, 30 October 1738, SRO, GD18/5009. R. Pococke, 'Tours in Scotland, 1747, 1750, 1760', *SHS*, vol. I (1887), p. 72; T. Pennant, *A Tour in Scotland and Voyage to the Hebrides, 1772* (1790), vol. I, p. 413; RCAHMS, *Argyll*, vol. 2 (1975), pp. 261–5.

Johnstone had previously been employed at Haddo House and Mavisbank and was later the wright at

Galloway House. SRO, GD18/5005/10; /1767; /5246/6/73.

61. Donald Campbell to Patrick Campbell of Barcaldine, Airds, 15 September 1738, SRO, GD170/765/13, 8. RCAHMS, op. cit., vol. 2, pp. 244–5.

62. Supra, n. 60.

63. Ardmaddy was built 'for the constant residence of the Chamberlain and Such as might be convenient for the Proprietor when visiting that estate'. SRO, GD112/20/5/11/1. RCAHMS, op. cit., vol. 2, pp. 248–52.

64. A. Palladio, *The Four Books of Architecture* (republished 1965), Bk. II, pl. XXXVIII.

65. O. Scamozzi, *Le Fabbriche e i Disegni di Andrea Palladio* (1796), Bk. 3, pl. 48.

66. 'Memo. for Mr Alison concerning business for Sir John and Lady Maxwell', Maxwell of Pollok MSS, T-PM106/243.

67. W. Fraser, *Memoirs of the Maxwells of Pollok* (1863), vol. I, p. 98; L. Weaver, 'Pollok House, Renfrewshire', *CL*, vol. XXXIII (25 January 1913), pp. 126–33.

68. Payments to Matthew Dreghorn, a merchant and possibly a relative of Allan Dreghorn, are recorded in the Maxwell of Pollok MSS, passim. Allan Dreghorn is best known as the architect of St Andrew's church, Glasgow, a handsome Gibbsian essay begun in 1740, in which the stunning display of the stuccoist's craft is by Thomas Clayton in 1753. In the previous year he may have worked at Dreghorn's mansion in Clyde Street and was possibly responsible for the plaster decorations at Pollok House. H. Colvin, *A Biographical Dictionary of British Architects, 1600–1840* (1978), p. 274; G. Beard, *Decorative Plasterwork in Great Britain* (1975), pp. 210–11.

69. William Adam, Edinburgh, 8 May 1725, Mellerstain Letters, vol. IX.

70. W. Kent, *Designs of Inigo Jones* (1727), vol. II, pl. 7.
    It may be worth noting that one of the subscribers was 'Mr John Craig of Glasgow', a builder who had a business relationship with Allan Dreghorn. Craig seems to have died early in 1745. Colvin, op. cit., pp. 238–9. Supra. n. 58.

71. W. and J. Halfpenny, R. Morris and T. Lightoler, *The Modern Builder's Assistant* (republished 1971), pl. 47.

72. J. Maclehose, *Old Country Houses of the Old Glasgow Gentry* (1878), p. 54.

73. J. Dunbar, *The Historic Architecture of Scotland* (1966), p. 124.

74. Maclehose, op. cit., p. 94.

75. *NSA*, vol. III, p. 215.

76. Maclehose, op. cit., p. 129.

77. Gibbs, op cit., pl. 34.

78. Lord Garlies to Sir John Clerk, Clary, 15 February 1738, SRO, GD18/5246/6/41.

79. Sir John Clerk, 'A Trip to Bonhill in the Shire of Dunbarton', SRO, GD18/2110.

80. Sir John Clerk, 'A Journey to Galloway, 1721', SRO, GD18/2101.

81. Sir John Clerk, 'Memoirs of a journie to Drumfrise-shire [sic] and Galloway in 1735', SRO, GD18/2112. J. M. Gray (ed.), 'Memoirs of the Life of Sir John Clerk of Penicuik, *SHS*, vol. XIII (1892), p. 144.

82. Lord Garlies to Sir John Clerk, Whithorn, 10 October 1739, SRO, GD18/5246/6/54.

83. Ibid., Clary, 27 September 1738, SRO GD18/5246/6/46.

84. Ibid., Clary, 29 December 1735, SRO, GD18/5246/6/36.

85. Ibid., Clary, 10 August 1737, SRO, GD18/5246/6/38.

86. Ibid., Whithorn, 13 December 1737, SRO, GD18/5246/6/40.

87. Ibid., Clary, 15 February 1738, SRO, GD18/5246/6/41.

88. Ibid., Holm, 7 June 1738, SRO, GD18/5246/6/43.

89. Ibid., Clary, 21 February 1739, SRO, GD18/5246/6/51.

90. Supra, no. 82.

91. Ibid., Clary, 1 November 1739, SRO, GD18/5246/6/55.
    When Lord Garlies mentions Sir John Clerk's plan he may be referring to the scheme marked, 'House for Ld. G-S, J.C.', which shows an elevation of three storeys with a plain five-bay front linked laterally to pavilions. Alongside the principal floor plan an alternative version has been pencilled in substituting a saloon for two bedrooms (RHP 3868). The scheme has almost the number of rooms specified by Lord

Garlies in his letter of 10 August 1737 but may subsequently have formed a basis for ideas about the house planned for Ponton two years later.

92. Ibid., Barclay, 18 June 1740, SRO, GD18/5246/6/64. John Baxter to Sir John Clerk, Whitehaven, 1 May 1740, SRO, GD18/5011.

93. Lord Garlies to Sir John Clerk, Barclay, 25 June 1740, SRO. GD18/5246/6/65.

94. Ibid., Clary, 27 May 1741, SRO, GD18/5246/6/72.

95. Ibid., Clary, 2 December 1741, SRO, GD18/5246/6/73.

96. Ibid., Clary, 16 June 1742, SRO, GD18/5246/6/82.

97. John Baxter to Sir John Clerk, Ponton, 15 June 1742, SRO, GD18/5011.

98. Gray, op. cit., p. 175.

99. John Baxter to Sir John Clerk, Ponton, 29 August 1740, SRO, GD18/5011.

100. Colvin, op. cit., pp. 99, 272. While building Haddo House, Baxter wrote to Sir John Clerk that Douglas had given him 'a hint of the Earle of Galloway's house but I did not seen the Draughts of it'. This, and other remarks, in the autumn of 1734 must refer to the rebuilding of the recently destroyed Glasserton House for it was not until 1739 that Lord Garlies settled on Ponton as the site of Galloway House. SRO, GD18/5005/8, 9, 10.

101. Sir John Clerk, 'Advices Concerning Building and Planting', SRO, GD18/1395.

102. *NSA*, vol. II, p. 142; Colvin, op. cit., p. 99.

103. Galloway House was altered by Robert Mylne in 1764, by Wiliam Burn in 1842 and by Sir Robert Lorimer in 1909. Colvin, op. cit., pp. 575, 165.

104. Supra, n. 92.

105. Supra, n. 97.

106. *VB*, vol. I, pls. 42, 91.

107. *NSA*, vol. IV, p. 280; Fraser, op. cit., vol. I, p. 447.

108. J Blackett, *Arbigland* (n.d.) p. 4.

109. 'Diary of George Ridpath, Minister of Stichel, 1755–61', *SHS*, 3rd Series, vol. II (1922), p. 269.

110. W. Craik to J. Graham, Arbigland, 13 December 1763 and January 1764, Graham of Mossknowe MSS.

111. Ibid., Arbigland, 14 January 1764, Graham of Mossknowe MSS.

112. W. Graham to J. Graham, Jamaica, Westmorland, 21 July 1764; W. Craik to J. Graham, Arbigland, 12 August 1764, Graham of Mossknowe MSS.

113. A. Williamson to J. Hoggan, Hopehouse, 1 December 1766; 'Articles of agreement between John Graham Junr. Mercht. in Dumfries and Andrew Twaddell Mason there', 9 February 1767, Graham of Mossknowe MSS.

114. A foundation stone at Ardwall is dated 5 April 1762.

115. S. Forman, 'Links with the Russian Court in Scotland', *CL*, vol. CXXVII (26 May 1960), p. 1174.

116. An undated and unsigned drawing shows the front elevation and plans of the first and second floors. Wolrige Gordon MSS.

117. The east wing at Craig Castle was altered in 1906 and again after a fire in 1942. Erected in 1767 and 1768 to the design of John Adam it has numerous masonry details comparable to those at Wardhouse. Gordon of Craig MSS.

118. Dunbar, op. cit., p. 84.

119. *NSA*, vol. XII, p. 447.

120. J. Davidson, *Inverurie and the Earldom of Garioch* (1878), pp. 368, 419.

121. Allardyce, op. cit., vol. I, pp. 110, 117; L. Melville, *Errol* (1935), p. 183; D. Walker, 'Glendoick, Perthshire', *CL*, vol. CXLI (30 March 1967), pp. 708–12.

122. Crawfurd, op. cit., p. 396; Millar, op. cit.

123. The date of Kippenross has been placed between 1772 and 1778. A. Barty, *History of Dunblane* (1944), p. 155.
    Perhaps an earlier date would be more correct if it is borne in mind that there is a ceiling by Thomas Clayton who died in 1760. In that same year Bishop Pococke passed by the house. Pococke, op. cit.,

vol. I, p. 292.

124. Ibid., vol. I, p. 180; J. Burke, *A Visitation of the Seats and Arms* (1852–3), vol. II, p. 16.

125. H. Mackenzie, *The Man of Feeling* (1970), p. 108.

126. University of Aberdeen, Arbuthnott MSS, Box 2764/9/2, bundle 3. H. G. Slade, 'Arbuthnott House, Kincardineshire', *PSAS*, vol. 110 (1978–80), pp. 432–74.

127. A. Grant of Laggan, *Letters from the Mountains* (1845), vol. I, p. 30.

128. Macky, op. cit., p. 33.

129. Halfpenny, Morris and Lightoler, op. cit., p. 28.

130. *NSA*, vol. XV, p. 94.

131. A. Carlyle, *Anecdotes and Characters of the Times* (1973), p. 257.

132. Allardyce, op. cit., vol. II, p. 98.

133. 'Advice by Sir John Clerk on the building of a family house', SRO, GD18/1855.

134. William Adam to Lord Marchmont, Edinburgh, 15 December 1724, SRO, GD158/1303/2.

135. Supra. n. 69.

136. Blair Castle was remodelled for the 2nd Duke of Atholl by James Winter with decorations by Abraham Swan and Thomas Clayton. A. Oswald, 'Blair Castle, Perthshire', *CL*, vol. CVI (4 and 11 November 1949), pp. 1362–6; 1434–8; Colvin, op. cit., pp. 199, 906–7; Beard, op. cit., pp. 11–12, 87–8.

137. 'Diary of George Ridpath, Minister of Stichel, 1755–61', *SHS*, 3rd Series, vol. II (1922), p. 143.

138. Newhailes was doubled in size before 1720. Clayton's accounts are dated 1742. NLS, MS 7228/455.

139. Supra, n. 134.

140. H. Thompson, *The Anecdotes and Egotisms of Henry Mackenzie, 1745–1831* (1927), p. 51.

141. Duke of Roxburghe to Lady Roxburghe, London, 26 July 1718, Duke of Roxburghe's MSS, bundle 756.

142. Supra, n. 134.

143. M. Plant, *The Domestic Life of Scotland in the Eighteenth Century* (1952), p. 34.

144. Supra, n. 138.

145. 'Accompt the Right Honble the Lord Dun to Willm. Adam Architect, 1742', SRO, GD123/136/29.

146. Supra, n. 132; T. Somerville, *My Own Life and Times, 1741–1814* (1861), p. 336.

147. J. Fyfe, *Scottish Diaries and Memoirs*, vol. II (1942), p. 276. 'Selections from the Family Papers Preserved at Caldwell', *Maitland Club*, Pt. I (1854), p. 261.

148. Somerville, ibid.

149. 'To James Watt, Smith in Alloa for work in the year 1718', SRO, GD24/5/4/34.

150. Allardyce, op. cit., vol. II, p. 65.

151. Somerville, op. cit., p. 337.

152. Ibid., p. 338; supra, n. 150; Carlyle, op. cit., p. 244.

153. C. Fiennes, *The Journeys of Celia Fiennes* (1947), p. 205.

154. Allardyce, op. cit., vol. I, pp. 211, 71; vol. II, p. 66.

155. Carlyle, op. cit., p. 194.

156. Duke of Roxburghe to 'Mr Bradfat', London, 30 April 1745, Duke of Roxburghe's MSS, bundle 548.

157. 'Selections from the Family Papers Preserved at Caldwell', *Maitland Club*, Pt. II, vol. I, p. 8. For an account of a similar gathering at Dalkeith House in 1739 see NLS, MS 2145, f. 23.

158. Supra, n. 15.

159. Duke of Roxburghe to 'Mr Bradfat', Braywick, 7 July 1745, Duke of Roxburghe's MSS, bundle 548.

CHAPTER FIVE

'Plainness and Utility'

On 25 June 1748 Robert Adam wrote to Lord Milton recording the death of his father, William Adam. 'Yesternight we were deprived of him for ever. My Brother John's untimely Absence Oblidges us to delay his Burial for a few days.'[1] Almost symbolically, William Adam's mantle had passed, in the absence of the eldest son, to Robert so that for historians and even for a contemporary, such as Clerk of Eldin, John Adam has remained a shadowed figure. As the self-appointed memorialist of the Adam family, Clerk of Eldin, a relative by marriage, lauds the achievements of Adam *père* before hymning a paean of praise for the genius of Robert Adam while passing over his elder brother with the comment that 'being left a considerable landed property by his father ... [he] Succeeded in Decorating with large and thriving plantations his Estate of Blair in Fife and Kinross-shires'. By implication, John became a country gentleman. Yet he was more than that, much more, although it was his misfortune, so far as his architectural reputation was concerned, to have a younger brother 'of such lively Genius and Spirit that from his youth, and thro' the whole course of his life, he was the admiration and darling of the numerous men of the Age resorting to his Father's House'.[2]

Throughout the last decade of his life William Adam had relied increasingly on the services of his eldest son, who had been 'bred up in the knowledge of Carpenter work, as well as Masons work and architecture',[3] and later, with increasing business, the latter was joined by Robert and, in time, by James, the third brother. On the father's death John 'immediately assumed Robert as a partner in the architecture',[4] a step which was essential if the family's business interests were not to fall away. Apart from the lucrative employment from the Board of Ordnance, which saw John Adam setting out, often for weeks at a time, on frequent tours of inspection to barracks and to forts in the Highlands,[5] there were the private commissions. In some cases, as does happen in architectural practice, a client, seeking alterations, came back to the firm so that in 1754 John Adam 'was obliged to go out to Arnistone';[6] and there were the unfinished commissions such as the Duke of Argyll's neo-Gothic castle at Inveraray on the west coast[7] or, nearer home, HOPETOUN HOUSE which 'had long been a Subject of employment for Mr Adam the father, and even for his sons after his death'.[8]

The 1st Earl of Hopetoun had died in 1742 having lived, for much of his life, in the country's most splendid building yard. His successor seems to have been immune from building fever and by 1746 had completed the bulk of the fabric. Thereafter, the wright, John Paterson, was paid £134:4:0 for the windows in the cupolas of the pavilions and a further £62:0:4 in 1748 for the staircase in the north cupola with minor works in the north wing being itemised in the next year when the 'Book of Jobbs' included 'To making Styles and putting them up in the Red [drawing] room'.[9] So the finishing went slowly on. Even ten years later the 'Note of Wright Work finish'd and allowed to John Paterson, standing in the Library, and not yet put into the Places to which it belongs' included the 'Venetian Window for South End of Library'. Such work, expensive as it is, causes despair in a client who reckons that the heavy outlays should be behind him. One can understand, therefore, why Lord Hopetoun queried Paterson's accounts for fitting up the hall, though the Vitruvian scroll on the chair-rail was a modest eight shillings and sixpence, the dining-room (now the yellow drawing-room) and the red drawing-room before accepting John Adam's verdict that 'there is no doing a thing in an extraordinary manner, without a price adequate to the pains',[10] which is small comfort to a client whose hand is never out of his pocket.

Apart from such minor jobs as 'Copeing the Court Wall and pedestals under the Sphynxes', the most pressing task for the Adam brothers should have been to raise William Adam's intended portico. That was abandoned by Lord Hopetoun, perhaps to speed up the day when he could be rid of tradesmen or perhaps to save costs, and instead he called for an 'Estimate for Altering the Middle breaking of Hopt. House' which meant inserting attic windows, reshaping those below and cutting Corinthian pilasters so that the entire centre would read as a design continuum rather than be counter-balanced by a free-standing portico without which there was no need for the curved forestairs. Perhaps because the Adams' interest had lessened or because, as has been suggested, John Adam was devoid of ideas, a list and commentary on published designs was selected from *Vitruvius Britannicus*, the *Designs of Inigo Jones* as well as from Gibbs and Desgodetz and sent to Lord Hopetoun that he might choose his own front steps.[11]

Evidently Lord Hopetoun had become a sound judge of building.[12] As one whose views were sought by his friends, he was consulted at an early stage about the preliminary designs for DUMFRIES HOUSE, Ayrshire, one of which 'received the Sanction of Lord Burlington's Approbation that puts it above Exception'. The estimate, though, Lord Hopetoun 'could not pretend to examine particularly, that being a long and laborious Work'.[13] Nevertheless, Lord Dumfries still hesitated to build, perhaps because of the cost, and it was not until 1754 that Allan Whitefoord and Andrew Hunter, an Edinburgh lawyer, sat down with John Adam to revise the building contract. 'Some alterations were made on it and a clean coppie to be made out and sent to your Lordship next post'[14] although, being too bulky, it had to go by the courier.[15] In July, to celebrate the laying of the foundation stones of the new house, there were day-long junketings ending with a ball, an account of which Robert Adam was eager to have published in *The Courant* in Edinburgh. Having agreed to that and having paid the architect £1,500, 'as the first moietie of the Contract', the lawyer could not help but express his anxiety when writing to Lord Dumfries. 'I wish I had also a receit for the last moietie and should put in the news papers that Dumfries House was finished.'[16] The earl was equally fearful about committing himself to building for ''tis certainly a great undertaking, perhaps more bold than wise, but necessity has no law'.[17]

The contract specified, for a sum of £7,979:11:2, 'a Body of a House, two Covered

Passages or Collonades ... Two Pavilions towards the South and Two Low buildings ... towards the North with Back Courts, Coall and Ash Yeards'. The house itself was to be 95 feet long by 65 feet broad with three storeys and garrets though these would be invisible except on the sides. On the ground floor 'The Porter's Lodge, Pantry, Butler's Room and Small Beer Cellar, Wine Cellars, Vally's Room and Closet and the Corridores or Passages are all to be vaulted with Stone But the Charter Room in the principal Story and the Doors and windows of the whole House to be Arch'd with Brick' as were the under-sides of the hearths 'to prevent them having any dependance upon Timber so as to Guard against the accident of Fire'. The floors were to be of fir deal except in the drawing-room, which was to be laid with 'wanscot Board', while the hall would be paved with polished freestone 'reduced to Squares with Black Marble dotts in the Corners'. Another interesting detail was the architects' specification 'to shoulder the Slates with plaster lyme and give them a proper overlap To prevent the wind from shaking them and the Rain from getting in'. At specific stages in the construction work the architects would be paid although Lord Dumfries was to meet the cost of excavating the foundations. He would also pay for the tradesmen's travelling time from Edinburgh and supply 'all Stones of Every kind, Bricks, Chalk, Stucco, hair, Lyme, Sand and Water ... and to Sour the whole Lyme, furnish all Scaffolding, Gangways, Cooms for Arches, Mortar Hods, Mortar Tubs, Barrows, tresses, etc. and Such Machines as may be necessary for hoisting up of Great Beams'.[18]

With construction, initially under the superintendence of Robert Adam,[19] proceeding steadily and uneventfully Lord Dumfries wrote in the spring of 1757 to a neighbour, 'The new House advances very fast; tis to be roofed in and sashed before the end of summer, and they talk of the House warming in August 1758',[20] an event that was, in the end,

107 DUMFRIES HOUSE, Ayrshire, principal floor plan, 1754

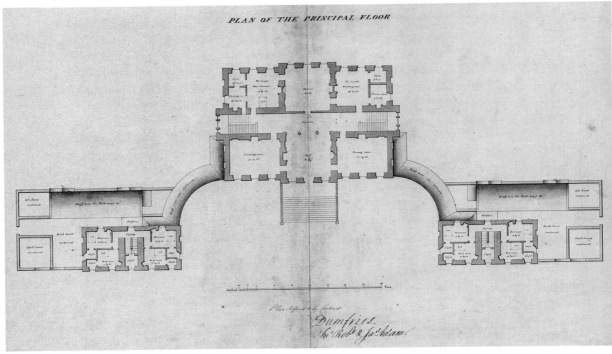

108 DUMFRIES HOUSE, Ayrshire

delayed for a year although long before then Lord Dumfries was considering the decorations
and furnishings chiefly for the drawing-room and dining-room which lay on either side of
the hall [107]. A cross-passage behind, running the full length of the house and terminated
at each end by a staircase, gave access to the family parlour with 'My Lord's Dressing
Room', a closet and the charter room on one side and a bedroom, dressing-room and closet
on the other.[21] As the hall was to be enriched with the Doric order, the Ionic order was to
be used in the dining-room which was to be lined with fir wood. The drawing-room, 'with
an Entablature for the Corinthian order and the Ceiling thereof with Stucco Ornaments',[22]
was to be hung at the ends 'with tapestrie Hangings which are here'[23] while 'All the Dressing
over the Marble Chimney is propos'd of Wood, with a picture fix'd in it' opposite which,
on the window wall, there should be five marble tables beneath which 'Jarrs or pieces of
China are very propper parts of Ornamental furniture'.[24] For the remaining furnishings,
Lord Dumfries had in mind 'a kind of silk furniture made at London like Damask generalie
of two culours, Green and gould culour, sky blew and white; My Lord Marchmont has a
good deal of it at Redbraes and I believe in his House at London ... I shall want eighteen
Elbow Chairs, tapestrie backs and botoms, and two settes to hold three people each, by the
two sides of the fire ... I would only have on[e] pateron Elbow Chair, and the two Settees
made at London, and the others I should chose to get made at Edinburgh.'[25] Other necessary
purchases were two dozen chairs and 'the best Wilton carpet' for the dining-room[26] as well
as 'four good [looking] Glases for the dining room and Drawing room'.[27]

Viewed from the south Dumfries House [108] presents a well-defined articulation and
massing of the component blocks which, in their simplicity and emphatic horizontality,
bespeak a study of contemporary Palladianism bringing to the habitual forms of William
Adam a taut discipline. Yet, the first independent commission of the young Adam brothers
has a deeper significance if it is read as a paraphrase of the ideas of James Gibbs, especially

125

109 AUCHINLECK HOUSE, Ayrshire

of the first two country-house designs in *A Book of Architecture*.[28] Thus, in an early scheme, the south elevation ha's four storeys with a pediment set before a hipped roof with the walling crowned by a parapet and urns and supported at the angles by quoins. A Chiswick-type staircase and an alternating sequence of pedimented voids on the piano nobile[29] may have won Lord Burlington's approval although there could have been no question of four storeys being revealed in elevation just as Lord Dumfries could not sanction excessive stone carving. That the built elevation of three storeys was a compromise can be seen on each side where the pediment, overall height and the retention of the fourth storey as garret lights epitomise the Bruce-Smith school while providing solutions to problems not answered by Gibbs in his published work. Such dual sources may be evident internally where a compact version of the plan published by Gibbs is utilised for the principal floor above which the architects, lacking further guidance, use a standard double-pile plan.

Any architect, robbed of the chance of using fancied novelties, reintroduces them at the earliest opportunity. Thus, the intended external effects for Dumfries House were transposed across the park to AUCHINLECK HOUSE, the seat of Alexander Boswell. Famous as the father of the biographer, he was himself a notable lawyer who was elevated to the bench as Lord Auchinleck although, 'Every moment of the vacation that could be spared from the circuit was spent by him at Auchinleck, of which he was passionately fond. There he built an excellent house, so slowly and prudently, that he hardly felt the expense.'[30] Like any good neighbour he would have been involved in the proposals for Dumfries House. 'On Wednesday', he wrote to a correspondent in August 1753, 'I din'd en famille at

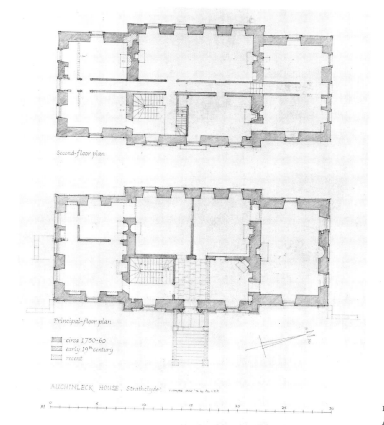

Second-floor plan

Principal-floor plan

circa 1750-60
early 19th century
recent

AUCHINLECK HOUSE, Strathclyde

110 AUCHINLECK HOUSE,
Ayrshire

Leifnorris where politicks and House building made the subject of conversation at a plentifull dinner and a copious desert furnished by my noble neighbour who is hospitality itself.'[31] Doubtless, too, the talk would have turned to the clever Adam brothers, especially as John Adam knew Lord Auchinleck's distant relation 'Mr Boswal who commonly does business for me'.[32] Therefore, it may be reasonable to credit Auchinleck House.[109] as an Adam work.

Any architect has to provide for a client's requirements and, on a subliminal level, for his aspirations. Thus, Lord Dumfries had need of a charter room, being a considerable landowner, as well as rooms of parade which could include the spacious entrance hall where the family crest and Thistle star alternate as metopes beneath the glitter of armorial bearings which repeat those on the tympanum outside. At Auchinleck, according to the sharp-eyed Duchess of Northumberland, 'the Pediment is terribly loaded with Ornaments of Trumpets and Maces and the Deuce knows what.'[33] Over these is the heraldic crest which reappears on the drawing-room ceiling alongside such emblems of pastoral classicism as the pipes of Pan, their thin notes shivering the Horatian couplet cut outside. 'What thou seekest here it is ... if contentment do not fail thee.' So, it must be no surprise to find that the grandest room is a library, set amidst the bedroom floor, below which is the dining-room and family bedroom, leading to a dressing-room and closet, which, with a morning-room, fill one side of the principal floor with the drawing-room occupying the other [110]. Something of the same spatial character occurred at nearby Ballochmyle but there the hall and staircase, being in axis, fill the centre, pushing the dining-room to one side with a bedroom, closet and breakfast-room on the other and a parlour on the garden side of the ground floor.[34] Ballochmyle, the property of Allan Whitefoord and described in 1760 as a 'new House very neatly fitted up and finish'd',[35] resembles many of William Adam's schemes for the gentry being neither a show seat nor a place of study and retiral but the establishment of a gentleman farmer in which sense it could compare with Moffat House, Dumfries-shire. As the latter was built for Lord Hopetoun's occasional residence during his visits of inspection, as curator of the Annandale estates, accommodation could be restricted to a low parlour and a drawing-room with a writing-room for estate business and a 'Little House in Park'.[36] John Adam engaged the masons and labourers but was 'not undertaker for said Building' though he was 'to have reasonable allowance for my trouble in planning and directing the said work'[37] which is why the final account, which put the cost of the house at £3,538:17:4, includes 'To Mr Adam for his Trouble and for Plans. £100.'[38] These provided, as at Ballochmyle, for a three-storey centre with a bowed rear, curved service passages and pavilions all of dark whinstone with dressings of smooth tawny-red sandstone.

The same general formula was drawn up for TOUCH HOUSE, the most important Georgian mansion in Stirlingshire [111], although it has earlier origins which are most obvious in the visible retention of the medieval tower and, less so, of the north range.[39] Tacked on to that a new front was expressive, even without the proposed wings, of the desire for more spacious accommodation with its regular plan suggested externally by the

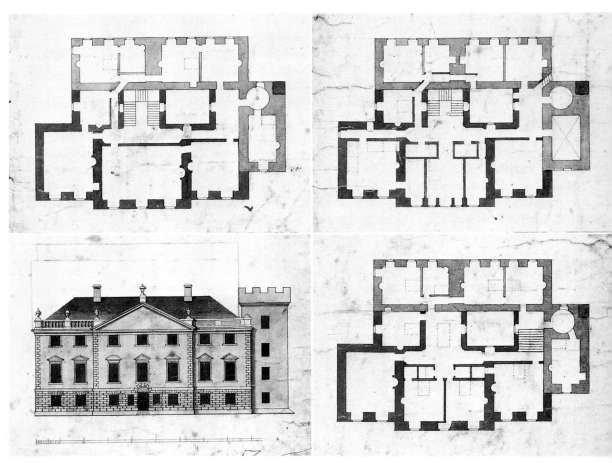

111 TOUCH HOUSE, Stirlingshire

112 TOUCH HOUSE, Stirlingshire, the library ceiling

outlines of the boldly cut stone enclosing the piano nobile above which the bedroom windows are run into the eaves cornice, an oddity of design found, as has been observed, at nearby Blairdrummond.[40] One writer, probably relying on family tradition, gives the dates as between 1757 and 1762[41] which means that the rococo ceiling of the library [112], on the topmost floor, is comparable in style and date to the drawing-room ceiling at Auchinleck.[42] Although it is tempting, in the absence of a proven architect, to ascribe Touch, because of its high quality and some particular characteristics, to John Adam,[43] there is no reference to him in the discovered accounts. These confirm the building dates and show how complicated the organisation of a building programme must have been with merchants in Stirling, Alloa, Dundee and Edinburgh all supplying materials. Perhaps the key document is the discharge 'for Building the House of Touch' in which Gideon Gray of Stirling acknowledges 'full payment of All the Mason Work done at Touch'.[44]

An earlier house, dated 1750 over the entrance, where it seems to be proven that John Adam did have a hand, is Largo House, Fife,[45] a belated version of Colen Campbell's Shawfield Mansion in Glasgow.[46] Perhaps it may be useful to speculate that Charleton and Durie in the same county could have been by the same designer.[47] Like many other Scottish mansions they display the fondness for the hipped roof which at Largo is given significance by the balustraded roof platform, a *passé* device yet one that would reappear in Ware's *A Complete Body of Architecture*,[48] while at Fordell balustrades finished off the canted bays filling out the side elevations.[49] The same design feature was proposed by John Adam in a set of plans produced for Captain John Ross after a visit to Balnagowan in Easter Ross in 1762. The architect wished to include the kitchen and offices within the house to save space and because the house would look better. When the client demurred, preferring to have the offices separate from the house, pavilions were suggested 'and by that means you can increase your Lodging both for Friends and Servants. You may, if you choose, have good sleeping places out of the Rooff [sic] which will serve excellently for people you are not in great ceremony with.'[50]

113 BANFF CASTLE, Banffshire

It would, of course, have been surprising if the more affluent northern landowners had not secured John Adam's services while he was about government business at Fort George. In 1750 the expenses for BANFF CASTLE [113] include, 'July 1. To Postage of a Letter to Mr Adams at Ardoirsire. 2d' and two years afterwards, 'To an Express for Mr Adam's to Ardoirsire. 5/6'[51] which hints at urgency although, by then, the new house was complete and the accounts settled save for a trifling sum which Lord Deskford would pay 'except My Lord Hopton upon considering the account should think that there is already enough payed'.[52] Despite the reslating and reglazing of the old castle in 1749, it was only a matter of months before 'the New House' was founded when two shillings were disbursed for drink money, although in October the allowance was more generous for 'the Masons at Chimney Heads' which meant that the offices could be begun in the next building season.[53] Such rapid progress, albeit the house was an unadorned five-bay block 'rough cast in order to defend the Storms',[54] should not obscure the obstacles that had to be overcome daily. Just about the only local supplies were birch trees, fashioned into wheelbarrows, and peat and broom which fuelled the lime kiln.[55] Everything else came in seventy boat-loads,[56] a hazardous undertaking as witnessed in the winter of 1750 with the cash entry, 'To Gathering Lymestone scattered by the Sea Storm. 1/–'. Some building stone came from Burghead along the coast[57] but most supplies were shipped from Leith including the bulk of the timber, 'Four Boxes Cutt [sic] English Window Glass', as well as slates, lead and nails.[58] Even so, there had to be such improvisations as making 'fourteen Rules to the Masons' or 'Seven Shafts for hammers and putting them on'[59] or 'To Carriage of Nails to and from Cullen borrowed till our own come home. 3d'.[60]

Many such trials would have been repeated at CASTLE GRANT, Morayshire, with the added disadvantage of distance from a harbour. With the old castle retained as a vertical core its compact U-plan was extended by two parallel ranges of offices, set on the cross-fall

114 CASTLE GRANT, Morayshire

to the south, thus achieving an elevated court reached by a steep stair [114]. Low in scale and anonymous in character, these domestic units are an attractive foil to the majesty of the tall castle unlike the barrack-like addition to the north which prompted Lord Fife to write, 'The road leads one on the angle of the new front, which rather should be hid.'[61]

Once again Lord Hopetoun played the role of architectural consultant for, having visited Castle Grant and next having pushed the commission towards the Adams, it was to him that John Adam first sent the plans for the new work in February 1753 along with a note saying that he had 'got about a dozen of hands engaged for it, and David Frew to oversee them, who is very capable for it. I doubt if Fraser would be, even for the Offices, as he is so confused a creature, besides his being almost perpetually drunk.'[62] Lord Hopetoun continued to promote the Adams by writing to Sir Ludovic Grant, his brother-in-law, that, 'Mr Adam will expect your Orders as to the time of sending North the Masons, who allways [sic] grow impatient to be at Work after the first of March',[63] although, because of frost and snow, it was to be April before they set out to shape dressings from the quarries. In the meantime, wood had to be collected for the centering of the ground-floor vault and for the masons' sheds.[64] As to David Frew, 'If there is any little place about the House where he could keep his papers, it would be much more convenient than at a distance ... And as he is very sober and uneasie lest he should be brought in the way of drinking in the publick house, in case he lys there, he would also be extreamly fond, if that place could hold a little bed for him.'[65]

In reshaping and extending Castle Grant the living accommodation was to be contained in the heart of the old castle with the entrance hall and staircases in the extension to the north where there was to be a nine-bay front. That was to have a projecting centre, an idea that was abandoned because of design problems with the roof form and its connection to the castle.[66] John Adam favoured a platform as against a single roof, with its heavier and larger timbers, or as against a valley roof in which water would collect. 'This was the case originally at Yester House, and this Marquess by my Father's advice, turn'd it into a Platform which answers to a wish.' He was, therefore, surprised that Sir Robert Gordon should have given contrary advice 'as I have been told that in order to prevent having a Platform, he cover'd his house at Gordonstoun with several small rooffs [sic] and gutters, all which rain in'.[67] Once more Lord Hopetoun allied himself with his protégé. 'I know there is a difficulty in keeping Platforms in order where Plumbers are at a distance, especially such as were made some time ago when that business was much less understood in this Country than it is now ... while you Potentates of the North allow the Forts to subsist, the Plumbers will always find business there.'[68] So it was settled and, in the autumn of 1754, a plumber was sent north to see to the leadwork for a platform[69] after which the wright, James Houston, could begin laying joists and flooring in the new building.[70] However, the death of Lady Grant brought about a hiatus and it was not until 1760 that Houston was back at the castle employed on finishing jobs as well as 'White Washing the 2 Stair Cases in the Nursery and Women House' in the west wing and 'Bottoming 6 Chairs for the Servants' which cost a shilling whereas 'ten Clos beds for servants' was itemised at £5:10:0,[71] while for Miss Grant he made a folding bed, drawing-desk and fire-screen.[72] There is no mention of the public rooms until the winter of 1765 when John Adam was considering sections and moulds[73] although, in the end, he opined that, 'The finishing I think should be very much of the same kind with that at Moy and the same Moulds may answer.'[74]

The MOY estate, on the Moray coast, had been inherited from an uncle in 1755. Once Sir Ludovic decided to replace the centre with a more distinguished architectural unit and better accommodation, he went in 1759 to Robert Adam and though his scheme remained a paper exercise it did provide ideas for much that was to come especially as the elevations displayed a degree of expertise and sophistication in the handling of Palladian motifs that put them in a class of their own. The older wings were retained as the plain descants to the fine tuning of rusticated basement and entrance above which a Venetian window graced a breakfast-room. With the greater part of the new block set to the north there was space on the side elevations for splayed bays which, being two-storeyed, eased the transition between roof and wall. Much of the ground floor was given over to cellarage but there was, as might be expected, a parlour or daily living-room and a housekeeper's room with the stores locked in the bay which, on the floor above, in the dining-room was transformed into a columned 'Nich for Musick'[75] perhaps in response to Ware's dictum that, 'A screen of columns may be fit in a dining-parlour or an alcove in a bed-chamber; but these are ornamental parts which cannot be admitted in other rooms.'[76] As for the plan, that was cribbed from *The Modern Builder's Assistant* though Robert Adam did reshape the side bays.[77] Perhaps, too, it is worth noting that these occur at Ham House where the entrance echoes that designed for the north front of Moy and later adopted by Colen Williamson

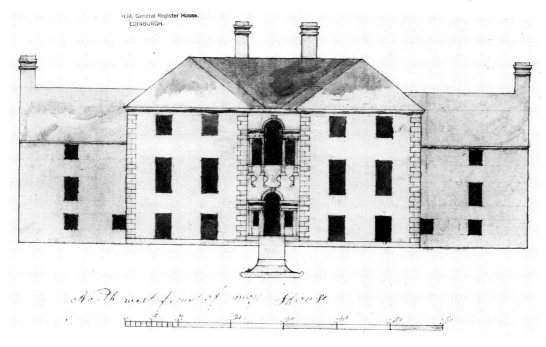

North west front of moy House

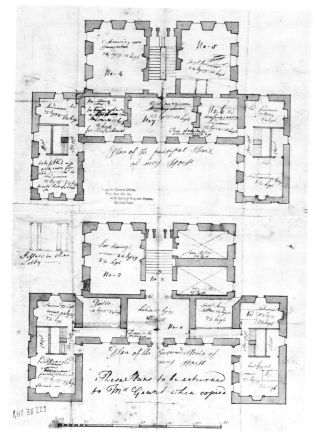

115 and 116 MOY HOUSE, Morayshire,
by Colen Williamson

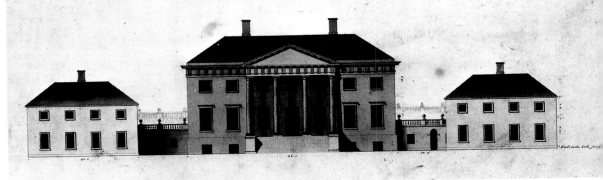

ELEVATION of the Principal Front of a *HOUSE* defign'd for
PATRICK HOME of *BILLY* Esqʳ at *PAXTON*

117 PAXTON HOUSE, Berwickshire

when he took over the commission.

Why there was a change of architect is a mystery. Certainly it was not a happy move since John Adam had to be called in later. Williamson, who was doubtless a local man, submitted charges in 1761 for demolishing and rebuilding the central block quoting prices as low as five pounds for the entrance doorway and for each Venetian window[78] of which there were to be two, piled one above the other, on each front [115]. Obviously, Williamson had seen Robert Adam's drawings but, lacking an educated taste, ignored the refinements of elevation and the subtle spatial exercises in favour of a flashier but crude external treatment and commonplace planning [116] so that, in the northward extension, the intrusion of the staircase so curtailed the accommodation that the dining-room was transferred to a new position over the front door. Although James Houston installed the joists,[79] no other internal work was done until the spring of 1763 when John Adam, who had been sent Williamson's plans,[80] despatched instructions to the wright for finishing the low parlour before drawing out sections and moulds for other public rooms where he wished to reduce the number of windows to give more wall space, especially in the drawing-room where 'A Venetian Windo [sic] on the broad side of the room, might do very well, but there is not height sufficient to make it of any tollerable Size.'[81] Also, 'The Dado in this Room ought to be flush, without any Panels ... To have a Ionic or Dentil Cornice with one or two members inriched in Plaister.' A flock wallpaper and marble chimney-piece would complete the ensemble. The best bedroom was to have flock paper of the same pattern as in the low parlour but the dining-room was to be painted sky-blue with the ornamental plasterwork in a stone colour and the hall and staircase were to be light yellow.[82] Despite these endeavours, the plan of the staircase was still not settled by spring 1765[83] and even some fifteen months later John Adam was writing to Sir Ludovic to say that, 'The Cast Iron ballusters for your Stairs have been at Fort George for several weeks past.'[84]

The majority of the Adam houses so far considered were planned as the seat of a country gentleman. 'His family is moderate: he intends to build for convenience more than magnificence, but he will have the house handsome though not pompous.' Such houses, 'without columns, or other expensive decorations', were usually free-standing blocks with the offices in the basement, a practice that Ware condemned. 'He is not to put the kitchen under the parlours, or the stables in a corner of the yard: a brick layer could do that ... these offices are far from being under a necessity to be hid, to be inconvenient or to be placed improperly ... and instead of a plain square house ... it will be possible, at a small advance in the charge, to add wings to the centre, and connect them by passages ... the whole regular and uniform.'[85] Most landowners, certainly in Scotland, could not afford either the capital outlay or the upkeep of the orthodox villa layout as monitored by Ware, the mid-century's most forceful contender for Palladianism both as author and architect of such a work as Amisfield, East Lothian, in 1756. It is surely not without significance that the most fully developed Palladian exercise by the Adam brethren was begun in 1757 at PAXTON HOUSE, Berwickshire.[86] By the next summer the mason, James Nisbet, was writing that 'the Building goes on very Well, I intend to Lay some of the Soalls (cills) of the Windows this Day. I have been Stopt with Rain ... there is no Accts. of the Ships arrival with the Slates as yet.'[87] That Nisbet was competent in his craft is borne out by a letter of March 1763 when the structure of house, colonnades and pavilions was complete. 'The Steps of the Stair are well wrought and ready to Lay ... an out Side Stair ought to be done with as much judgement as any pice [sic] of Masonry I know ... as the Pedestals of your Stair is very massy I intend jogling the Steps together in Such a manner that the Weather can have no pour to move them, this practice I in a great Measure owe to the Execution of the Cornice.'[88]

With a tetrastyle portico and extended entablature Paxton [117] was indisputably a work 'of a higher kind' since the introduction of an order 'is a great addition of dignity'[89] while 'the continuing the entablature strait and entire has a look of a strength'.[90] Initially, there may have been hesitation in choosing between the Doric and the Ionic[91] although the former was urged by Ware since 'its use is in no instance so proper or so happy as in the manner of porticos ... in the real office of supporting some considerable part of this fabrick'. Besides, as 'there is none in which the great article of proportion is more perfectly seen', the columns, for which the architect should 'select the Attic base', were to be 'raised a little above the eye'. Unfortunately, in 'the disposition of its triglyphs and metopes' the Doric order had its peculiar difficulties which 'have so embarrassed the common race of architects, that the order has been much less used than its natural beauty deserves'.[92]

As Paxton was an exact commentary in stone and lime on Ware's text, who was the exegetist? That it was John Adam can be fairly assumed since in the years after 1748 he was the evident head of a family firm that was 'John and Robert Adam's Architects' at Hopetoun in 1750[93] and four years later at Dumfries House included James.[94] In view of his later fame it is, of course, tempting to fix on those early years and conjure up Robert as the gifted leader of a design team. Thus one, otherwise cautious, writer claims that the Dumfries House designs 'were mostly by Robert and that he was responsible for the scheme of interior decorations as well'[95] although in every recorded instance, save one, it is John Adam who acts as *chef d'œuvre*. Certainly, Henry Mackenzie recollected that Robert, 'then a very young artist', had presented his father with a plan for a house in Nairn.[96] That apart, he was the firm's man although, as in a modern practice, each partner would have a responsibility for his own projects. Thus, Gunsgreen House, Berwickshire [118], was built to the designs of

118 GUNSGREEN HOUSE, Berwickshire,
by James Adam

James Adam whose other schemes included Moy House, Inverness-shire, for Captain Aeneas Mackintosh. As usual, the three-storeyed compact block was rectangular on plan since 'a long square is preferable. It pleases the eye more, it 'admits more variety in the inner division'[97] which was a dining-room and drawing-room on the principal floor.[98] However, 'Invercald says that a single house with no sunk story and two Colonads will be much cheaper', a view supported by the captain's wife who wanted 'the Dineing Roome in on[e] of the collonads' which would be constructed with the materials from the old house.[99]

James Adam's sketch designs are typical of the output from the Adam office though, considered as juvenilia, they reveal the germ of inventiveness which would be developed under the influence of Robert in the early sixties. By then one would have hoped to have seen in John Adam's architectural devising something of those novelties and syntheses which had made Robert's London career a triumph. Yet, as has been remarked before,[100] that was not so. One can accept that John Adam was not an inspired architect; what is distressing is his lack of creative design or an interest in new ideas. Faced with practical problems he could give advice; for design decisions he resorted to pattern books. His elevations are comparable with his father's but, without the latter's gusto and *bravura*, they become a

119 CULLODEN HOUSE, Inverness-shire

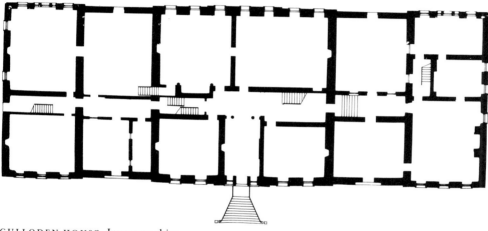

120 CULLODEN HOUSE, Inverness-shire

stripped-down Palladianism although that accorded with mid-century taste, 'preferring Plainness and Utility to Gaiety and Ornament',[101] and suited the pockets of the lairds. Having to count the coppers they would have agreed with Palladio that 'for gentlemen of a meaner station, the fabrics ought also to be less, of less expence and have fewer ornaments'.[102]

Perhaps, however, there was a tentative acceptance of Robert Adam's innovations in the projected elevations for Broomhall, Fife, where the entrance is contained in a semi-engaged domed cylinder,[103] or at Cromarty House, where the garden front has an elliptical bow, while, in the manner of Robert Adam's unexecuted treatment of Moy House, Morayshire, the wings are clapped on to the sides of the house for which there was a Palladian precedent,[104] despite Ware's stricture that lateral wings had 'no grace, no variety, nor elegance: the eye is tired with the same dull formal look, and all has a poor dead aspect'.[105] At Culloden house, Inverness-shire [119], all three virtues are present since wings and house are held apart by link corridors [120] which, on the rear elevation, have statues of philosophers in niches as in the octagonal entrance hall at Cromarty [121]. Since both mansions

121 CROMARTY HOUSE, Ross and Cromarty.

were begun in 1772,[106] they have much in common including a rather straight-laced Gibbsian look about the centre although at Culloden the high-fashion Adamesque details are continued internally though lacking the *jeu d'esprit* that might be expected. Bearing in mind these considerations and John Adam's north-east connections, it is probably a reasonable assumption that he was the architect of both Cromarty and Culloden at a time when Robert Adam's London practice was opening up in Scotland.

Notes to Chapter 5

1. Robert Adam to Lord Milton, Edinburgh, 25 June 1748, NLS, MS 16665, f. 15.
2. J. Clerk of Eldin, 'Life of Robert Adam', SRO, GD18/4981.
3. William Adam to Lord Milton, Inveraray, 25 September 1746, NLS, MS 16596, f. 46. Supra, n. 2.
4. J. Clerk of Eldin, 'Life of Robert Adam', SRO, GD18/4982.
5. John Adam to Lord Milton, Edinburgh, 20 August 1750, NLS, MS 14551, f. 116.
    Besides building Fort George, John Adam was heavily involved between 1747 and 1750 at Fort Augustus and Fort William, the castles of Mar, Corgarff, Blackness, Stirling, Edinburgh and Dumbarton and the barracks at Inversnaid and Bernera. NLS, MS 10693.
6. John Adam to Lord Milton, Edinburgh, 13 October 1755, NLS, MS 14551, f. 137. Also SRO, GD248/49/1. John Adam was fitting up the uncompleted western portion of Arniston House with a lofty, coved dining-room and drawing-room. RHP 5248/12. H. Colvin, *A Biographical Dictionary of British Architects, 1660-1840* (1978), p. 46; C. McWilliam, *Lothian* (1978), pp. 80-1; M. Cosh, 'The Adam Family and Arniston', *Architectural History*, vol. 27 (1984), pp. 220-3.
7. J. Macaulay, *The Gothic Revival, 1745-1845* (1975), pp. 43-4.
8. Supra, n. 2.
9. Hopetoun MSS, bundle 385.
10. Ibid., bundle 373.
11. Ibid., bundle 639. J. Fleming, *Robert Adam and His Circle* (1962), pp. 91-2; A. Rowan, 'The Building of Hopetoun', *Architectural History*, vol. 27 (1984), pp. 194-9.
12. Lord Hope to Lord Tinwald, 'Hopt-house', 11 and 13 April 1739, NLS, MS 5074, ff. 163, 167.
13. Lord Hopetoun to Lord Dumfries, 'Hopt-house', 12 April 1751, Bute MSS.
    Discussions with John Adam seem to have commenced in 1748. Two years later Lord Hopetoun was reported to have 'finished his observations upon the plan'. Andrew Hunter to Lord Dumfries, Edinburgh, 19 November 1748 and 12 July 1750, Bute MSS.
14. Andrew Hunter to Lord Dumfries, Edinburgh, 9 February 1754, Bute MSS.
15. Ibid., Edinburgh, 20 February, 1754, Bute MSS.
16. Ibid., Edinburgh, 27 July 1754, Bute MSS.
17. Lord Dumfries to Lord Loudon, Leifnorris, 5 June 1754, Bute MSS.
18. Contract between Lord Dumfries and John, Robert and James Adam, 24 April 1754.
    According to the building certificates of Robert Neilson, the clerk of works, and John Mitchell, the foreman mason, the vaults of the ground storey were in place by August 1755, the principal storey was joisted in the following building season and the roof was on by August 1757. By the end of that year the east pavilion and colonnade were also roofed. After the west pavilion and colonnade had been roofed by August 1758 the back courts, coal and ash yards were finished in the winter of 1759. Bute MSS.
    Lord Mountstuart wrote in 1772 that Robert Adam 'said he had but thirty pounds for the plans of Lord Dumfries's'. 'Selections from the Family Papers Preserved at Caldwell', *Maitland Club* (1854), Pt. II, vol. II, p. 201.
19. Supra, n. 2.
20. Lord Dumfries to Lord Loudon, Leifnorris, 17 May 1757, Bute MSS.
    On 14 May John Adam wrote to his brother James, 'I have spoke to My Lord Dumfries about the transportation of his Sashes ... I believe the Carts must also have a covering of Sail Cloath in case of Rain.' SRO, GD18/4836.
21. 'Plan of the Principal Floor', Bute MSS. Cf. *VS*, pl. 19.
22. Supra, n. 18.
23. Lord Dumfries to Lord Loudon, Leifnorris, 26 July 1758, Bute MSS.
24. 'Memorandum for the Right Honble The Earl of Dumfries ... 3d Novem. 1755', Bute MSS.
25. Supra, n. 22.
26. Lord Dumfries to Lord Loudon, Edinburgh, 30 December 1758, Bute MSS.
27. Ibid., Leifnorris, 30 November 1758, Bute MSS.

28. J. Gibbs, *A Book of Architecture* (1728), pls. 37, 38.

29. 'South Front of Leifnorris House towards the Court. One of the Seats of the Right Honble the Earl of Dumfries', Bute MSS.

30. A. Allardyce, *Scotland and Scotsmen in the Eighteenth Century* (1888), vol. I, pp. 165–6.
    Building accounts, now among the Boswell papers at Yale University, show that slates were delivered from Ayr in 1758 and 1759 when one shilling was paid 'To mending a window and Dressing the Mock window in the Pedement of New House.' Window tax was paid for the year beginning Whitsunday 1759. Auchinleck was probably begun after Alexander Boswell became a Lord of Justiciary in 1756.

31. Alexander Boswell to Lord Loudon, 30 August 1753, Bute MSS, bundle 3.

32. John Adam to Lord Milton, London, 5 January 1764, NLS, MS 16730, f. 1.

33. J. Greig, *The Diaries of a Duchess* (1926), p. 25.
    Elizabeth Percy, Countess and later Duchess of Northumberland, visited Ayrshire during a short tour of southern Scotland in August 1760. Early in that month Lord Auchinleck wrote from Edinburgh to Lord Loudon, 'I hear the Earl of Northumberland is to be at Leifnorris and I was yesterday applyed to by our ffriend [sic] Allan and the E. of Dumfreis's desire to get some road helped which these great people are to pass and tho' it is not on my grounds I am just now to write about it that it may be got done.' Bute MSS.

34. *VS*, pl. 63.

35. *Supra*, n. 33.

36. 'Account of Painting the Earl of Hopetoun's House at Moffat by Runciman and McLaurin. 1786', Hopetoun MSS, bundle 322.

37. 'From Mr Adam Relating to the Building the House at Moffat. 20 April 1762. Edinr.', Hopetoun MSS, bundle 342.

38. 'General Accot. of Debursements for building, finishing and furnishing The Right Honble Earl of Hopetoun's House at Moffat from 1760 to 1768 inclusive', Hopetoun MSS, bundle 642.

39. Drawings, unsigned and without a date, are still at Touch House.
    Although the visible retention of the tower might seem odd, it should be noted that all the designs, including a set by John Adam in 1764, for Gordon Castle, Morayshire, incorporated a tower, a remnant of the former castle, as the centre-piece of the garden front. Macaulay, op. cit., pp. 152–3.

40. J. Cornforth, 'Touch, Stirlingshire – I', *CL*, vol. CXXXVIII (19 August 1965), pp. 440–3; RCAHMS, *Stirlingshire* (1963), vol. II, pp. 376–9.

41. J. Gibson, *The Lands and Lairds of Touch* (1929), p. 47.

42. The design sources for the drawing-room ceiling at Auchinleck and the library ceiling at Touch are to be found in W. and J. Halfpenny, R. Morris and T. Lightoler, *The Modern Builder's Assistant* (republished 1971), pls. 80, 81. The plasterer at Touch was Thomas Clayton whose accounts are preserved in the house.

43. It may be worth noting that in 1758 John Adam attempted to procure a partnership in the wine trade for his youngest brother William and that Hugh Seton of Touch was the son of a prosperous wine merchant. John Adam to Lord Milton, Edinburgh, 23 March 1758, NLS, MS 16703, f. 5; Gibson, op. cit., p. 46.

44. The building accounts are at Touch House. They show that Gray was employed for 'mason work' on many estate jobs throughout the 1760s and 1770s. However, it has to be recorded that the drawing, showing the plans and elevation of Touch as built, bears a label inscribed, '1747 Took House by James Steinson'.

45. A receipt, signed by John Adam, for two chimney-pieces supplied to James Durham of Largo in 1759 is at Arniston House. A. Millar, *Fife: Pictorial and Historical* (1895), vol. II, p. 31.

46. *VB*, vol. II (1717), pl. 51.

47. Charleton House was built in 1759 and Durie three years later. *NSA*, vol. IX, pp. 326, 268; Millar, op. cit., vol. II, p. 45.

48. I. Ware, *The Complete Body of Architecture* (1756), pl. 33.

49. There is no evidence for John Adam's involvement at Fordell. However, the 'Plan of a Small House for Capt. Hugh Dalrymple of Fordle. 1756', reputedly drawn by James Adam, shows a small three-bay house with a square projection, one of which contained the staircase, on each side. SM, vol. VII, no. 17.
    A. Bolton, *The Architecture of Robert and James Adam* (1922), vol. II, Index of Adam Drawings, p. 14. Fordell was demolished in 1963.

50. John Adam to Captain John Ross, Edinburgh, 14 and 28 January 1762, SRO, GD129/7/7.
51. 'Book of debursements On Account of the Right Honourable James Lord Deskfoord for His Lordship's Buildings at the Castle of Banff. 1749'. SRO, GD248/1169.
52. 'Augt. 28th 1752. Obligement Lord Deskford to John Adams Architect for £37 Ster.', SRO, GD248/984/4.
53. Supra, n. 49.
54. John Adam to Sir Ludovic Grant, Edinburgh, 1 January 1754, SRO, GD248/176/3/5.
55. Supra, n. 49.
56. 'To Lord Deskford from Jas. Bartles, Banff', SRO, GD248/Box 905, bundle 7.
57. Supra, n. 49.
58. 'In the Happy Return of Banff, George Abernethy Mar. from Leith', SRO, GD248/Box 905, bundle 5.
59. Supra, n. 54.
60. Supra, n. 49.
61. W. Fraser, *The Chiefs of Grant* (1883), vol. II, p. 483.
62. John Adam to Lord Hopetoun, Edinburgh, 12 February 1763, SRO, GD248/176/1/12.
    RHP 9047, a drawing for proposed offices, may be by Fraser. Was he the Alexander Fraser who designed the additions for Balvenie House in 1725?
63. Lord Hopetoun to Sir Ludovic Grant, 'Hopt. House', 27 February 1753, SRO, GD248/176/1/16.
64. John Adam to Sir Ludovic Grant, Edinburgh, 22 March 1753, SRO, GD248/176/1/21.
65. Ibid., Edinburgh, 29 March 1753, SRO, GD248/176/1/25.
66. RHP 9046. See also RHP 9048, 9050 and 9052 showing the executed alterations.
67. John Adam to Sir Ludovic Grant, Edinburgh, 1 January 1754, SRO, GD248/176/3/5.
68. Lord Hopetoun to Sir Ludovic Grant, 'Hopt. House', 2 January 1754, SRO, GD248/176/3/4. In this same letter Lord Hopetoun gave his approval 'of the Aisler Front which no doubt will have a very good effect'. Perhaps he was referring to the ink drawing with Gibbsian details pencilled over the entrance doorway. SRO, GD248/79/8/17.
    Despite the assurances about the platform roof, John Adam was writing in the winter of 1765, 'I am sorry the New Rooff should need Sclating already.' SRO, GD248//49/3/16.
69. John Adam to Sir Ludovic Grant, Edinburgh, 12 October 1754, SRO, GD248/176/3/9.
70. 'Abstract of James Houston's Accompts, 1760', SRO, GD248/251/3/1/1. See also SRO, GD248/251/3/3/6.
71. 'Accott. The Honble Sir Ludovick Grant of Grant Barrtt. [sic] To James Houston', SRO, GD248/251/3/1/4.
72. 'Accot. of Jobb Work Wrought by James Houston', SRO, GD248/251/3/2/1.
73. John Adam to James Grant of Grant, Edinburgh, 13 February 1765, SRO, GD248/49/3/16.
74. Ibid., Edinburgh, 27 June 1765, SRO, GD248/49/3/25.
75. SM, vol. 30, nos. 39–42. RHP 9062 and 9063 are client's copies of floor plans inscribed 'R.A. 1759'. Moy was visited in 1758 by Sir William Burrell who described it as 'a small old house'. NLS, MS 2911, f. 27.
76. Ware, op. cit., p. 297.
77. Halfpenny, Morris and Lightoler, op. cit., pl. 52.
78. 'Proposals for Building To the Honable Sir Loudivic Grant of Grant by Collen Williamson 22 Sept. 1761', SRO, GD248/79/1/19.
79. 'Act. Betwixt the Honble Sir Ludovick Grant of Grant Bart and James Houston Squar[e] Wright for 1761 and 1762. Moy', SRO, GD248/251/3/7/1.
80. RHP 38228 and 38229 are inscribed, 'These plans to be returned to Mr Grant when Copied.' RHP 38227 and 9061 are part of the same set.
81. John Adam to James Grant, Edinburgh, 14 May 1763, SRO, GD248/178/2/13.
82. 'Copy directions for finishing the House at Moy', SRO, GD248/181/3/67.
83. John Adam to James Grant, Edinburgh, 13 February 1765, SRO, GD248/49/3/16.
84. John Adam to Sir Ludovic Grant, Forres, 1 September 1766, SRO, GD248/185/1/27.
85. Ware, op. cit., p. 406.
86. Walter Scott of Harden entered in his cash book a small payment 'for Paxton Mason and Workmen' on 31 December 1757. SRO, GD157/813.
    Although there is no proof of an Adam involvement at Paxton, it is accepted that the surviving drawings,

which include an astylar elevation, are from the Adam office. *NSA*, vol. II, p. 153; A. Rowan, 'Paxton House, Berwickshire', *CL*, vol. CXLII (17 and 24 August 1967), pp. 364–7, 422–5.

87. James Nisbet to Patrick Home of Billy, Paxton, 28 July 1758, SRO, GD267/16/9/9.
88. Ibid., Paxton, 29 March 1763, SRO, GD267/16/9/11.
89. Ware, op. cit., p. 355.
90. Ibid., p. 371.
91. 'Estimate of Prices of Mason work for Patrick Home of Billy Esquire by James Nisbet Mason', SRO, GD267/16/9/10.
92. Ware, op. cit., pp. 403–5.
93. 'Accompt the Right Honble The Earl of Hopetoun To John and Robert Adams for Dealls. 1750'. Hopetoun MSS, bundle 639.
94. Supra, n. 18.
95. Fleming, op. cit., p. 95.
96. H. Thompson, *The Anecdotes and Egotisms of Henry Mackenzie, 1745–1831* (1927), p. 121.
97. Ware, op. cit., p. 304.
98. James Adam's sketch book, no. 3, Clerk of Penicuik MSS.
99. Captain Aeneas Mackintosh to Lord Loudon, 16 October 1754 and 15 February 1755. Also John Adam and James Adam to Lord Loudon on 6 November 1754 and 10 May 1755 respectively. Bute MSS.
100. Macaulay, op. cit., p. 153.
101. R. Morris, *Rural Architecture* (1750), preface.
102. A. Palladio, *The Four Books of Architecture* (republished 1965), Bk. II, p. 37.
103. J. Crook, 'Broomhall, Fife', *CL*, vol. CXLVII (29 January 1970), pp. 242–6.
104. Palladio, op. cit., Bk. II, pl. XXXVI.
105. Ware, op. cit., p. 407.
106. Cromarty House is built on the site of Cromarty Castle which was razed to the ground in 1772. *SA*, vol. XII, p. 258; F. Groome, *Ordnance Gazetteer of Scotland* (1894), vol. I, p. 309; J. Nightingale, 'The Threat to Cromarty', *CL*, vol. CLXII (11 August 1977), pp. 338–40.

It should be noted that Robert Adam prepared drawings for a church in Cromarty for George Ross of Cromarty, who subscribed to *Ruins of the Palace of the Emperor Diocletian at Spalatro in Dalmatia*. SM, vol. XLV, nos. 44–9.

Culloden House was erected after the death of John Forbes in 1772 by his son who in 1783 married an heiress. J. Mitchell, *Reminiscences of My Life in the Highlands* (1883), vol. I, p. 62; J. Burke, *A Visitation of the Seats and Arms* (1852), vol. II, p. 108.

CHAPTER SIX

'Beyond the ignorant present'

During thirty-four years of practice, after his return to England from Italy in 1758, Robert Adam was commissioned to produce over a hundred schemes for classical country-houses. Many were never executed; others were modifications to existing houses. It has not been previously noticed, however, that a third of all the schemes were for clients in Scotland. In the seventeen-sixties and seventies Scotland does not figure prominently in Robert Adam's practice. Within those decades he designed over fifty projects in England, half his output of classical country-houses, whereas in Scotland, out of ten commissions, four were built. After 1780 the difference in weighting north and south of the Border changes dramatically. England provided ten commissions: in Scotland there were twenty-six with more than half that number, compared to one solitary example in England, being designed in the short period between 1790 and the architect's death two years later.

In view of these figures it is surprising that Robert Adam's later classical houses in Scotland have been all too often ignored by scholars. Perhaps, though, there have been good reasons. Of the total number of thirty-six projects more than a third remained as paper schemes. Also the fates have not spared those that were built. Kirkdale in Kirkcudbrightshire was gutted internally by fire; Balbardie, near Bathgate, was sold to pay an eldest son's debts and a court case and subsequently demolished; others, such as Walkinshaw, on the outskirts of Glasgow, having been engulfed by urban expansion, have disappeared; some were demolished after the Second World War; some, such as Archerfield, remain as empty shells while Dunbar Castle became a military barracks in the mid-nineteenth century. Only half a dozen houses remain intact but usually with modifications. Balavil in Inverness-shire has later alterations and Letterfourie in Banffshire has plasterwork by another contemporary architect.[1] That leaves Newliston, West Lothian, as the sole example of an unaltered late classical house by Robert Adam although it has wings added by David Bryce in 1845.

The difficulties in evaluating the houses are further complicated by a lack of information. Apart from Archerfield and Dunbar Castle, there is a paucity of contemporary documentation. The printed sources are just as deficient. In the two volumes of Woolfe and Gandon's *Vitruvius Britannicus*, published in 1767 and 1771, only three of Robert Adam's country-houses are delineated but they are all in England; in the *New Vitruvius Britannicus* of 1802 there are two with Gosford House, East Lothian, being one. Clearly Adam was not held in the overriding esteem which his present fame would suggest. Not surprisingly, therefore, travellers in late eighteenth- and early nineteenth-century Scotland tended to pass by his houses which were, in any case, the homes of the gentry rather than the aristocratic palaces of England, although Heron in 1792 did record that 'the house of Kirkdale rises with a sort of magic effect. It is newly built, of grey granite quarried from the adjacent hills; the edifice stately and spacious; after a most elegant plan by Mr Adams [sic]; the granite beautifully polish'd.'[2] On the whole, though, the usual sources, such as the *Statistical Account* and its successor and the *Ordnance Gazetteer of Scotland* are uninformative. Even *Country Life* which, so far as country-houses are concerned, can be considered as the *omnium gatherum*, has little to offer. Fortunately, there are the Adam drawings.

In looking at the experimental architecture of Robert Adam it is all too easy to forget that he had been brought up as a Palladian and that he remained one at heart. Thus, when adding to the 'Body of the House' at AUCHENCRUIVE in Ayrshire, the conventional solution was quadrant corridors and kitchen and stable pavilions. The scheme was then smartened up by redrafting the entire layout. Straightening out the links gave a sense of greater size and of movement with a slight but subtle recession in the centre, whereas on the garden side a generously spaced bay was introduced to indicate what, in an earlier generation, would have been the saloon but which, having fallen in social status, was become the drawing-room entered off-centre thus blocking the through vista from the hall where the side position of the staircase was counter-balanced by a screen of columns.[3] The Auchencruive estate having been sold in 1764 to Richard Oswald, a wealthy merchant,[4] it was probably he who built the house, modifying the external treatment and omitting the stable pavilion as there was an existing stable court nearby. By 1766 he was ready to commission ceiling and chimney-piece designs.[5] For the hall Adam worked from a mid-century copy-book for the beam and panel ceiling[6] in which the divisions isolate the compartments of details, producing a static effect, whereas in the design for the drawing-room ceiling the geometry of circles is more open, diminishing the chunkiness of the antique details. Perhaps, however, the experimentation is best appreciated in the dining-room where the foliated wreaths of ornament have lost the curvaceous waywardness of their rococo precedents and where low-relief linearisation unifies the larger design compartments while holding apart the voids.

Oswald may also have built Cavens, Kirkcudbrightshire,[7] a boxy astylar villa of four storeys with a pyramidal roof, features which were to be re-used at Woodburn House, Midlothian, in 1792,[8] a date accounting for the dexterous planning and Greek Doric porch. While both designs may indicate Scottish economy in building high, they also demonstrate that the villa, if conceived as a single unequivocal block modelled on the occasional residences of the metropolitan cognoscenti, did not allow for the necessities of a permanent dwelling on a farm or estate. So, for Polton, Midlothian, in 1768[9] the lineaments of a villa were faithfully reproduced, including a tetrastyle pedimented frontispiece, but with the addition of Kentian single-bay wings containing in one the kitchen on the ground floor and in the opposing wing the eating-room with a combined library and drawing-room above. Although Champfleurie has the same characteristics in 1790,[10] the impact of height in the centre is lessened by pulling out the elevation so that, with domes over the wings and a semicircular bay in the rear, the composition becomes fluid. Adam usually preferred straight links between the units of accommodation as at JERVISTON in Lanarkshire in 1782[11] which

122 JERVISTON HOUSE, Lanarkshire

may have served as the prototype for Champfleurie and other villas. As Jerviston survived into the present century it can be seen that any hint of gauntness in the composition [122] was overcome by fine stonework and proportions notably on the pilastered entrance front which is an adaptation of Palladio's Villa Ragona[12] although his claim, that 'one may go every where under cover',[13] is not fulfilled at Jerviston since one had to go outside the house to reach the separate male and female privies in one of the meagre links [123]. As these and the adjacent courts served no essential domestic purposes that could not have been contained

123 JERVISTON HOUSE, Lanarkshire, ground-floor plan by Robert Adam

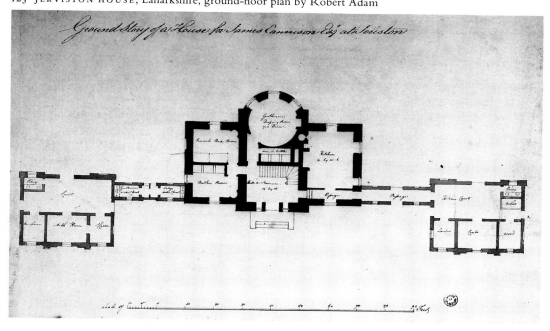

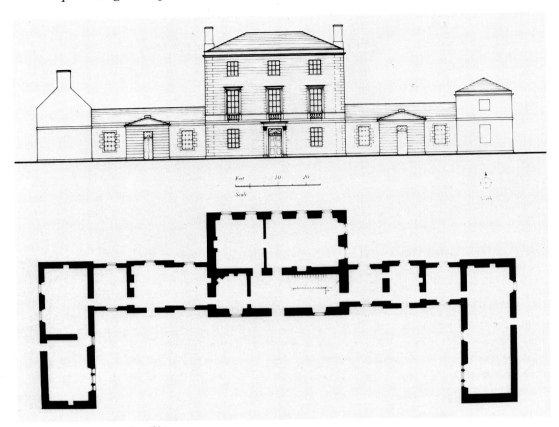

124 LETTERFOURIE, Banffshire

within the house, one can assume that they were designed to support and to replicate in miniature the central design element perhaps in response to Lord Kames's affirmation that 'the form of a building spread more upon the ground than raised in height, is always preferred for a dwelling-house'.[14]

In Edinburgh on 13 December 1791 the finishing touches were put to the drawings for Lint House[15] so that a month later Robert Adam 'Received a Draft from Mr Spreull in full of Plans. £21'.[16] Though the exterior followed to the letter the precept of Robert Morris, that 'Country Seats are generally divided into three Stories . . . as the Ground or Basement for Conveniency or Use, the State for Pleasure and Delight, and the Attick for Sleep and Retirement, or Study',[17] in response to changing fashion the two public rooms and study were at ground level leaving the finely detailed central window above to light nothing more than a closet. Deep links gave through communication from the centre to kitchen and bedroom wings beyond which Adam sketched in kitchen and stable courts three-quarters the area of the centre. However, it was only at Letterfourie, Banffshire [124], in 1773[18] that a stable was incorporated, creating a compact half H-plan at the front, although at the rear the fall in ground level and the need for a sub-basement allowed for a towering silhouette of loosely knit forms looming over the distant bounds of the sea-girt estate [125].

146

125 LETTERFOURIE, Banffshire

Most of Adam's Scottish clients tended to be either successful lawyers or merchants. Rather pushing, it seems, in their ways they would require substantial residences but without too many frills. William Douglas, a merchant in Glasgow, had interests in Kirkcudbrightshire where he founded the burgh of Castle Douglas and purchased the Newton Stewart estate for £7,500 in 1784.[19] Three years later he had commissioned designs for CASTLE STEWART.[20] The main block with hipped roof, rusticated basement and attached pedimented portico is in the mainstream of eighteenth-century villa design within which the recessed apsidal balconies on the rear elevation are a reinterpretation of the Palladian loggia while the trefoil spaces at the junction of the central block and the wings are a recurrent Adam device which he had discovered at Spalato and took to be Diocletian's bedroom. For an up-to-date source there was Ware who had laid down that, 'Where the proprietor has spirit, and the chosen spot allows of a due extent, the house should have a court before it, and a garden behind it.'[21] At Castle Stewart the court was to be U-shaped with the wings returned and containing a separate male and female servants' bedroom.

Of the same genre was Barholm or Balhazy, Kirkcudbrightshire, of 1788[22] for the servants were once again to be in the wings. As in most of the previous designs, the principal floor of the *corps de logis* has three rooms with a drawing-room to the left of the entrance and a dining-room to the right: behind the staircase the breakfast-room is no longer a circle but an octagon. The front elevation, with an attached distyle portico, instead of the more

147

common tetrastyle, is Palladio's Villino Giovanile improved.[23] While the same general features occur at Ninewells, Berwickshire, in 1790,[24] the planning is more stilted and less Cartesian since Adam seems to have been designing an addition and wings for an existing house, an exercise he had already gone through twenty years before when he wrote of his client's kinsman, the playwright and author of *Douglas*, 'I saw John Home yesterday. He is obliged to add to his Cottage and I have schemed 2 Wings for him to give the Conveniencys necessary for a Married Man!'[25]

It was not unusual for Adam to refurbish a scheme. When in September 1791 Adam 'Dined at Carmile with Mr Dunlop after Visiting Rosebank'[26] he may have substituted a rather pedestrian offering by the 'New Design' in 1792[27] with an entrance elevation which is blood brother to any number of villas, as descended from Palladio, in the engravings and reinterpretations of the early eighteenth century. What, however, makes Adam's designs of particular interest is that every now and again the eye is startled by a shift of emphasis. For example, Rosebank, as a composition, may be compared with Letterfourie of two decades earlier since the architectural episodes are similar. At Letterfourie these are integrated as a totality, a unitary composition; at Rosebank there are disparate geometric blocks,

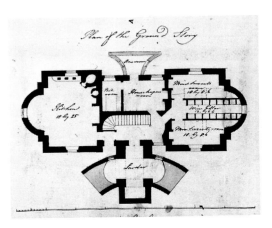

126 and 127 SUNNYSIDE (LIBERTON) HOUSE, Edinburgh, by Robert Adam

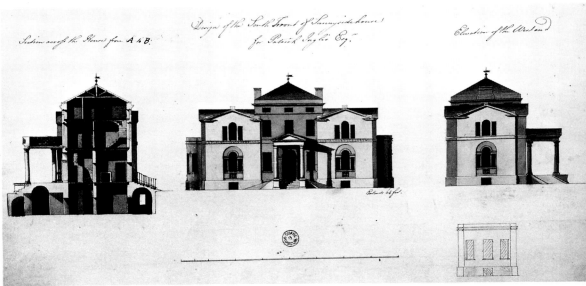

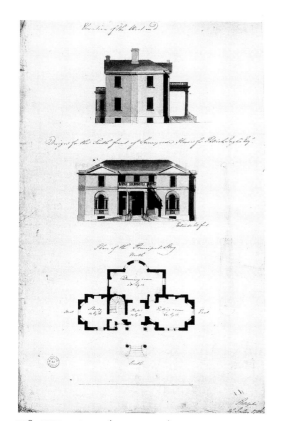

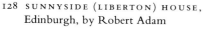

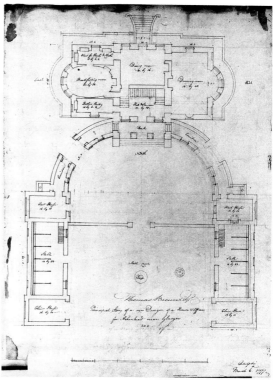

128 SUNNYSIDE (LIBERTON) HOUSE,
  Edinburgh, by Robert Adam

129 AITKENHEAD HOUSE, Glasgow,
  by Robert Adam

playing in loose conjunction, so that the separateness, the elemental identity of each is maintained. Internally, the diversification in the plan, reaching such a pitch of contrivance that no two areas are alike, creates explosive tensions as though the restraints imposed by operating within the discipline of a symmetrical casing would be blown asunder. One sees Robert Adam struggling to contain the planning components and their formulation in the alternative versions of SUNNYSIDE (now LIBERTON) HOUSE in 1785 and 1786.[28] Though the first scheme is portrayed in plan [126] as a rectangle with bowed ends, in volumetric terms [127] it is a series of vertical units pulling away from a taller core which, in the succeeding scheme, is reduced and swallowed up in an acceptable horizontality [128] even if the bland façade does hide the complicated, zonal interlocking achieved by Adam who, as a visitor to Sunnyside noted, had 'given so much foundation for producing variety in ye form of ye general plan'.[29] This variety found prophetic fulfilment in the achievement at Glencarse, Perthshire of separate and identifiable functional zones for business, family and public use.[30] Even if the time had not yet come for a relaxation of the inherited ordering of external volumes, one could acceptably ease the tensions by loosening the planning bonds, as witnessed in the proposed approach in 1777 to AITKENHEAD HOUSE, a suburban retreat in the leafy environs of Glasgow for a rich London doctor.[31]

Within the house [129] there is the customary trio of public rooms. Outside, there is a tetrastyle porch, extended on each side as a curved colonnade, terminated at either end by a coalhouse and a wash-house. At that point all the plans previously mentioned stopped. At Aitkenhead the forward movement is continued with stables. At other Adam houses, with the exception of Letterfourie, these were detached and at a distance from the house for, as Ware had written, 'The offices ... must be disposed where they shall be least observed.'[32] On the other hand, the practical-minded Mrs Grant of Laggan was surprised to find at Inveraray Castle 'that they should place the offices at such a distance as to require such roads'.[33] Perhaps economy dictated that house and stables should be joined at Aitkenhead, an arrangement adopted by other architects when plotting a great country-house. At Vanbrugh's last house, Seaton Delaval, the opposed stables provide the same elongated approach as at Aitkenhead. That architect was particularly admired by Adam for the quality of movement which Adam sought in his own work, considering it necessary to 'increase the scenery and add to the movement' even indoors.[34] Certainly, there is the feeling at Aitkenhead that the internal plan forms have been brought into the open air to lend drama to the site. Whether that was an accident of design or otherwise, Adam may subsequently have heeded the injunction of Sir Joshua Reynolds in his Thirteenth Discourse of 1786. 'It may not be amiss for the architect to take advantage sometimes of ... the use of accidents: to follow when they lead, and to improve upon them, rather than always to trust to a regular plan.'[35]

130 ARDKINGLAS, Argyll, proposed principal floor plan by Robert Adam

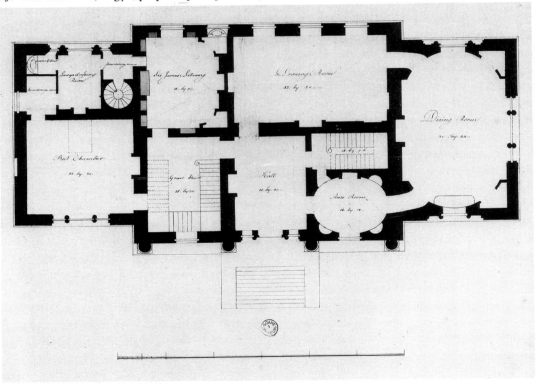

131 WALKINSHAW, Renfrewshire

In the later seventeen-eighties the courtyard theme became a dominant one with Adam and, if it was developed more with the castles, it does appear as early as 1773 in the scheme drawn up for ARDKINGLAS, set by the wooded shores of Loch Fyne.[36] By adding single-storey wings, for a family bedroom suite and large oval dining-room, Adam was able to loosen the planning in the three-bay centre [130]. Attached laterally to the semi-exposed basement was to be an elliptical kitchen court making the outline plan a reminder of Trajan's Forum. Or is that too positive a statement for what may be at best a subliminal relationship? At Balmakewan in Kincardineshire in 1789[37] a stable court was to be attached to one side of an otherwise conventional plan producing not only an asymmetrical layout but one where the extent of building would appear greater than it was especially on the entrance front. A more balanced scheme was proposed in the following year for Congalton, East Lothian,[38] where the sunk court was an extension of the domestic offices but retaining the stables as a detached block. That stables already existed at Newliston, as the sole fragment of the grand Palladian mansion projected by William Adam, may have governed his son's intention to extend the house into a domestic court,[39] an architectural development best summarised some years later by Uvedale Price. 'Much of the naked solitary appearance of houses, is owing to the practice of totally concealing, nay sometimes of burying all the offices underground ... in general, nothing contributes so much to give both variety and consequence to the principal building, as the accompaniment, and, as it were, the attendance of the inferior parts in their different gradations.'[40]

Although Ware preferred a rectangular plan for his 'principal building', he did concede that, 'A perfect square is a plan on which a very good house may always be constructed.' Not surprisingly, Adam used both plans in equal measure for his smaller classical country-houses with the exception of WALKINSHAW in Renfrewshire [131] where 'variety and

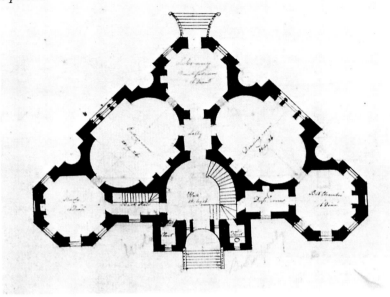

132 WALKINSHAW,
Renfrewshire,
principal floor plan by
Robert Adam

consequence' came from clustered towers and a triangular plan.[41] It is well known that Adam experimented with a variety of plan shapes, especially with his castles, which have attracted some attention from writers. Yet from the Renaissance onwards architects had wrestled intellectually with strict geometric shapes and that was no less true in the eighteenth century which saw a number of triangular designs being built. Nevertheless, they were novelties at best, as is Walkinshaw [132], though summing up an age of architectural experiment by the external revelation of the plan forms. Just as significant as the internal sequences of octagons and ovals is the appearance of towers, which are paired at the entrance, a leitmotif which Adam had introduced at Luton Hoo in Bedfordshire after 1771. Of course, the use of towers on a classical frontage could be justified by referring to Adam's own description of Diocletian's palace, where the entrances were guarded by towers which 'seem to have been intended for ornament, rather than for defence; ... we learn from Pliny, that towers were no uncommon ornament even in the villas of private persons'.[42]

Even including Walkinshaw, Adam's smaller classical houses are recognisably villas, a type which, apart from the precocious example of Mavisbank, had made few significant appearances until John Adam received a commission from Andrew Pringle, the Solicitor-General, later raised to the bench as Lord Alemoor. 'He made a beautiful villa at Haw[k]hill, near Edinburgh, in which he took much delight, and where he appeared to much advantage as a host in the company of a few easy friends. Everything bespoke elegance and propriety.'[43] Within a compass of 60 by 45 feet, the ground floor held an octagonal entrance hall, ingeniously giving access to a bedroom and study, and, at the rear, to a taller dining-room and saloon [133] in which was a set of ten landscape paintings.[44] As with Pope's villa, HAWKHILL was the home of a bachelor man of letters, one who, with a sense of detachment, could espouse friendship, learning, politics and the arts, a combination of hedonistic and humanistic values which became so marked among the literati in the second half of the

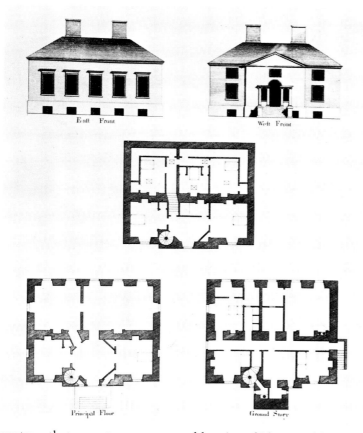

East Front   West Front

Principal Floor   Ground Story   133 HAWKHILL, Edinburgh

century that a contemporary could write of 'the republic of letters' in which the Greek and Roman classics 'were still universally read and admired',[45] so much so that another judge, the eccentric Lord Monboddo, 'enthusiastically partial to classical habits', garlanded his wine flasks and strewed his table with roses 'after the manner of Horace'.[46]

Although the descriptions of the villas of Horace and of Pliny would have been the inspiration of Hawkhill, its proximity to the capital and its restricted layout meant that as a *villa urbana* it 'was only a Country-House of Pleasure, built without any regard to the Villa Rustica, or any thing relating to Agriculture or Pasturage'.[47] It was indeed for that very reason that the 'frescoed villa' had been condemned by the poet Martial. 'Ought this to be called a farm, or a town-house away from town?'[48] And it was the luxurious suburban villa, divorced from the life-support system of the cultivated countryside, which prompted an outburst from Varro. 'Why your villa is plastered with paintings, not to speak of statues: while mine . . . has many a trace of the hoer and the shepherd.'[49] Such were the villas of the majority of Robert Adam's clients for they were not the elegant dilettanti sweeping into town in gilded coaches, to hand down legal sentences or manipulate politics, before going on to routs and balls. Though some were wealthy, the most part were country lairds whose income and status depended on the possession and the working of their land. By referring to William Adam's drawings for Haddo House,[50] it is seen that, below the grandeur of the piano nobile, a charter-room and counting-room are set side by side while there were stables for hunters, coach-horses and work-horses with the floor above reserved as a 'Victual Granary'. Nowhere is the idea of the country-house, as a self-supporting centre of economic

153

activity, rather than a rural retreat for self-indulgent pleasure, so neatly expressed. Although, by building on their lands, the lairds were following centuries of tradition, their atavism was bolstered by Augustan writers who saw the landowners as the inheritors of a classical tradition. 'For the wealthy Roman citizens did indulge their humour of Building more on their Estates, or out of Town, than in the City.'[51] Indeed, the most admired Roman poets had affected to despise city life, with its vicious wealth and corrupting vices, whereas, by contrast, 'not only is the tilling of the fields more ancient – it is more noble'.[52] Not only was the social superiority of hereditary landownership thereby acknowledged but it was reinforced by an interest in and the financial gains of the Agrarian Revolution for which again there was classical precedent since 'there remains ... one method of increasing one's substance that befits a man who is a gentleman and free-born, and this is found in agriculture'. In that pursuit 'the farmer, then, should build handsomely, but without letting building become his passion'.[53]

It would seem that the genesis of Adam's villas lay with Castell whose influential *Villas of the Ancients Illustrated* was published in 1728. 'A *Villa*, according to *Columella*, consisted of three Parts, viz. *Urbana*, *Rustica* and *Fructuaria*. The first of which was that Part of the House, set apart for the Master's Use; the Second was for the Cattle and Servants ... and the last consisted only of Repositories for Corn, Wine, Oyl, etc.'[54] Thus, behind the concept of the laird working his land, there seems to have been the notion of the *villa rustica* 'particularly with relation to the Farm-House, which in this Sort of Buildings, according to the more ancient Roman manner, was always join'd to the Master's House, or but very little remov'd from it'.[55] Yet, while it was acceptable for the residential block to have an urban style,[56] the gospel of Palladio laid down that 'plain and simple things are more suitable than those that are delicate',[57] so that 'Profuseness of Ornament, especially external, is carefully to be avoided',[58] while internally, according to Lord Kames, the friend of Adam, 'in dwelling houses that are too small for variety of contrivance, utility ought to prevail'.[59] With such a weight of tradition, it is scarcely surprising that the greater number of the villas are lacking in complicated shapes, both internally and externally, which, coupled with an almost complete absence of elaborate interior decoration, would accord with the clients' strong desire, even need, for economy. Yet listen to Pliny writing of his own villa near Laurentum. 'The house is large enough for my needs, but not expensive to keep up.'[60] The sentiment was echoed by Horace, the other Roman whose writings were the model for the civilised life of a cultured country gentleman.

> No gold or ivory gleams
> On panelled ceilings in my house; no marble beams
> Hewn on Hymettus press
> Great columns quarried from the Libyan wilderness;
> . . .
> My one dear Sabine farm is wealth enough and bliss.[61]

One wonders if such sentiments were in the mind of Roger Hogg of Newliston who, 'amongst other economical habits, used to dispose of his poultry, and in order to superintend the trade himself, he usually brought them to market in his carriage'.[62]

Such a man might pay grudgingly for the decoration of his hall and for a few chimney-pieces[63] but for no more, leaving the silk panels in the drawing-room to be worked by his wife.[64] If few of the clients for Adam's classical houses could afford or were interested in his decorative schemes, there was an exception at Sunnyside in 1788 where, though 'the plaisterers are at work in ye upper story', the dining-room and drawing-room were 'not to be touched till Mr Robert comes down in July' since the client, 'laying aside his more oeconomical Ideas has some little desire of having both as tasty as possible', having been to view James Playfair's nearby Melville Castle where 'there are little Gimcracks of variety of form going on in which he would not like Sunnyside to be deficient'.[65] Of course, Adam's decorations cost a lot of money so that the owner of ARCHERFIELD, wishing to refurbish the interiors, was charged £170:10:0, for 'my own time in Inventing, my Expences in Journeys etc. in the years 1789 and 1790', although Adam did deduct ten guineas 'As Mr Nisbet is not to execute the present dining room, or drawing room'. The former was to become the library with the existing ceiling cove lightened by lunettes, their ornaments repeated in panels set above the bookcases [134]. Adam also supplied 'a design for the present

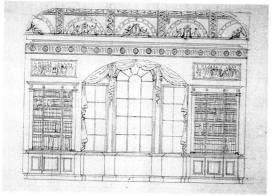

134 ARCHERFIELD, East Lothian, design for the library by Robert Adam

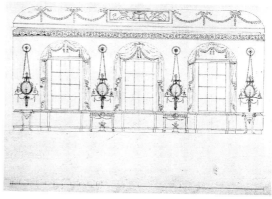

135 ARCHERFIELD, East Lothian, design for the drawing-room by Robert Adam

Coved Drawing room Cieling and manner of finishing the four sides of that Room [135] ... these drawings shall be compleatly shaded and Coloured in London'.[66] Such drawings show the 'Circular Anti-Room' with a dark-green skirting and light-cream walls with green being repeated as a background in the ornamental strings in the dome. Dark colours, blue against buff and purple against green, were to be used in limited zones in 'the New Eating room to the East', the biggest of the rooms.[67] Perhaps the client 'did look upon a tolerably large eating-room as one of the necessaries of life'.[68]

Like his father before him, Robert Adam had begun his career working on several large commissions such as Hopetoun House and Dumfries House. In Scotland, after his return from Italy in 1758, no such commissions came along until almost the end of his life, although there was one abortive scheme. In 1770 he spent two days at Buchanan Castle on Loch Lomondside discussing, no doubt, the proposed new mansion[69] which, though nine bays long and four storeys high, was a blown-up version of what would appear later and with more power in the condensed villa plans.

136 KIRKDALE HOUSE, Kirkcudbrightshire, by Robert Adam

137 KIRKDALE HOUSE, Kirkcudbrightshire

138 KIRKDALE HOUSE, Kirkcudbrightshire, section by Robert Adam

If built as drawn, the austere exterior of Buchanan would have been softened only by a few firm horizontal divisons so that in time it might have merited the criticism which Adam directed in 1789 at Yester. 'But those lines of flat ashlers running from end to end and from top to bottom of both fronts of the House, dazzle the Eye, and render them a mass of Confusion.'[70] In the same year, at Alva, while the broad divisions are those of Buchanan, Adam, in 'altering and decorating' the south front, introduced a giant order and entablature and crowded the three-part centre with incident.[71] To gain the same effects of 'light and shade', to use his own words,[72] Adam intended a giant order [136] at Kirkdale House, on

139 KIRKDALE HOUSE, Kirkcudbrightshire

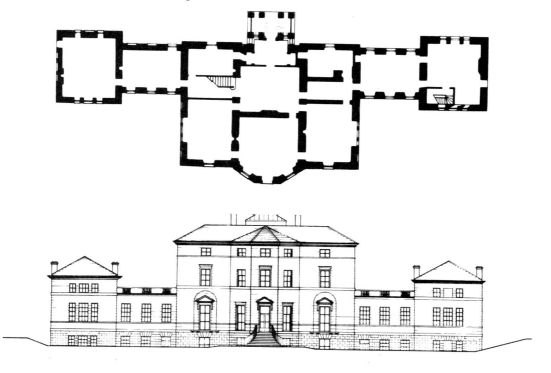

the Solway coast,[73] which, as a traveller noted in 1789, 'will cost no less than £25000. What cannot an Indian fortune do!'[74] Perhaps the nabob balked at the cost or perhaps the granite [137] was too unyielding for in the end all the architectural trimmings were omitted [138] so that, to reduce the lumpishness of the centre, the middle of the sea front was canted, which was a gain in the prospect from the house of the expansive bay [139].

Such was the local fame of the granite that 'Admiral Stewart also got all the principal stone here for Glasserton House which he carried across the bay in boats',[75] although the finished mansion, replacing his grandfather's, was modified in elevation. Adam had designed a half H-plan but, to counter the forceful thrust of the short wings, he proposed a centre where the stacked columnar screens would be concluded with a thermal window.[76] Omit all that, and though certain classical allusions are lost, the plainer composition gains a neo-classical strength, since the ends become dominant and, as the centre recedes, so the entrance is diminished. It is the same reductive process at Glencarse with a design, conceived not so much as volumes as in separate units, where the outer edges, the wings with their tetrastyle frontages, matter most leaving a friable centre pinned down by a blocking course.[77] This fractured composition, typical of Burlingtonian Palladianism, was repeated at BALAVIL, Inverness-shire, the home of 'Ossian' Macpherson who, having made a fortune in India, in 1788 had 'bought three small estates within these two years, given a ball to the ladies, and made other exhibitions of wealth and liberality'.[78] Overlooking the Great North Road from a bluff on the hillside, the house, though seven bays long, was only one room deep. By doubling the ground area to the north, one could provide new domestic offices while retaining part of the south frontage as the owner's study and bedroom. This was the show front, to be marked off by a giant order bearing an attic storey. However, with a steep declivity in the foreground it was sensible, if the giant order was to have visual impact, to lift it above the ground storey using a reduced number of pilasters to frame up the ends. Despite the intention to have a three-storey block, Adam did a remarkable thing by omitting the top floor in the centre so that the end bays rose free, like the pyramid-capped towers of Croome Court, where Adam had been employed thirty years before.[79] And perhaps older memories were stirring since the bases, pilasters and architraves, pieced together as a skeletal frame, are characteristic of Serlio. Yet, remove the linear armature from the north elevation and the impact is the solid geometry of neo-classicism to be repeated [140] at Dunbar Castle[80] for which Adam received 'to accot. of plans and surveying £52:10:0' in May 1791.[81]

140 DUNBAR CASTLE, East Lothian, by Robert Adam

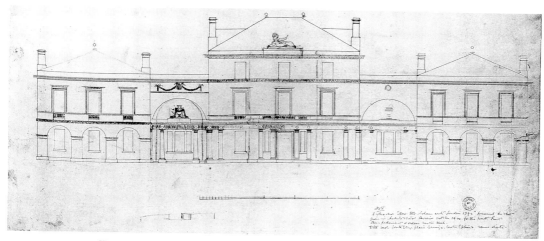

141 BALBARDIE, West Lothian, by Robert Adam

As Adam turned, in the sere years, to the tower-houses of Scotland as the inspiration for his own castles, in the late classical mansions there is a welling up of Palladianism as though, like all old people, the architect found that the distant rather than the recent past held greater clarity and significant meaning. Balbardie in West Lothian, described disapprovingly by a minister as 'a shewy house, Mr Marjoribanks new built',[82] if stripped of its graceful swags and paterae, becomes a boxy villa, loosely connected to lateral wings, though sturdy arches, blind recesses and the filtering of planes into one another [141] anticipate an architecture that Adam would not live to see.[83]

In his last years, Adam had on hand a number of public and domestic works in the Lothians which, besides Balbardie, included Newliston [142], Archerfield, Dunbar Castle and GOSFORD HOUSE. The 7th Earl of Wemyss had purchased the Gosford estate in 1784. The land was barren and treeless; the house was old.[84] Doubtless the new owner would

142 NEWLISTON, West Lothian

159

143 GOSFORD HOUSE, East Lothian
144 GOSFORD HOUSE, East Lothian, principal floor plan

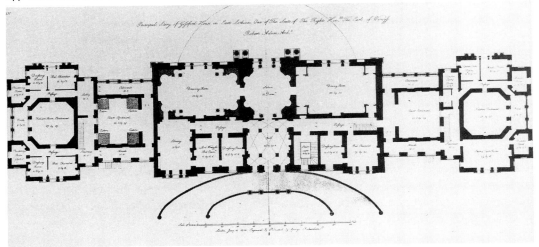

have agreed with Mr Rushworth in *Mansfield Park* that, 'I never saw a place that wanted so much improvement in my life.'[85] Still, it was not until 1790 that Robert Adam was called upon to produce plans for a new house[86] because, so the story goes, the earl was tired of travelling the six miles from Amisfield, a maternal inheritance, to the shore of the Firth of Forth to play golf.

Lady Louisa Stuart commented on the design of Gosford: 'There is a *corps de logis* and two pavilions all with domes, so at a distance, it looks like three great ovens, but the front is really a very pretty one. They say the plan is absurd. Three rooms in the middle of fifty feet long, each lighted with one huge Venetian window and unconnected with the rest.'[87] The windows [143] were to light a celebrated collection of pictures housed, in what was, in effect, a gallery, along the west or seaward front, top lit by a dome over the saloon [144]. Although domes had appeared on some centrally planned villas and were much used for garden buildings, so far as the great country-house is concerned, they were a rare external feature appearing at Vanbrugh's Castle Howard and at Kedleston in which Adam recreated

160

the main apartments of the Emperor Diocletian's palace at Spalato. Clerk of Eldin described Gosford as 'a magnificent Palace'[88] and indeed it was fulfilling, as it did, Sir John Clerk's criteria of sixty years before,

> Where airy Logios, stately Porticos
> High tow'ring Cupola's, bold Pediments
> Are Scattered round, and Skillfully disposd.[89]

The location of Gosford House, by the sullen waters of the Forth, must have forcibly reminded Adam of the imperial palace, which he had measured, by the shores of the Adriatic and perhaps, too, of the ordinance of Columella that, 'A villa is always properly placed when it overlooks the sea and receives the shock of the waves and is sprinkled with their spray; yet never on the shore but not a little distance removed from the edge of the water.'[90] Thus, the sea front of Gosford is not only the more harmonic of the two main elevations but it has arcades and a Palladian window in each pavilion. These elements are found at Spalato where, on the seaward side, the 'Crypto-Porticus', as Adam called it, 'like our modern galleries, was probably adorned with pictures, statues and bas-reliefs'[91] and the Roman theme was further demonstrated by placing a cold bath in the south wing with a hot one positioned between a heating-room and a bedroom as described by Pliny in his villa at Tifernum.[92] Perhaps it was not only Lord Monboddo who 'anointed his body with oil, after the manner of the ancients'.[93]

The main block was mostly taken up by the gallery for which Isaac Ware had laid it down that, 'The rule is universal, that if only one be required, it must be in the centre of the house, either in the fore or back front.'[94] The gallery at Gosford was approached through a hall, roofed with a Roman groin vault, with the centre filled by the saloon as the mid-point of a triple sequence of rooms which Adam had introduced previously at Newby Hall in Yorkshire. At Gosford, the saloon was modelled on the *vestibulum* at Spalato and a similar apartment appears at Archerfield where, locked in the body of the house, it becomes a tribune. That it did not appear in other Adam works was because, as Ware had explained, 'The antients ... knew the capacity and beauty of a circular figure therefore ... they employed it to the noblest purposes.'[95] On either side, the dining-room and drawing-room were each of the same dimensions, making a vista of 136 feet in all, though the former, with its decorated groin vault, was more severe whereas the drawing-room was a giddy exercise of undulating walls and reflective glass beneath an oval dome, stabilised at the corners by four marble columns so that the inside finishing must have been 'splendid yet pure, rich yet light', words originally applied to the interior of Kedleston,[96] the only English work to stand comparison with Gosford since both, in their planning, were directly inspired and modelled on the maritime palace of a Roman emperor. Gosford, 'one of the last and favourite works' of Adam,[97] even when shorn of its wings,[98] so that it stood like one of Rome's basilicas, was as instructive as the Adam villas to those enthused by the *gravitas* of Rome since, in the words of Sir Joshua Reynolds, 'The mind is to be transported ... beyond the ignorant present, to ages past.'[99]

Notes to Chapter 6

1. The drawing-room ceiling at Letterfourie may have been designed by John Baxter, junior who worked nearby at Gordon Castle from 1769 to 1782. J. Macaulay, *The Gothic Revival, 1745–1845* (1975), pp. 158–9.

2. R. Heron, *Observations Made in a Journey through the Western Counties of Scotland; in the Autumn of 1792* (1793), vol. II, p. 242.

3. SM, vol. XLIV, nos. 60–5.

4. A. Carlyle, *Anecdotes and Characters of the Times* (1973), pp. 45, 285; J. Burke, *A Visitation of the Seats and Arms* (1852), vol. I, p. 121; A. Oswald, 'Auchencruive, Ayrshire', *CL*, vol. LXXII (17 December 1932), pp. 690–5.

5. SM, vol. XI, nos. 219–23.

6. W. and J. Halfpenny, R. Morris and T. Lightoler, *The Modern Builder's Assistant* (republished 1971), pl. 79.

7. *NSA*, vol. IV, pp. 238–9. SM, vol. XLIV, nos. 39–44.

8. SM, vol. XXX, nos. 97–102.

9. SM, vol. XLVI, no. 55.

10. SM, vol. XXXIV, nos. 69, 70.

11. SM, vol. XLII, nos. 42–7.

12 A. Palladio, *The Four Books of Architecture* (republished 1965), pl. XL.

13. Ibid., Bk. II, p. 51.

14. Lord Kames, *Elements of Criticism* (1762), vol. III, p. 324.

15. SM, vol. XXXI, nos. 91–6.

16. Miscellaneous account book of Robert Adam, 1791, SRO, GD18/4968. M. Sanderson, 'Robert Adam's Last Visit to Scotland, 1791', *Architectural History*, vol. 25 (1982), pp. 35–46.

17. R. Morris, *An Essay in Defence of Ancient Architecture* (republished 1971), p. 76.

18. A keystone on the south front is dated 1773, SM, vol. XLV, nos. 90–3.

19. P. McKerlie, *History of the Lands and their Owners in Galloway* (1870–9), vol. I, p. 317; F. Groome, *Ordnance Gazetteer of Scotland* (1894), vol. V, p. 113.

20. SM, vol. XXXIV, nos. 39–45; vol. XXXVI, nos. 94–8.

21. I. Ware, *The Complete Body of Architecture* (1756), p. 322.

22. *NSA*, vol. IV, pp. 334–5. SM, vol. XXX, pp. 112–18.
    Robert Adam's scheme for Barholm is identical in its essential part to an earlier scheme by 'Adams Archts.' *VS*, pl. 94.

23. R. Ceves, *I Modelli della Mostra del Palladio* (1976), pp. 35–6.

24. SM, vol. XXXVI, nos. 109–13.

25. Robert Adam to Baron Mure of Caldwell, Edinburgh, 5 November 1770, NLS, MS 4945, f. 58.
    John Home's house was Kilduff, East Lothian. It has been demolished. A. Bolton, *The Architecture of Robert and James Adam* (1922), vol. I, p. 116.

26. Supra, n. 15.

27. SM, vol. XXXIX, nos. 46–52.

28. SM, vol. XLVI, nos. 13, 14; vol. XLVIII, nos. 90–4. A. Rowan, 'Sunnyside and Rosebank, Suburban Villas by the Adam Brothers', *AA Files*, no. 4 (1983), pp. 29–39.

29. J. Clerk of Eldin to Miss Margaret Adam, Edinburgh, 2 June 1788, SRO, GD18/5486/17.

30. SM, vol. XXXVI, no. 107.

31. J. Maclehose, *Old Country Houses of the Old Glasgow Gentry* (1878). SM. vol. XLII, nos. 20–5.

32. Supra, n. 20.

33. A. Grant of Laggan, *Letters from the Mountains* (1845), vol. I, p. 19.

34. R. and J. Adam, *The Works in Architecture* (1975), p. 48.

35. J. Reynolds, *Discourses on Art* (1969), pp. 212–13.

36. SM, vol. XLV, nos. 1–4.

37. SM, vol. XXXI, nos. 81–90.

38. SM, vol. XLV, nos. 81–5.
39. *NSA*, vol. I, p. 131; Burke, op. cit., vol. II, p. 119; Groome, op cit., vol. V, p. 110; J. Small, *Castles and Mansions of the Lothians* (1883), vol. II; Bolton, op. cit., vol. II, pp. 284–5; C. McWilliam, *Lothian* (1978), pp. 355–7; A. Bolton, 'Newliston, West Lothian', *CL*, vol. XXXIX (26 February 1916), pp. 270–7. SM, vol. XXXII, nos. 67–76.
40. U. Price, *Essays on the Picturesque* (republished 1971), vol. II, p. 180.
41. *NSA*, vol. VIII, p. 19. SM, vol. XXXI, nos. 56–62.
42. R. Adam, *Ruins of the Palace of the Emperor Diocletian at Spalatro in Dalmatia* (1764), p. 17.
43. A. Allardyce, *Scotland and Scotsmen in the Eighteenth Century* (1888), vol. I, p. 326, n. 1; J. Simpson, 'Lord Alemoor's Villa at Hawkhill', *Bulletin of the Scottish Georgian Society*, vol. I (1972), pp. 2–9.
   In 1745 the Duke of Cumberland considered that Belle-mont, on the outskirts of Edinburgh, was the handsomest villa he had met with north of the Tweed. Belle-mont was rebuilt by W. H. Playfair in 1828. A. Campbell, *A Journey from Edinburgh through Parts of North Britain* (1811), vol. I, p. 6.
   William Adam had constructed the small villa, Hamilton-House at Fala in Midlothian. *VS*, pl. 121. It has been demolished. Perhaps the most distinguished of the early villas was John Adam's North Merchiston.
44. *VS*, pl. 123.
45. Allardyce, op. cit., vol. I, pp. 2, 7.
46. W. Knight, *Lord Monboddo and Some of His Contemporaries* (1900), p. 17.
47. R. Castell, *The Villas of the Ancients Illustrated* (1728), p. 1, n. (a).
48. Martial, *Epigrams*, vol. I (1927), p. 197; W. McClung, *The Country House in English Renaissance Poetry* (1977), p. 14.
49. M. Varro, *On Agriculture* (1934), p. 431; McClung, op. cit., p. 13.
50. *VS*, pl. 54.
51. G. Leoni, *The Architecture of A. Palladio* (1742), p. 96.
52. Varro, op. cit., p. 425.
53. Columella, *On Agriculture* (1941), vol. I, pp. 9, 57.
54. Castell, ibid.
55. Ibid., preface.
56. Columella, op. cit., p. 65.
57. Palladio, op. cit., Bk. II, p. 53.
58. R. Morris, *Rural Architecture* (republished 1971), introduction.
59. Kames, op. cit., vol. II, p. 322.
60. *The Letters of the Younger Pliny* (1974), p. 75.
61. *The Odes of Horace* (1976), p. 127.
62. J. Kay, *A Series of Original Portraits and Caricature Etchings* (1877), vol. I, p. 45.
63. SM, vol. V, no. 86 and vol. XXXII, nos. 185, 195, 218.
64. Bolton, op. cit., p. 276.
65. Supra, n. 28.
66. 'William Nisbet Esquire to Robt. Adam. September 25th 1790', SRO, GD6/1644. As the interiors of Archerfield have been gutted it is now impossible to say what work was executed.
67. SM, vol. XXVII, nos. 1–27.
68. J. Austen, *Northanger Abbey* (1974), p. 171.
69. Supra, n. 24.
   Although successive Dukes of Montrose contemplated building a new seat at Buchanan nothing came of the schemes until after a fire in 1850. William Adam was paid ten guineas in 1731, a further twenty-five guineas in 1743 'for a Plan and Estimate made by him Ao 1741' and in 1745 payment was made 'for carrying in to Edb. the large plan of Buchanan to Mr Adams Architect in order to his making out, a new plan for a house and policy at Buchanan'. SRO, GD220/6/13, pp. 1, 6, 10; /32, p. 681; /33, pp. 791, 794, 826.
70. Robert Adam to Professor Dalziel, London, 24 March 1789, NLS, MS 14829, f. 19.
71. SM, vol. XXXIV, nos. 57–63.

72. Adam, op. cit., p. 53.

73. SM, vol. XXXV, nos. 32–40.

74. 'A Travelling Journal' (1789), NLS, MS 1080, f. 32. *SA*, vol. XV, p. 553; *NSA*, vol. IV, p. 334; Groome, op. cit., vol. IV, p. 426.

75. *SA*, ibid.; Burke, op. cit., vol. II, p. 91; *Jones' Views of the Seats, Castles, Mansions.*

76. SM, vol. XLV, nos. 63–9; vol. XLVI, nos. 97–9.

77. SM, vol. XXXVI, nos. 101–8.

78. Grant of Laggan, op. cit., vol. I, pp. 236, 286; Allardyce, op. cit., vol. I, p. 553; *NSA*, vol. XIV, p. 70.

79. SM, vol. XXX, nos. 63–76. J. Fleming, 'Balavil House, Inverness-shire', *The Country Seat* (1970), pp. 178–80.

80. SM, vol. XLVIII, nos. 49–56.
    Lord Lauderdale's house at Dunbar which was possibly late seventeenth century, judging by the ground plan, was remodelled and enlarged by Adam. His earliest design is dated 31 March 1790 but the north elevation was drawn in October 1792. After Robert's death, earlier that year, James Adam travelled to Scotland to inspect the works on hand including Dunbar Castle. SRO, GD18/4965.
    SA, vol. V, p. 476; J. Miller, *The History of Dunbar* (1830), p. 235; Groome, op. cit., vol. II, p. 403; J. Irvine, *Parties and Pleasures* (1957), p. 94.

81. Supra, n. 15.

82. Diary entry for 27 September 1795 by the Revd J. Hastie, minister of Edrom, Berwickshire. Inf. ex W. L. Marjoribanks of that Ilk. Robert Adam noted on 30 May 1791, 'Went to Mr Marjoribanks at Balairdy near Bathgate' and he returned there in August. A later entry reads, 'Novr. 25th Received from Mr. Marjoribanks to Accot. £31:10:0.' Supra, n. 15.
    T. Marwick, 'Balbardie House and Robert Adam', *AR*, vol. XLVIII (1920), pp. 81–5.

83. SM, vol. XXXII, nos. 87–9. The working drawing for the north elevation was drawn out in Edinburgh in May 1793. Another drawing is in the possession of Sir James Marjoribanks.

84. 'Gosford House, East Lothian', *CL*, vol. XXX (2 September 1911), pp. 342–8; J. Hunt, 'Gosford, East Lothian', *CL*, vol. CL (21 October and 4 November 1971), pp. 1048–50 and 1200–2; Small, op. cit., vol. I; A. Bolton, *The Architecture of Robert and James Adam*, vol. II, p. 196.

85. J. Austen, *Mansfield Park* (1972), p. 40.

86. Although there are no drawings for Gosford House in the Soane Museum, plans and elevations were illustrated by G. Richardson, *New Vitruvius Britannicus* (1802), pls. 43–50.
    Drawings at Gosford House include a plan of the principal floor, sections and two elevations for the wings engrossed, 'Edinr. 2d. July 1791'. In his account book on 6 August Adam itemised, 'To expense at laying the foundation stone of Gosford on Thursday the 4th.' Supra, n. 15.

87. 'Gosford House, East Lothian.' Supra, n. 84.

88. J. Clerk of Eldin, 'Life of Robert Adam', SRO, GD18/4981.

89. Sir John Clerk of Penicuik, 'The Country Seat', f. 11. SRO, GD18/4404/1.

90. Columella, op. cit., p. 61.

91. Adam, op. cit., p. 9.

92. *The Letters of the Younger Pliny*, p. 141.

93. Allardyce, op. cit., vol. I, p. 354; Knight, op. cit., p. 254.

95. Ware, op. cit., p. 333.

95. Ibid., p. 302.

96. A memoir by John Clerk of Eldin, SRO, GD18/4982.

97. Richardson, op. cit., p. 14.

98. The builder of Gosford House was the 7th Earl of Wemyss who died in 1808. His grandson, the 8th Earl, demolished the wings to improve the sea view from old Gosford House, and so the house remained until the 10th Earl succeeded in 1883 when he commissioned William Young of London, the architect of Glasgow's City Chambers, to replace the wings and courtyards. Supra, n. 84.

99. Reynolds, op. cit., p. 207.

164

CHAPTER SEVEN

'The language, though plain, was strong and unaffected'

'The Union with England carried many of our nobility and gentry to London ... From the Union many of our younger sons became merchants and went abroad. It likewise became the fashion for our young men of fortune to study for some years in Holland, after which to make a tour throw France.'[1] Earlier, Holland had been a place of refuge for opponents of the Catholic King James VII. One such was the 1st Earl of Marchmont whose son studied at the University of Utrecht when a boy. Some thirty-five years later he returned to the Low Countries as ambassador at the protracted Congress of Cambrai where, in the summer of 1724, he succeeded to the earldom.[2] In the New Year he had written home to his brother-in-law, Sir James Hall, 'To show you that my thoughts are all homeward I have been thinking and taking advice about the house at Red-breas', the family castle in Berwickshire. 'To make it a house then, the Steeple, Closets upon the Roof, great Stairs and Balasters upon the Leads and other great weights must be taken quite away.' By partly infilling the ground storey 'with Rubbish or Gravel for to make the Principal Story wholesome and habitable' one would have 'a magnificent Apartment 19 or 20 feet high and save a good deal of money'. Sir James was to consult 'Ld. Hopeton's Architect [William Adam] who no doubt is the best in Scotland' and have a survey made of the castle for despatch to London to Lord Binning,[3] another Berwickshire landowner, who would 'pray advise with Mr Campbell and Mr Gibbs ... and get Plans from them. I'll do the same here and if I can at Paris [perhaps from Lord Mar] and will take the cheapest and best.' Even so Lord Marchmont already had 'a draught and a notion of my own'[4] and a month later sent a plan to Lord Binning with the request that he forward a copy to Sir James Hall.[5]

When William Adam's proposals reached Cambrai in late summer they were well received although 'the design is great, especially that of the Offices, and would cost more money than I would desire to lay out that way'. So Adam was asked to provide two estimates, one for a new house and a second calculated to modernise the castle for, 'What is necessary must be preferred to what is only convenient and both, in my opinion, to what is only magnificent.'[6] Lord Marchmont next sent 'another Plan as the House stands, with little or no addition, at present only taking away the first floor that was to be done by the other Plan'.[7] This Adam accepted although, since the north wall had to be taken down, he projected that front by 12 feet which gave 'a Compleit Appartment on each Side' which 'compleits the State of the first floor and affords two Ante Chambers or waiting rooms for Serts. in the most propper places'.[8] Even that scheme seems to have come to naught since, apart from some minor work,[9] Lord Marchmont determined that 'to go to the expence of

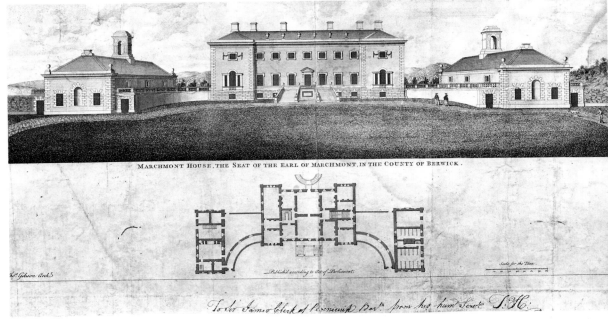

MARCHMONT HOUSE, THE SEAT OF THE EARL OF MARCHMONT, IN THE COUNTY OF BERWICK.

145 MARCHMONT HOUSE, Berwickshire

5 or 6000£ for a House in the Country I think not adviseable',[10] so leaving it to his son to build.

The 3rd Earl of Marchmont succeeded his father in 1740 but did not undertake a new house until a decade later when his own son was born. Despite the sale of his mother's estate in Ayrshire, funds may have been limited since the work is supposed to have extended over ten years.[11] As the plasterwork began in 1753[12] a neighbour could write three years later that, 'The saloon is a grand room, and finished in high and good taste. The fine furniture of Lady Marchmont's room was covered with paper and the library locked up, which were great wants.'[13] Externally, the finish was less fine with rubble walling rather than costly dressed ashlar. When asked why, Lord Marchmont retorted, 'Because I intend to live in the inside of my house and not on the outside.'[14]

Like many others, Pope thought highly of the 3rd Earl, once reporting that Lord Chesterfield 'tells me, your Lordship is got ahead of all the gardening Lords; that you have distanced Lord Burlington and Lord Cobham, in the true scientific post; but he is studying after you, and has here lying before him those Thesauruses from which, he affirms, you draw all your knowledge, Millers Dictionaries; but I informed him better, and told him, your chief lights were from Johannes Serlius.'[15] Perhaps then, in designing Marchmont House, what was needed was not so much an architect as a draughtsman and clerk of works. He was Thomas Gibson, who is credited on a rare engraving of the house [145] as being the architect[16] and whose name first appears in Lord Marchmont's accounts in November 1750 and thereafter intermittently[17] and of whom a correspondent wrote in September 1751, 'I saw Mr Gibson this day who can walk but not so firmly as formerly.'[18]

'Drink Money at laying the Foundation of the House, £3:3:0' was paid on 13 June 1750 and by the autumn there was work to be done 'pulling down and redding out Corner of old house'.[19] As Lord Marchmont wrote to his wife, 'The foundation of the House goes on

166

146 AMISFIELD, East Lothian

very well, the ground extremely good, the walls well laid and very broadly founded, and the mortar as good as can be ... So that I hope, beside the lodging my Betty has in my heart to place her in the best house in Britain.'[20] In the next season, with the earl in London, instructions were sent to James Pringle of Bowland, a landowner and principal clerk of the Session, who acted in a supervisory capacity. Early in the spring the earl was looking ahead to the new season's operations. 'You must by all means take care to gett the Sclates home this Summer, a thing done is not to do'; lime was to be fetched, 'whilst the Berwick kilns will furnish it', and timber and stone; and the accounts were to be scrutinised including those from the masons, especially 'the measure of their work in the foundations which being under ground no stranger can determine'.[21] A week later Lord Marchmont was lifting his thoughts higher. 'We want here the dimensions of the several marble chimnies at Redbraes, that of the openings and the breadth of the marble in a little sketch, that in drawing the Sections for finishing the rooms, the chimnies may be placed in the rooms they will best suit, and the finishing may be adapted to the chimnies respectively. I fancy some of the Masons at their leisure hours may be able to do it.

'I am enquiring here into the prices of hinges, you must try also, into the prices they can be had at, in Scotland, that I may see whether it will be best to gett them here.'[22] Next he was concerned about 'the form of the Doors in any of the Drawings of the Sections',[23] which had been 'Sent down this winter', all of which 'should be given in a portefeuille large enough to hold 'em to the Masons ... And all the former Drawings ... which are

167

now out of use, having been alter'd and might puzzle the Masons, must be deliver'd to you.'[24] Such were the trials of building from a distance!

In view of the friendship with Lord Burlington, it is no surprise that Marchmont House was a model of Burlingtonian Palladianism from 'the broacht work of the Basement', the supply of which had caused Lord Marchmont some anxiety,[25] to the flat unaccentuated centre and the Venetian window in each projecting end bay. The Villa Mocenigo[26] was the inspiration for the setting of offices and centre locked in parallel by closed quadrants with the internal planning and elevations cribbed from Houghton Hall as it appeared in the third volume of *Vitruvius Britannicus*, to which the 2nd Earl had subscribed in 1725,[27] perhaps lending weight to the statement that Marchmont House was planned by both him and his son.[28]

Marchmont was the first of a trio of large country-houses which heralded the Indian summer of Palladianism in mid-eighteenth-century Scotland. The second was AMISFIELD, East Lothian, built to the design of Isaac Ware[29] by John Baxter between 1752 and 1758[30] so that Bishop Pococke went out of his way to view 'a large house of red freestone, with a Paladian Ionick logis on the first floor of the grand front, a bow window in the middle of each side. There is a fine galery on the second floor.'[31] Though the published elevation [146] shows a conventional block, composed of such familiar elements as the triple-arched entrance, some variations in execution altered subtly the overall proportions indicating an easing of the rigours of the Palladian canon. Most notably the canted side bays reinforced the vertical accents of the loggia which, though meant to dominate the approach, failed to do so since the exposed basement of channelled masonry bearing down on rustic piers was so overwhelming that the elevation read as two equal parts and not as triple horizontal layers. To judge by the height and the chance comment of a visitor[32] the basement [147] was used for family living which must have meant, as Lord Fife would write of Duff House,

147 AMISFIELD, East Lothian, basement plan

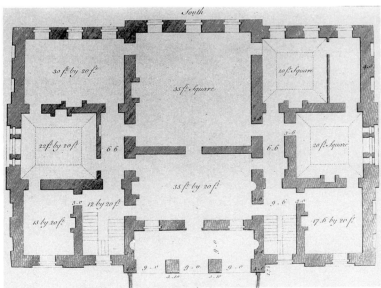

148 PENICUIK HOUSE, Midlothian, after the fire in 1899

that, 'Untill the Pavilions are built, I shall always be pinch'd for Room for the family.'[33]
At Amisfield such necessary appendages were later added[34] for, according to Sir John Clerk,

> These usefull wings supply her daily wants
> And ease the Burden of Domestick Cares.[35]

On inheriting PENICUIK in 1722 Sir John had thought 'to have made it a very fine
Uniform house but I found that the old house Was to be pull'd down or that Very little
could stand of it so I contented myself with what was done ... It has many Conveniences
and looks better in my opinion in its Antique figure than if it was all new built.'[36] Such
was the sentiment of the antiquary. Although his son added a few rooms and a library in
1752,[37] within a decade he was founding a new family seat [148] using John Baxter, his

149 PENICUIK HOUSE, Midlothian, design for the principal floor plan by Sir James Clerk of Penicuik

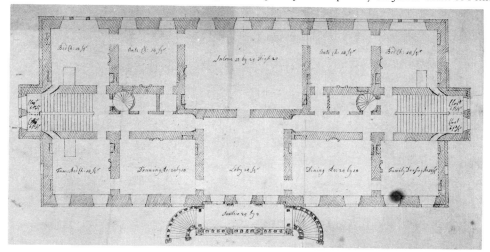

father's mason at Mavisbank, not only as builder but as amanuensis for, like his father, Sir James was governed by architecture, inventing scratchy designs [149] which were then worked up by the professional with rendering, skiagraphy and those fiddly bits and pieces which so dismay the impatient amateur.[38] Thus in January 1761 Baxter was paid four guineas 'for Copying my draughts and making estimates of the same'. Outside advice was also sought for in June Sir James's journal of expense included, 'To Mr Adams A Consultation. £5:5:0', an association which was continued a year later when 'Mr Adam Architect' (probably John) was paid £230:8:3 for timber.[39]

Some months before Robert Adam, cock-a-hoop with the acclaim of the London beau monde, had poured cold water over the proposals for Penicuik using a freedom of expression which would have astonished his father. 'I believe that it is the only house in the world in which there are six cube rooms upon a floor. It is impossible not to laugh.' He then gave a rare insight into how the plan of a country-house should be organised. 'In France where Men and Women live always together and their pleasures are never separate, the Dining room and Drawing room must be both large and are better next one another . . . . But in England, and more so in Scotland, where Men's pleasures in Women consist chiefly in Matters of fact . . . it is proper that the Dining room should be a capital good room particularly in the Country and that it should not be next any room in which there is or can be any company. The Drinking and the conversation after dinner make this absolutely necessary . . . In the Country there ought to be another room upon the principal floor which I call a loitering room and it ought to be a library and large. There people spend their time with pleasure who neither like to drink or be with the Ladies. There they may take up one book and then another and read a page of each; others may like the children look at a picture book or read the title page and afterwards with importance talk of the book and the goodness of the adition [sic].' Other points of criticism were the dimensions of the drawing-room and dining-room.[40]

The riposte from Sir James was lengthy. He refuted the contiguity of the chief public rooms. 'Even in France this must be inconvenient as the fracas, necessarily occasioned by servants for several hours every day in the Dining room must be very inconvenient to the inhabitants of the Drawing room.' There could be no charge about the smallness of the dining-room which would be in the saloon. 'Our Usual Residence will be in the Parlour . . . in our Cold Climate a good fire cannot keep a larger room in a tolerable degree of heat.' Above the saloon was the library 'where the free air and prospect from the windows sufficiently apologise for going up one pair of Stairs to it, which I hope too will have the good effect of freeing it, from turning out to be the loitering resort of the whole of the family.

'Now as to the Portico. It serves as a retreat from the inclemency of the weather, where a dry and clean walk with fresh air may be had in a bad day, it likewise prevents the rain and the snow from beating into your house by the principal door.'[41]

At first, Sir James had contemplated retaining much of the old house, especially the new portions, but, like his father before him, found that to be impractical and went all out for new work. His first shy at an elevation was a crude mixture of late seventeenth- and early eighteenth-century tectonics. The prominent hipped and platformed roof had an open lantern, the attic story was raised in the centre to hold a pediment, as at Yester, but the fenestration of the end bays was Palladian. The side elevations, cribbed from Melville House, testified to Sir James's limited drawing skills for it bore a note that, 'This Lanthorn looks greatly misplaced here but will have a better effect in work as it stands 45 feet backwards from the two Chimney heads.' Not surprisingly, it was soon displaced although Sir James did incorporate, in the ultimate resolution of his designs, features which his father would have found acceptable. Thus:

> Above the Attick Floor a Platform Roof
> May be extended like a spacious Field
> From whence the many pleasant Landskips round
> May be with Ease and with Delight Survey'd.[42]

Other constants were the emphatic piano nobile, the bedroom floor treated as an attic storey, the oblong mass and the overall astylar severity since

> That House is justly deem'd of greatest use
> That least incumber'd is with gaudy State.[43]

Such an austere programme did not preclude a portico which heralded

> A Floor of well proportioned Rooms, to which
> By a large open Stair or Portico
> We may ascend from a neat Spacious Court
> Here may a Loby or Salon be placed.[44]

Such accredited arrangements became in turn constraints pricking out the length and number of bays thus allowing the portico to be stretched to hexastyle for

> No Structure can be (justly called) Great
> But where with polished Shafts huge Columns rise.[45]

Baxter's drawings, technically proficient, also show a rejection and assimilation of Sir James's aspirations so that one elevation has a range of Ionic pilasters which are omitted in the next, thus redefining the portico's essential role

> Since all Brittania now enjoys the Bliss
> That ev'ry private house a Temple is.[46]

So paternal influence and private study and inclination honed the designs thereby restating Burlingtonian principles. Yet the placing within the portico of statues of Druids, albeit they were the family's armorial supporters, protected by a Roman order was not only an anthropomorphic expression of those strands of history dearest to Sir James but presaged later eighteenth-century associationism whereby the search for the origins of society was expressed architecturally by the plainest of classical forms.

In the hall, alongside genuine Roman antiquities, found in southern Scotland, was statuary commissioned from Rome using the services of John Baxter junior. Early in January 1765, he wrote home to his father, 'I sett to work to find out the best antique Masculine figures in rome, as companions to stand in niches. I have sent you scetches from the sculptor, of four figures,' including the Medici Apollo and the Borghese Piping Faun, copies of which

150 PENICUIK HOUSE, Midlothian, Ossian's Hall

would eventually arrive at Penicuik. Below the nude drawings there was a postscript: 'They are to have dresserie on their Middle parts.' In the meantime, 'There is two of the Chimneys finished and the third is advancing ... the one with the Cariatides may serve for any Room in Europe ... there is one thing I would advise Sir James to, which is 2 Marble Tables, to Accompany his Statues. They are very elegant furniture and made of different pieces of the finest Antique Marbles, of different Collours, they cost about £30 a pair and every English Gentleman that comes hear carreys home some of them.'[47]

Also in Rome were the Runciman brothers, having been sent out by Sir James on the understanding that, once back in Scotland, they were 'to paint all the ornament work in my great room and two staircases'.[48] Alexander Runciman thought that 'the Salloon will be best in the Taste of some of ye Baths of Titus or Lodge of Rafalei [the Vatican loggia] that is Light Ornaments with small Pannells or Pictures'.[49] Sir James had other subject matter in mind so that the saloon became Ossian's Hall [150] with a thematic programme of paintings by Runciman on the coved ceiling derived from James Macpherson's epic poems. Allegorical figures in the corners depicted the principal rivers of Scotland with Ossian at the centre playing on his harp to the people grouped in attendant neo-classic poses.[50] Once again Rome's art and the history of his native land were portrayed by Sir James as the handmaidens of Scotland's civilisation.

In advising about the design of Penicuik, Sir James's cousin had wanted ramps leading

172

up to the portico so that 'a Coach may be driven up under cover so as to go out dry into the hall, whereas by a Stair people are wet to the Skin at particular times. If you go in by the ground floor it is not so convenient and makes a miserable entry which however people will fall into the habit of out of indolence and the principal Stair only serves by way of a prospect and the fine hall is in a manner lost.'[51]

Possibly it was the logic of such a practical approach that went some way to producing a revolutionary masterpiece at DUDDINGSTON HOUSE, designed by Sir William Chambers, perhaps on the recommendaton of Queen Charlotte,[52] for the 8th Earl of Abercorn.[53] Though descended from the ducal house of Hamilton, the family had given up its territorial base in Scotland until Lord Abercorn bought back the Duddingston estate on the outskirts of Edinburgh in 1745.[54] Only after the land had been improved by enclosures and by subdivision into farms and a park was embellished with temples, canals, lake and cascades[55] was the set ready in 1762 for a centre-piece [151]. In October Chambers was sending 'the plans for the house and by the end of the Week Shall Send the plans for the offices but I fear the Climate of Scotland is by no means fit for building in winter'.[56] In the next summer Lord Abercorn was writing to his architect about the possibility of a visit. 'I am afraid you will think us very backward. We are only this day beginning to lay the joists of the main house, and have hardly finished setting the plinth of the kitchen offices.'[57] Then, with the autumn coming on and no slates on the site, the decision had to be taken to have 'the Whole building Covered with Thatch ... by Wch means we shall Save much time as the inside finishing may be carrying on during the Winter'.[58] And indeed, when there was a late fall of snow in February 1765, 'The Plaisterers have and still keep at work, and hope by keeping their Rooms close they will be able to continue.'[59]

151 DUDDINGSTON HOUSE, Edinburgh

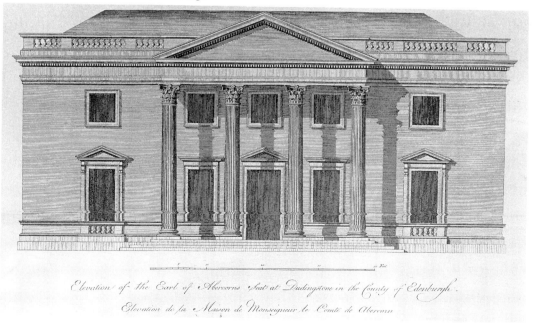

Elevation of the Earl of Abercorns Seat at Dudingstone in the County of Edenburgh.

Elevation de la Maison de Monseigneur le Comte de Abercorn

When all was finished in 1767, at a reputed cost of £30,000,[60] there was an ensemble of 'a park, a real park five miles round, a spacious modern-built house, so well placed and well screened as to deserve to be in any collection of engravings of gentlemen's seats in the kingdom'.[61] Not that the house was large for Lord Abercorn was a bachelor and, as it was a secondary residence in a suburban location, it was very properly a villa, its antecedent being Campbell's Newby Park, as illustrated in *Vitruvius Britannicus*, where, by omitting the basement, full prominence was given to the piano nobile and its interplay with the attached tetrastyle portico.[62] All that and more Chambers took from Newby. His main change was the fluted Corinthian order, 'proper for all buildings, where Delicacy, Gayety and Magnificence are required',[63] which, set on a crepidoma, is not only a surprising concession to the newly published *Antiquities of Athens*,[64] and therefore the first hint of the Greek revival in Scotland, but isolates and gives pre-eminence to the portico which reads like a true temple front rather than being emasculated by assimilation into the surrounding domestic architecture. The result was a greater truthfulness in the role of the architectural parts pointing ahead to the archaeological scholasticism of the French neo-classicists.

The limited accommodation of Duddingston House was indicative of Lord Abercorn's few needs as well as the practicality of the architect's design methodology as expressed by Lord Kames in the dictum that 'utility requires that the rooms be rectangular for otherwise void spaces will be left of no use'.[65] The largest and most decorated space was the hall,[66] partly to reflect the scale and dignity of the portico, and because 'in the country . . . the hall may be an elegant room.

152 DUDDINGSTON HOUSE, Edinburgh

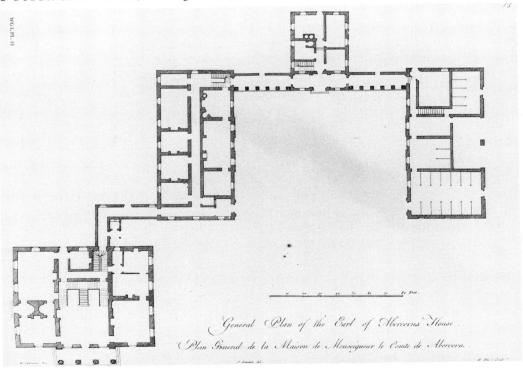

General Plan of the Earl of Abercorns House.
Plan General de la Maison de Monseigneur le Comte de Abercorn.

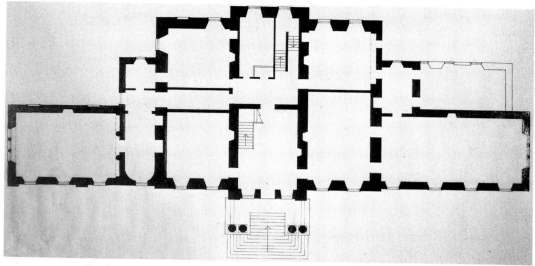

153 ROSSDHU, Dunbartonshire. The wings and portico are a later addition

'It serves as a summer-room for dining; it is an anti-chamber in which people of business, or of the second rank, wait and amuse themselves; and it is a good apartment for the reception of large companies at publick feasts.'[67] Thus did Isaac Ware amplify Palladio's text.[68]

Perhaps it could have been said of Lord Abercorn that, 'if he had a vanity, it was in the arrangement of his offices'.[69] To these he directed his most pointed criticism when writing to Chambers. 'I imagine the columns of the Colonnade are intended to be without bases. I am afraid I should not like them so, and wish it was altered ... I imagine your design was to make freer entrance to the colonnade.' A year later, in July 1764, he was vexed about the clock pavilion over the offices as the columns were 'too detached', he was not sure about the dome, 'But I object principally to putting the dial in the pediment.'[70] Chambers stuck to his guns. The columns would have 'a much lighter appearance than if they were engaged in the Walls', above which 'The top of the turret last sent Your Lordship finishes a la Chinoise. I thought I might take that liberty as well as Michael Angelo whose Lantern of St Peter's finishes in that manner.'[71] That the offices were unique, in being offset from one side of the house as a U-shaped court [152], may have owed something to a study of Lord Kames. 'A building intended for utility solely, such as detached offices, ought in every part to correspond precisely to that intention.'[72] Thus, the Duddingston layout not only suggests the Picturesque, but the use of the Tuscan order, 'Carrying with it', as Chambers wrote, 'An idea of strength and rustic simplicity',[73] unites the workaday service block recalling Varro's concept of the villa as 'a farmhouse and city residence'.[74]

Though there were lessons to be learnt at Duddingston, it would have been foreign to the conservative nature of the Scottish artistic temperament if the supremacy of orthodox Palladianism had been shaken. Thus, Sir James Clerk may have been able to repeat in some measure his virtuoso performance at Penicuik House by ghosting the designs for ROSSDHU in Dunbartonshire. Although Pococke had seen 'the Castle of Lus; to which there is

154 ROSSDHU, Dunbartonshire

adjoyning a good mansion-house' in 1760[75], within a dozen years John Baxter junior was
paid £9:7:0,[76] presumably for drawings for which his architectural mentor, Sir James Clerk,
would have given guidance.[77] As the foundation stone for a new house [153] was laid in
September 1773 it was not until the opening of the next building season that Sir James
Colquhoun 'Sent Mr Thomas Brown Architect at Renfrew for his attendance about my
Building.' Throughout that season the latter had charge of twenty-six masons whose
progress must have been sufficiently rapid to justify the payment 'To the Masons for Drink.
£5.' And so the payments multiplied until in June 1778 Sir James, 'Payd, the Masons for
putting up the Cattacombs in the House'.[78] By the close of that year Rossdhu seems to have
stood complete though, to a knowing eye, it would have appeared old-fashioned with its
steep pitched roof, lofty piano nobile and cluster of Gibbsian details around the entrance
[154].

Other architects, lacking foreign travel and educated patronage, had no recourse but to
stick closely to a standard text. For his first commission, Ednam House [155] on the outskirts

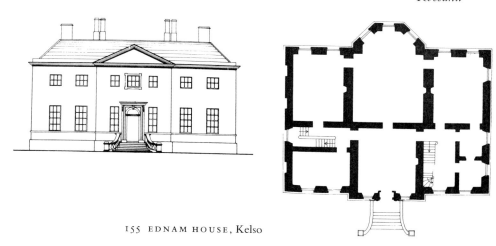

155 EDNAM HOUSE, Kelso

of Kelso, James Nisbet not only modified a plan and elevation in *The Complete Body of Architecture* but borrowed from the same source for the drawing-room ceiling[79] where winged Apollo's chariot is drawn by his four horses whose hooves clip marshmallow clouds bowling along above a spiky rococo edging. Such *passé* decoration would have amused Robert Mylne when he sketched the plan of the house during a summer visit to Scotland.[80]

Mylne was one of that generation of Scottish artists and architects who looked upon a Roman sojourn as a prerequisite for 'fixing a standard for Beauty and rules for composition'.[81] While still in Rome, he was writing early in 1759 to Lord Garlies, the son of the builder of Galloway House, now back in London from his Grand Tour, 'I have sent you as you desired me, a sketch for Mr Murray's house, which I am hopefull he will be so good as to think as the bad digested principalls that a house should be built upon, rather than a house that I say is fit for him.' And he enclosed plans and an elevation for a four-storey seven-bay block.[82] This was for Cally House, Kirkcudbrightshire, to which William Adam had been summoned in 1742 'to concert a Plan, of what you propose to be built betwixt the two Pavilions'[83] and for which Ware had published a design in 1756.[84] That Mylne's less sophisticated and cheaper version was executed, albeit with the jumbled planning given some rhyme and reason, was perhaps because of the continued interest of Lord Garlies, a cousin of Murray of Broughton. As the latter was frequently in London his architect dutifully 'Attended Mr Murray on chimney-pieces' or 'Gave Mr Murray two drawings in lines of the front of the house; one of pediment cornice at large and a long letter on the execution thereof' or in the summer of 1765 'Attended Mr Murray to the ironmongers.' Civility paid off for Mylne retained his client to whom he 'Gave a section for library and drawing of bookcases' in 1774.[85]

In that summer Mylne paid one of his periodic visits to Scotland. From Edinburgh he 'Went over to Fife' and 'Surveyed the situation for a new house' for General Skene at PITLOUR near Strathmiglo. Within two years Mylne was back after which there was a long interval until 1783 when he spent three days 'in altering plan of approach, etc.'[86] after the contract drawings had been signed by 'Robert Mylne, Surveyor'.[87] The old L-plan

156 PITLOUR HOUSE, Fife

house was to be retained as brewhouse, wash-house, laundry and dairy connected by a 'Subterranean Passage underneath Covered Way' to the new mansion [156]. Within its 60-foot square, the basement included the housekeeper's room with a 'Place for Bed', maids' room with two beds and closets, servants' hall and 'Footman's Room for Plate, Shoes and Clothes' leading into the 'Butler's Room' with its 'Deal Presses and Closet'. There was the kitchen with its scullery and also beer and wine-cellars. Over all these there was the dining-room with a 'Niche, Glass and Table' between the pair of windows opposite the fireplace. Colour was restricted to blue walls and a paler blue for the frieze. In the drawing-room one wall was apsidal with attendant niches. To the right of the entrance was a 'Dressing Closet' and water closet beyond which was a 'Study or Parlour' furnished with bookcases and writing-table leaving the south-west corner to be filled by a bedroom, dressing-room and closet. Such indications of social organisation and working practices are as interesting as the composition of the plan.

Externally, Pitlour is a stripped-down version of the aristocratic villas of the earlier part of the century with the difference that the basement is sunk, allowing the owner and his family the immediate delight of closer contact with nature. In social terms Pitlour is an early example of the villa, fallen from its high estate as the occasional residence of a nobleman, becoming the habitual residence of a gentleman commoner. More interesting would have been Mylne's alternative scheme[88] with the centre crowned not by a pediment but by a parapet and blocking courses. Perhaps Mylne had been turning his eyes to France and in particular to the pavilion at the château of Louveciennes by Ledoux.[89] Such a francophile taste would become the guiding inspiration in the later work of James Playfair.

178

157 BOTHWELL HOUSE, Lanarkshire

Having set up in practice in London, Playfair's early Scottish commissions were conventional enlargements of existing houses, such as Langholm Lodge, Dumfries-shire, 'Begun to be built in 1787',[90] or Buchanan Castle, Stirlingshire,[91] or BOTHWELL HOUSE, Lanarkshire [157], hard by the ruins of the medieval castle 'out of Part of which the good Lord Forfar built a pretty neat Box at a little Distance'.[92] In 1759 the Duke of Douglas was adding pavilions and stipulating that the 'Wainscott for all the windows to be made (out of the Dealls and Wainscott which are lying at Douglas Castle) and Trees for Laths (out of Bothwell Park)'.[93] A generation later and workmen were 'taking down the inside of the old house' which was followed by the demolition of the front wall although four months later it could be reported that, 'The Masons have got all the Rock work round the house putt on and are setting off the windows.'[94] A year later Playfair was working on details, including the 'Portico to Bothwell Castle: and a new front to Wings etc.'[95]

In August 1787 Playfair made his first visit to Paris after which his architecture has an intellectual rigour, the razor-edged sharpness and the plasticity of French neo-classicism, which is why CAIRNESS in Aberdeenshire, a grey knuckle of granite drawn from the cold Buchan soil, is as sophisticated and as urbane as a Parisian *hôtel* except that the court is to the north, leaving the southern aspect open across the park [158].

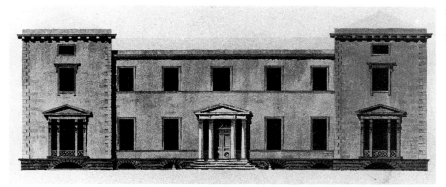

158 CAIRNESS,
Aberdeenshire,
by James Playfair

179

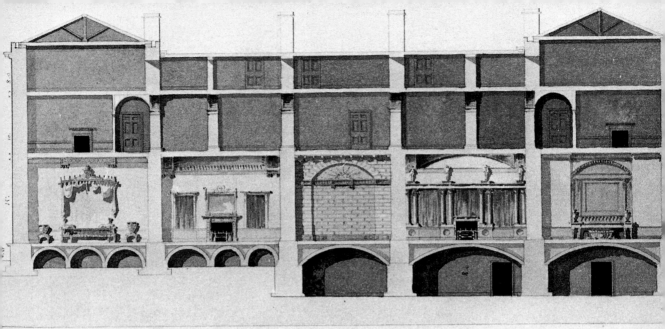

159 CAIRNESS, Aberdeenshire, section by James Playfair

In the summer of 1789 Playfair was intending to be in the north in October when he would wait on Charles Gordon 'at Cairness at that time'.[96] The outcome was that in the following spring Playfair 'Sent off Estimate and proposals', amounting to £5,886:16:0, followed by 'Copies of Plans for Tradesmen to estimate by'[97] after which he acknowledged the receipt of 'a Draft for one Hundred pounds to account for designs etc. in Architecture',[98] which would have included the bound set of elevations, a section and plans which show a square service court.[99] As these were client's copies, once 'The Wrights began work at Cairness on Monday 21 March 1791'[100] there would have been the usual rush to keep up with the demand for working drawings. By 1793 the construction must have been well forward since Playfair detailed coloured studies for the finishing of the public rooms which had strong classical allusions [159]. In the dining-room, where the south window reaches

160 CAIRNESS, Aberdeenshire, design for the drawing-room by James Playfair

to the floor, the illusion is created of looking out through a Doric temple porch. The drawing-room [160] was similarly treated but with 'The Frieze and Ionic Order as in the Temple of Apollo Didymaeus in Ionia', an effect to be heightened by dressing the proposed granite columns with marble bases and capitals, while in the billiard-room a coved ceiling would replicate that in 'Nero's Baths at Baia'.[101] With the death of Playfair in 1794 and of his client soon after, the full scheme of decoration may never have been executed. Thus, in the billiard-room the overall masonry pattern was more cheaply and more effectively gained by framing the room *à l'Egyptien*, with wood coated with sand and indented with mock hieroglyphics, a scheme inspired perhaps by the plates in Piranesi's *Diverse Maniere*. This may be the first Egyptian revival interior in Britain and it is indicative of the eclecticism that appears in Playfair's mature work just as the court of offices, antique forms swelling from obdurate granite, are the most authentic statement of French neo–classicism in Britain. Imagine a hemicycle, penetrated by a single downswept arch in the manner of Ledoux, sweeping round to clasp the house and ending in pavilions sheltering stumps of Doric columns beneath enfolding arches [161].

161 CAIRNESS, Aberdeenshire

Even more francophile were the unfulfilled designs for ARDKINGLAS, Argyll, which Playfair reconnoitred, at a cost to his client of five guineas plus £21 for drawings and an estimate, in October 1790.[102] As the Robert Adam scheme had remained on paper only and as, 'The old house of Ardkinglas has become unfit for the accommodation of the family', the decision had been made 'to raise another for the sum of between three and four thousand pounds'.[103] Like Adam, Playfair, was inspired by the lochside setting to conjure up 'A Marine Pavilion', which was envisaged as a rectangular block with a flat centre beyond which the ends were marked off by a strong vertical accent. Deep eaves, lunettes and thin, tensile pediments were a response to Ledoux as was the cylindrical lantern tower,[104] especially after Playfair was 'Ordered by Sir. A. Campbell to make Elevations to his building without the dome',[105] which overtopped a circular court of offices probably imitating such Parisian landmarks as the Halle au Blé or the circular stables of the Duc de'Infantado.[106]

Prior to engaging Playfair, Charles Gordon had already built a house at Cairness.[107] The funds allowing such expenditure were the profits from a sugar plantation in Jamaica, a

162 PRESTON HALL, Midlothian

staple of wealth in the eighteenth century. It was, however, in the subcontinent of India, with its confused tangle of trade, politics and war, that the greatest riches could be amassed by a man of spirit. Thus, when Alexander Callander, a younger son of a Stirlingshire laird, left Bombay, after close on thirty years' service with the East India Company, it was with a fortune in excess of £100,000. Already, in 1784, the estate of Crichton in Midlothian had been purchased for him though its mansion was so old and small as to be unworthy of a returning nabob. By good fortune the contiguous estate of PRESTON HALL was also for sale 'on which there is a very great house surrounded by extensive pleasure grounds laid out with very good taste. This estate has long been on the Market, but as the greatest part of the estate is laid out in pleasure grounds, rides, etc., and of no consequence, would yield an annual income very inadequate to the price.' On the other hand, a fellow nabob saw the 'comfortable house' of Preston Hall in quite another light as 'such a monstrous, unwieldy straggling and detached fabrick ... were it mine, with your fortune, I declare I would pull it to the ground'. Understandably, Callander was reluctant to buy and held back until 1789 when his friend was quick to advise on how he should spend his Indian gains by building 'a compact, elegant Mansion on the improved stile of the times' for 'I never knew yet a person who patched up an old house that did not in the end most thoroughly regret it.' Once the old house was demolished, the foundation stone of the new one was laid with some ceremony on Friday, 18 March 1791 for, 'I propose Friday', the factor reported, 'As it is Comon [sic] for the men to get a drink we would lose only Saturday if any of the men took a Ramble.'[108]

Despite its date and the splendour of the concept, Preston Hall, considered stylistically, is a bit like the curate's egg. The *corps de logis*, a seven-bay block with an implied tetrastyle portico, has a solemn square-faced look which stamps it as belonging to the regular mid-century school [162]. Equally characteristic is its alignment, to give direct communication, with the reshaped and cut-down William Adam wings now considered 'as pleasing objects seen from the drawing and breakfast rooms ... This arises in some degree from the rich sculpture, paintings and gilding of the rooms, contrasted with the architecture seen through

182

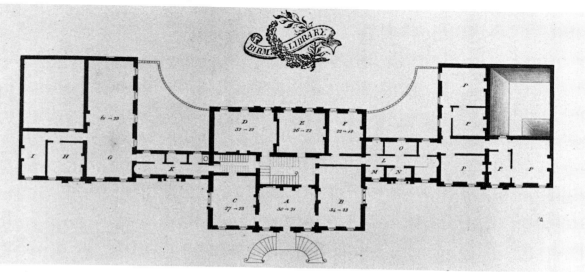

163 PRESTON HALL, Midlothian, principal floor plan

the windows, as a picture is found to be improved by the richness of the frame.'[109] Although it may have been for such a reason that Robert Mitchell favoured the mid-century formula for country-house planning, the rear elevation of Preston Hall is a neo-classical astylar composition of differing rectangles with each component having a partial identity and, therefore, a sense of separateness from its neighbour. The low pavilions, shallow-pitched and each with a tripartite window (unusual in contemporary British architecture), rouse memories of Cairness. Yet why was this design not carried through to the front? Perhaps because the client remembered and preferred what had been fashionable when he was a young man in Britain.

Within the augustan shell the plan [163] is looser and more comfortable than might have been expected. There is no through vista and, instead of a chilling saloon, there is a library,

164 PRESTON HALL„ Midlothian, upper stairhall

165 IRVINE HOUSE, Dumfries-shire,
proposed elevation by Henry Holland

166 IRVINE HOUSE, Dumfries-shire, proposed site plan by Henry Holland

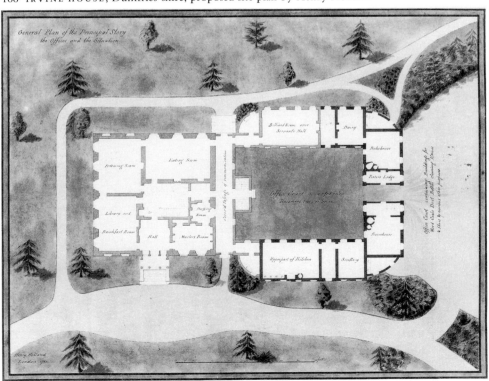

while off the hall there is the now fashionable breakfast-room, implying a casual informality at the start of the day, while in the furthest corner of one wing, beyond the gallery and billiard-room, is a writing-room.[110] All are rectangular, reflecting Lord Kames's notion that 'a square room of great size is inconvenient, by removing far from the hand, chairs and tables, which, when unemploy'd, must be ranged along the sides of the room'.[111] While the rooms are 'frugal in ornaments',[112] the staircase, 'as an elegant composition, greatly surpasses any other part of the house'.[113] At the upper level the bedroom corridors are parclosed on each side by a pair of Greek Corinthian columns *in antis* between which stands a Coade-stone female figure holding a lamp [164]. At Cairness one looked out from the temple; at Preston Hall the arrangement of internal porches linked by a domed lantern suggests a Roman atrium. One almost expects to hear the rain-water dripping into the impluvium.

It was, of course, inevitable that, just as Scottish architects settled in London, English architects would move into Scotland. Thomas Atkinson, a convert to Catholicism, was summoned from York in 1788 to design the rather bleak Terregles House in Kirkcudbright-shire for a Catholic landowner whose main estate was in Yorkshire.[114] More fashionable, with its French overtones, was Henry Holland's unexecuted design for Irvine House, Dumfries-shire, a shooting-box of the Duke of Buccleuch [165]. Although the 'Master's Room' [166] overlooked the entrance, the windows on that side of the 'Library and Breakfast Room' were blind to ensure the family's privacy.[115]

The most significant of the English neo-classical architects was Thomas Harrison of Chester who is credited, in 1795, as the designer of K E N N E T H O U S E, Clackmannanshire,

167 K E N N E T H O U S E, Clackmannanshire

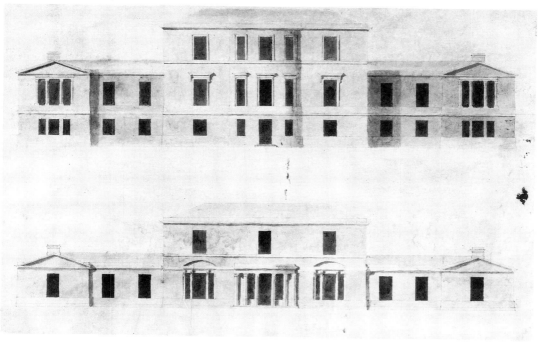

'built in a style of superior elegance to most of the houses to be met with in Scotland; and exhibits in all its parts an equal attention to convenience and utility, as it does elegance and taste'.[116] With a linear plan and sunk basement, all the accommodation could be on one floor with the public rooms overlooking the gardens and the bedrooms ranged on either side of the entrance hall. A semicircular porch, treated as a tholos, was cleverly flanked by segmental-headed tripartite windows [167] which, on the garden elevation, became miniature Grecian temples when capped with a pediment.[117]

Although the 7th Earl of Elgin, a relation of Bruce of Kennet, was said to be 'building an elegant modern mansion' in 1799,[118] what he was about was altering a house of 1702. That was against the advice of his mother for 'considering your Taste and style of living a prodigious House will be a monstrous burden'. As there was a shortage of ready money, so that Lord Elgin had to borrow heavily, and as 'no plans have yet appeared from Mr Harrison', it should have been evident from the start that a happy outcome would be unlikely. So, in the end, it proved for, while 'a partial plan of the rustic Basement of the House' arrived in March 1796, there was little progress over the next two years so that the sole important alteration remained the elliptical bow with its pairs of Ionic columns sheltering classical reliefs of Coade stone. Even a personal plea in 1799 from Lord Elgin, who was about to set off on his famous mission to the Levant, provoked no satisfactory response from Harrison so that, for 'having neither come himself nor sent any answer and having omitted or neglected to give instructions by any other channel for finishing the house at Broomhall', he was sacked.[119]

Although Lord Elgin would pass his remaining years toying with designs for the completion of Broomhall,[120] he was, in a sense, a *passé* figure for, after the middle of the century, the old aristocratic families, by now equipped with classical mansions or, in a few instances, with neo-Gothic castles, were not the notable patrons of architecture. That was left to the new men. 'The fortunes ... brought from the East Indies alone in the course of the last fifty years, have been so large, and have been so greneally applied to the purchase of estates, that the property thus acquired now bears a great proportion to the whole landed property in Scotland.'[121] With capital to spare, the returned exiles 'picked up estates thro' the Country, and lived in a higher style than the old Gentry',[122] some of whom looked askance at those who had 'drained the treasuries of the Nabobs'.[123] Perhaps typical was the 2nd Earl of Fife's reflection that 'when I laid myself on my pillow, I blessed God that I had not Asiatic wealth, for such a forfeit of conscience as these Nabobs must feel'.[124]

In the opening years of the century there must have been numerous estates 'in the hands of gentlemen having from £500 to £800 a year, there being at the Union few commoners of larger fortune'.[125] Although there would be a considerable augmentation of personal wealth, few of the landed gentry ever had a sufficient superfluity of funds which could be set aside for a new family seat no matter how modest. Sometimes there was little choice but to build. The laird of Castle Lachlan in Argyll, 'finding it inconvenient for a family residence, he has just now built a good modern house close by the castle'.[126] Such a house would be unpretentious and, 'as a composition it would not have disgraced a gentleman; the language, though plain, was strong and unaffected'.[127] With little variety in plan or elevation and with minimal decoration there was, nevertheless, a decorum which was acceptable until well into the Regency period.

In 1750 Wrightpark, Stirlingshire, had what was basically the familiar tripartite plan with a curved staircase at the far end of a ground-floor hall.[128] There is some kinship with Quarter, in the same county and dating from 1776, which has a dining-room and drawing-room, filling most of the ground floor on either side of the hall, with a central staircase round which five bedrooms are expertly grouped on the floor above.[129] Externally, all the features are characteristic of the early Georgian period and these continued in use in various parts of the country until late in the century. Saddell, Argyll, has a piended and platformed roof in 1774[130] as does Barbreck which, even as late as 1790,[131] has a familial resemblance to the earlier seaboard mansions of that area of the west Highlands. Many houses, thick with *retardataire* details, never saw an architect. Weems in Roxburghshire of *c*.1775 typifies a number of such houses in the Borders including Torwoodlee for which a complete set of painstaking drawings still survives.[132] Nearby is Yair, which Alexander Pringle of Whytbank, 'pressed by the expenses of a numerous family', was obliged to part with in 1759 but which twenty-five years later his son, having served with the East India Company, was rich enough to buy back and found a new family seat with a bayed centre and balustraded parapet.[133]

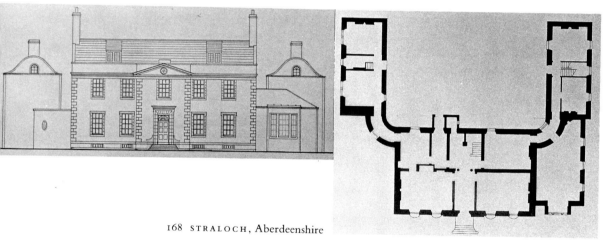

168 STRALOCH, Aberdeenshire

Early Georgian plan forms also persisted. In 1793 it was stated that, 'New and elegant houses were built within the last three years at Elrick and Straloch' in Aberdeenshire.[134] At the latter [168] the back-swept wings form a courtyard at the rear. Harling, contrasted with thin granite margins, and curly gables carrying panelled chimney-stacks, all evoke an earlier building age. However, not only was the north-east deficient in architects but in 1783 John Baxter wrote 'that some of the Masons have left Ellon Castle and they give such a dreadfull Account of the place that I shall be difficulted to get men to supply their place'.[135] At Bayfield in Easter Ross [169] there is a lateral plan with one-storey wings set against a three-storey box further heightened by tall chimney-stacks. As the same pattern was used at Embo, Sutherland, the rooms can be enfilade for the full length of the front [170]. However, there is no external definition of a piano nobile, the pediment carries a chimney [171] and

187

'The language, though plain, was strong and unaffected'

169 BAYFIELD,
Ross and Cromarty

over-large Gibbsian surrounds are reserved for the single-bay corridors. Compare that with Tarbat House, Easter Ross, with its fine-jointed ashlar, careful calculation of proportional niceties including a slight forward movement of the centre so that the effect is more Regency than Georgian [172]. Unusually, there is no family accommodation on the ground floor, where the hall and staircase separate the servants' hall and 'Mens Bedroom' on one side from the housekeeper's room and the 'Maids Bedroom' on the other. The domestic offices

170 EMBO HOUSE, Sutherland

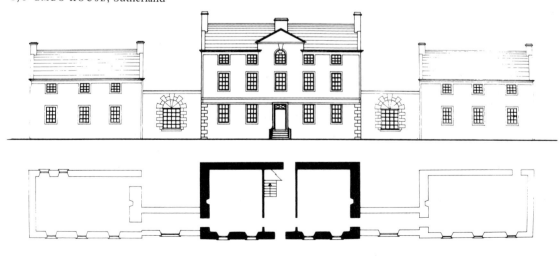

188

171 EMBO HOUSE, Sutherland
172 TARBAT HOUSE, Ross and
Cromarty, by James McLeran

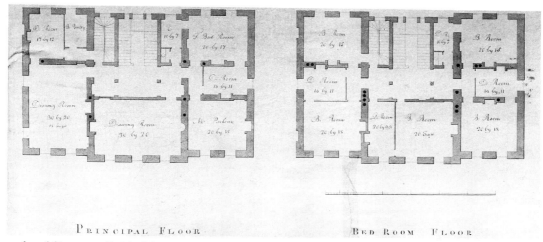

PRINCIPAL FLOOR   BED ROOM FLOOR

and stabling are divided between the wings which, set back from the frontage, are entered directly from the house. The architect was James McLeran of Edinburgh[136] who supervised the construction of Netherurd House, Peebles-shire, designed by the owner with neighbours' advice.[137]

It was inevitable that the passage of time would show an increasing influence from the Adam brothers. Rozelle, now in Ayr, purchased in 1754 and originally named Rochelle 'from a property of that name in Jamaica',[138] has an astylar treatment in the manner of John Adam with a five-bay harled centre, quadrants and two-storeyed pavilions. At Annick Lodge a Palladian layout, embellished with key blocks and globe finials, is dated 1790. However, the two-storeyed centre and bowed side may be a partial justification for the contemporary description of the house as 'a complete specimen of the English ferme ornée'.[139]

189

173 DUNLUGAS HOUSE, Banffshire

Throughout the century there was a persistent taste for the detached block of which a charming example is Dunlugas, completely in scale with its miniature park [173]. 'With the exception of Duff House, perhaps no residence in the county of Banff is more delightfully situated.'[140] Skews, rubble walling and gabled chimney-stacks offset the dignified entry of pilasters and Adamesque entablature [174]. Omit the pediment and one has the long lines of Glenae, Dumfries-shire, for which the architect, Thomas Boyd of Dumfries, was a party

174 DUNLUGAS HOUSE, Banffshire

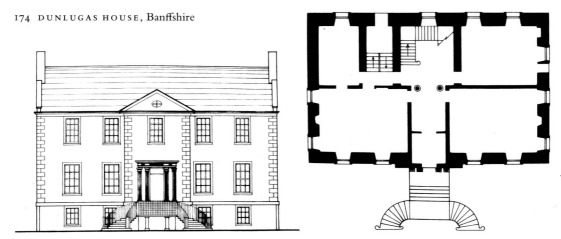

175 ARDVORLICH, Perthshire, before 1890

to the building contract whereby the mason agreed to execute the work 'in the most regular manner' and, among other costs, 'to polish in the completest manner the Steps for the hanging stair and to build the same at the rate of Seven Shillings and Sixpence Sterling for each step'.[141] An equally 'plain and unpretending' seat was Ardvorlich, Perthshire,[142] which, in its original state in 1790, had a minuscule windowed pediment peeping over the wallhead and Adamesque urns at the corners and vertex [175].

176 CHESTERS, Roxburghshire

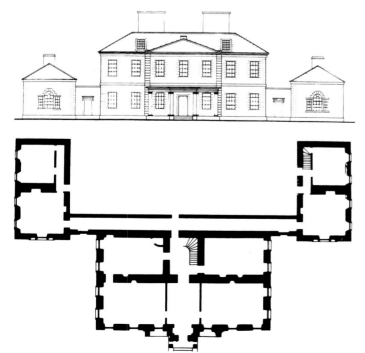

191

It is instructive to compare Ardvorlich, the seat of a Highland chieftain, with Chesters House, Roxburghshire, built for Thomas Elliot Ogilvie who, having returned from India, purchased the estate in 1786. His architect, William Elliot, was a local man with up-to-date ideas[143] so that the spreading pediment is supported by rustic pilasters while a bold Doric porch marks an easy transition between indoors and outdoors [176]. More grandiose was his Ladykirk House, Berwickshire, an enlarged villa with tapered pilasters and a foliate frieze. Just as austere is Ardgowan House, Renfrewshire, designed by Hugh Cairncross, once a clerk of works for Robert Adam [177]. Curved forestairs led to a perron beneath which was an entry to a 'lobby' and family staircase. At the centre of the principal floor is a bowed saloon, hung with red damask, with a billiard-room above on the bedroom floor over which, in the centre of each front, there was a 'Barrack Room' with four beds. Altogether there were seventeen servants' beds in the garrets.[144] Monreith, Wigtownshire,[145] also has a bowed garden front; at Naughton House, Fife, it is on the entrance and leads through the hall to a circular stairwell. At Seggieden, Perthshire, John Paterson, another former Adam clerk of works, displayed his fondness for complex spatial sequences with a Greek Doric porch defining a square hall leading to a top-lit saloon with its ovoid plan being repeated in the drawing-room which was marked externally by pairs of columns on a shallow bow.[146] Only once, however, was there a scheme resembling the trilobate plans of Robert Adam's later villas.

LEUCHIE HOUSE, East Lothian, was designed by an Edinburgh architect, Alexander Peacock, who 'was at Leuchie all last week', as was reported in January 1781 and again in March.[147] Site work had begun two years before on 1 February when, 'As our winter is remarkable mild the masons began this day to cut stones for the house.'[148] The work would have proceeded uneventfully for, by spring 1782, 'The Plaisterer is to be out nixt week in order to Set About the Plaistering of the upper Drawing Room and the dinning room below.'[149] An advantage of having an employer who was resident for much of the year in London was that, 'As soon as Mr Peacock comes to the Country will remember to inquire at him the prices of the Marble Chimney pieces'[150] so that Flaxman was paid fifteen guineas

177 ARDGOWAN, Renfrewshire, by Hugh Cairncross

178 THE BURN, Angus,
the stairhead ceiling

for the chimney-piece tablet in the upper drawing-room.[151] For the big drawing-room on the ground floor Sir Hew Dalrymple's son wrote from London that, 'From what enquiries I have made the Tablet and Cornish in the Chimney should be same as those in the room.'[152] The design of the looking-glasses also conformed to the frieze pattern.

What is noticeable in the decoration of these late eighteenth-century country-houses is the absence of ornamental plasterwork apart from over-simplified cornices. Leuchie and The Burn, Angus, are exceptions. At the latter the double-height staircase hall [178] has a ceiling composed of the Adam formula of two rectangles bounding a square and incorporating panels of trophies and the Huntly crest.[153] At Leuchie there is fine work in the Adam style, especially in the upper drawing-room with a cobweb ceiling, garlands in the frieze and pendant arabesques in slender panels with Corinthian pilasters breaking through the dado to create spatial zones. Not only was Leuchie an exception to Mrs Elton's complaint 'at the want of two drawing-rooms'[154] but it was to have a library, with books costing £2,000,[155] 'however it might be avoided by the family in general'.[156] Not surprisingly, the future overheads of Leuchie alarmed one member of the Dalrymple family. 'One will want a Number of People to fill it and a pretty Deal of Expence to furnish and fit it up ... which makes me almost shudder to think of what a Number of Candles to light it up.'[157]

One reason for the diminished number of public rooms may have been that the former strict separation of use was breaking down. 'To the Great House accordingly they went, to sit the full half hour in the old fashioned square parlour, with a small carpet and shining floor, to which the present daughters of the house were gradually giving the proper air of confusion by a grand piano forte and a harp, flower-stands and little tables placed in every direction.'[158] At Cairness the breakfast-room had '2 Mahogany Tea Tables, 1 Card Table, 1 Work ditto, 1 Tea Urn Stand' plus a sofa and eight red leather chairs. The dining-room had '3 Mahogany dining Tables', fourteen red leather chairs, wine-cooler and a sideboard 'with a break in front, a Pot Cupboard at Each End and drawer in Center Cross'. There was a yellow or brown floor-cloth lined with green baize and '3 Rod window curtains and Draperys of your chints calicoe lined with white' though the best bedroom had 'A festoon window curtain of yellow damask calicoe lined with white ditto and fring'd'.[159] At Terregles there was yellow damask in the drawing-room. Brought from the London house, and 'tho' Cleaned looks as well as new', it was preferred to wallpaper which 'wou'd have been half Cover'd with the looking Glasses'.[160] An innovation in many country-houses was the water closet. At Leuchie, 'a force Pump' piped water from the well by the kitchen door up to a cistern.[161] At Cairness there was a 'Framed Box for Pipes' and three closets with mahogany seats, all at £15,[162] although the best bedroom had 'A Mahogany Night table and Stone pan'.[163]

After having built, decorated and furnished a country-house there were the never-ending domestic cares. The 2nd Earl Fife's letters to his factor at Duff House are heavy with admonitions. 'You are to be particularly attentive to everything about the House ... to see all Doors and Windows of the House locked every night, every person about the House regularly to Bed, that the Iron Gate be always locked ... You are to see all the Chimneys cleaned, particularly that of the Charter Room ... the Inner Charter Room to be frequently opened, and the air therein to be lett out.' Or more particularly, 'Pray look into my Library some times, as my things are loose and no locks on my Presses ... and when you put up or do anything to the Books, pray put the Chairs in the middle of the room, otherwise they will stand upon them.'[164]

Besides such cares, there was the worry for many lesser men of a sufficient future income to maintain one's home for, as Lord Chesterfield wisely observed, 'Estates in land ... fall infinitely shorter of the rental, than any body unacquainted with them could imagine.'[165] That noblemen and country gentlemen were prepared to rebuild their family seats and were emulated in doing so by lawyers, merchants and nabobs was because, 'Your new house', as a correspondent wrote to Sir Hew Dalrymple, 'will be a monument to your Successors of your taste and judgemt. ...You by a well regulated Economy, lived Suitable to your Rank, provided for your Son, assisted your Relations, built a Convenient Usefull and Orna-mental Family Mansion ... and left your Estate much more considerable than when you found it.'[166]

Notes to Chapter 7

1. 'Selections from the Family Papers Preserved at Caldwell', *Maitland Club* (1854), Pt. I, pp. 266–7; A. Allardyce, *Scotland and Scotsmen in the Eighteenth Century* (1888), vol. II, p. 64.
2. J. B. Paul, *The Scots Peerage*, vol. VI (1909), pp. 17–18.
3. Earl of Marchmont to Sir James Hall, Cambrai, 8 January 1724, SRO, GD158/2505, f. 268.
4. Earl of Marchmont to Lord Binning, Cambrai, 8 January 1724, SRO, GD158/2505, f. 266.
5. Ibid., Cambrai, 10 February 1724, SRO, GD158/2505, f. 278.
6. Earl of Marchmont to W. Adam, Cambrai, 12 September 1724, SRO, GD158/2515, f. 119.
7. Earl of Marchmont to Sir James Hall and to W. Adam, Cambrai, 15 December 1724, SRO, GD158/2515, ff. 173, 175.
8. W. Adam to Lord Marchmont, Edinburgh, 19 January 1725, SRO, GD158/1303/3.
9. W. Hall to Lord Marchmont, Edinburgh, 3 July 1729, SRO, GD158/1282/2/26, f. 63. J. Dickson to Lord Marchmont, Redbraes Castle, 31 August 1730, SRO, GD158/1340, f. 106.
10. Supra, n. 7.
11. Paul, op. cit., vol. VI, p. 20; C. Hussey, 'Marchmont, Berwickshire', *CL*, vol. LVII (28 February 1925), pp. 310–18.

12. Substantial payments for unspecified work were made to the plasterer Thomas Clayton between 1753 and 1757. SRO, GD1/651/7 and 8.
13. 'Diary of George Ridpath, Minister of Stichel, 1755–61', *SHS*, 3rd Series, vol. II (1922), p. 57.
14. M. Warrender, *Marchmont and the Humes of Polworth* (1894), p. 99.
15. G. Rose (ed.), *A Selection from the Papers of the Earls of Marchmont* (1831), vol. II, p. 298.
16. Clerk of Pencuik MSS.
17. 'Earl of Marchmont's Investments and Private Accounts', SRO, GD1/648/4.
18. J. Grant to J. Pringle of Bowland, Edinburgh, 17 September 1751, Torwoodlee MSS.
19. Journal, 1749–50, SRO, GD1/651/13.
20. Lord Marchmont to Lady Marchmont, Redbraes, 18 August 1750, SRO, GD158/2584/18/1.
21. Lord Marchmont to J. Pringle of Bowland, London, 9 March 1751, Torwoodlee MSS.
22. Ibid., London, 16 March 1751, Torwoodlee MSS.
23. Ibid., London, 16 April 1751, Torwoodlee MSS.
24. Ibid., London, 23 April 1751, Torwoodlee MSS.
25. Ibid., London, 30 March 1751, Torwoodlee MSS.
26. A. Palladio, *The Four Books of Architecture* (republished 1965), pl. LVIII.
27. *VB*, vol. III (1725), pl. 29.
28. Supra, n. 14.
29. I. Ware, *The Complete Body of Architecture* (1756), pls. 39, 45.
    One possible reason for the choice of an English architect to design Amisfield House may be that the original family seat of the Charteris family in Dumfries-shire is not far from Carnsalloch which may have been built to a Ware design, *c.*1754, by Alexander Johnstone. H. Colvin, *A Biographical Dictionary of British Architects, 1600–1840* (1978), p. 866.
30. The workmen's books are among Lord Wemyss's MSS at Gosford. C. Hussey, 'Made by Chippendale? The Amisfield Day Beds', *CL*, vol. CXXXVIII (15 July 1965), p. 184.
31. R. Pococke, 'Tours in Scotland, 1747, 1750, 1760', *SHS*, vol. I (1887), p. 318.
32. 'A Tour in Scotland', NLS, MS 1021, f. 44.
33. Lord Fife to W. Rose, Paris, 21 December 1765, A. and H. Tayler, *Lord Fife and His Factor* (1925), p. 23.
34. Wings were added to Amisfield by John Henderson in 1785. J. Miller, *The Lamp of Lothian* (1844), p. 527; J. Small, *Castles and Mansions of the Lothians* (1883), vol. I; C. McWilliam, *Lothian* (1978), p. 76.
35. Sir John Clerk of Penicuik, 'The Country Seat', f. 22, SRO, GD18/4404/1.
36. Sir John Clerk of Penicuik, 'Memorandum of the building the house of Pennycuik', SRO, GD18/1758.
37. J. M. Gray (ed.), 'Memoirs of the Life of Sir John Clerk of Penicuik', *SHS*, vol. XIII (1892), p. 228.
38. The drawings, some of which are subscribed by Sir James Clerk, are among the Clerk of Penicuik MSS. A. Rowan, 'Pencuik House, Midlothian', *CL*, vol. CXLIV (15 and 22 August 1968), pp. 383–7, 448–51.
39. Further payments to 'Mr John Adams' are recorded in November 1764, in June 1765 for '1500 weight of Stucco', in October 1766 and finally in February 1769 'To Mr Adam's Marble work for Dove Coloured Slabs for tables'. Sir James Clerk of Pencuik 'Journal of the Expenses of My New house and Office houses', SRO, GD18/1758a.
40. Robert Adam to Sir James Clerk, SRO, GD18/1758b.
41. Copy letter from Sir James Clerk to Colonel Robert Clerk, Penicuik, 4 March 1762, SRO, GD18/5014.
42. Sir John Clerk of Pencuik, op. cit., f. 13.
43. Ibid., f. 20.
44. Ibid., f. 21.
45. Ibid., f. 11.
46. Ibid., f. 19.
47. John Baxter to John Baxter senior, Rome, 3 January 1765, SRO, GD18/5014.
    The three chimney-pieces cost Sir James £85 and the tables £75 plus freight charges and customs dues on all the goods, which had arrived early in 1768, totalling £188:10:10. Supra, n. 39.
48. Ibid.
49. A. Runciman to Sir James Clerk, Rome, 12 January 1770, SRO, GD18/4682.

50. J. P. Neale, *Views of Seats*, 2nd Series, vol. II (1825).
    The painted ceilings of Ossian's Hall and the main staircase, depicting episodes from the life of St Margaret, were destroyed in the fire which gutted Penicuik House in 1899. Drawings for the ceilings are in the National Gallery of Scotland. E. Croft-Murray, *Decorative Painting in England, 1537–1837*, vol. II (1970), pls. 138–9, pp. 70, 272.

51. Colonel Robert Clerk to Sir James Clerk, London, 16 February 1762, SRO, GD18/1758b.

52. Lord Abercorn had entertained Queen Charlotte at his Essex seat in September 1761. Paul, op. cit., vol. I (1904), p. 65.

53. J. Harris, *Sir William Chambers* (1970), pp. 46–8, 206–7; D. Walker, 'Duddingston House, Edinburgh', *CL*, vol. CXXVI (24 September 1959), pp. 358–61.

54. G. Crawfurd, *A General Description of the Shire of Renfrew, 1710* (1818), p. 321; W. Baird, *Annals of Duddingstone and Portobello* (1898), pp. 83–4.

55. R. Forsyth, *The Beauties of Scotland* (1805), vol. I, p. 353.

56. W. Chambers to Lord Abercorn, 19 October 1762, PRONI, D623/A/53/25.

57. Lord Abercorn to W. Chambers, Duddingston, 25 August 1763, British Architectural Library, CHA/2/17.

58. W. Chambers to Lord Abercorn, London, 2 September 1763, PRONI, D623/A/53/69.

59. W. Key to Lord Abercorn, Duddingston, 27 February 1765, PRONI, D623/A/53/193.

60. *SA*, vol. XVIII, p. 364; *NSA*, vol. I, p. 389; Small, op. cit.; J. Grant, *Old and New Edinburgh* (1880), vol. II, p. 317.

61. J. Austen, *Mansfield Park* (1972), p. 36.

62. *VB*, vol. III, pl. 46. For a comparison with Duddingston House see J. Woolfe and J. Gandon, *VB* (1970), pls. 14–17.

63. W. Chambers, *A Treatise on Civil Architecture* (1759), p. 31.

64. J. Stuart and N. Revett, *Antiquities of Athens*, vol. I (1762), Ch. V, pl. III.

65. Lord Kames, *Elements of Criticism* (1762), p. 324.

66. 'The usual method, in buildings where beauty and magnificence are preferred to oeconomy, is to raise the Hall and Salon higher than the other rooms, and make them occupy two Stories.' Chambers, op. cit., p. 82.

67. Ware, op. cit., p. 335.

68. Palladio, op. cit., Bk. I, p. 27.

69. J. Austen, *Northanger Abbey* (1974), p. 188.

70. Lord Abercorn to W. Chambers, 25 August 1763 and 1 July 1764, British Architectural Library, CHA/2/17 and 18.

71. W. Chambers to Lord Abercorn, London, 9 and 26 July 1764, PRONI, D623/A/53/128, 134.

72. Kames, op. cit., p. 321.

73. Chambers, op. cit., p. 16.

74. M. Varro, *On Agriculture* (1934), p. 433.

75. Pococke, op. cit., p. 62.

76. Account of book of Sir James Colquhoun, Colquhoun of Luss MSS.

77. Colvin, op. cit., pp. 220–1.

78. Supra, n. 76.

79. Ware, op. cit., pls. 42, 49, 81, 82.

80. The sketch is contained in Mylne's diary for 1776. Photograph in NMRS.

81. James Adam to Lord Kames, Rome, 9 May 1761, SRO, GD24/1/553, f. 24.

82. R. Mylne to Lord Garlies, Rome, 26 January 1759, SRO, GD10/1421/287, 288A.
    Lord Garlies, later 7th Earl of Galloway, was both cousin and brother-in-law of James Murray of Broughton. Paul. op. cit., vol. IV (1907), pp. 164–5.

83. W. Adam to the Hon. Alexander Murray of Broughton, Edinburgh, 25 September 1742, SRO, GD10/1421/212.

84. Ware, op. cit., pls. 56, 57.

85. A. Richardson, *Robert Mylne* (1955), pp. 62, 67, 71.

86. Ibid., pp. 98, 108, 120.

87. NLS, Adv. MS, Ch.B.2226.

88. Richardson, op. cit., p. 159.

89. A. Braham, *The Architecture of the French Enlightenment* (1980), p. 177.

90. SM, vol. 2N, no. 3.

91. Playfair was at Buchanan Castle in the summer of 1788 and in February 1789 was working 'long hours' on plans, sections and elevations. By the end of the month, 'Lord Graham's works are begun under my direction but at present no new house is to be built at Buchanan.' J. Playfair, 'Journal of Architecture, 1783–91', NLS, Adv. MS 33.5.25. Also SRO, GD248/588/15/41 and /589/2/97.

92. J. Macky, *A Journey Through Scotland* (1723), pp. 294–5.

93. 'Agreement between His Grace the Duke of Douglas and Messrs Gowans and Paterson about Bothwel House. 9 Janr. 1759', Douglas-Home MSS, Box 48/1 and 6.

94. J. Lorimer to A. Douglas, Bothwell Castle, 23 January 1787, and correspondence of W. Stodert, 30 January and 5 June 1787, Douglas-Home MSS, Box 49/5.

95. Playfair's journal includes entries for further work in 1789 and 1790. Bothwell House was demolished in 1926.

96. J. Playfair to C. Gordon, London, 8 August 1789, University of Aberdeen, Gordon of Buthlaw and Cairness MSS, 1160/28/3/1 and 2. D. Walker and C. McWilliam, 'Cairness, Aberdeenshire', *CL*, vol. CXLIX (28 January and 4 February 1971), pp. 184–7, 248–51.

97. Playfair, 'Journal'.

98. J. Playfair, Cairness, 25 October 1790, University of Aberdeen, Gordon of Buthlaw and Cairness MSS, 1160/28/3/3.

99. University of Aberdeen, Gordon of Buthlaw and Cairness MSS. Also SM, vol. 26, nos. 1–11.

100. University of Aberdeen, Gordon of Buthlaw and Cairness MSS, 1160/28/2/2.

101. 'Design by James Playfair Architect for Public Rooms at Cairness, 1793', University of Aberdeen MSS.

102. Playfair, 'Journal'.

103. R. Heron, *Observations Made in a Journey through the Western Counties of Scotland; in the Autumn of 1792* (1793), vol. I, pp. 334–5.

104. SM, vol. 2U, nos. 1–4. Client's drawings are at Ardkinglas and photographs in NMRS. C. McWilliam, 'James Playfair's Designs for Ardkinglas', *The Country Seat* (1970), pp. 193–8.

105. Playfair, 'Journal'.

106. Braham, op. cit., pp. 108, 110, 239.

107. 'Accot. of the Wrightwork of the High Part of the building at Cairness 1782 and 1783 Years', University of Aberdeen, Gordon of Buthlaw and Cairness MSS, 1140/28/2/1.

108. M. Girouard, 'Preston Hall, Midlothian', *CL*, vol. CXXX (24 and 31 August 1961), pp. 394–7, 454–7; C. McWilliam, *Lothian*, pp. 395–8.

109. R. Mitchell, *Plans, and Views in Perspective, with Descriptions, of Buildings Erected in England and Scotland* (1801), p. 6.

110. Ibid., pls. 9–11.

111. Kames, op. cit., p. 325.

112. Mitchell, op. cit., p. 9.

113. Ibid., p. 5.

114. Terregles House, now demolished, was built between 1788 and 1794. References to the progress of the building are contained in letters from members of the family. University of Hull, Maxwell-Constable MSS, DDEV/60/60/20. Colvin, op. cit., p. 74.

115. Holland's designs, dated 'London, 1783', are among the Duke of Buccleuch's MSS.

116. *SA*, vol. XIV, p. 616; A. Drummond, *Old Clackmannanshire* (1953), p. 35.

117. Drawings in NMRS.

118. J. Stoddart, *Remarks on Local Scenery and Manners in Scotland During the Years 1799 and 1800* (1801), vol. II, p. 237.

119. J. Struthers, 'Broomhall, Fife, with Particular Reference to Thomas Harrison' (1974), pp. 3, 4, 30–8.
120. J. Crook, 'Broomhall, Fife', *CL*, vol. CXLVII (29 January 1970), pp. 242–6.
121. T. Somerville, *My Own Life and Times, 1741–1814* (1861), pp. 359–60.
122. 'Selections from the Family Papers Preserved at Caldwell', Pt. I, p. 270.
123. H. Mackenzie, *The Man of Feeling* (1970), p. 103.
124. Tayler, op. cit., p. 192.
125. Allardyce, op. cit., vol. II, p. 46.
126. *SA*, vol. IV, p. 566.
127. J. Austen, *Emma* (1966), p. 77.
128. RCAHMS, *Stirlingshire* (1963), vol. II, p. 367.
129. Ibid., vol. II, pp. 335–6.
130. RCAHMS, *Argyll*, vol. I (1971), p. 191.
131. Barbreck is dated 1790. There are measured drawings in NMRS.
132. Drawings at Torwoodlee. *NSA*, vol. I, pp. 417–18.
133. J. Burke, *A Visitation of the Seats and Arms* (1853), vol. II, p. 132.
134. *SA*, vol. VI, p. 475.
135. J. Baxter to Dr W. Thom, Edinburgh, 22 August 1783, Haddo MSS, Box 8/2.
136. Three signed plans and an elevation are among the Earl of Cromartie's MSS at Castle Leod. *SA*, vol. VI, p. 186; *NSA*, vol. XIV, p. 306; F. Groome, *Ordnance Gazetteer of Scotland* (1894), vol. VI, p. 427; W. Fraser, *The Earls of Cromartie* (1876), vol. I, p. cclviii; vol. II, p. 435.
    Tarbat House replaced a courtyard mansion begun in the mid-sixteenth century and enlarged in the sixteen-eighties. As it resembled Panmure House the architect may have been Robert Mylne, the designer, perhaps, of the 1685 extension of Caroline Park, Lord Tarbat's residence near Edinburgh. Fraser, op. cit., vol. I, pp. 55–6; vol. II, pp. 430–5. RHP 45193.
137. *SA*, vol. X, p. 179; RCAHMS, *Peebles-shire* (1967), vol. II, p. 300.
138. J. Paterson, *History of the Counties of Ayr and Wigton* (1863), vol. I, Pt. I, pp. 152–3.
139. Stoddart, op. cit., vol. II, p. 315.
140. *NSA*, vol. XIII, p. 164.
141. The contract, dated 7 April 1789, is at Glenae.
142. Burke, op. cit., vol. II, p. 186.
143. Colvin, op. cit., p. 289.
144. Drawings, signed by Cairncross in 1797, are in the Paul Mellon collection as are the drawings for a scheme by Claud Cleghorn. Photographs are in NMRS.
145. Monreith House was built in 1791 for Sir William Maxwell under the terms of the 'Acts of Parliament past in the year 1768 for encouraging the improvement of lands held under settlement of strict entail in Scotland'. The architect was Alexander Stevens and the foreman mason was William Elliot. SRO, SC19/65/1.
146. *Scots Magazine*, vol. LXV (June 1808), p. 403; L. Melville, *Errol* (1935), p. 185; Colvin, op. cit., p. 624.
    Paterson's work at Seggieden, c.1794, may have been a remodelling of a house constructed by Andrew Watson, mason, and 'John Young Wright in Perth' for which marble chimney-pieces were supplied by Alexander Whyte. Drummond-Hay of Seggieden MSS, Sandeman Library, Perth.
    Seggieden has been demolished but there are photographs of drawings in NMRS.
147. A. Burn to Sir Hew Dalrymple, Bonnington, 18 January and 1 March 1781, SRO, GD110/783/3 and 5. M. Girouard, 'Leuchie House, East Lothian', *CL*, vol. CXXX (12 October 1961), pp. 826–9; McWilliam, op. cit., pp. 282–3.
148. H. Dalrymple to Sir Hew Dalrymple, North Berwick, 1 February 1797, SRO, GD110/1056/12.
149. The plasterwork at Leuchie House was executed by James Nisbet. A. Burn to Sir Hew Dalrymple, Edinburgh, 23 April 1782, SRO, GD110/783/16.
150. Ibid., Bonnington, 27 March 1781, SRO, GD110/783/11.
151. J. Flaxman to Sir Hew Dalrymple, 27 Wardour Street, Soho, 21 October 1782, SRO, GD110/1072.
152. H. Dalrymple to Sir Hew Dalrymple, Bruton Street, 7 March 1785, SRO, GD110/1056/18.
153. After selling Preston Hall to Alexander Callander, Lord Adam Gordon purchased the estate of The Burn,

Angus, paying £300 for the same number of acres with a rental of £5:11:1½. On his death this land, and the small estate of Woodton, was sold for £20,000. *NSA*, vol. XI, pp. 26, 122.

154. Austen, op. cit., p. 291.

155. M. Dalrymple to Sir Hew Dalrymple, Tonbridge, 15 September — , SRO, GD110/1071/4A.

156. J. Austen, *Northanger Abbey* (1974), p. 330.

157. Supra, n. 155.

158. J. Austen, *Persuasion* (1978), p. 67.

159. Account from Thomas Seddon. London, 23 November 1794 and 'Inventory of Household Furniture', 1814, University of Aberdeen, Gordon of Buthlaw and Cairness MSS, 1160/28/4/7, 11.

160. T. Constable to M. Maxwell, Terregles House, 9 May 1796, University of Hull, Maxwell-Constable MSS, DDEV/60/29.

161. Supra, n. 147.

162. 'A Rough Sketch of an Estimate to Finish the Different Apartments at Cairness', University of Aberdeen, Gordon of Buthlaw and Cairness MSS, 1160/28/4/5.

163. Supra, n. 159.

164. Tayler, op. cit., pp. 50, 100.

165. *Letters of Lord Chesterfield to Lord Huntingdon* (1923), p. 35.

166. W. Dalrymple to Sir Hew Dalrymple, Cadiz, 30 April 1779, SRO, GD110/965/54.

EPILOGUE

With the deaths in London of Robert Adam in 1792 and of James Playfair two years later, British architecture lost two of its most original practitioners. Despite a recent claim, it is difficult to concede that Adam, in his sixty-fourth year when he died, would have produced further significant architectural advances had he lived as he seems to have had little interest in the nascent Greek revival or the antiquarian Gothic revival. The loss of James Playfair at the age of thirty-nine was another matter as Cairness, Aberdeenshire, was the signpost of a new direction in its mix of archaeological and eclectic Egyptian and Greek motifs with contemporary French massing. Such a complex stylistic polyphony is not found in Adam's work or that of his successors. Perhaps the latter were in a difficult situation since architecture *per se* no longer existed but was classified into styles, of which the most vigorous in Scotland, in the countryside at least, was Gothic.

It has been noted that the largest country-houses were those commissioned by the higher ranks of the nobility at the start of the eighteenth century. At its close and for the first decades of the next century the patrons of country-house architecture were the lesser landowners and the new men, the merchants, lawyers and retired officers who required decent-sized, unpretentious dwellings of the kind that numerous contemporaries had already built. Thus, it has been written that Yair in Selkirkshire, begun in 1784, 'is representative of a fairly numerous group of late Georgian and Regency villas erected in Tweeddale'. Much the same could be said of other houses in other localities.

It is odd, however, that, given the fame of Robert Adam even in his lifetime, his villa style was seldom imitated albeit that so few of his concepts were realised. Certainly, little of Adam's inventiveness was displayed at Ardgowan, Renfrewshire, by Hugh Cairncross, the former Adam clerk of works. Another was John Paterson. While faithful to many of the Adam canons, such as the use of varied plan shapes, his restrained decoration and refined detailing are best defined as Regency as in the now destroyed Montgomerie House, Ayrshire. After 1794, when he set up in independent practice, Paterson received ten large country-house commissions. Tellingly, seven of these were in the Gothic style.

From the commencement of Inveraray Castle, Argyll, the first major Gothic revival building in Britain, in 1746, to the close of the century, thirty castles were constructed in Scotland of which thirteen were by Robert Adam. In the nineteenth century the pace of castle building quickened; in the first decade thirty castles were under way. Symbolic witnesses in stone of lineage and landownership, they are spectacularly represented by Taymouth Castle, Perthshire, built by a cadet branch of clan Campbell and therefore a derivative, like several others, of Inveraray Castle. Hence, too, the symmetrically composed and regularly disposed elevations. Elsewhere these would be dissolved when variety, intricacy, and irregularity overlaid organic planning. Once that formula was set out in the publications outlining the tenets of the Picturesque and in the writings of Gilpin, Scotland came to be seen as the castle country *par excellence*. In time, the demand for more accurate representations of the vernacular castles led to the emergence of Scots Baronialism from the office of William Burn. Nevertheless he was, on occasion, an inventive exponent, like Archibald Simpson and John Smith in the north-east, of the Greek revival that was best served by religious, professional and corporate needs in the town.

If the significant history of the classical country-house in Scotland lasted for little more than a hundred years, that does not mean that it should be seen as an extended interlude between two phases of castle building. Nor was it a pale reflection of what was happening south of the Border. What is remarkable is how frequently new architectural concepts were first promoted in Scotland either by an architect, such as James Smith, working within the country or by others, such as Robert Adam and James Playfair, working from London. It is the combination of such concepts with influences from Holland, France, Italy and England that give the Scottish classical country-house its distinctive interest.

Envoi

For there is nothing in the course of one's duties so fatiguing as . . . seeing a great house, dawdling from room to room – straining one's eyes and one's attention – hearing what one does not understand – admiring what one does not care for. – It is generally allowed to be the greatest bore in the world.

Jane Austen, *Mansfield Park*

BIBLIOGRAPHY

BOOKS

Adam, Robert, *Ruins of the Palace of the Emperor Diocletian at Spalatro in Dalmatia*, London, 1764.

Adam, Robert and James, *The Works in Architecture*, 3 vols., London, 1773–1822, re-issued London, 1975.

Adam, William, *Vitruvius Scoticus*, Edinburgh, n.d., reprinted Edinburgh, 1980.

Allardyce, Alexander, *Scotland and Scotsmen in the Eighteenth Century*, 2 vols., Edinburgh and London, 1888.

Atholl, John, 7th Duke of, *Chronicles of the Atholl and Tullibardine Families*, 5 vols, Edinburgh, 1908.

Austen, Jane, *Emma*, Penguin English Library, Harmondsworth, 1966.

Austen, Jane, *Mansfield Park*, Pan Classics edn., London, 1972.

Austen, Jane, *Northanger Abbey*, Penguin English Library, Harmondsworth, 1974.

Austen, Jane, *Persuasion*, Penguin English Library, Harmondsworth, 1978.

Baird, William, *Annals of Duddingstone and Portobello*, Edinburgh, 1898.

Barty, Alexander, *History of Dunblane*, Stirling, 1944.

Beard, Geoffrey, *Decorative Plasterwork in Great Britain*, London, 1975.

Blackett, J., *Arbigland*, Dumfries, n.d.

Bolitho, Hector, and Peel, Derek, *The Drummonds of Charing Cross*, London, 1967.

Bolton, Arthur T., *The Architecture of Robert and James Adam*, 2 vols., London, 1922.

'The Book of Record. A Diary Written by Patrick, First Earl of Strathmore, 1684–9', *Scottish History Society*, vol. IX, Edinburgh, 1890.

Braham, Allan, *The Architecture of the French Enlightenment*, London, 1980.

Burke, John B., *A Visitation of the Seats and Arms of the Noblemen and Gentlemen of Great Britain*, 2 vols., London, 1852–3.

Burke's Peerage, Baronetage and Knightage, 105th edn., London, 1970.

Campbell, Alexander, *A Journey from Edinburgh Through Parts of North Britain*, 2 vols., new edn., London, 1811.

Campbell, Colen, *Vitruvius Britannicus*, 3 vols., London, 1715–25, re-issued New York 1967.

Carlyle, Alexander, *Anecdotes and Characters of the Times*, James Kinsley ed., London, 1973.

Castell, Robert, *The Villas of the Ancients Illustrated*, London, 1728.

Cato, Marcus Porcius, *On Agriculture*, trans. by W. D. Hooper, revised by H. B. Ash, London and Cambridge, Mass., 1934.

Ceves, Renato, *I Modelli della Mostra del Palladio*, Venezia, 1976.

Chambers, Robert, *Domestic Annals of Scotland from the Reformation to the Revolution*, 5 vols., Edinburgh, 1859–61.

Chambers, Sir William, *A Treatise on Civil Architecture*, London, 1759.

Columella, Lucius Junius, *On Agriculture*, trans. by H. B. Ash, E. S. Forster and E. H. Heffner, London and Cambridge, Mass., 1941.

Colvin, Howard M., *A Biographical Dictionary of British Architects, 1600–1840*, London, 1978.

Colvin, Howard M., and Harris, John (eds.), *The Country Seat*, London, 1970.

Crawfurd, George, *A General Description of the Shire of Renfrew, 1710*, Paisley, 1818.

Croft-Murray, Edward, *Decorative Painting in England, 1537–1837*, 2 vols., London, 1962–70.

Cruden, Stewart, *The Scottish Castle*, Edinburgh and London, 1963.

Davidson, John, *Inverurie and the Earldom of the Garioch*, Edinburgh and Aberdeen, 1878.

Defoe, Daniel, *A Tour through the Whole Island of Great Britain*, 2 vols., 1724, reprinted London, 1927.

'Diary of George Ridpath, Minister of Stichel, 1755–61' *Scottish History Society*, 3rd Series, vol. II, Edinburgh, 1922.

Dictionary of National Biography.

Drummond, A. I. R., *Old Clackmannanshire*, Alva, 1953.

Du Cerceau, Jacques, *Des Plus Excellents Bastiments de France*, 2 vols. Paris, 1576 and 1670, republished Farnborough, 1972.

Dunbar, John G., *The Historic Architecture of Scotland*, London, 1966.

Dunbar, John G., *Sir William Bruce, 1630–1710*, Edinburgh, 1970.

Fiennes, Mrs Celia, *The Journeys of Celia Fiennes*, Christopher Morris ed., London, 1947.

Fittler, James, and Nattes, John C., *Scotia Depicta*, London, 1804.

Fleming, James S., *Ancient Castles and Mansions of Stirling Nobility*, Paisley, 1902.

Fleming, John, *Robert Adam and His Circle in Edinburgh and Rome*, London, 1962.

Forsyth, Robert, *The Beauties of Scotland*, 5 vols., Edinburgh, 1805.

Fowler, John, and Cornforth, John, *English Decoration in the 18th Century*, London, 1974.

Fraser, Sir William, *The Chiefs of Grant*, 3 vols., Edinburgh, 1883.

Fraser, Sir William, *The Earls of Cromartie*, 2 vols., Edinburgh, 1876.

Fraser, Sir William, *Memoirs of the Maxwells of Pollok*, 2 vols., Edinburgh, 1863.

Fyfe, James G., (ed.), *Scottish Diaries and Memoirs*, 2 vols., Stirling, 1928 and 1942.

Gibbs, James, *A Book of Architecture*, London, 1728.

Gibson, John C., *The Lands and Lairds of Touch*, Stirling, 1929.

Good, George, *Liberton in Ancient and Modern Times*, Edinburgh, 1893.

Graham, Henry G., *The Social Life of Scotland in the Eighteenth Century*, 2 vols., London, 1899.

Graham, John M., *Annals and Correspondence of the Viscount and the First and Second Earls of Stair*, 2 vols., Edinburgh and London, 1875.

Grant, James, *Old and New Edinburgh*, 3 vols., London, 1880.

Grant of Laggan, Mrs Anne, *Letters from the Mountains; between the Years 1773 and 1803*, 3 vols., 6th edn, London, 1845.

Gray, John M., (ed.), 'Memoirs of the Life of Sir John Clerk of Penicuik', *Scottish History Society*, vol. XIII, Edinburgh, 1892.

Greig, James, (ed.), *The Diaries of a Duchess*, London, 1926.

Groome, Francis H., *Ordnance Gazetteer of Scotland*, new edn., 6 vols, London, Edinburgh and Glasgow, 1894.

Gunther, Robert T., *The Architecture of Sir Roger Pratt*, Oxford, 1928, reissued New York 1972.

Halfpenny, William and John; Morris, Robert; and Lightoler, Thomas, *The Modern Builder's Assistant*, London, 1757, republished Farnborough, 1971.

Hannan, Thomas, *Famous Scottish Houses*, London, 1928.

Harris, John, *Sir William Chambers. Knight of the Polar Star*, London, 1970.

Heron, Robert, *Observations Made in a Journey Through the Western Counties of Scotland; in the Autumn of 1792*, 2 vols., Perth. 1793.

Hill, Oliver, and Cornforth, John, *English Country Houses. Caroline, 1625-1685*, London, 1966.

Hume Brown, Peter, *Tours in Scotland, 1677 and 1681 by Thomas Kirk and Ralph Thoresby*, Edinburgh, 1892.

Irvine, James, (ed.), *Parties and Pleasures. The Diaries of Helen Graham, 1823–26*, Perth, 1957.

Jones' Views of the Seats, Mansions, Castles, etc. of Noblemen and Gentlemen in England, Wales, Scotland and Ireland, Series of Scottish Seats, London, n.d.

'Journal of Henry Kalmeter's Travels in Scotland, 1719–20', *Scottish History Society*, 4th Series, vol. 14, Edinburgh, 1978.

Kames, Lord, *Elements of Criticism*, 3 vols., Edinburgh, 1762.

Kay, John, *A Series of Original Portraits and Caricature Etchings*, 2 vols., London, 1877.

Kent, William, *Designs of Inigo Jones with Some Additional Designs*, 2 vols., London, 1727.

Knight, William, *Lord Monboddo and Some of His Contemporaries*, London, 1900.

Lees-Milne, James, *English Country Houses. Baroque, 1685–1715*, London, 1970.

Leighton, John M., *History of the County of Fife*, 2 vols., Glasgow, 1840.

Le Muet, Pierre, *Manière de Bien Bastir Pour Toutes Sortes de Personnes*, 2nd edn., Paris, 1681.

Leoni, Giacomo, *The Architecture of A. Palladio*, 3rd edn., London, 1742.

Letters of Lord Chesterfield to Lord Huntingdon, London, 1923.

The Letters of the Younger Pliny, trans. by Betty Radice, Penguin Classics edn., reprinted Harmondsworth, 1974.

'Lord Mar's Legacies, 1722–7, *Scottish History Society*, vol. XXVI, Edinburgh, 1896.

Loveday, John, 'Diary of a Tour in 1732 thro' Parts of England, Wales, Ireland and Scotland', *Roxburghe Club*, London, 1889.

Macaulay, James, *The Gothic Revival, 1745–1845*, Glasgow and London, 1975.

McClung, William A., *The Country House in English Renaissance Poetry*, Berkeley and London, 1977.

MacGibbon, David, and Ross, Thomas, *The Castellated and Domestic Architecture of Scotland*, 5 vols., Edinburgh, 1887–92.

Mackenzie, Henry, *The Man of Feeling*, Oxford English Novel Series, London, 1970.

Mackenzie, William C., *The Life and Times of John Maitland, Duke of Lauderdale*, London, 1923.

McKerlie, Peter H., *History of the Lands and Their Owners in Galloway*, 5 vols., Edinburgh, 1870–9.

Macky, John, *A Journey through Scotland*, London, 1723.

Maclehose, James, *Old Country Houses of the Old Glasgow Gentry*, 2nd edn., Glasgow, 1878.

McWilliam, Colin, *Lothian, Buildings of Scotland*, Harmondsworth, 1978.

Marshall, Rosalind, *The Days of Duchess Anne. Life in the Household of the Duchess of Hamilton, 1656–1716*, London, 1973.

Martial, *Epigrams*, trans. by W. C. A. Ker, 2 vols., London and Cambridge, Mass., 1927 and 1968.

Melville, Lawrence, *Errol*, Perth, 1935.

Millar, Alexander H., *Castles and Mansions of Renfrewshire and Buteshire*, Glasgow, 1889.

Millar, Alexander H., *Fife: Pictorial and Historical*, 2 vols., Cupar (Fife), Edinburgh and Glasgow, 1895.

Millar, Alexander H., *The Historical Castles and Mansions of Scotland*, Paisley and London, 1890.

Millar, Alexander H., *Historical and Descriptive Accounts of the Castles and Mansions of Ayrshire*, Edinburgh, 1885.

Miller, James, *History of Dunbar*, Dunbar, 1830.

Miller, James, *The Lamp of Lothian*, Haddington, 1844.

Mitchell, Joseph, *Reminiscences of My Life in the Highlands*, 2 vols., London, 1883–4.

Mitchell, Robert, *Plans, and Views in Perspective, with Descriptions, of Buildings Erected in England and Scotland*, London, 1801.

Moncrieff, Frederick, and Moncrieffe, William, *The Moncrieffs and the Moncrieffes*, 2 vols., Edinburgh, 1929.

More Nisbett, Hamilton, *Drum of the Somervilles*, Edinburgh, 1928.

Morris, Robert, *An Essay in Defence of Ancient Architecture*, 1728, republished Farnborough, 1971.

Morris, Robert, *Rural Architecture*, 1750, republished Farnborough, 1971.

Mylne, Robert S., *The Master Masons to the Crown of Scotland*, Edinburgh, 1893.

Neale, John P., *Views of the Seats of the Noblemen and Gentlemen in England, Wales, Scotland and Ireland*, 2nd Series, 5 vols., London, 1824–9.

New Statistical Account of Scotland, 15 vols., Edinburgh, 1845.

The Odes of Horace, trans. by James Michie, Penguin Classics edn., reprinted Harmondsworth, 1976.

Omond, George W., *The Arniston Memoirs: three centuries of a Scottish house edited from the family papers*, Edinburgh, 1887.

Palladio, Andrea, *The Four Books of Architecture*, republication of the 1738 edn. by Isaac Ware, New York, 1965.

Paterson, James, *History of the Counties of Ayr and Wigton*, 3 vols., Edinburgh, 1863–4.

Paul, Sir James Balfour, *The Scots Peerage*, 9 vols., Edinburgh, 1904–14.

Pennant, Thomas, *A Tour in Scotland, 1769*, 3rd edn., Warrington, 1774.

Pennant, Thomas, *A Tour in Scotland and Voyage to the Hebrides: 1772*, 2 vols., London, 1790.

Piranesi, Giovanni B., *Diverse Maniere d'Adornare i Cammini*, Rome, 1769.

Plant, Marjorie, *The Domestic Life of Scotland in the Eighteenth Century*, Edinburgh, 1952.

Pococke, Richard, 'Tours in Scotland, 1747, 1750, 1760', *Scottish History Society*, vol. I, Edinburgh, 1887.

Price, Sir Uvedale, *Essays on the Picturesque, as Compared with the Sublime and the Beautiful*, 1810, republished Farnborough 1971.

Reynolds, Sir Joshua, *Discourses on Art*, Collier Books Reissue edn., 4th printing, 1969.

Richardson, Sir Albert, *Robert Mylne, Architect and Engineer, 1783–1811*, London, 1955.

Richardson, George, *New Vitruvius Britannicus*, 2 vols., London, 1802–8, reissued New York, 1970.

Rose, Sir George, (ed.), *A Selection from the Papers of the Earls of Marchmont*, 3 vols., London, 1831.

Royal Commission on the Ancient and Historical Monuments of Scotland, *Argyll*, vols. 1 and 2, Edinburgh, 1971 and 1975; *Peebles-shire*, 2 vols., Edinburgh, 1967; *Stirlingshire*, 2 vols., Edinburgh, 1963.

Rubens, Peter Paul, *Palazzi di Genova*, Antwerp, 1622, reissued New York and London 1968.

The Satires of Horace and Persius, trans. by N. Rudd, reprinted Harmondsworth, 1976.

Scamozzi, Ottavio B., *Le Fabbriche e i Disegni di Andrea Palladio*, Vicenza, 1796, republished London 1968.

'Selections from the Family Papers Preserved at Caldwell', *Maitland Club*, 2 Parts, Glasgow, 1854.

Serlio, Sebastiano, *The Book of Architecture*, London, 1611, reissued 1970 and reprinted New York, 1980.

Serlio, Sebastiano, *Tutte l'Opere d'Architettura et Prospetiva*, Venice, 1619, republished 1964, 2nd impression Farnborough 1968.

Skrine, Henry, *Three Successive Tours in the North of England and Great Part of Scotland*, London, 1795.

Slezer, John, *Theatrum Scotiae*, London, 1719.

Small, John, *Castles and Mansions of the Lothians*, 2 vols., Edinburgh, 1883.

Smout, T. C., *A History of the Scottish People, 1560–1830*, 2nd edn., London, 1970.

Somerville, Thomas, *My Own Life and Times, 1741–1814*, Edinburgh, 1861.

Statistical Account of Scotland, 21 vols., Edinburgh, 1791–9.

Stoddart, John, *Remarks on Local Manners and Scenery in Scotland During the Years 1799 and 1800*, 2 vols., London, 1801.

Stuart, James, and Revett, Nicholas, *Antiquities of Athens*, vol. I, London, 1762.

Stuart, John, (ed.), *Registrum de Panmure*, 2 vols., Edinburgh, 1872–4.

Summerson, Sir John, *Architecture in Britain 1530–1830*, 4th edn., Harmondsworth, 1963.

Tayler, Alistair and Henrietta, *The Book of the Duffs*, 2 vols., Edinburgh, 1914.

Tayler, Alistair and Henrietta, *Lord Fife and His Factor, Being the Correspondence of James, 2nd Lord Fife 1729–1809*, London, 1925.

Thompson, Harold W., *The Anecdotes and Egotisms of Henry Mackenzie, 1745–1831*, Oxford and London, 1927.

Varro, Marcus Terentius, *On Agriculture*, trans. by W. D. Hooper and revised by H. B. Ash, London and Cambridge, Mass., 1934.

Ware, Isaac, *The Complete Body of Architecture*, 3rd edn., London, 1756.

Warrender, Margaret, *Marchmont and the Humes of Polworth*, Edinburgh and London, 1894.

Watts, William, *The Seats of the Nobility and Gentry*, London, 1779–86.

Webb, Geoffrey F., (ed.), *The Complete Works of Sir John Vanbrugh*, vol. IV, London, 1927.

Woolfe, John, and Gandon, James, *Vitruvius Britannicus*, 2 vols., London, 1767–71, reissued New York 1970.

Wordsworth, Dorothy, *Recollections of a Tour Made in Scotland, A.D. 1803*, 2nd edn., Edinburgh, 1874.

ARTICLES

'Balcaskie, Fife', *Country Life*, vol. XXXI, 2 March 1912.

Binney, Marcus, 'Thirlestane Castle, Berwickshire', *Country Life*, vol. CLXXIV, 11 and 18 August 1983.

Bodie, W., 'Introduction to the Rothes Papers', *Proceedings of the Society of Antiquaries of Scotland*, vol. 110, 1978–80.

Bolton, Arthur T., 'The Drum, Midlothian', *Country Life*, vol. XXXVIII, 9 October 1915.

Bolton, Arthur T., 'Mellerstain, Berwickshire', *Country Life*, vol. XXXVIII, 13 November 1915.

Bolton, Arthur T., 'Newliston, West Lothian', *Country Life*, vol. XXXIX, 26 February, 1916.

'Caroline Park, Midlothian', *Country Life*, vol. XXX., 19 August 1911.

Colvin, Howard M., 'A Scottish Origin for English Palladianism?', *Architectural History*, vol. 17, 1974.

Cornforth, John, 'Mertoun, Berwickshire', *Country Life*, vol. CXXXIX, 2 June 1966.

Cornforth, John, 'Touch, Stirlingshire'. *Country Life*, vol. CXXXVIII, 19 August 1965.

Cosh, Mary, 'The Adam Family and Arniston', *Architectural History*, vol. 27, 1984.

Crook, J. Mordaunt, 'Broomhall, Fife', *Country Life*, vol. CXLVII, 29 January 1970.

'Dalkeith Palace, near Edinburgh', *Country Life*, vol. XXX, 7 October 1911.

Dunbar, John G., 'The Building Activities of the Duke and Duchess of Lauderdale, 1670–82', *The Archaeological Journal*, vol. 132, 1975.

Dunbar, John G., 'The Building of Yester House, 1670–1878', *Transactions of the East Lothian Antiquarian and Field Naturalists' Society*, vol. XIII, 1972.

Forman, Sheila, 'Links with the Russian Court in Scotland', *Country Life*, vol. CXXVII, 26 May 1960.

Girouard, Mark, 'Drumlanrig Castle, Dumfries-shire', *Country Life*, vol, CXXVIII, 25 August 1960.

Girouard, Mark, 'Kinross House, Kinross-shire', *Country Life*, vol. CXXXVII, 25 March and 1 April 1965.

Girouard, Mark, 'Leuchie House, East Lothian', *Country Life*, vol. CXXX, 12 October 1961.

Girouard, Mark, 'Mellerstain, Berwickshire', *Country Life*, vol. CXXIV, 4 September 1958.

Girouard, Mark, 'Preston Hall, Midlothian', *Country Life*, vol. CXXX, 24 and 31 August 1961.

'Gosford House, East Lothian', *Country Life*, vol. XXX, 2 September 1911.

'Hatton House, Midlothian', *Country Life*, vol. XXX, 16 September 1911.

Hunt, John, 'Gosford, East Lothian', *Country Life*, vol. CL, 21 October and 4 November 1971.

Hussey, Christopher, 'Haddo House, Aberdeenshire', *Country Life*, vol. CXL, 18 August 1966.

Hussey, Christopher, 'Made by Chippendale? The Amisfield Day Beds', *Country Life*, vol, CXXXVIII, 15 July 1965.

Hussey, Christopher, 'Marchmont, Berwickshire', *Country Life*, vol. LVII, 28 February 1925.

'Kinross House, Kinross', *Country Life*, vol. XXXII, 20 July 1912.

Marwick, Thomas, 'Balbardie House and Robert Adam', *Architectural Review*, vol. XLVIII, 1920.

'Melville House, Fife', *Country Life*, vol. XXX, 30 December 1911.

Nightingale, John, 'The Threat to Cromarty', *Country Life*, vol. CLXII, 11 August 1977.

Oswald, Arthur, 'Auchencruive, Ayrshire', *Country Life*, vol. LXXII, 17 December 1932.

Oswald, Arthur, 'Blair Castle, Perthshire', *Country Life*, vol. CVI, 4 and 11 November 1949.

Rowan, Alistair, 'The Building of Hopetoun', *Architectural History*, vol. 27, 1984.

Rowan, Alistair, 'Kilkerran, Ayrshire', *Country Life*, vol. CLVII, 1 May 1975.

Rowan, Alistair, 'Paxton House, Berwickshire', *Country Life*, vol. CXLII, 17 and 24 August 1967.

Rowan, Alistair, 'Penicuik House, Midlothian', *Country Life*, vol. CXLIV, 15 and 22 August 1968.

Rowan, Alistair, 'Sunnyside and Rosebank, Suburban Villas by the Adam Brothers', *AA Files*, no. 4, 1983.

Rowan, Alistair, 'Yester House, East Lothian', *Country Life*, vol. CLIV, 9 August 1973.

Sanderson, Margaret, 'Robert Adam's Last Visit to Scotland, 1791', *Architectural History*, vol. 25, 1982.

Simpson, James, 'Lord Alemoor's Villa at Hawkhill', *Bulletin of the Scottish Georgian Society*, vol. 1, 1972.

Slade, H. Gordon, 'Arbuthnott House, Kincardineshire', *Proceedings of the Society of Antiquaries of Scotland*, vol. 110, 1978–80.

Tait, Alan A., 'William Adam and Sir John Clerk: Arniston and "The Country Seat"', *Burlington Magazine*, vol. CXI, March 1969.

'Thirlestane Castle, Berwickshire', *Country Life*, vol. XXVIII, 6 August 1910.

Walker, David, 'Duddingston House, Edinburgh', *Country Life*, vol. CXXVI, 24 September 1959.

Walker, David, 'Glendoick, Perthshire', *Country Life*, vol. CXLI, 30 March 1967.

Walker, David, and Dunbar, John G., 'Brechin Castle, Angus', *Country Life*, vol. CL, 12 August 1971.

Walker, David, and McWilliam, Colin, 'Cairness, Aberdeenshire', *Country Life*, vol. CXLIX, 28 January and 4 February 1971.

Weaver, Lawrence, 'Pollok House, Renfrewshire', *Country Life*, vol. XXXIII, 25 January 1913.

UNPUBLISHED DISSERTATION

Struthers, James, 'Broomhall, Fife, with Particular Reference to Thomas Harrison', Diploma dissertation, Scott Sutherland School of Architecture, Aberdeen, 1974.

FAMILY MANUSCRIPTS QUOTED

Private Collections
The Marchioness of Aberdeen's MSS at Haddo House
The Marquess of Bute's MSS at Dumfries House and Mount Stuart
Mr Malcolm Colquhoun, Yr. of Luss's MSS at Rossdhu
The Earl of Cromartie's MSS at Castle Leod
Graham of Mossknowe MSS at Mossknowe
Gordon of Craig MSS
The Earl of Haddington's MSS at Mellerstain
The Duke of Hamilton's MSS at Lennoxlove
Lord Home of The Hirsel's MSS at The Hirsel
The Hopetoun Papers Trust
Mr P. Johnstone's MSS at Glenae
The Earl of Kintore's MSS at Keith Hall
Montcoffer MSS
The Earl of Moray's MSS at Darnaway Castle
Mr A. Munro Ferguson of Novar's MSS at Raith
Mrs D. Pringle's MSS at Torwoodlee
The Earl of Rosebery's MSS at Dalmeny House
The Duke of Roxburghe's MSS at Floors Castle
The Earl of Wemyss and March's MSS at Gosford
Capt. R. Wolrige Gordon's MSS at Esslemont House

British Architectural Library
Sir William Chambers's MSS

Kirkcaldy Art Gallery and Museum
Rothes MSS

National Library of Scotland
Erskine Murray MSS
Minto MSS

Bibliography

Newhailes MSS
Stuart Stevenson MSS
Yester MSS

Perth and Kinross Archives
Drummond-Hay of Seggieden MSS

Public Record Office of Northern Ireland
The Duke of Abercorn's MSS

Scottish Record Office
Abercairny MSS (GD24)
Biel MSS (GD6)
Breadalbane MSS (GD112)
Broughton and Cally MSS (GD10)
Bruce of Kinross MSS (GD29)
Buccleuch (Dalkeith) MSS (GD224)
Campbell of Barcaldine MSS (GD170)
Clerk of Penicuik MSS (GD18)
Dalhousie MSS (GD45)
Erskine of Dun MSS (GD123)
Fea of Clestrain MSS (GD31)
Fergusson of Craigdarroch MSS (GD77)
Glencairn MSS (GD39)
Haddo House MSS (GD33)
Hamilton-Dalrymple of North Berwick MSS (GD110)
Home of Marchmont MSS (GD158)
Home of Wedderburn MSS (GD267)
Leven and Melville MSS (GD26)
Lothian MSS (GD40)
Mar and Kellie MSS (GD124)
Marchmont Estate MSS (GD1/651)
Montrose MSS (GD220)
Mylne MSS (GD1/51)
Ross of Balnagowan MSS (GD129)
Scott of Harden MSS (GD157)
Seafield MSS (GD248)
Shepherd and Wedderburn MSS (GD242)
Tods, Murray and Jamieson MSS (GD237)

Strathclyde Regional Archives
Maxwell of Pollok MSS

University of Aberdeen
Arbuthnott MSS
Duff of Braco MSS
Gordon of Buthlaw and Cairness MSS
Kelly Building Accounts

University of Hull
Maxwell-Constable of Everingham MSS .

University of Yale
Boswell of Auchinleck MSS